The Beginning of the Rise of Bob Hamilton...

With an appeal to his father's prejudices, he described his vision for a revival of American values. "I want to live in a nation that honors God, family and flag again. We have fallen so far. The country you fought to save doesn't exist anymore. It's overrun by immigrants, feminists and faggots. It's up to people like you and me to bring America back. With any luck, I'll be in the Senate in a few years and then, God willing, the White House. I'm going to need your help. You know so many people in this state. It would mean a lot to me if we could work as a team to make this happen."

Robert III had never been prouder of his son than he was in that moment. Wiping away tears with the back of his hand, his voice shaky, he said, "Well, of course I'll help you Bobby. I'll do anything I can. Jesus Christ. President Robert David Hamilton. I like the sound of that."

Prince
of the
Pharisees

JOHN RILEY MYERS

Published in the United States by Breur Media Corporation.

ISBN-13: 978-0-9819474-2-6
ISBN-10: 0-9819474-2-5

Printed in the United States of America

Cover art: Nick Myers
Cover design: Arthur Breur

Breur Media Corporation
2643 Narnia Way, Suite 102
Land O' Lakes, FL 34638

813-868-1500
www.BreurMedia.com

I dedicate this novel to my 92-year-old parents,
Raymond and Dorotha Myers, who taught me volumes
about unconditional love, tolerance of other viewpoints
and lifestyles, and the true essence of heavenly spirit.

Thanks to all of my family members and friends
who read drafts of my novel and offered
helpful comments and much needed support;
to my son, Nick, for his great cover art;
to my daughter, Erica, for her encouragement;
to Barack Obama, for giving me the opportunity
to work on his Senate campaign and
inspiring me to make a difference;
to my publisher, Arthur Breur, for
taking a leap of faith with a new author;
to Doug Birkeheuer, for making me look
better than any sixty-year old deserves;
and, last, but not least, to Madeline Archer,
an accomplished author and good friend,
who advised me throughout my journey.

PRINCE OF THE PHARISEES

Prologue

Christmas Eve 1957 - London

Lizzie Hoffmeier held her breath when she heard the knock at the door of her room at Brown's Hotel. She had thrown her things into one large bag in a mindless panic. She remembered her instructions: "A gentleman is going to come to your room to escort you to a safe place. Ask who sent him. He will tell you 'Miss Boone.' Then ask him what we called the mother superior at St. Gert's. When he answers that correctly, let him in and do what he asks you to do."

When the man at the door answered " 'Mad Dog,' " Lizzie removed the chain and opened the door. Her visitor was holding a dark gray cloth overcoat and a black travel case. He smiled and said, "Nice to meet you, Lizzie."

She began to relax. His voice was deep and authoritative. She couldn't determine the accent, but she knew he was not British. His close-cropped salt-and-pepper hair suggested he might be ex-military. "This is the coat you'll be wearing," he said, handing it to her. "Please show me what you have packed."

Despite her fear, Lizzie perked up. He was fortyish, fit, and firm with her. "That won't be necessary. I have my fur coat," she said.

"You'll have to leave your coat and wear this one. It's best. For you and your baby."

Suddenly, her beloved mink seemed trivial. "Whatever you say. Here," she said, pointing to her bag on the bed.

He grinned as he surveyed its jumbled contents. She loved the way his skin crinkled around his blue eyes when he smiled. Opening his travel case next to hers, he quickly sorted through her bag, extracting only a few items. "This is all we can take. Is there one other thing you would like to add?"

"Oh, my God, yes. I can't believe I forgot." Hurrying over to the closet, she brought back an old hat box and retrieved a red silk hand bag. Checking to make sure the emerald brooch was inside, she handed it to him. It was the last piece of her mother's jewelry. Her only real asset. "What's your name?" she asked.

"You can call me Hank," he said as he locked the case. "Shall we go? There's a scarf in the coat pocket. Use it to cover your head. When we leave, hold my arm and keep your head down."

Once inside the car, she exhaled deeply. "Everything's going to be fine, Lizzie," Hank said. "You're safe now." She took his hand and held it tightly. Hank put his other hand on top of hers and gave it a squeeze.

As he pulled into traffic, she asked, "Are you married, Hank?"

He smiled. "No. Are you proposing?"

"If I did, would you accept? Make me an honest woman?"

"You're charming, Lizzie. That's very flattering. But I'm not good husband material, I'm afraid."

"Do you have a brother?"

Hank laughed softly. "No more personal questions. Try to get some sleep. We've got a long drive ahead of us before we get on the boat."

Chapter 1

December 1971 – September 1972

"Come on, Emily. We're going out to celebrate your last night as a maiden," Ruth Schmidt whispered in her sister's ear.

It was the night before Emily Schmidt's wedding to Lieutenant Lawrence McIntyre. The rehearsal dinner at Leo's Steakhouse, the best restaurant in Mt. Jehoshaphat, Pennsylvania, had just concluded. It had been six months since Larry and she had graduated from Penn State. Emily had spent the time working in the marketing department of the McIntyre family business, McIntyre Steel, in Pittsburgh. She had been living with her future in-laws while Larry had completed his training at Fort Benning, Georgia. He was shipping out to Vietnam in five days.

"Oh, I don't think I should," Emily said, knitting her brow. The bride-to-be had her father's healthy German nose and high forehead and her mother's close-set hazel eyes and long neck. Her straight brown hair draped over matronly breasts that were cantilevered up and out by an industrial strength brassiere.

"Yes, you should," Ruth said. "It's your last night of freedom. Come on. Larry's going out with the boys. Marjorie's coming too. It'll be fun."

"Where would we go? Neither of you is old enough to drink. Marjorie's only eighteen." Emily was holding a stack of wedding gifts just received from Larry's relatives. They were heavy boxes. Sterling silver, she hoped. The McIntyres could afford the good stuff on the bridal registry. Her mother had been scandalized by the prices. "Surely, you can find something more sensible in silver plate," she had said to Emily.

Ruth rolled her eyes. "Marjorie's the one who found this place. It's a roadhouse in the next county. They don't card. It's ladies night. Half-price drinks."

Emily set down the booty and looked over at her mother. Hannah Schmidt was busy, talking with Larry's mother. She was in heaven. Her oldest daughter was about to marry a God-fearing patriot from a family with money and good manners. She would not be happy, knowing her girls were taking off to celebrate the end of Emily's virginity in a bar filled with lecherous drunks. "What do we tell Mom?" Emily asked.

"You keep your mouth shut. I'll tell her we're taking you out. She won't be able to object in front of Larry's mother. Now, go get in the car before she can give you the evil eye."

The three Schmidt girls sat on stools in the half-empty saloon. Tommy's Bar and Lounge was a smoky, tired-looking watering hole. Largemouth bass and deer antlers were mounted on knotty pine next to neon beer signs and a lighted clock with a rippling mountain stream on its face. A string of multi-colored lights blinked over the bar, and Perry Como was singing *It's Beginning to Look a Lot Like Christmas* on the jukebox. Under other circumstances, Emily would not have been impressed, but on the night before her wedding, the atmosphere was perfect. Just the right amount of tawdriness. Ruth and Marjorie seemed at home in Tommy's, and Emily wanted to be one of the girls.

The sisters had been close when they were younger, playing dolls and board games, baking cookies and riding bikes. But early on, Hannah had cut Emily out of the herd for special attention. Emily suffered the brunt of her mother's rigidity and fearfulness. Hannah didn't have the energy to indoctrinate all three girls, but she felt if she scared Emily sufficiently, she would pass along the lessons, much as her older sister had done with her. Emily enjoyed the special bond she had with her mother, and she was very protective of her sisters, but she didn't have the mother gene. Try as she might, she couldn't browbeat her sisters into following the rules of wholesome ladyhood. Both of her sisters were children of the Sixties. They were much less willing to put up with Hannah's hand wringing. Emily was convinced that twenty-year-old Ruth had been smoking pot and sleeping around for most of her five semesters at Penn State. She suspected that Marjorie, a freshman at Slippery Rock, was a libertine in the making.

Ruth ordered a bottle of champagne, and the bartender managed to find an old bottle of California pink brut in the back of the cooler. He delivered the bottle with three smoked glass wine goblets. Emily examined her glass, blew in it to remove the dust and then wiped it out with her cocktail napkin. "Cheers," Ruth said, holding her goblet aloft. The pink brut looked blood red in the smoked glass. "To my sister, Emily. May you never leave the bedroom on your honeymoon."

"To multiple orgasms," Marjorie said. The three girls clinked glasses and took a sip of the flat wine. The bubbles had long since popped.

"Thank you," Emily said. "I feel like the prize pig at the county fair."

Ruth and Marjorie exchanged glances. "What do you mean?" Ruth asked.

"Well, it's just that my virginity seems like such a public matter. I'm embarrassed in front of my own sisters."

Marjorie patted Emily's back. "Oh, don't be embarrassed. We're proud of you. You've stood by your beliefs and look what you got. Larry's a hunk. Is it true that he's a virgin, too?"

"Marjorie!" Ruth exclaimed.

"That's all right," Emily said. "I knew you couldn't keep a secret, Ruth."

"Wow," Marjorie said. "How do you guys know if you'll be sexually compatible?"

"We're compatible in every other way. I'm sure we'll be fine. Marriage is not only about sex, little sister."

"Now, you're sounding like Mom," Marjorie said as she poured herself some more fizzless vino.

"I hate to admit it, but I have a lot of her in me," Emily said. "I envy you two. You seem so relaxed about sex. I wish I could be more like you, but I'm not. I know you think I'm silly, but I worry about you two. Be careful you don't get pregnant. Mom would be devastated."

"Don't worry about me," Marjorie said. "I use birth control. I keep condoms where Mom can't find them."

"I'm taking the pill," Ruth said. "I got a prescription at the university clinic. It's great. I don't have to worry about rubbers breaking, and the boys are happier."

Emily took a big gulp of what now seemed like sacrificial wine. She was an over-ripe vestal virgin waiting to be penetrated to assuage the gods of fertility. Gods that her sisters had gladly chosen to defy. She had presumed her sisters were playing around. Especially Ruth. But being confronted with the reality of their licentiousness on the night before her wedding, the night before Christmas Eve, made her feel particularly ridiculous. She was both shocked and fascinated. Neither of her sisters was markedly different than Emily in her features or coloring. And they didn't have the advantage of Emily's prodigious mammaries. Yet, they presented and carried themselves in a much more provocative and appealing manner. Their make-up, hair and clothing were all carefully programmed to attract not just a man, but men. Even as they celebrated with her, they were furtively cruising the few likely candidates at Tommy's.

"What kind of birth control have you two planned on using?"

Marjorie asked.

"We really haven't talked about it. I suppose we'll take our chances. If I get pregnant, then it was meant to be."

"Yes, but do you want to have a baby right away?" Ruth asked. "While he's in Vietnam? Wouldn't you rather wait until he comes back? It would be so hard to raise a child alone."

Emily really hadn't thought about it. She had compartmentalized her wedding separately from her life in Pittsburgh, living with Larry's parents. It was as if she were a single woman again. Larry had been home only once in the last six months, and there had been no time for just the two of them during his visit. Her married life would start after he returned from the war. And she was fine with that. She would miss Larry, but the major task would have been accomplished. She would be married to a near-perfect man, the seal would be broken and her life would be launched. Though, as the alcohol began to take effect, she decided that bearing him a child would be just the thing to do while he was away killing gooks. The child would bond them together forever.

The following evening, the newlyweds were ensconced in a heart-shaped pool in their own private suite at a resort in the Poconos Mountains of northeastern Pennsylvania. Emily had insisted they wear their bathing suits. Larry had reluctantly agreed. She had met him in the campus library when he had given her a brochure for Students for Jesus. She had declined his invitation to a prayer meeting, but he had been persistent. Blonde, blue-eyed and buff, he was every bit the hunk her sister had admired. As he wrapped his arm around Emily and caressed her right breast, she stiffened and then tried to relax. She reminded herself that this was what the honeymoon was all about. The beginning of their sex life together. She wanted to send him off to war happy. She didn't want to appear too skittish. He was making her feel good as he rubbed her nipple through the wet fabric. This part she liked, though she would have preferred to close her eyes and play the narcotized princess. She forced herself to look into his eyes and smile. He kissed her and pulled her hand down to his crotch. It was much larger and harder than she had expected. Still, in the abstract, underwater in the subdued lighting, it was exciting. It thrilled her that she could make this man so eager and ardent.

Larry picked her up out of the water and climbed out of the pool. He carried her dripping to the large round mattress. It seemed to Emily more like a stage than a bed. How, she wondered, did they find sheets to fit? "Let's dry off first," she said. But Larry ignored her. He threw her onto the center of the circle and landed on top of her. Starting with her neck, he began kissing her, inch by inch, pulling the straps off her shoulders and slowly revealing her nakedness as he made his way down to her pudendum. Emily closed her eyes and began breathing deeply. "It's the best advice I can give you," her mother had said as she buttoned up her wedding dress. When he spread her legs and tried to lick her labia, she pulled him up to her and kissed him hard. With that encouragement, Larry positioned himself and slowly pushed inward.

The pain was excruciating, but she bit her lip and endured it. Her mother had warned her about this, too. Like Hannah, Emily had an unusually thick hymen. She bled profusely, but Larry didn't notice. The blood was all the lubricant he needed. He rocked above her and grunted so violently that she opened her eyes, fearful that he was having a heart attack. What she saw repulsed her. This good Christian man was straining every muscle as he plunged deep into her. His sweat dripped off his brow on to her breasts as he rose and fell in an ape-like rhythm. Surely, she thought, this was not how it was done, rocking to and fro in such a mechanical, piston-like pounding assault. She saw the two of them in the mirror on the ceiling above her and closed her eyes as quickly as she could. But it was too late. The image was frozen in her mind for all time. His butt tensing as he ground himself into her. The horrified look on her face. The hapless female splayed out for the man's pleasure. Her mother had not prepared her for this. This degradation and defilement. No wonder it was called original sin. Nothing could be further from God than what Larry was doing to her.

Just as she thought it couldn't get any worse, Larry started groaning and gasping at a quickened rate as he increased his pummeling of her loins. His face constricted into a mask of pain and pleasure as he exploded inside her. She was sure she felt his semen strike against her cervix as wave after wave of sticky goo spattered inside her once-pure vagina. He collapsed onto her, all wet and slippery, panting in her ear. Thank God, it's over, she thought. Seconds later, he began to stiffen inside her, and without even asking for permission, he began his barbaric thrusting again. After his second ejaculation, he fell off of her, mumbling his thanks and passing out almost simultaneously.

Emily gathered up her bathing suit and held it between her legs as she made her way to the bathroom. She closed the door and looked at herself in the mirror. She looked ten years older. Haggard, in pain, stretched and torn, violated. She sat down on the toilet to urinate as blood and semen dripped out of her. Cursing Eve and the serpent, she cried into a towel, muffling her sobs as best she could. Then, she remembered it was Christmas Eve. She wanted to be home with her parents and sisters, sleeping in her own bed, alone, waiting for Christmas morning. She wanted to be a little girl again.

The balance of the honeymoon was a nightmare. Larry was like Dr. Jekyll and Mr. Hyde. Outside the motel room, he was a perfect gentleman, more attentive than ever. Holding her, touching her gently, giving her little kisses every few minutes. However, in their suite, the pleasure pit, as he called it, he became possessed, filled with such seething surges of testosterone that he was barely capable of speech. It was if twenty-two years of pent-up desire had burst out of him with a force so volcanic that he could not resist it, even if he had prayed on his mother's soul for temperance. Emily imagined him breaking down doors, pulling down temple pillars and raping the Sabine women, one after another, all of them her.

Finally, finally, finally their three day marathon of sexual torture came to an end. They drove home to Pittsburgh in his '57 Chevy, his hand on her thigh most of the way, him smiling at her from time to time as if they shared the most precious secret on earth. He was spent and she was in pain, barely able to sit. They headed straight to the airport, where his parents met them. At the gate, he kissed her good-bye and whispered in her ear, "Whenever you get sad, just think about our honeymoon, the two of us naked, me inside you. I'll do the same. That memory is a gift from God. It will sustain us until I return." With that, he squeezed her butt and headed down the gangway in his crisp green uniform.

Emily couldn't even muster a tear. She was so glad to see him go that she had to hold herself in place, sadly waving for a respectable length of time, to convince his parents that she would be appropriately bereft until he returned the conquering hero. Five weeks later, she learned she was pregnant, and nine months later, she gave birth to Lawrence Jr. The birth trauma was only slightly more terrorizing than sexual intercourse. She figured that the whole process might help her better accommodate Larry's penis once it returned. She had just arrived home from the hospital with Larry's parents and Larry Jr. when two young men in Army uniforms stepped out of a government car and grimly marched up to the front door. Both of them looked barely old enough to be out of high school. The taller one, a baby-faced blonde, asked, "Ma'am, are you Mrs. Lawrence McIntyre?"

"Yes," she said, half fearing, half hoping that her husband had been paralyzed from the waist down in combat. Her mother-in-law burst into tears.

"We are sorry to report that Lieutenant McIntyre was captured by the enemy three days ago. The United States Army believes that Lieutenant McIntyre is alive. He is a prisoner of war. We want to assure you that we are doing everything possible to obtain his release."

The thought of her husband, tied to a rack, or paraded through Hanoi or starving in a small cold room, fighting off rats trying to steal a moldy piece of bread, finally broke through her shell. As much as she hated what he had done to her womanhood, she could not help but feel compassion for the sad, scared boy on the other side of the planet, wishing he were in her arms at that very moment. She handed Larry Jr. to Larry's dad and ran upstairs to her room to cry alone. She had held it all in for nine months, but she could not hold it in any longer. Picking up the phone, she called her folks. "Mom, it's Emily. I'm coming home."

September 23, 1972

Robert David Hamilton III and his son, Bob, were golfing at Elysian Fields, Robert III's private white Protestant male-only golf club near the old family plantation, Hamilton Oaks, outside of Atlanta. Robert III's graying hair was still in the pompadour style of his youth. His round belly drooped over his white leather belt by a couple of inches. In the moist heat, he was at his pinkest.

As they drove away in their golf cart from the twelfth hole, Robert III said, "I've made an important decision, Bobby."

"What's that?" Bob asked, his voice cracking. He was a half foot taller than his father. Slender, with dark curly hair and the random pimple, he carried himself with the cocky self-assurance of the lone heir to two fortunes, Hamilton Industries and his maternal grandfather's even larger empire, Boone Enterprises.

"I'm switching political parties."

"Why?"

"We Hamiltons have been Democrats forever, but the party has deserted us, deserted the South actually. They're trying to destroy our way of life. It's been a long time coming. I used to play golf at the

Bobby Jones public course in the city back before you were born. Then, some upstart niggers filed a lawsuit, demanding they be able to tee up right next to us. The Supreme Court ruled in their favor. Mayor Hartsfield tried to save the public courses, offered to sell them to private individuals, keep them white-only. But it didn't happen. It's been going downhill ever since."

They pulled up to the next tee. "How so?" Bob asked.

Using his cane, Robert III slowly stepped out of the cart. "Well, everywhere you look, you see it. The races are mixing in the stores, restaurants, movie houses, schools. They've polluted the music young people listen to."

Bob selected his club and his father's club and put a tee and a ball down for his father. "What's Nixon going to do about it?"

Robert III tried a practice stroke. "Well, he can't exactly reverse it all, but he can slow it down. Pick the right judges, make it harder for them to file lawsuits, let them know we're still in charge. It's too bad. Everyone was better off the way it was." He swung and his ball sailed off to the right. "Damn Japs. If I had two good legs, I could shave twenty strokes off my game."

Bob swung and hit his ball two hundred yards down the middle. "Did I tell you I'm running for class president?"

Robert III wiped his brow. "No, you didn't. That's wonderful, Bobby. You're a born leader."

"Thanks. I thought I'd give it a try. See how it goes."

Robert III put his hand on his hip and looked up at his son, beaming. "I'm sure you'll win. You're so handsome and smart. All the girls will vote for you."

"Yeah, I'm kinda hoping for that. Chip Cotter's running against me."

Robert III climbed back into the cart and took a swig of bourbon from his flask. "Well, let me know if I can do anything to help. Cotter's dad does a lot of business with one of our companies. Maybe I could talk to him."

Bob looked at his father. "You serious?"

"Absolutely. I'd do anything for you, Bobby."

"I should be okay. Chip's kinda dumb. I've been working on my own stealth strategy, making nice with the girls, especially the plain janes. Nobody pays much attention to them." Bob stopped the cart and ran out to find his father's ball.

Robert III smiled. "Except for you."

"Except for sweet ole Bobby Hamilton." Bob sang as he headed into the rough.

April 4, 1973

On March 29, 1973, the last of the American POWs walked out of the North Vietnamese prison they called the Hanoi Hilton and headed home. Larry McIntyre was the last man out the door and onto the truck. He had been in captivity for six months. His capture was a quirk of fate that he had accepted as a test from God. A Daniel in the lion's den catechism. His commanding officer would have called it a death wish. Without the knowledge of his parents or his fiancé, Emily, Larry had taken every step possible to assure that he would be placed in harm's way. Most of his ROTC buddies at Penn State were being decommissioned shortly after graduation because the war was winding down. Larry had to make a determined and persuasive appeal to keep his commission and to be attached to one of the few combat units still fighting in Vietnam.

Once in Vietnam, he had taken every opportunity to get assigned to the most dangerous missions. By September 1972, there was little else to do on the ground, but assist South Vietnamese troops in secondary roles. The American military presence had been restricted largely to providing air support. Captain Jessie Grant had told Larry, "Lieutenant, if you keep it up, you're going to get yourself killed. I'd advise you to keep your head down from now on out. Let some other poor son of a bitch take this one."

"This one's mine, Captain. I'm ready to go." Grant had shaken his head and handed Larry orders to accompany a column of South Vietnamese troops headed north to Quang Tri City. They were to take part in the final stages of an effort to reclaim the province lost to the North Vietnamese in the Easter Offensive earlier that year. A few miles short of their objective, they had been ambushed. Larry got caught in a spray of machine gun fire and had fallen into a deep ditch next to the road. Just before he passed out, he had seen a vision of a golden temple on a hill ablaze with light. When he awoke, he was in a makeshift prison hospital with bandages covering half his body. He was able to move his arms and legs, but he was in excruciating pain. As he drifted in and out of delirium, he had seen the golden temple each time. He was sure it was a sign of God's favor.

Larry had become more and more desperate in his last year at

Penn State because he had not yet experienced transcendence, an encounter with God so strong that it would transform him and show him the path he must take to fulfill God's will on earth. He was pretty sure that if he returned to his father's steel fabrication business in Pittsburgh and raised a family in Upper St. Clair he would not have the holy epiphany he was seeking. One cold, gray Saturday morning in January, he had been particularly despondent after masturbating. He had defiled himself yet again, and he was sure that he would not be chosen. He had turned to his Bible and opened it by chance to Zechariah nine, verses fourteen through seventeen, where he read:

> Then the Lord will appear over them, and his arrow go
> forth like lightning; the Lord God will sound the trumpet,
> and march forth in the whirlwinds of the south.

> The Lord of hosts will protect them, and they shall devour
> and tread down the slingers; and they shall drink their
> blood like wine, and be full like a bowl, drenched like the
> corners of the altar.

> On that day the Lord their God will save them for they are
> the flock of his people; for like the jewels of a crown they
> shall shine on his land.

> Yea, how good and how fair it shall be! Grain shall make
> the young men flourish, and the new wine the maidens.

Larry had been convinced that he was being called to battle where, drenched in the blood of his enemies, he would receive a revelation from God. Based on similar random Bible selections, he had spoken to Emily in the library and later asked her to marry him. If he had read verses eleven and twelve that day, he might have had some warning about his capture by the Viet Cong and the Lord setting "prisoners of hope" free from their "waterless pit" so that they could return to their "stronghold."

As he recovered from his wounds and settled into the humdrum existence of life in solitary confinement, the golden temple vision had faded from his dreams. He was afraid he had failed God in some way. The only blood he had drunk was his own when a guard whacked him with a rifle butt, cracking his tooth and splitting his lip. Time was slipping away. He had been afraid the warring parties would sign an agreement at the Paris Peace talks before God could give him some clarification on the whole golden temple thing. He needed to confront his enemy and was perplexed that he hadn't been dragged into an interrogation room for waterboarding or cattle prods. No matter how much of a ruckus he made or how foul his epithets were, his captors had ignored him.

One day, when the guard brought him his daily ration of rice, Larry had hurled a bucket of urine and feces in his face. That move got their attention. After being beaten and kicked by three guards in a storm of angry Vietnamese profanity, he had been hauled naked into a small room and strapped into a chair. While an officer looked on, two guards had attached electrodes to his nipples, testicles and penis. For good measure, they had dropped the bottom out of the chair and stuck one up his anus. Finally, Larry had thought, we're getting somewhere. Sure enough, at some point between the tenth and twentieth jolt of electricity, the golden temple had come into focus. He had seen the grand house of worship in all of its glorious detail on a magnificent wooded hill. The massive golden doors had opened and out had walked Emily in a flowing white robe holding their son, Larry Jr., also in a white robe. She had been smiling and waving at him and motioning him to follow her into the temple. It was then that he knew. Despite the pain, he had smiled. And then he had heard the laughter and opened his eyes. The officer and the guards were pointing at his crotch where his penis stood at attention. Just then he had ejaculated. That, too, he had taken as a sign from God.

In Pittsburgh, he limped off the plane to a hero's welcome. Emily, Larry Jr., Larry's parents, Emily's parents and half of Upper St. Clair were there to greet him. At the welcome home party at his parents' country club, he took Emily aside and said, "I had a vision over there. It was a message from God."

"Really, dear. What did He tell you?" She was holding six month old Larry Jr. who was ready for his nap. She had learned early on that she had very little patience with his pre-nap fussiness. Her mother had been spelling Emily in the afternoons so that she could take her own nap. At that point of the party, both mother and child needed a dark, quiet room.

"He wants us to build a church, a golden temple actually. On a hill. He wants us to minister to his flock and bring his message to

Upper St. Clair and, eventually, to the rest of the world."

Emily had never seen Larry like this. Before, he had always spoken like some well-behaved Boy Scout with an earnest devoutness that could be irritating at times. But now, he was speaking with an aggressive confidence that made her perk up. "What about your father's business?" she asked. She was tired of living with his parents and her parents. She was ready for the big home in the suburbs. Every minister she knew lived in a modest parsonage. Every minister's wife she knew wore rummage sale dresses.

"Oh, we can't do it right away. I'll still work for Dad for the time being. I've got to get a divinity degree or at least take some classes. But we can get started. Maybe rent some space nearby. I want to build a congregation of true believers."

Larry Jr. was starting to whine and arch his back. He was overtired and over-stimulated. Emily felt like whining, too. "But Larry, surely there's some church we could find that would suit you."

"There's not one church in Pittsburgh that's worth a damn. They're all sleepy little excuses for tax exemptions. None of them is awake spiritually. I bring a new message of redemption, a redemption born of fire and blood. There's a battle coming, Emily, and we have to be ready for it."

Larry Jr. opened his mouth as wide as he could and used the full volume of his little lungs to announce his unhappiness with life as he knew it. He was wet, tired, hungry and scared of the crazy man talking to his mother. "We'll talk more later. I've got to find my mother," Emily said. She turned on her heels and marched off with her son screaming in her ear. His tears were staining her new silk dress. It was lavender, her favorite color, and it was her first designer dress. The first of many, she had hoped, now that Larry was home. She was every bit as unhappy as her son. She did not want to be a preacher's wife. Surely, Larry's father could talk some sense into him.

Later that night, after many heartfelt speeches of praise for Larry's heroics and bravery and many toasts to the future happiness of the reunited couple, Larry climbed into bed next to Emily, who was covered from neck to ankle in her lavender flannel nightgown. She was reading Ira Levin's *The Stepford Wives*. He reached down to pull up her gown. She put her hand on his to stop him. "Not tonight, Larry. I'm having my period." She had been so glad when she started bleeding just before she had left for the airport that morning. She figured she had at least four days before they would have intercourse.

"I could tell," Larry said. "I swear I could smell your hormones. It makes me want you even more."

She kept her hand firmly over his. "Yes, but, I'm all bloody down there, and I've got cramps and it would be such a mess on the sheets. Your parents' sheets."

"Don't worry. Sex is good for your cramps and I'll get a towel to put underneath you. I didn't tell you the other revelation I received from God. He told me that sex between a man and his wife is His gift to us. We celebrate Him when we make love. It's a form of prayer and worship. The more we do it, the more favor He shows to us. We are so blessed to have found each other, you and me. We're two healthy attractive adults, each of us turned on by the other. There's no reason why we can't have sex every night for the rest of our married life." He gave an extra tug on her gown.

She used both hands to stop him. "Larry. This is not right. It's against the Bible. We're not supposed to have sex during my period," she said, relying upon the laws of Leviticus to protect her from his assault.

"Now, Emmy, don't Bible verse me in bed. You can't win that one," he said as he forced her hands away from her gown. "You know how you love your jumbo shrimp. The Bible's against shellfish, too, but you still eat them." He stroked her inner thigh and pulled out her tampon. "I am the head of our house just as Jesus is the head of our church." As he slipped inside her bloody vagina, the image of her favorite appetizer, dipped in thick red cocktail sauce, almost made her vomit.

Moments later, he ejaculated, mixing his semen with her uterine slough. "There, that wasn't so bad, was it?" he asked. "Sorry about getting blood on your gown." He rolled off of her on to his back and fell asleep. She opened her eyes and caught a glimpse of his shrunken penis covered in her menstrual blood, some of it pooling in his navel. She never ate shrimp cocktail again.

November 1975

Eulalia Gibson awoke with the first contraction, but she waited to see how soon the next one would be. With her first child, James, the labor had dragged on for twenty hours. The hospital had sent Sam and her home when they had come to the emergency room with no cervical dilation and contractions an hour apart. She wasn't going to make the same mistake twice. Sam was snoring. She decided to check on James. The three-year-old boy was a light sleeper. Sometimes, when she got up in the middle of the night, she heard him singing in his room. No Motown tonight. She smiled. James' version of *Respect* put Aretha to shame.

She walked through the kitchen and onto the back porch. It was an unusually mild November night for Baltimore. The Japanese maple and sycamore in the back yard of the small townhouse were dropping the last of their leaves in the light breeze. The half moon cast a silvery glow across the yard. She needed to get James' toys out of the sandbox. Now was as good a time as any she decided and waddled out to the box with a bushel basket. She was larger this time. James had been small, barely six pounds. The doctor had told her this baby would probably be more than eight pounds. Another boy, she suspected. Leaning over to pick up a half-buried plastic bucket, she felt the next contraction. It was stronger than the first. Maybe five minutes had passed. That was close. She continued to fill the basket with scoops and shovels and dump trucks. The next contraction made her straighten up and cry out in pain. Dropping the basket, she shuffled back to the house as fast as she could, but before she could reach the back door, her water broke with one immense contraction. She yelped again. "Sam," she cried out.

They dropped off James at her sister's place and headed to the University of Maryland Hospital. By the time they reached the admissions desk, Eulalia was fully dilated and fighting the urge to push. Orderlies helped her on to a gurney and rushed her back to a delivery room. Sam sat down in the fathers' waiting room. He was short of breath, and he had a pain in his gut that he'd never felt before. Probably stress, he thought. The pain passed. He lit a cigarette and tried to relax.

Sam Gibson had grown up in Pea Ridge, Maryland and joined the Marines one step ahead of his draft notice in 1965. After three tours in Vietnam, he'd landed a job as a Baltimore city bus driver and met Eulalia Scott at a wedding the following year. Sam nodded off in his chair and the next thing he heard was the television in the waiting room. Before he opened his eyes, he heard Bill Cosby say:

> On this day two hundred years ago, November 12, 1775, General Washington signed an order prohibiting all black Americans, slave and free, from participating

in the armed conflict with the British. Washington, a slave owner, and other leaders feared that Negroes, once armed and allowed to defend themselves and their country, would refuse to return to servitude and would demand equal rights. Thus, blacks, who had already fought bravely at the battles of Lexington and Concord, Bunker Hill and many other battles, were stripped of their arms and sent home. This Bicentennial Minute was sponsored by the John Hancock Life Insurance Company.

Sam couldn't believe what he was hearing. Normally, the Bicentennial Minutes were self-congratulatory patriotic pap. Opening his eyes, he saw Barbara Walters and Jim Hartz smiling out at him from their set on the Today show. He checked his watch. It was a little after seven o'clock. It had been three hours since they had arrived at the hospital. Something was wrong, he was sure. Just then, a young black man in surgery greens opened a door. "Mr. Gibson?" he called out.

Sam scrambled to his feet. "I'm Gibson."

The young man smiled and stepped forward to shake his hand. "Hi, I'm Doctor Magembe." He spoke in a lilting Commonwealth English. "Congratulations. You have a beautiful baby girl. Your wife and daughter are both fine. She's a big girl, Mr. Gibson. Nine pounds. Come on back to see them."

"I was worried. What took so long?" Sam asked as he followed the doctor down the hallway.

"Your daughter decided to take her time. She has a mind of her own."

Eulalia was holding her baby when Sam entered the room. She looked tired, but happy. She saw Sam and smiled. "Hey, Daddy. Here's your little girl."

"Not so little, I hear." He took his daughter from Eulalia and rocked her in his arms. "Should we call her Rosa or Rosie?"

"Let's call her Rosa. See if it sticks. No use giving her the name if we don't use it."

Sam held Rosa up and she opened her eyes. "So, great things, huh?"

"Yes," Eulalia said. "She's going to move mountains. You'll see."

In the doctor's lounge down the hall, Magembe was sitting on a beige Naugahyde sofa, relaxing with a cigarette. His friend, Doctor Tambo, walked in and sat down next to him. "You wanted to see me?"

Magembe crushed his cigarette and leaned in to talk privately. "There was a female born this morning. I assisted. She has the Sign of the Leopard."

Tambo's eyes widened. "That's not possible."

Magembe sipped cold coffee from a paper cup. "I know. That's what I thought. But I saw it with my own eyes. It's the right shape in the right place."

"But her parents?"

"They're not African as far as I can tell. Blacker than you or me, but they came over on the boats, I'm sure."

"So both of them?"

Magembe lit another cigarette. "It's the only explanation. Pure bloods."

"What are the chances of that?"

"One in a million." Magembe took a long drag and exhaled. "But, this is not random. I felt the heat of the cat's breath on my neck when she came out."

Tambo smiled. "Then, she will have the power."

Magembe sat back. "Yes."

"Have you talked to the parents?"

"No, and I won't. They can't help her. And her father is sick. He won't last long."

"It seems a shame. Not to provide instruction for such a child."

"She's here for a reason. She will find her way."

Rosa Parks Gibson left the hospital with her parents three days later. Sam gave her a bath that evening. Her brother, James, sat on the counter next to the kitchen sink. "Look," he said. "Kitty."

"No, James. She's a baby. She's your sister."

"No, Daddy. Kitty." James pointed at Rosa's right shoulder blade.

Barely discernible against her dark skin was a birthmark. Sam didn't notice it. He was too nervous with the slippery little girl to pay much attention to a three-year-old's gibberish. "Whatever you say, son." Just then, his gut wrenched in pain. "Eulie, can you come in the kitchen?"

Chapter 2

June 6, 1976

"I've lost him," Martha Hamilton said. Marion Randolph and she were riding along a creek bed at Hamilton Oaks. It was late morning, and they were headed for their favorite spot to picnic, a large flat boulder near a small waterfall.

Martha's auburn hair was just beginning to gray. Her green eyes were still sharp. And she'd held her figure in middle age. A disdain for southern cooking, she would say. But, mostly it was her insecurity. She had never fully accepted the fact that Marion found her attractive. They had fallen in love thirteen years before on another trail ride. He had been the new stable hand, barely twenty-one, and she had been the mistress of the big house. She had been sleeping alone since she'd kicked her husband, Robert III, out of the bedroom for having an affair with his secretary.

"What do you mean?" Marion asked, looking back at her. He was everything Robert III was not. Tall, lean, intelligent, and thoughtful. As black as Robert III was pink.

"He's his own person," Martha answered. "And I don't like what he's becoming. The older he gets, the sharper he comes into focus. What I thought were childhood traits have hardened into rather unpleasant permanent fixtures of his personality."

They reached the boulder and tethered their horses to a willow tree. "Oh, come on," Marion said. "He's a teenager. All teenagers are obnoxious. It's what they do."

They sat down on the boulder in the cool shade. "No, it's more than that," Martha said. "He's actually not very teenagerish. He's well-mannered, respectful, even sweet."

Marion opened a saddle bag and pulled out their lunch. "Well, then, what are you complaining about?"

"It's not real. It's an act. He's covering up what I'm afraid is an almost pathological narcissism. He feigns humility and compassion, but he's actually super competitive and judgmental. He uses his friends, his classmates, his grandmother to get what he wants with a steely charm that scares me. You should see how he handles Robert. The poor man doesn't know what hit him."

"But he hasn't fooled you, huh? I don't see it. I've spent a lot of time with him. He seems like—"

"A perfect Southern gentleman."

"No. I was going to say a nice kid. Maybe this is your stuff. You were a rebel. Maybe you're projecting."

"Remind me to stop lending you my psychology books. I've thought about that, hoping that's what I was doing, but I don't think so. I know what a genuinely good kid looks like. My sister, Charlotte, was for real. Bob is another breed of cat altogether."

Marion pitched his apple core into the ferns on the other side of the creek. "Give me some examples."

"Well, his political campaigns, for one. You know. Class president every year. This last year, he was student body president, too. I overheard him once, on the phone to his friend, Lisa Brown, his so-called campaign manager. The two of them are like Haldeman and Erlichman, plotting their next move. Dirty tricks, the whole thing. But what I heard only confirmed what I already felt in my gut."

"Is it so bad he's a born politician? A lot of great men have been assholes in their private lives."

"No mother wants her son to be an asshole, whether he's loved by the masses or not."

Marion took a bite of his sandwich. "True enough. So what can you do about it?"

"That's where I started. I don't think there is anything I can do about it. I've lost him. He's almost eighteen. He's going off to Duke this fall. He's fully baked."

October 9, 1976

"One more wedding," Ben Stein said. "The last of four daughters. I'll have to take a second job and rob your piggy bank." Ben and his son, Josh, were sailing off Sydney's Bondi Beach on a clear spring day. There was very little breeze and the water was calm. At fifty-one, Ben still had the wiry frame of his youth. His hair had thinned and grayed so he had taken to wearing a Greek fisherman's cap to protect his scalp. Dressed in cut offs and a T-shirt, he looked barely forty. Josh was wearing a pair of lime green board shorts and sunglasses. He'd trimmed his curls back for football earlier that year and decided he liked the shorter look.

"Good luck. I'm tapped out," Josh responded. "I spent my last cent at the record store."

"I should have opened a record store. You kids spend all your money there. What did you buy?"

Bohemian Rhapsody. It's a single by Queen."

"What's Queen?"

"It's a British rock band. But this song is like rock opera. I'll play it for you when we get back."

"Why do they call themselves Queen?"

"I don't know." Josh smiled. "What about your music? The Modernaires, the Pied Pipers, the Four Aces? How did they choose those names?"

"Hey, those were great groups. They really knew how to sing."

"But they had goofy names. I bet you never asked why the Modernaires called themselves the Modernaires."

"Still, what's Queen? Why not the Queens or the Four Queens?"

Josh smiled again. "Talk to me before you buy a record store, okay? I think you should stick to real estate."

Ben waved off his son. "Don't worry. Sarah's reception will put me in the poor house. You want some lunch? I made tongue sandwiches."

"Sure." Josh lowered the sails while his father unpacked the cooler.

The conversation drifted on to Josh's sisters and their respective husbands and Sarah's fiancé, Cliff, the only gentile in the lot, and the hope that he'd feel welcome in the family. Ben quizzed Josh about the utility of studying English literature at the University of Sydney the following year, and Josh defended his choice in the manner typical of children of successful entrepreneurs. "I don't really care how much money I make."

Then, Ben asked, "It's just a couple months 'til the senior dance. Have you thought about who you'd like to ask?"

"Yes, I have, but it's not going to happen."

"What do you mean?"

"I want to take Jeremy Logan."

There was a long silence. The wind had started to pick up. "What, you're not good enough for Jeremy's parents?" Ben asked.

Josh studied his father. He hadn't intended to come out to his father that particular day, but he had decided that he would have the conversation before graduation. His father sometimes used humor to hide discomfort, and Josh wondered if Ben were making a joke because he was too hurt to say how he really felt. "Jeremy's parents don't know about us," Josh said. "They don't know about Jeremy. He's afraid they'll kick him out."

Ben lifted his cap and looked at his son. "How long have you been with Jeremy?"

"Since the beginning of high school."

Ben sat up. "How long have you known?"

"Since I can remember."

"Does your mother know?"

"Yes."

Ben nodded. "How long has she known?"

Josh hesitated. "Since I was eleven. She caught me with Stu Rosen."

"And she told you not to tell me because I would be upset."

"Pretty much."

Ben leaned over and patted Josh's hand. "You're a good son, Josh, but you underestimate me. I love you no matter what."

"I know that, Dad. I wanted to tell you first thing. But, Mom wanted me to wait."

"Poor woman. I'm afraid she's the one who's upset. And all these years, she's kept it to herself."

"That's what I figured."

"You know you never have to keep a secret from me. I will always love you. I loved you the minute I held you in my arms in that airport."

"I know, Dad. I'm sorry. I'm glad I finally told you."

June 12, 1979

Eulalia Gibson was sprinkling soil on her husband's casket with her free hand. In her other arm, she held one-year-old Althea, her third child. Standing next to her at the graveside were James, six, and Rosa, three. James was holding the American flag, folded into a tight triangle by the contingent of U.S. Marines who had served as the color guard at the service in Arlington National Cemetery. The little boy was grim faced. Rosa was simply perplexed. "Where's Daddy?" she asked as she hugged her mother's leg, not sure what to make of the men in uniform who had fired the rifles three times to salute their fallen comrade.

"Daddy's in heaven, honey," Eulalia replied as she looked up at the deep blue sky of a perfect summer day.

It had been ten years since Sam Gibson had left the jungles of

Vietnam. The nightmares had become less frequent as time had passed, but another residue of the war had become more apparent. Sam was an early victim of exposure to Agent Orange, the U.S. military's defoliant of choice. Twenty million tons of the white powder had been dropped from aircraft to strip trees and bushes of their leaves and deprive the Viet Cong of their cover. The first noticeable symptoms, nausea, diarrhea and brown urine had shown up just after Eulalia had become pregnant with Althea. The dioxin poison ultimately had concentrated in his liver, causing a large cancerous tumor that metastasized and killed him in three months.

Rosie wandered away from her mother and looked behind the young Marines, two of whom were almost as black as her father. They were wearing the same uniform her father had worn in the photograph that hung on the wall in her parents' bedroom. She was hoping to find Sam hiding behind the Marines. She suspected he might be playing the game where he used to hide from her, before he was too sick to get out of bed. When she would find him, he would put her on his shoulders and carry her around while she shrieked with laughter. She wanted her father, and she wanted to laugh. The mood in the Gibson household had been dark for some time. Rosa didn't find her father, but she did catch a glimpse of the leopard. The animal sat on a hill just fifty feet from the grave. She looked into Rosa's eyes and then turned and disappeared behind the hill.

"Kitty cat," she squealed and toddled up the hill after her.

May 11, 1981

"It's almost like the closer to God he gets the more he wants sex," Emily McIntyre said to her sister, Ruth. The two women were walking through the freshly planted garden on the grounds of the newly constructed Church of the New Faith in Upper St. Clair, just outside of Pittsburgh. Emily was dressed in a new lavender suit from a local boutique, modest, but elegant. Appropriate for the minister's wife at the dedication ceremony that was about to take place in the Golden Mount sanctuary. She wore her brown hair short and permed in the style of fortyish suburban women, not too tight, but stiff enough to hold in a breeze. In the last five years, she had been wearing more makeup. She preferred the foundation and powdered look of her mother's generation. Merle Norman was the gold standard.

"That's great," Ruth exclaimed. "Dick and I have less and less sex as time goes by. What with the kids and everything else, we're exhausted at the end of the day."

"Well, Larry's mom takes care of the boys, but I'm tired too, when I get home from work. It was bad enough at the steel company, but now that I'm working fulltime promoting the church, I expect I'll be even busier. Night meetings, weekend meetings. And now, of course, Sundays too. Larry's working even harder than me, but he has the sex drive of a teenager."

When Larry McIntyre arrived home from Vietnam, he had gone to work for his father's steel fabrication business. At the same time, he had launched his church in an empty strip mall storefront. Two years later, his father had died of a heart attack, and Larry had inherited the bulk of the stock in McIntyre Steel. He had sold the company and poured the money into building the golden temple of his dreams on a hill in Upper St. Clair. When Emily had objected to the expense, Larry replied, "Don't worry, dear. God will return our gifts tenfold."

Ruth shook her head. "That figures. You're the prude and you get the sex machine. He's in great shape, too. Does he have a big one?"

"Ruth! You keep asking and I'm not telling."

"Well, does he? I've always suspected he did."

"He's too big for me. But I have nothing to compare him to. He's the only man I've ever been with."

The McIntyres had three sons. After Larry Jr., Joe was born in 1975, and Luke was born in 1978. Emily had called a halt to procreation. She was afraid they would keep making boys. She found boys over-sexualized, playing with their penises and getting erections even as babies. She was glad her mother-in-law was willing to raise them. Larry's mother had moved in when Larry and Emily had built their new parsonage, a small estate, a half-mile from the temple.

Sexual intercourse had never lost its grotesqueness for Emily, but she had managed to limit Larry to twice a week after Joe was born, and then for not much more than ten minutes from beginning to end. While Larry was humping away, she would check out mentally, closing her eyes and visualizing the garden she had been planning for the new church. She groaned every so often so that Larry would think he was pleasing her, but she never had to fake an orgasm. She had convinced Larry that she was incapable of having an orgasm, a congenital defect common to the women in her family, she had claimed.

The sisters sat down on a bench under a crab apple tree. Emily had found a variety with lavender blooms, and the petals were falling gently in their hair as they chatted. She took a deep breath and then plunged ahead. "You know I love Larry dearly, and I feel so lucky to be married to him. He puts me on a pedestal so much of the time with his old-fashioned chivalry. So rare these days. And, he has awakened in me a faith I never had in our parents' church. I believe he has been sent by God to heal this country, and I'm glad I can be part of his mission. I truly believe God brought us together, and I would do almost anything to please him. Heaven forbid if I ever lost him. I could never find another man like him."

Ruth turned to face her. "Why are you worried about losing him?"

Emily dabbed away a tear. "There has been only one moment in our entire marriage that I had any doubt about him. The other night, for the first time ever, he asked me to...you know..." Emily shivered and looked away.

Ruth smiled. "He wanted a blow job? You've been married how long and he's just now asking for a blow job?"

Emily grimaced. "I hate that term. Please don't use it again."

"What did you do?" Ruth asked.

"Well, I said no, of course. I couldn't believe this sweet, devout man could be led astray. I told him I couldn't possibly do such a disgusting thing. I told him I was insulted that he would even suggest that his wife do such a bestial act. Then I ran into the bathroom and locked the door and cried like a baby."

"What did he do?"

"He stood at the door and ordered me to come out." Emily spat out her words in a torrent. "He started talking about being head of the household. I quoted the Bible to him about the abomination of sodomy. I got so angry when he insisted I 'submit' to him. Even now, thinking about it, I get furious at him all over again." Emily pounded her knees with her fists as she finished.

Ruth patted Emily's back. "Don't you think you're overreacting? He's not the first man to ask his wife to do that. Most men love it. My Dick can't get enough of it. I swear he'd rather do that than intercourse."

"I know, I know." Emily dabbed her eyes again. "I just thought Larry would be different. As you know, I have trouble with intercourse. The whole messy business. And the thought of that oozing thing anywhere near my mouth..." Emily shivered again. "Mother said sex is to be endured, but I'm sure she never meant doing that."

Ruth laughed. "I'm sure you're right. Poor Daddy. So what happened?"

"I stayed in the bathroom until he stopped spouting off about my submitting to him. Then, we prayed together for guidance on either side of the door. Me crying the whole time. Finally, he promised that he would never mention it again if I would come out."

"Well, then, why are you still so mad at him?"

The church bells had started ringing, announcing that the dedication service was about to begin. "I'm angry he even thought he could ask me to do that, but I'm afraid he resents me for saying no. We've never fought like that. I'm scared. I want him to love me." Emily got up and brushed the petals out of her coiffure. "Come on, we better hurry."

The women started walking toward the mammoth golden structure. Ruth nudged Emily's arm and asked, "Who's that?" At the back door to the sanctuary was a tall buxom blonde in a scarlet, form-fitting dress with a plunging neckline. She was waving at them and smiling, motioning them toward the open door.

"Ugh!" Emily said. "That's Priscilla Luse. She's the new music coordinator. She's *so* dramatic all the time. I can't stand her. And she fusses over Larry like an infatuated school girl. 'Yes, Reverend McIntyre. Whatever you say, Reverend McIntyre. May I call you Larry, Reverend McIntyre?'"

"Can't you just tell her to back off?"

"She won't back off. I know her type. She'd just do it behind my back. I've got her number. She won't be here long."

April 1984

Rosie Gibson walked into her mother's bedroom in the McCulloh Homes public housing project and asked, "Whatcha doin'?" She was big for nine and already awkward with her size. She sat on the foot of her mother's bed. As soon as Eulalia Gibson came home from her housecleaning job at the Lord Baltimore Hotel, she always put up her feet and took a nap. Her children knew not to disturb her for the first hour, but it was well into the second hour and almost time for dinner. Rosie was hungry.

"I'm just lying here talking to Daddy," Eulalia said. The couple's wedding photo sat on the bed stand. Eulalia had placed photos of Sam Gibson throughout the apartment so that she could talk to him wherever she went.

"Whatcha tellin' him?"

Eulalia smiled. "What good kids you are. He's so proud of you. He's so glad you do what your Momma tells you to do. And you try hard in school. He wants you all to go to college."

Rosie smiled to herself. She loved getting reports from her father. She could barely remember him, but her mother painted such a vivid picture of his spirit that she often felt his presence when her mother had her "little talks" as she called them.

"Momma, can we not use my full name when I'm baptized on Sunday?"

"Now, why would you want to do that, child?"

Rosie looked at the floor. "You know. It's an old lady name. And kids laugh when they hear it."

"Don't you listen to them. They don't know nothing. Rosa Parks was a brave woman. I gave that name to you because you're going to do great things some day."

"I know she was a great lady. And maybe someday I'll do those things. But, I'm just a kid now. That name's too big for me. I'm just Rosie."

Eulalia sat up next to her daughter and gave her a hug. "Now, don't you worry. Folks will be clapping too loud for anyone to hear those kids snickering."

Every Sunday, Eulalia took her children to the Calvary Baptist Church. Eulalia insisted they put on their best clothes and walk the five blocks to the red brick Romanesque fortress. Reverend Marcus Washington was Rosie's first impression of a man of God. He made clear that he did not suffer fools or sinners. His God was a judgmental male force who growled like thunder from on high, much as the reverend did on Sunday mornings.

Washington's sermons gave Rosie nightmares. She lived in fear that she would never enter the pearly gates. Unlike Rosie, her friends were unfazed by the threat of eternal damnation. They paid no attention to the minister. During services, they were drawing pictures, playing games, poking each other, or in the case of Alice Johnson, discreetly masturbating with the hymnal between her legs. But Rosie had been born an old soul. She lived in a spiritual world.

On Easter Sunday, along with twenty-two other nine-year-old children, Rosie was going to be publicly soaked. She was nervous, but also excited, expecting to come out of the water free of nine years of sin, reborn and ready to start life anew. Mature for her age, Rosie already had grown a couple of very healthy buds on her chest. They had been a source of embarrassment for some months, especially with the boys at school, who called her Rosie Boobs. Even in a blousy white cotton choir robe, they were apparent from the back row of the church. When she marched up the steps of the altar and then down three steps into the tepid water of redemption, she had a nervous smile on her face.

Wet to his thighs, dressed in a white-on-white dress shirt and dark trousers, Reverend Washington was waiting for her and nodded approvingly as she stepped toward him. He was a big man with big appetites. His belly stretched his too small shirt and sweat poured off his high forehead. It was an extra warm spring day, and three hundred cardboard fans, courtesy of Nelson Funeral Home, were flapping in the pews. Rosie stood in front of the minister and faced to the side where she saw the familiar jungle cat crouching beneath a row of Easter lilies. She had learned early on not to mention the big kitty to her mother.

Washington put his left hand on the middle of her back and held his right hand above her, summoning God and all His angels to witness. "Do you, Rosa Parks Gibson, accept Jesus Christ as your Lord and Savior? Do you repent your sins and promise to serve Him all the days of your life? Do you forsake all other false gods and believe that, through Christ, you will be granted eternal life?"

"Yes, Sir, I do," Rosie answered clearly and firmly.

"Then, I baptize you, Rosa Parks Gibson, in the name of the Father and the Son and the Holy Ghost."

At this point, Rosie knew to pinch her nose with one of her father's folded white handkerchiefs and relax so that Washington could dip her backward into the cleansing water. She held her breath as Washington placed his right hand over hers and slowly lowered her. Just as Rosie dropped below the surface, Washington dropped his right hand to caress her left breast ever so lightly. Frightened and frozen, Rosie did not move when he touched her, but she opened her mouth in horror and sucked in almost a cup of water. Jerking violently, attempting to breathe, she broke free from Washington's hold and sank to the bottom of the tub. Panicking, she thrashed until she caught her footing and then launched herself upward. Her head struck

Washington's testicles with such force that he buckled in pain. Still under water, Rosie did not hear him cry out "Motherfucker!" But she broke the surface in time to hear the uproar from the congregation.

Eulalia came running down the center aisle, holding her broad-brimmed Easter hat in place with one hand and dragging James and Althea with the other. The organist hurriedly struck up the hymn, "Christ the Lord is Risen Today, Alleluia." The choir director took his cue and frantically gestured the choir to commence singing. Anything to drown out the oaths that Washington was stringing together over the public address system. Rosie coughed and gasped for air as she made her way up the steps and out of tub. The assistant minister quickly turned off the microphone and tried to no avail to quiet his boss.

Rosie did not return to the sanctuary that morning for her first communion, nor did she ever return to Calvary Baptist despite her mother's worst threats. It was then that Rosie found God. Just as her mother had lied to her about the tooth fairy, Easter bunny and Santa Claus, she figured her mother, though well meaning, was off the mark about the true nature of God. This revelation was not at all disturbing to Rosie. In fact, it was hugely liberating. If she could reject Washington's warped vision of a cranky, short-tempered, unloving God, she was free to come to her own conclusions. It seemed to her, at the tender age of nine, that if God created humans in Her own image, then She understood and was forgiving of weaknesses inherent in the human condition. If God is love, then God loved her no matter what she did or who she was. At the time, Rosie could not put her philosophy into so many words, but she knew it intuitively, and, in some ways, she had always known it. And so, she came to understand why the leopard goddess was in her life.

Chapter 3

July 14, 1986

"Now, remember, we get seventy percent of the offering. Don't give them an extra penny. They wouldn't have a pot to piss in if it weren't for us," Reverend Larry McIntyre said. He was sitting in his pastoral office in Upper St. Clair overlooking the valley below.

"Don't worry. Remember, I'm the one who got seventy-five percent in Erie," his wife, Emily responded. She was dressed for intimidation in her navy suit and heels.

Larry smiled. "You're my tigress. I don't know what I'd do without you, honey bun. Go show them who's boss."

Emily headed out the door for the cab waiting to take her to the airport. She was flying to Charleston, West Virginia to meet with the minister of the independent Holy Path Church, a faltering congregation with a large old building that was the perfect location for the fourteenth branch of the Church of the New Faith. After the contract was signed, a large projection screen would be installed at the front of the sanctuary, so that another thousand true believers could be held in the thrall of Reverend Larry's theatrics every Sunday morning.

Larry's vision of redemption, born of fire and blood, had grown into the largest church in a five state area, offering remote live feeds of his spell-binding sermons to tens of thousands of worshippers. It was a gospel of submission to the Word of God, as interpreted by Reverend Lawrence McIntyre. Evil and sin were clearly demarcated and included abortion, homosexuality, adultery, premarital sex, Hollywood values and New York City values. The weekly love offerings had grown exponentially, allowing the church to build an entire wing dedicated to producing a slick, professional show each week, along with a mail order house for distributing tapes of the services and a growing library of spiritual self-help books written by the man himself.

As the church's marketing director, Emily had been the first to see that its revenue curve would flatten if they did not expand beyond Pittsburgh. "We need to act now, Larry, or our competitors will copy our business model and beat us to the punch," she had said. When she wasn't prospecting for new locations in Pennsylvania and neighboring states, she was traveling around the country, discreetly sitting in on services of the most successful churches in the land, fastidiously taking notes and names. She had hired away some of the best talent in holy music performance, lighting, make-up and camera work.

She had told the assembled creative team, "I want the highest production values of any church service in the nation. I want his close-ups scripted to emphasize certain parts of his message. I want the music to be Carnegie Hall quality. I want congregation members pre-screened for reaction shots. I want lighting that looks like it came directly from heaven. I want each service to sizzle. Have I made myself perfectly clear?"

When Emily was home, she saw her sons once a day at dinner time. The boys went to a private church school that required uniforms. Emily liked the clean, standardized look they gave her bumptious boys, so she insisted they wear the uniforms to dinner, which was cooked and served by a housekeeper Emily had hired because she had never liked her mother-in-law's menus.

"Lawrence, why don't you tell us something new you learned at school today?" was the way she opened the inquisition at the dinner table. The boys had learned to come prepared with something innocuous, but sufficiently meaty to satisfy Emily that Larry and she were getting their money's worth at the fancy private school. Once, the youngest, Luke, had offered in elaborate detail the reproductive practices of the Bornean Orangutan as witnessed that day on a class field trip to the Pittsburgh Zoo.

"That's enough, Luke," Emily had said, turning red with anger. She was convinced Luke's older brothers had coached the six-year-old to embarrass her. "I don't want to hear another word about the Bornean Orangutan." She had studied Larry Jr.'s and Joe's faces for telltale signs of guilt or glee, or both. Finding none, she had presumed they were responsible nonetheless and denied them dessert for a week.

"I don't think the boys like me," she had confessed to Larry one night as they were getting ready for bed.

Larry had been buttoning up his pajama top. "Nonsense. Of course, they like you. You're their mother."

"I'm afraid they think I'm too strict. But I feel like I have to be. I mean, after all, they're boys. By nature, they're more rambunctious and devilish. Sometimes I wish we had girls. I know about girls. I had two sisters, and I helped raise them."

"The boys love you in their own way. They just don't show affection like girls do. Don't worry. Just do God's work and the rest will follow."

"That's my other concern. I'm gone so much, I feel like I barely know them. Your mother is their real mother. They listen to her. They look at me like I'm from Mars."

"You're a modern woman working outside the home. They'll be grateful when they get older that you did so much for the church. Not only for your holy work, but also for the financial security that it will bring them."

Edna Roberts toddled into Larry's office. She was a heavy-set woman with small breasts and a pear shape who wore loose shifts to hide her figure. With mousy brown hair and dull gray eyes, there was nothing in particular to recommend her for romance. Never married, she had worked long hours as Larry's secretary at the steel company and the church. She was loyal, smart and discreet. Closing the door and flipping the lock, she asked, "Is she gone?"

Larry checked his Rolex watch. "She's in the air. She won't be back until tomorrow evening."

Edna smiled. She had very sexy lips. They were full and voluptuous. Normally, she wore the palest pink lipstick, but for these moments, she applied a ruby red shade that Larry loved. Larry pushed a button, and the curtains closed. He rolled his desk chair back, unzipped his trousers and retrieved his penis which was already starting to stiffen in anticipation. Edna positioned herself between his legs and dropped to her knees on a cushion that Larry kept under the desk. She placed her hands, one on each thigh, breathed in the aroma of his crotch and sighed.

"You smell good today," she said, her voice tight with excitement.

"Thank you. I've been working up a sweat down there waiting for Emily to leave."

She looked at him with mock disapproval. "What did I tell you about mentioning her name?"

He stroked her temple. "I'm sorry. Another fine?"

"Yes. That one will cost you five hundred. But enough about her. Let's get down to business."

November 2, 1987

Martha Hamilton put the phone back on the hook and turned to Marion Randolph. "That was Bob. He's up to something." The two of them were standing in the kitchen at Hamilton Oaks, making breakfast.

In the preceding weeks, Robert III had sold off all but one

hundred acres of the grand estate to developers, and then sold all the horses. The night before, Robert III had told Martha, with considerable satisfaction, "We won't need Marion any more. I let him go this afternoon."

The next morning, Robert III came down to the kitchen to find Marion scrambling eggs for Martha. "What's going on?" he had asked.

"The cook quit yesterday, so I hired Marion to take her place. He's quite a gourmet. We're having chateaubriand tonight to celebrate."

"How would you like your eggs, sir?" Marion had asked with a smile.

Robert III had made a face and said, "Never mind. I'm late for the office."

Just after Robert III had slammed the front door, the telephone had rung. It was her son, Bob, calling from New York. After Duke and Wharton Business School, Bob had made a small fortune as an investment banker on Wall Street.

"He says he's decided to join the Peace Corps," Martha said to Marion.

"What makes you think he's up to something?" Marion asked as he dished the eggs onto their plates. Alone together, they were like an old married couple, easy and comfortable, reading each other's thoughts and moods, touching often.

"Because I know my son. He doesn't have an altruistic bone in his body. A college buddy got him interested. This is so unlike him."

Marion pulled a coffeecake out of the oven, and the two of them sat down. "Maybe he's had some sort of crisis of faith."

Martha took her vitamin pill and washed it down with fresh squeezed orange juice. "He's no more capable of a crisis of faith than I am. I mean I love him, but I don't trust him. He's carrying on about taking a break from the rat race and helping the less fortunate. I felt like saying: 'This is your mother. Don't bullshit me.' But, I suppose there's a one percent chance of redemption. And, it's not as if he won't be doing good."

The kitchen was warm from the morning's baking. Marion leaned over and cracked the window to let in a breeze. It was a pleasant November morning. "Maybe the experience will transform him," he said. "The Peace Corps can have that effect."

"We can only hope. Robert will be apoplectic. He wants Bob to come home and take over the business. It's not as if he's ever done much but keep out of the way at the office, but he has this vision of turning over the reins to Bob, just as his father did with him."

Marion sliced a couple big pieces of homemade pecan coffee cake. "You better hope that doesn't happen. Then, he'll be home all the time."

"I know," she said, as she stroked his arm. "That will never do."

July 4, 1988

With one big breath, Roger Webber blew out the thirty candles on his birthday cake. His two roommates, Roland and Ned, cheered and clapped.

"What did you wish for?" Ned asked.

"I can't tell or it won't come true," Roger said He was too embarrassed to admit that he'd wished to be thirty pounds lighter, to have a place of his own, to be starring on the London stage, to have a handsome boyfriend and to have the love of his father and brothers. It was a pathetic and ridiculously unrealistic list. He would be lucky if he could stop gaining weight, let alone lose a pound.

"More champagne?" Roland asked. He was a tall, slender redhead with long fingers and a puckish smile.

"Sure. I'm only thirty once. It's all downhill from here." Roger offered up his glass. They were on their third bottle of cheap sparkling wine.

As he was pouring, Roland asked, "You know what I think we should do to celebrate? We should dress up and enter the drag contest down at the Manhole."

Roger groaned. "Not on my birthday." He took a big swig of bubbly.

"I think that's a fabulous idea," Ned said. He was a chubby young man with a shaved head and a pug nose. I'm in a Sophie Tucker mood tonight."

"I'm thinking Liza," Roland said as he sat down and helped himself to the coconut cake.

"Must we?" Roger asked. "I was thinking naked men dancing on a pole would be more fun."

"Oooh." Ned shivered. "Strippers make me nervous. I like Roland's idea. We'll have much more fun in drag. And who knows? You might win. Then you could pay for a private lap dance."

"I'd never pay for it," Roger said. "But I could use the cash."

Roger had been living with Roland and Ned since his mother had kicked him out. Six months after he had arrived in Toronto from London, she had caught him smoking pot in his room. His sister, Elaine, had managed to patch things up between them, but Bernice did not want him back in the house. "You're almost twenty-five," she had said. "You shouldn't be living with your mother."

Up to that point, Roger had been unemployed. Forced into the workforce, he had found a job as a waiter at The Cloud Room, an upscale restaurant at the top of one of Toronto's tallest buildings. Roland and Ned were actor/waiters, too. Roger had met them at an audition for a punk rock version of *A Little Night Music* put on by the Snakepit Theatre Troupe. Roger had landed the part of Count Carl-Magnus Malcolm, and Ned had been selected to play Madame Leonora Armfeldt. It had been Roger's first acting job in Toronto, and he had been thrilled. He had thought he was finally on his way. But then Stephen Sondheim's lawyers had shut down the show after the second week for copyright infringement and defamation. In the next three years, he had managed to pick up small parts in neighborhood theatres, but nothing had topped his reviews for Count Malcolm.

One of the benefits of working at a fancy restaurant was that, at the end of the night, there were often some tasty dishes that would go to waste unless the staff filled their plates. The venison and veal were even better with vintage wine from half-empty bottles abandoned by diners who'd pickled themselves with too many aperitifs. The rich food and fine wine had soothed Roger's depression, but it had begun to collect around his midriff. In the last couple years, he had been losing parts because he was too "thick" or "beefy" as some casting directors had put it.

He'd landed in Toronto with a firm determination to find himself a boyfriend. Tall and handsome, he'd had some luck at first, but none of the relationships had lasted. "I need someone to complete me," he had told his sister Elaine. But none of the men he had met had been willing to complete him, or fix him or put up with his baggage. As he would tell anyone who would listen, he had grown up in Cape Town, South Africa, the son of Piet and Bernice Webber. They had adopted him because they had thought they could not have children. And then they had proceeded to have three children, Dirk, Claus and Elaine. Piet had been a wife-beating, racist cop, and Bernice had begun treating Roger like another woman's child once she had learned she was pregnant with Dirk. His brothers were blonde bulldogs like their father and would have nothing to do with skinny, dark, sensitive Roger. Only Elaine would listen to him. In high school, drama club had been his escape from reality. And with a scholarship to Cambridge University, he had fled Cape Town, never to return. After he came out, his father had disowned him and his brothers had refused to speak to him. When Roger's acting career had faltered in London and Bernice finally had divorced Piet and moved to Toronto with Elaine, Roger had joined them, broke and broken.

Drag had been a strictly private indulgence for Roger. He had jammed a second-hand dressing table into his small bedroom and, when he was alone on a night off, he'd perch on the edge of the bench, lean forward and apply his eyeliner. It was a skill he'd picked up at Cambridge, where the British boys did drag revues at least once a term. He'd taped one of his London head shots in the upper left hand corner of the dressing table mirror and would gaze up at it from time to time as he transformed himself. When he put on his wig, he'd look up at the photo and say, "Don't worry, Roger. This is just for fun. Soon, we'll be out this rat hole and on our way back to London."

One night, he'd forgotten to lock his door and Roland had walked in as he was lip-synching *Hello Dolly*.

"Carol, darling, you look fantastic," Roland had said.

Roger, in a dynel blonde wig and white sequins, had curtsied and said "Why thank you, kind sir."

At the Manhole, the night of his thirtieth birthday, Roger was the last act. He stepped out from behind the shiny gold curtain into the spotlight wearing a large curly red wig and a low-cut green satin dress, the bodice of which was filled with every sock he owned. He was the third and tallest Bette Midler of the night. Unlike the other contestants, he'd asked to perform *a cappella*.

When he started to sing in Bette's husky, soulful style, the bar went quiet. "She was forty-one and her daddy still called her baby. Everyone in Brownsville thinks she's crazy."

Cheers and whistles went up from the crowd, and the applause swelled, allowing Bette to take a dramatic pause and acknowledge her people. Roger continued with the heart-wrenching story of the once beautiful woman who for decades had carried her suitcase down to the train station each day to wait for a mysterious dark-haired stranger, a man of low degree who had promised to take her as his bride.

When he reached the chorus, the entire bar was singing with him, "Delta Dawn, what's that flower you have on? Could it be a faded rose from days gone by?"

Roger gathered confidence with each phrase and stretched each note for maximum effect. Every man in the bar was watching him and he knew he owned the room. A rush of emotion made him choke up momentarily. All of which came off as the perfect dramatic effect for the rockabilly sonnet. By the time he hit the final refrain, "He's gonna take you to his mansion in the sky," he was drowned out by cheers and applause that lasted until he agreed to an encore from the Divine Miss M, with an eerie rendition of *Do You Want to Dance?*.

Not only did he win the two hundred dollar cash prize, but he kissed and hugged scores of men that night, many of whom bought him drinks to celebrate his victory and his birthday. When he awoke in his bed the next afternoon, he discovered that he'd lost his wig and most of his socks. He thought about sitting up to unzip his satin dress, but his head was pounding too severely to allow him to move. In the dressing table mirror, he could see himself, mascara smeared and lipstick uneven. Despite the pain and dishevelment, he smiled.

"You're a star, Roger. You're a star."

December 15-17, 1988

"Are you getting excited?" Pearl Busby asked her daughter. They were sitting at the kitchen table of a ranch house in Pembroke, Georgia, tying up little bags of uncooked minute rice with squares of yellow cellophane, squares of blue netting and pink ribbons.

"Yes, I guess. Mostly I just want to get it over with. It's embarrassing. Getting married twice in four years."

Pearl patted her daughter's hand. "Now, June, don't be like that. The first one doesn't count. It barely lasted a year. There were no children, thankfully. You've always loved Billy. This is the real thing. I know I'm excited for you." Pearl was a plumper version of June, with more freckles and Clairol-enhanced strawberry blonde forever hair. She was wearing dark green polyester pants and a red and green teddy bear Christmas sweater.

"No, Momma. The first one does count. Everyone in Pembroke's saying, 'Oh, poor June Busby. She went off and married Dwayne Skiles after she dumped Billy Short. But, then she realized what a jerk Dwayne was, so she divorced him, and waited around, hoping Billy would take her back.'" June tightened the tiny bow, threw the bag in the basket and started another one. She was sitting on one foot, wearing levi cut-offs and a purple tube top. Her big hair mane cascaded down her back, partially obscuring a small rose tattoo on her left shoulder. She'd lost her cheerleader cuteness and grown into a young woman of the South, with an even December tan and perfect velvet rose lacquered nails. The lawyers at Holcum & Streff were going to miss her when she left her job as secretary/receptionist to join her new husband, Captain Billy Short, at Fort Bragg in North Carolina.

Just short of six feet, Billy Short had a lean, sinewy frame, big feet and near perfect balance. He was made to catch fast pitches and throw out runners at second, but he had torn up his shoulder after painting "Class of 83" on the Lake Pembroke spillway. Dwayne Skiles and he had been celebrating winning the baseball conference title with a case of Budweiser. Michael Jackson had been singing *Beat It* on Dwayne's boombox, and Billy had been doing the moonwalk when he fell off the spillway footbridge. His major league career prospects in ruins, Billy had decided to join the Special Forces because he had always dreamed of doing something "big." June had reacted by throwing his class ring in his lap as they sat outside her house in the cab of his father's Chevy pickup truck. She had run into her house in tears and he had said good-bye to his dad, a widowed peanut farmer, and boarded a Greyhound bus that would take him to basic training.

For four years in the U.S. Army Special Forces, Billy had picked up a variety of women at honky-tonk bars near the bases where he had been assigned. But there had been no girlfriends since June. At twenty-two, he had decided that he would never marry, because he lived a dangerous life and he didn't want to leave a young widow. Then, he had run into June at a party in Pembroke when he was home on leave over the Christmas holidays. His heart had melted.

Pearl measured rice onto a cellophane square. "It's been almost a year since Billy proposed. Nobody's thinking about Dwayne anymore. All they talk about is how sweet it was the way he asked you to marry him under the mistletoe on New Year's Eve."

June smiled. "That was sweet, wasn't it? In his uniform and all. He's such a man now." She clenched her thighs together and squeezed her arms against the sides of her breasts. "I'm not much for second weddings, but I'm going to love my second honeymoon. Three days in Disney World. I can't wait."

Pearl shook her head. "He must love you. To take you there. Why not go to some quiet beach? Some place more romantic?"

"Like you've been to a quiet beach with Daddy. I've never been to Disney World. I've been asking to go since I can remember. Finally, Billy's going to take me. I know it's not his first choice, but I'll make it up to him." She clenched her thighs again and smiled.

Pearl smiled and threw another rice bag in the basket.

Two days later, June Busby and Billy Short were married in Pembroke's First United Methodist Church. He was favoring his left knee as he walked down the aisle. "Just twisted it," he had told June the day before. But the truth was he had re-injured his knee parachuting into a jungle in Mozambique. Two years before, in Nicaragua, he had torn it up in a firefight while he had been training Contra rebels.

Rice hailed down on them as they ran from the reception in the church's fellowship hall and jumped in Billy's Pontiac Trans Am. That night, in the Ramada Inn five miles from Disney World, Billy and June were cuddling after their second round.

"Thanks," Billy said.

"For what?" she asked, lifting her head. Without his uniform, he was no longer a warrior. He was the farm boy she had fallen for in high school, with his impish smile, button nose and sandy-haired cowlick.

"For giving me a second chance."

June was running her hush pink nails through his pubic hair. "You're welcome. Thanks for giving me a second chance."

"Hey, what are you doing down there?" he asked.

She smiled as she reached underneath his scrotum. "Just checking things out."

"Be careful. Your nails are sharp."

"Don't worry. I trimmed this one while I was in the bathroom. Now, just relax. This won't hurt." She started nibbling on his nipple as she probed deeper. His penis came to life.

"Damn, girl. Where'd you learn to do that?"

"*Cosmo* magazine," she said and resumed nibbling.

Chapter 4

September – October 1989

"Rosie, come here," Charise Woods called out.

Rosie Gibson had left the locker room at Baltimore's Woodrow Wilson High School, still sweating from volleyball practice. She was the tallest girl on the freshman team, but the least coordinated. That day, she had stepped on one girl's foot and knocked another one over when she jumped to spike. The coach had put her on the bench to hold down the injuries. Rosie looked over and saw her friend, Charise, smiling from a crack in the supply room door. "What you doing in there?" she asked.

"Shhh. Get in here." Charise was the shortest girl on the team. She had the most talent, but the least discipline, the coach had said. Which, of course, made her the most fun.

Rosie checked to make sure no one could see her and then snuck into the supply room with Charise.

"What are we doing in here?" Rosie asked. "This room's like a furnace. Let's get out of here."

"Shhh. Come back here in the corner on these mats and sit down."

"What for?"

"Sit."

Rosie sat down in the dark. There was a glimmer of light coming from the crack under the door. Then, Charise gently took Rosie's face in her hands and kissed her.

Rosie pushed her away. "What you doing that for?"

"We're going to practice kissing," Charise said in Rosie's ear.

"Why?"

"So we'll be ready when it comes time to kiss a boy."

"Maybe I don't want to kiss a boy."

"Well, then you can learn how to kiss a girl." Charise put a cool hand on Rosie's cheek and lightly kissed her forehead and then her eyelids, nose and lips.

Rosie began to object, but then she stopped herself. She was hot, dripping with sweat, sticking to the smelly wrestling mat, worried that the coach would find them, worried her mother would wonder where she was, and turned on. She laid back and pulled Charise on top of her and they kissed and hugged until the last bell of the day announced the doors would be locked in five minutes. The two girls scrambled to their feet and giggled all the way down the hall to the exit. Walking home together, Rosie asked, "How'd you get in there?"

"My older sister had a key. She gave it to me when she graduated."

"What are you going to do with it?"

"Sneak in there with you."

"How do you know I'll sneak in there with you again?"

Charise lifted her chin and looked away. "All right, don't. I'll find someone else to kiss."

"Maybe you will."

Two days later, the girls were back in the supply room. After an hour, Rosie said,

"We've got to do this somewhere else or I'm going to pass out from the heat."

After that, the girls took to fooling around during study sessions in each other's bedrooms, on sleepovers, in the back rows of theaters and any other semi-private nook or cranny they could find. One day, when Rosie stayed home from school with the cramps, Charise came over and they played all morning. After a long hot shower, they stepped out of the tub and wiped the fogged bathroom mirror clear so that they could admire their bodies. Aretha Franklin was demanding respect at full volume on Rosie's vintage stereo system. Posing in front of the mirror, Charise said, "You know, we should get our picture taken like this, all artsy like."

Rosie smiled. "Well, which position do you think would be the sexiest?"

The two girls vamped for the mirror and then decided that demure was better than brazen. Each girl placed a hand over the other's crotch and smiled chastely at the fantasy camera. It would have been a museum quality work of art, a study in contrasts and curves. Rosie's queenly blue-black frame entwined around Charise, a caramel-colored princess waif.

They didn't think they were doing anything wrong, but they knew enough to keep their fun a secret. "Does this make us lesbians?" Rosie asked Charise after one particularly steamy interlude.

"Noooo," Charise answered. "Lesbians are all white women."

"Well, what does it make us then?" Rosie asked as she hooked her bra.

Charise snickered. "Just a couple of girls from the projects having fun without the shuck and jive of the all mighty black man's dick."

Rosie's mother, Eulalia, was oblivious. "I'm so delighted Charise and you are so close and you study so much together. She keeps you off the streets and away from all the drugs and gangbangers."

"Yes, Momma."

"Maybe she'd like to come with us for Christmas when we go see your daddy's family in Pea Ridge. Your Aunt Gladys has enough room. You two could share a bed. And Althea could sleep with me."

"I'll ask her tomorrow. I'm sure she'd love to come."

November 2, 1989

When the nurse handed the baby to Emily McIntyre, she shrieked and dropped him. Fortunately, the nurse caught him before he hit the delivery room floor. Emily continued to wail until the anesthesiologist sedated her. What had horrified her was not the child's male sex organs, but his telltale Down syndrome facial characteristics. "He's a mongoloid," she screamed just before she went under.

After she turned forty, Emily had known that she was at increased risk for a Down Syndrome child, but, ten years after Luke, she had wanted one last chance to produce a little girl. Larry was all for it and had insisted on multiple fertilization efforts. As soon as she learned she was pregnant, she had cut him off. "It's bad for the baby," she had lied. "The doctor says, at my age, intercourse could trigger a miscarriage." She had declined all the tests that would have told her the gender of the child or the likelihood of Down Syndrome. Partly because Larry preached against them as the tools of abortionists. But mostly because she wasn't concerned. She just knew God was going to give her a healthy baby girl, as requested.

When she came to, she was back in her private hospital room, and her new baby, Frances, named after her mother's mother, Francis, was in the nursery. "I don't want him to have her name," she told Larry, who had been waiting patiently for her to surface.

"It's too late, Emmy. I already told your mother, and she's tickled pink. I thought we agreed, boy or girl, to name him after your grandmother. I told the doctor. They can change the hospital records, but we can't talk you mother off the ceiling."

"Yes, but did you tell her he's a mongoloid? I can't believe she would want him bearing Grandma's name."

"Yes, she doesn't care. Just as long as you're fine and he's healthy."

"But I'm not fine, and he's not healthy." She started to cry.

"He's healthy as a horse. You should hear him. He's got great lungs."

"Am I the only sane one in this family? I wanted a beautiful little girl. A perfect little angel of a baby. Instead, I've got a mentally retarded boy who will be ten times the trouble of the other three combined."

"Now, Emmy. Frankie is God's gift to us. He's here for us to love just as much as our other sons. And he's here to teach us to appreciate the gift of life for ourselves and for him for however long he may be with us."

Her spirits lifted. "What do you mean? Is there a chance he won't live very long?"

"No, don't worry. The doctor says there's a good chance that he will live a normal life span. Now, no more tears. Rejoice. I'm going to ask the nurse to bring him in."

"No, don't," she said, but Larry had already left the room.

"Oh, God," she prayed. "What have I done to deserve this? I've tried to love the sons you have given me, but I just don't understand little boys. Please don't punish me for coveting my sisters' daughters. They're raising them like little hellions and don't have a clue how precious they really are. Grant me this one wish, and I will do whatever you ask of me. Take this child from this earth before I leave this hospital. Take him quietly in the night and bless his soul to eternal paradise. In Jesus name, I pray. Amen."

June 15-16, 1990

"I don't think I can do this," Roger Webber said to his sister, Elaine. "They hate me."

"I know it's hard, but you'll be fine. I've told them to behave or I'll ban them from the wedding." Elaine was checking herself in the three way mirror at the True Love Bridal Shoppe in Toronto. This was the final fitting. Their mother, Bernice, was picking up relatives at the airport, and Elaine had insisted that Roger join her. At twenty-six, she was a beautiful bride, with long dark hair and a slim figure.

"I mean, it's just a rehearsal and dinner. You don't really need me there. I know where to stand. Next to the best man." Roger was sitting in the "mother's" chair in the fitting room. He was wearing dark sweatpants and a hooded jacket, his latest attempt to hide his bloated waistline. He'd wanted to lose weight before the wedding, but had gained five pounds instead.

"Don't let them scare you off. You belong there more than they do," Elaine said. She was marrying Mike Griffin, who had just graduated from the University of Toronto Law School. She was a Toronto police officer. They had met when she pulled him over for speeding.

"Is Dad bringing Louise?"

"I'm sorry. I thought I'd told you. She filed for divorce last week."

"I'm not surprised. Are Dirk and Claus bringing their kids?"

"As far as I know. If the airline lets them on the plane."

"This is hard. I haven't seen any of them in ten years. Promise me you'll only get married once."

Elaine laughed and twirled to face him. "I promise. How do I look?"

Roger smiled and said, "Divine. I'm going to miss you."

"I'm going to miss you, too. Promise you'll come visit."

"Promise."

Elaine had met the perfect man. Mike was kind, intelligent, passionate, handsome and generous. And, as Roger liked to add, "thrifty, brave, clean and reverent." To top it off, his parents were loaded. "Something to do with paper mills," Elaine had told Roger. The only thing wrong with Mike, as far as Roger was concerned, was that he was taking Elaine away from him. Mike had accepted a position with a big law firm back home in Vancouver. Two thousand miles away. Elaine was Roger's one true friend. She was his "Lanie." He couldn't imagine not seeing her smile for months on end.

At the rehearsal that night at the St. James Cathedral Anglican Church in downtown Toronto, Roger stood nervously awaiting the arrival of his father, Piet, and his two brothers. When they stepped through the door, Roger was surprised to see how little his father had aged. At sixty-four, he was one year away from retirement from the police force, and he was still as trim and virile as he had always been. His two brothers had grown into handsome, tawny men, all blonde and tan, barely taller than Piet. The three of them moved as one, striding into the sanctuary like hyenas, seeking their prey. Once, they spotted Roger, they walked up to him, all three of them, staring him down, fiercely, Roger thought. But, in truth, they were miserably unhappy to be in the same room with the fairy. They were following strict orders from Elaine to be "nice" to Roger.

Piet extended his hand grimly. "Roger," he said.

Roger shook his hand stiffly. "Dad."

In quick succession, Dirk and Claus went through the same ritual with the same forced civility. Dirk squeezed his hand a little too hard for comfort, and Claus half-smirked when he gave him a limp wrist. Roger made it through the rehearsal without too much pain, but the dinner that followed was excruciating. It was held at the Cloud Room, where Roger worked. His six nieces and nephews, all towheads, stared at Roger as if he were a freak and refused to talk to him. After Roger gave his toast to the happy couple, they all went snickering off to the restroom.

Sitting across the table, Dirk shrugged his shoulders and said, "Kids." Which Roger took to mean, "How can you keep kids from laughing at a bugger?"

Piet didn't speak to him for the rest of the night, and Roger was too afraid to go up to him. He downed glass after glass of wine, but he couldn't screw up the courage. By the end of the dinner, he was devastated and drunk.

Later that night, he sat down at his dressing table and did his best to reincarnate Judy Garland. He had a regular gig at Manhole on Fridays, and normally he did Barbra or Cher, singing upbeat ballads that boosted liquor sales. But that night, he was in no mood for gaiety. He was a tortured soul and he only wanted to sing the blues. He brought tears to the eyes of his audience with *The Man That Got Away*, *A Foggy Day*, *After You've Gone*, *Stormy Weather* and *Over the Rainbow*.

In the two years that had passed since his debut as Bette, he'd become a celebrity of sorts in the gay community, and worked his little piece of fame to get close to the hunkiest men in the bar, men who wouldn't look at him twice if he were in street clothes. He craved every bit of attention they paid him, whether it was sincere, alcohol-induced or mocking. It had reached the point where he only felt good about himself when he was trussed up in his girdle and wonder bra. As soon as he got home and sat down at the dressing table to apply the cold cream, he began to deflate. By the time the last bit of mascara was wiped away, he was in the dumps again, searching out his cosmetic drawer for a roach or stealing some of Roland's vodka and replacing it with water. It wasn't that he couldn't afford his own cheap booze. It was just that he had constructed an elaborate fiction that he did not have a drinking problem because he did not buy alcohol. Leftover wine at The Cloud Room didn't count, free drinks at Manhole didn't count, pilfered roomie stock didn't count. He was not a drunk.

He severely tested that premise the night of Elaine's wedding rehearsal. Between the never empty glass of wine at dinner and the complimentary cosmopolitan martinis at Manhole, he managed to get so fried, he would have passed out standing up, if his roommate, Ned, hadn't stopped by for a nightcap. Ned poured him into a cab and pushed his silver lamé butt up three flights of stairs. When Elaine finally reached him the next day, it was noon. He had missed the family brunch and she was beginning to panic. The wedding was at two, and she could tell he was smashed.

"Roger, how could you do this to me? This is the most important day of my life."

"Lanie, I can't do it. I can't be in the same room with them. I love you and I want to be there for you, but I just can't."

She took a deep breath. "Roger, honey, you are the most important person in the world to me. I love Mike, but no one, not Mom, not anyone has been there for me like you have been. Every day of my life. You have been the one I've always gone to with all of my hopes and dreams, all my pain and disappointments. You never judged me. You always said the right thing to make me feel good. You got me through my childhood. And now, I need you to be there for me one more time. I swear I won't go down the aisle until I see you standing at the other end."

Roger pulled off his wig and threw it across the room, knocking the pink silk shade off one of the dressing table lamps. "Promise to name your first born after me?"

She laughed. "I've already told Mike, if we have a boy, his name will be Roger."

He sat up and took the icepack that Ned had just carried into the room. Pressing it against his forehead, he said, "Fair enough, and if you have only girls, the last one will be Rogerina."

She laughed again. "Regina."

"It's a deal."

Stoked by a couple of Bloody Mary's, Roger arrived at the church on time and cried quietly, like the mother of the bride, through most of the ceremony. The reception that followed at the Windsor Arms Hotel in Toronto's posh Yorkville district was an elegant affair with a hundred guests and a pianist playing popular dance tunes. Roger managed to ignore the South African contingent, spending much of his time freshening his drink and relieving himself. After dancing with the bride, his mother, his aunt, the groom's mother and the groom's sister, he took a break and stepped into the hotel lobby just as Roland's friend, Pierre, headed for the door. Pierre had helped serve their meals, but his work was done and he was going home in his waiter's tux. Just before he reached the revolving door, Roger called out, "Pierre, wait up."

Pierre was a tall, handsome French-Canadian-Lebanese mix with dark oily hair, blue eyes and a quick smile. "What's up Roger?" he asked.

"Are you in a rush? Do you have five minutes?"

Pierre checked his watch and said "I have maybe ten minutes. My boyfriend is picking me up. What's going on?"

"Dance with me. Just one dance. Right now. Please." Roger didn't look half-bad in his rented tux, patent leather shoes and full body corset.

Pierre smiled. "I saw you on the dance floor. You've got some good moves."

"This will be a slow dance. Just hold me in your arms and let me lead."

Pierre checked his watch again and said, "Sure, why not?"

They entered the banquet room together. Roger stuck a twenty dollar bill in the pianist's breast pocket and whispered his request. As Pierre and he took to the dance floor, the pianist began to sing "As Time Goes By." The other couples on the floor stopped dancing and looked on in amazement. Dirk and Claus immediately huffed off the parquet, dragging their wives with them. When she heard the first notes, Elaine stopped talking to her mother mid-sentence and turned to see the two men alone in the middle of the dance floor. She knew it was one of Roger's favorites. Pulling Mike away from his law school friends, she said, "Hurry. Roger needs us."

Soon Mike's parents joined them and then Mike's sister and her husband. By the time the pianist had reached "You must remember this, A kiss is just a kiss," several other couples were on the floor. The pianist, a friend of Dorothy himself, changed the lyrics from "Woman needs man and man must have his mate" to "We all need love and we all must find our mate."

No one noticed Dirk and Claus herding their wives and kids out the door, while little Lars screamed, "Why's Uncle Roger dancing with that colored man?"

Piet had been watching the spectacle from the bar where he had just ordered a cognac to go with his cigar. He steamed as he watched Bernice coax her sister out of her seat and onto the edge of the now crowded floor. "Come on, Hyacinth," she said. "I want to see Piet's face when he sees me in the arms of another woman."

"But I'm your sister," Hyacinth protested.

"Hush. Hold me tight and smile."

1990 - 1992

Bob Hamilton returned from his Peace Corps stint in Peru in June 1990. He immediately set up New Life, a non-profit agency to save South American babies from abortion and place them in comfortable North American homes. Then, he set out to woo Kathleen O'Malley. She had rejected Bob's advances when they were classmates at Wharton Business School, but when he showed up in Chicago after five years on Wall Street and two years in the jungle, he was a new man, she thought: mature, focused and compassionate.

He'd read Larry McIntyre's autobiography about his jungle epiphany and morphed it into his own. "I saw too many babies die," he said to Kathleen on their first meeting. "I had nightmares the whole time I was there. One morning, I woke up and I knew what I had to do. I think we're put on this earth for a purpose. Mine is to change the way the world cares for its children, before and after they're born."

Six months later, they were married, and, on their honeymoon, Bob told Kathleen, "The only way I can change the world is to run for political office." They had just left the New Life office in Lima, Peru, and she was too overcome with the sight of a tearful, pregnant fourteen-year-old named Beatriz to object.

Shortly after they returned from their honeymoon, Bob and Kathleen visited his folks at Hamilton Oaks outside of Atlanta. On a knoll overlooking the exurban sprawl that had once been the family plantation, Bob laid out his plans to Robert III. Kathleen and he would be moving to Atlanta. He would help his father run the family businesses, but only long enough to re-establish himself as a Son of the South. He intended to run for Congress.

Then, with an appeal to his father's prejudices, he described his vision for a revival of American values. "I want to live in a nation that honors God, family and flag again. We have fallen so far. The country you fought to save doesn't exist anymore. It's overrun by immigrants, feminists and faggots. It's up to people like you and me to bring America back. With any luck, I'll be in the Senate in a few years and then, God willing, the White House. I'm going to need your help. You know so many people in this state. It would mean a lot to me if we could work as a team to make this happen."

Robert III had never been prouder of his son than he was in that moment. Wiping away tears with the back of his hand, his voice shaky, he said, "Well, of course I'll help you Bobby. I'll do anything I can. Jesus Christ. President Robert David Hamilton. I like the sound of that."

The Hamiltons settled into Atlanta society with ease. In a matter of months, they had become the toast of the town. Bob was tall, dark, handsome, smart, gregarious and rich. More importantly, he was old South and old money, from two family trees. Kathleen was gorgeous, bright, charming, and "different," the word some used to describe her Irish Catholic Yankee heritage. They bought the perfect Tudor home on a large wooded estate on one of the winding roads of Atlanta's affluent Druid Hills neighborhood. Then, they joined just the right stripe of conservative Baptist church. Everyone was impressed that Kathleen would sacrifice her papist past for the righteous faith of the Confederacy.

Twenty months after the wedding, Robert David Hamilton V was born. At the christening party at Hamilton Oaks, Robert III lurched toward Kathleen, unsteady even with his cane. "Give me a big ole hug, Kathy." Smelling of bourbon and tobacco, he reminded her of an overripe Big Daddy in his wrinkled linen suit and straw hat. As always, his hug was too familiar for a father-in-law. And, as he stepped back, she could have sworn he was appraising her milk-filled breasts.

"I hope your boy will make you as proud as I am of Bobby," Robert III said, gazing down at the sleeping infant in the bassinet.

"I just want him to be happy," Kathleen said.

Robert III leaned over to stroke the baby's cheek. "I'm sure he'll be happy once his daddy sets the world straight."

November 1992 – November 1993

The day after Bill Clinton was elected president the first time, Emily McIntyre stormed into her husband's office just as his secretary,

Edna Roberts, was leaving. "Emily, what brings you in so early?" Larry asked as his penis quickly wilted.

"We're going to Washington," she said, standing before him, too distracted to notice the open curtains were swaying.

"What do you mean?"

"We're going to launch a national family values organization to counter the moral decay in this country. The American Family First Foundation."

"But why can't we do that here, in Pittsburgh?"

"We have to be where the power is, and we have to establish a national image. No one's going to take us seriously if we stay here. It's the next logical step in our progression. I've been watching our numbers and we're beginning to flat line again. Our market is saturated, Larry. We have to start building a national revenue base and a national constituency. Our message is too important to stay regional."

"But there must be a dozen organizations doing the same thing. Why do we have any credibility to start another group?"

Emily bristled with contempt. "Because you're the only one with credibility. You're the one who's been chosen by God. You're His messenger. Most of our competitors are hucksters, glad to see themselves on television and in the news. The rest are well meaning, but incompetent."

It was a hard sell at first, but eventually Larry came around, especially after Emily showed him the likely revenue projections. The first person he told was Edna Roberts, just after they had concluded an afternoon delight. "Put your house on the market, Edna. We're moving to D.C."

A year later, on November 30, 1993, Bill Clinton's compromise protection for gays in the military, the "Don't Ask, Don't Tell" policy, became law. The statute prohibited same-sex physical or romantic relationships in the military, prohibited homosexuals from publicly declaring their sexual orientation and prohibited the military from investigating the sexuality of any member of the armed forces.

The timing couldn't have been better for the McIntyres. They held a news conference the same day in Washington, D.C. to announce the formation of the American Family First Foundation.

At the press conference, all four McIntyre boys stood behind Larry and Emily. Twenty-one-year-old Larry Jr. was in charge of keeping four-year-old Frankie from acting up. Emily had already given Frankie half a valium, but she had warned Larry Jr., "If he so much as peeps, take his hand and quietly leave the stage. If anyone asks, I'll explain he needed to go to the restroom. Am I making myself clear?"

Just as Larry cleared his throat to speak, Frankie began to hoot and wave at Edna who was taking pictures from the back of the room. Emily turned and gave Larry Jr. a forced smile. Larry Jr., a senior at Virginia, paid her no attention, picked up Frankie and waved at Edna, too.

Larry ignored the commotion as he began. "My friends, members of the press, my wife Emily and I have traveled a long road together doing God's work for the Church of the New Faith, but He has called us to a new and much more difficult task. To do battle with the devil right here in our nation's capital. A new law took effect today that, for the first time in the nation's history, will allow homosexuals to serve in our military alongside our brave sons and daughters. They will be allowed to eat with them, shower with them and sleep next to them, all the while secretly desiring to have ungodly sodomy with them. This statute threatens to destroy the very moral fiber of our military and to destroy the family values upon which this great nation was founded. It is just one example of the insidious putrefaction of our government by the forces of evil that hold sway in this country."

Frankie yelled out, "Hi, Miss Roberts."

The room broke out in laughter. Smiling, Larry walked over and took Frankie from Larry Jr. He carried him back to the podium. "Here's another reason why Emily and I are standing before you. Not a day goes by that we don't give thanks to God for our little Frankie."

Larry tousled Frankie's thick black hair. Frankie kissed his dad's cheek and said, "I love you, Daddy." The entire crowd, including the hard-nosed Washington press corps, gave a collective "Awwww."

Larry continued, no longer smiling. "Need I say more? I love you, Daddy. How many of God's children are in heaven, never given the chance to utter that simple statement of affection to their father? Millions upon millions of babies, murdered in the name of personal irresponsibility. Love has its consequences, and Frankie is living proof of the love between my wife, Emily, and me. We must love all of our children as we ask God to love us. Emily and I will not rest until we have brought an end to the scourge of abortion and homosexuality in this land, and changed the laws so that the American family comes first."

At Emily's nod, a contingent from the Church of the New Faith choir, resplendent in new royal blue robes, burst into, "God Bless America," all of them smiling like Mormons on Prozac. Frankie continued to wave at Edna as he sang along with the choir, his earnest off-key warbling amplified by the podium microphone. The grizzled press corps veterans shook their heads in amazement. Never had they seen such a cleverly staged bit of theater. Captured on the Foundation's own video cameras, the poignant moment became a centerpiece of fundraising drives for years to come.

December 1993

The black Cadillac limousine pulled up to the curb along a busy commercial street in Atlanta, and Robert Hamilton III stepped out. "Keep the motor running. I won't be long," he told his chauffeur, Gus. It was a sunny morning, and Robert III was flushed pinker than usual, dressed for the golf course in red, white and blue plaid slacks and a red sweater that stretched against his Buddha belly. He'd recently graduated to a three prong metal cane and was moving a step slower. His yellowed white pompadour was already damply disheveled in the unusual late autumn heat.

Before him stood the local office of Congressman Harry Fisher, a longtime incumbent. First elected in the Nixon landslide of 1972, he had slowly mellowed his public views on race as Atlanta had become the capital of the New South, but Robert III knew how Harry truly felt about keeping the niggers in their place.

"Robert," the congressman bellowed with a cigarette voice as he rose from his desk. "Look at you, all decked out for the links, I see. How's my old friend?" Harry had dressed for comfort that morning in tan Sansabelt pants, a canary yellow polo shirt and a Kelly green cardigan sweater. He displayed a slight tremor as he extended his hand.

"Yes, I'm headed to the club from here," Robert III said with a gravelly drawl. "With Bobby in charge now, I can take a day off here and there."

"That's wonderful. I know how much you had hoped he would join you. You must be very proud. Come on, sit down. Would you like a cup of coffee? Betty, can you come in here?"

"No, that won't be necessary," Robert III said as he closed the door in Betty Higgins' face and took a seat.

"All right then," Harry said as he sat down hard in his chair, his arthritic knees giving out with loud cracks. "So this is a business call. What can I do for you?"

"I'm here to talk about your retirement."

"You and my wife both. Did she send you here?"

"No. I'm here on behalf of my son's campaign. He will be announcing for your seat in two weeks. We want you at the press conference to announce your retirement and to endorse him as the best man for the job."

Harry studied Robert III's face, looking for any sign of mirth. Robert III was a notorious practical joker. But his old friend was stone-faced. "I can understand you want to help your son, but I'm not ready to give up my seat. I figure a couple more terms, and I'll be joining you on the golf course. Tell your boy to relax. In four years, I'll be his number one supporter."

"We're not going to wait. It's time for you to step down. Look at you. You're falling apart as fast as I am. Do the gracious thing and step aside for the next generation."

Harry pointed a shaky finger at Robert III. "Now, you listen here. I've built up quite a reputation and I've done a lot of favors for folks in this town. You may have an old family name, but I've got the business community behind me, the party organization and some of the wealthiest men in Atlanta."

"Every single one of those men is on Bobby's finance committee. You won't get a plug nickel from any of them. You're done, Harry."

"I don't believe you."

"Go ahead, pick up the phone. I doubt any of them will even take your call."

"Why you little prick. You think you can scare me? I'll run without their money and I'll still beat your son."

"No you won't. If you don't do exactly as you're told, I will personally call the newspapers and tell them about Harry Junior's drug bust and your pressure to get the police to drop the charges and cover it up."

Harry stood and leaned over his desk. "Get out of my office before I throw you out, you little weasel."

Robert III pulled himself to his feet and faced down the congressman. "If I'm a weasel, you're a jackass. You will endorse Bobby or I will ruin you and your boy. Don't be stupid. Go home. Talk to Lois Ann. She'll be glad to have you home." He pulled a folded paper out of his hip pocket and handed it to Harry. "Here's your statement. Look it over and call Bobby's press secretary with any comments. His number's at the bottom."

If there hadn't been a desk between them, Harry would have slugged Robert III in the jaw. He made his way around the desk as quickly as he could, swearing a blue streak, but Robert III practically trotted out of his office, his cane aloft, wheezing as he waved at a perplexed Betty Higgins.

Two weeks later, in a joint press conference, Harry Fisher announced his resignation and endorsed Bob Hamilton, stating, "I pass the torch to a new generation and look forward to spending more time with my long suffering wife, Lois Ann, and my grandchildren. I can't think of a better candidate to take over my seat than Bob Hamilton. I am particularly delighted that he is also the son of my dearest and oldest friend, Robert Hamilton." With that, the three men clutched hands and held them aloft, smiling, Bob in the middle between the two old coots.

At Hamilton Oaks, Martha Hamilton watched the television coverage in bed with Marion Randolph. "Look at Robert," she said. "The little kingmaker. I've haven't seen him so happy since our wedding day."

"So you're okay with Bob running for Congress?" Marion asked as he nuzzled her neck.

"Hell, no. I hired a private investigator yesterday. We'll see what he can find to slow him down."

Chapter 5

December 1993

"Okay, time is up. Put your test booklets on my desk and a have a great holiday." Josh Stein stood at the front of the lecture hall, looking decidedly un-professorial in jeans and a tight black shirt that showed off his pecs and biceps. After many years teaching English Literature at the University of Melbourne, he had accepted a one-year fellowship at Columbia University in New York City. He was a visiting professor lecturing on Shakespeare's sonnets to undergraduates and the more obscure English poets to graduate students.

The last student to leave was his favorite, Vince Scavullo, a handsome Italian boy from Brooklyn. He was that rare English Lit graduate student who still had red blood coursing through his veins. "What are you doing over break, Professor?"

Josh was leaning against his desk. He smiled and shrugged. "I'm not sure. I was headed to LA, but my sister and her family decided to go skiing, and I don't ski, so…"

"So you're stuck in town for the next month." Vince had a short compact Mediterranean body — olive skinned, hairy, and beefy.

"Actually, I'm looking forward to it. I love this city, but I haven't had time to explore it." Josh held up a handful of blue test booklets. "And, of course, I'll be reading these to help me fall asleep."

"Let me buy you a drink."

Josh blushed as he ran his hand through thick dark curls. Vince had been flirting with him the entire semester. He had never said anything. It was all in the way he smiled and nodded each day as he came and went. His almond brown eyes, dark buzz cut and three day stubble made him hard to resist. "I'm not sure that's a good idea," Josh said as he stood and stretched his six foot frame.

Vince smiled and stepped closer. "Come on, the semester's over. You know I wrote the best exam, so I'm not pulling for a grade. It's just two guys going for a beer."

"Well, as long as we're clear on that." Josh stuck the blue books in his briefcase and they headed out to a nearby bar.

On the second beer, Vince said, "I think you're the hottest professor at Columbia. Not that there's much competition. But, you know what I mean."

Josh laughed. "Thanks. I guess I'm flattered."

"Sorry, I screwed that up. What I meant to say is I want to sleep with you."

"Damn, you don't waste any time, do you?"

"Well, you're only here one more semester, so I figure I better act fast."

Josh sipped his beer. "I think you're a very sexy young man, and I emphasize the word young, because I think you should find someone more your own age."

"You're what? Thirty-three, thirty-four?"

"Thirty-five. And you're twenty-four, twenty-five?"

"Twenty-seven. I worked a few years before I went back to school. Guys always think I'm younger because I'm short."

"Still that's eight years. That's a big difference."

"Big difference for what? I'm not talking about picking out china patterns. I just thought we could have some fun over break, keep each other company, pal around, get naked." Vince smiled lasciviously.

"Don't you have a boyfriend?"

"No, do you?"

"No."

"Then, we're set. Two single guys. Seeing how it goes. Taking it slow. One day at a time. No expectations."

That night, they made love at Josh's place, and they spent the rest of the holidays together. Josh went to the Scavullo family gathering on Christmas Day and towered above Vince's relatives. "Vinny's been telling me about you for months," his mother, Daniella said. "I'm so glad to finally meet you. I've read both your novels and I loved them."

Josh looked over at Vince who lifted his glass of limoncello and smiled. A moment later, Josh said to Vince, "I feel like I'm being stalked. What have you been telling your mother and why's she reading my novels? They're gay love stories."

They had their backs against a wall in the crowded dining room. Vince ran his hand across Josh's buttocks. "I tell my mother everything, and I told her I had a big crush on you the first day of class."

"Where did you find my books? I didn't think they sold outside of Australia."

"A second-hand book store. I paid a buck a piece. Probably some queen from Manhattan picked them up in Sydney to read on the plane and pitched them when he realized there were no graphic sex scenes. By the way, you write well, but you shouldn't give up your day job. My mother likes Danielle Steele, too."

"You're on very thin ice, Mr. Scavullo. I haven't turned in my grade report yet."

Vince squeezed Josh's butt. "Jeez, Professor Stein. What can I do to improve my grade? I'll do anything you ask, Sir. I have to pass your class in order to graduate."

Josh was starting to get hard. "We may be able to work something out, as long as you're willing to do what you're told."

Vince kissed Josh on the cheek. "Yes, Sir. Whatever you say, Sir."

November 8, 1994

"Hey, baby, are you ready to make history?" Bob Hamilton asked his wife, Kathleen, as he buttoned his suit coat. Bob had been born to kiss babies and spellbind the masses. At thirty-six, his curly black hair was still thick and shiny. His brown eyes were clear and intelligent. His square jaw and aquiline nose made him naturally photogenic. His smile was irresistible. And he spoke with an easy charm and confidence that was unmatched in the political world.

"Make history?" Kathleen asked.

"Yes, I just won with seventy percent of the vote. Five points more than Harry Fisher's best year. Can you believe it?" The Hamiltons and their political entourage were holed up in the Royal Suite of the Hyatt Hotel in downtown Atlanta. The news analysts had just called the race, and Bob was preparing to deliver his clarion call for a return to American family values.

"That's fantastic, Bob. How long 'til we go out? I need to nurse Martha, and Robbie is falling asleep. Do they need to be there for your speech? My mother can watch them."

Bob looked at her as if she were crazy. "Honey, we have to be out there as a family. That's my whole platform. They want to see us, you and me and the kids." He turned to Robert III. "Dad, is Mom ready?"

Robert III was smiling away as he watched the election returns, a bottle of bourbon by his side. He looked up when he heard his name called. "Oh, Bobby, your mother went home an hour ago. She's got a headache."

"I've got a headache," Kathleen said. "Can I go home?" She was too pretty to be a politician's wife. With raven hair, turquoise blue eyes and fair skin, she looked radiant in spite of her fatigue.

Bob smiled at her. "Very funny. Lonnie, can you get Kathleen some aspirin?"

"Just kidding. I'll be fine. Let's get this over so we can get the kids to bed. Give me five minutes with Martha." Kathleen took her six month old daughter into the bathroom to nurse. Her mother, Mary O'Malley, tried to follow her. Mary had flown in from Chicago for the victory party. She had bought a new black and white Christian Dior number for the evening, but managed to look frumpy in spite of the haute couture.

Kathleen blocked Mary from entering. "Mom, can you look after Robbie? I'll be right out."

"Okay, Kathleen. I'm just so excited for you. I can't believe you're really going to be a Congressman's wife."

"Me neither, Mom," Kathleen said from behind the closed door.

As they headed back to the suite after Bob's crowd-pleasing victory speech, Bob patted Robert III on his back and said, "We did it, Dad."

"Yes, we did, Bobby. We kicked butt." The old man was weaving, leaning on his cane more heavily than usual.

"I couldn't have done it without you, Dad. Thank you for all your help, especially with Fisher. That was masterful. The way you put the screws to him."

Robert III was glowing. He had embellished the story of his meeting with Fisher to heroic proportions, leaving out the part about his hasty retreat with Fisher in hot pursuit. "Aw, it was nothing any father wouldn't do for his son. I'm so happy I could do my part. Now, go up there to Washington and fight the good fight. Take no prisoners."

December 1994 – January 1995

When Emily McIntyre found her husband's body slumped back in his desk chair, she screamed loud enough to be heard over the sacred music playing on the office's public address system. At the American Family First Foundation's Washington, D.C. headquarters, the staff Christmas party was in full swing. *Hark the Herald Angels Sing* had just started when Emily's banshee wail pierced the conviviality of the affair. Several staffers rushed in, called 911 and helped a hysterical Emily into the next room.

Later, some wondered why Larry McIntyre had disappeared into his office just as the party was getting under way. Maybe he had felt pangs in his chest. Maybe he had left to take a call from a large donor. Maybe he had been praying. No one guessed that he had met up with Edna Roberts. He'd been out for two weeks, touring the country, raising money during the Advent season. Edna was set to leave the next day to visit her sister in Florida for two weeks. Those few private moments before he died had been their only opportunity to celebrate the nativity in their own special way.

No one noticed that Edna had forgotten to zip him up in her panic. The coroner never thought to check his urethra for recent sexual activity or swab his penis for traces of Revlon's Ravishing Rose Colorstay Lipstick. The heart attack was so massive and the family history was so evident, what with his father's early death, that once they opened his chest and found what they were looking for, they sewed him back up and shipped him off to Pittsburgh for services and burial. Back in Upper St. Clair, the embalming assistant, Ophelia Wainwright, who was something of a fetishist, was slightly more curious. She took photos of dead penises for her private collection. When she noticed the tiny smudge of Ravishing Rose, she smiled. It wasn't the first time a good blow job had triggered an acute myocardial infarction.

After the funeral, Emily went into seclusion for days. Larry and she had just bought a grand red brick colonial style home in Virginia, with eight bedrooms on twenty acres. It was their dream home, big enough to someday host their grandchildren and big enough to entertain members of the Platinum Heaven Club, the elite tier of the Foundation's donors. As Co-President of the Foundation, Emily had run the organization while Larry was out giving speeches, buttonholing Congressmen and talking to the press. She'd never been much of an orator or advocate. After weeks of prayer and reflection, she decided that, with the Lord's help, she would carry on in Larry's name. In speaking to the Foundation's board of directors the following month, she humbly offered to fill her husband's big shoes.

"I'm sure many of you are wondering how I could possibly inspire millions of followers and intimidate weak-kneed legislators like Larry did. I can only tell you that I have prayed on this and I know that the Lord will give me the words to say when the time is right. I share Larry's conviction to do battle and I carry his passion for victory in my heart. I will devote myself to this Foundation in Larry's memory to bring into reality his vision of a Christian nation committed to defending our values. On this Bible, I swear to you and to the Foundation my solemn oath to stop the killing of our babies and to lock the homosexuals back in their closet and throw away the key. So help me God."

The boardroom erupted in applause and cheers. Edna Roberts could hear the huzzahs from her desk, where she was packing to leave. She had submitted her letter of resignation right after Emily reassigned her to the photocopy department. Sobbing quietly, she put a framed photo of Larry in the box. She planned to stay with her sister in Fort Myers while she searched for a new home. Her pension money from the steel company, church and the Foundation would allow her to retire comfortably. And her nest egg from Larry's gifts would allow her to live in luxury.

1995

After ten years at the University of Melbourne, Josh Stein decided he wanted to be back in Sydney, closer to his parents and his sisters, Esther and Deborah, and their families. When his alma mater, the University of Sydney, offered him a full professorship, he accepted. He bought a one bedroom condo in Darlinghurst, one of Sydney's gayer neighborhoods, and a pre-owned Porsche sports car. On weekends, he sailed with his father, Ben, and drank beer with his old friend, Jeremy Logan, recently single again. Vince Scavullo came to visit from New York and put a smile on his face. Life was good.

For Ben's seventieth birthday party, Josh's sister, Sarah, and her family flew in from Los Angeles and his sister, Rachel, and her family flew in from London. There were red heads everywhere. Jeremy joined Josh at the celebration at a local restaurant, and gave a toast.

"Through my friendship with Josh, I've had the good fortune to know his father, Ben Stein, for over twenty years. He has been like a second father to me, especially after I came out to my parents and they disowned me. In many ways, he is my hero. He lied about his age to join the Royal Australian Air Force when he was sixteen, showed incredible bravery flying scores of bombing runs over Nazi Germany, came home and married his first and only love, Naomi, helped raise four amazing women and last, but not least, loved his gay son, Josh, as a father should, with his whole heart, without conditions or restrictions, knowing that all of his children are gifts from God, celebrating each of them for their uniqueness, and bringing me into that circle of love when I needed it most. Thank you, Mr. Stein. May you live another seventy years."

There was not a dry eye in the room. And then, Ben stood and lifted his glass. With his lean frame and creaseless face, he looked too young to have so many candles. Only his wispy white hair gave him away.

"Thank you, Jeremy, for your kind words. And thank you for being such a good friend to my son. You have my blessing if you should ever convince him to settle down."

Three weeks later, Ben Stein was dead. Josh was paralyzed with sadness, remorse and self-pity. He could not believe that his youthful father could simply stop breathing in the middle of the night from a brain aneurysm. It seemed cruel and unfair. He took his father's gentle presence and hearty laughter for granted.

"I always thought he would be here," he told Jeremy. "I have so much more I want to say to him and learn from him. I thought we could catch up now that I'm back in town. I'm not ready for him to be gone."

After sitting shiva with his mother and sisters for too many hours of reminiscing with well-meaning friends and relatives, Josh drove home and headed to the nearest bar. He drank gin martinis until he was drunk and then went home and passed out. The next day, he was the dutiful son and thoughtful brother, and then he went back to the bar until he was once again shit-faced. The pattern continued for a week, until he drove his sister, Sarah, to the airport. As she was getting ready to board the plane to Los Angeles, she handed him a piece of note paper with a phone number on it.

"I want you to call this number as soon as you get home."

"Why? What is it?"

"It's the number for Alcoholics Anonymous."

"Thanks, but I don't have a drinking problem."

"Yes, you do."

"I'm just going through a hard time with Dad's death."

"We all are, but we aren't getting tanked every night. Get some help now before it's too late.

"I can stop any time I want. I don't need AA."

"Do it for Dad. He worried about you, but he was afraid to confront you. You're a drunk, Josh. Good-bye.

June 15, 1996

"Oh, Roger, it's absolutely beautiful," Elaine Webber Griffin said to her brother as she held up the frilly white christening gown. "Heather will look so precious in it."

Roger was standing in the Griffins' nursery in Vancouver, holding six week old Heather. "I'm glad you like it. I've never made such a tiny dress."

"And all the fancy stitching and lace and these darling little mother of pearl beads. It must have taken you hours. I just love it."

At thirty-two, Elaine had evolved into the classic North American upper-middle class mom. With three-year-old Roger and newborn Heather, she was at the beginning of, long, carefully-planned parenting career. Roger could already envision his sister crying at Heather's wedding. Elaine had found her little piece of heaven and she would devote her life to tending it, nurturing her children, working hard to keep the romance alive in her marriage, and generally making the world a better place. As far as Roger could tell, Elaine and Mike were happily married. He was deeply envious. Still, he wondered if their sex life were as perfect as everything else. He suspected it was fairly vanilla. A typical gay man, he assumed most straight couples barely touched the surface of sexual pleasure. He toyed with the idea of giving Elaine a few tips to keep her man happy, but decided nipple clamps and butt plugs were not appropriate topics while he was holding his niece.

"So Mom says she's moving out here at the end of the year," he said with an air of studied indifference.

"Yes, can you believe she'll be sixty-five? You should come with her. I miss you so much."

"I miss you, too, but we talk almost every day, and I come out every summer. Vancouver's very pretty, but it's too small for me. And now that I've got the new job. I don't think I could find a position out here that would pay me as well."

"I'm sure your right. I can't believe my brother is a costume designer at The Princess of Wales Theatre."

"Well, I'd rather be on stage, but I've got to start somewhere. I've made so many dresses for myself the last few years, I figured I might as well get paid for it."

"So no more Bette, no more Cher?"

"Honey, look at me." Roger held his free hand above his head and twirled with Heather. He was wearing black, but there was no hiding his bulk. "I'm afraid that ship has sailed. There were more catcalls than cheers my last time out."

"Are you still seeing that guy?"

"Which one?"

"The older one."

"They're all older. Someday, I suspect I will date the oldest gay man in Toronto. And even they are losing interest. I don't suppose my attitude helps. I get lonely and I go to this one bar where the daddies congregate. At my age and with my girth, I'm invisible to anyone under the age of fifty. Occasionally, I find some middle-aged gentleman who's interested. And we share a moment. And then I'm repulsed by him and me both, and I leave. And guess what? They never call after that."

"I'm sorry. I wish you could find someone special."

"Me too." He put the back of his hand to his forehead and sang, "Someday my prince will come. Someday I'll find my love."

Elaine chimed in. It was their favorite song from Walt Disney's *Snow White and the Seven Dwarfs*. "And how thrilling that moment will be when the prince of my dreams comes to me. He'll whisper I love you and steal a kiss or two."

Roger put his sleeping niece in her bassinet, and he waltzed around the nursery with Elaine, the two of them singing all three verses, finishing with "and the birds will sing and wedding bells will ring someday when my dreams come true." The two of them laughed, incredulous that they had remembered every word from their childhood.

The next evening, after the christening ceremony and the fancy dinner at the elegant Lumiere restaurant, Roger went back to his hotel and put on his gear. Venturing forth to his favorite leather bar, he headed to the back room and found a dark corner. By two the next morning, he had swallowed the royal seed of several Canadian princes.

Chapter 6

December 1997

Josh Stein rang the buzzer of his friends' apartment. The last thing he wanted to do was spend a long evening with a room full of high energy gay men. But it was Ralph Hudson's fortieth birthday party, and Ralph and his partner, Oscar Fuentes, were two of his best friends. So despite the hangover from the night before, he had rallied, cleaned himself up and walked over to their place in Sydney's Darlinghurst district.

Josh had arrived late enough to avoid the cocktail hour and claimed a chair at the foot of the table, as far from the birthday boy as possible. Normally, he would have enjoyed Ralph's banter, but with his throbbing headache, all he wanted to do was fade into the background and go home at the earliest possible juncture.

"Ta da!" Oscar exclaimed as he carried the huge dish of paella into the dining room. "My mother's secret recipe."

It was a pleasant summer evening, and the windows were open to catch the breeze. Yet, Josh was sweating, as his body labored away, attempting to metabolize seven gin martinis. Sitting next to him was a stranger, a friend of a friend. Mark Cross, Josh remembered from the introduction as they sat down. He had a shaved head, dark, intense eyes, a prominent nose and a small gold ring in his left ear. Mark sat back in his chair, lean and tanned, looking very relaxed in a black tank top, camouflage cargo pants and leather sandals. Josh had noticed his neighbor, but he couldn't muster enough energy to act on his hormones.

At thirty-nine, Josh was no slouch, himself. Rock hard from almost daily trips to the gym, he prided himself on staving off the ravages of time. His hair was still thick and black, his eyesight was near perfect, and his erections were frequent, firm and long lasting, drunk or sober.

As the sangria pitcher made its way toward him, Josh chugged his first glass. Pouring himself another, he caught the stranger smiling at him.

"Hair of the dog?" Mark asked.

"How'd you know?"

"I've been there. Many times."

"Any suggestions?"

"Yeah. Stop drinking."

"I've tried that."

"How many times?"

"More than I can count. How about you?"

"I had my last drink nine years, three months and twelve days ago."

Josh grinned. "Day by day, then?"

Mark smiled back. "Exactly. I can still taste it. What I wouldn't give for a long neck right now."

"How'd you do it?"

"I had no choice. I got pissed as a parrot one night and got sacked."

"That's harsh. Where did you work?"

"The Australian Ballet Company. I missed my cue. We were doing Sleeping Beauty. I was the prince. The director was as mad as a cut snake."

"That was nine years ago?"

"Three months and twelve days."

"Sorry to hear it."

"It's not so bad. I was an aging prince. In ballet, you're an old man at thirty-five. I teach dance now. What do you do?"

Josh glanced down at his newly empty glass. "Well, I drink too much. I teach at the University of Sydney and I write fiction. For a very small group of enlightened readers."

"What's your last name?"

"Stein. Of the Bondi Beach Steins. Old Australian family. We were here before the Dingoes."

"I've got you beat. I've got a splash of aborigine. And I'm one of your enlightened readers."

Josh studied Mark with new interest. He did indeed have a distinctive, not quite Caucasian, look to him, a sexy feral quality. Josh couldn't stop himself. "Which books have you read?"

Mark had read them all and was perceptive enough to identify the linking theme of the protagonist as an outsider. The sangria was kicking in, and Josh was beginning to enjoy the party. He told his story about growing up tall, dark, gay and adopted in a household of height-challenged redheaded females. "Don't get me wrong. I love my family, but I felt like I was from another planet half the time.

Mark nodded. "I know exactly what you're saying. I was the apple eater with black blood and dance shoes trying to fit in at university with all the ockers."

"Ah. A Tasmanian boy. I wondered about your accent."

"And then, for the last ten years, I've been positive. So, I know something about feeling like an outsider."

In Josh's head, the cathedral-sized pipe organ playing Felix Mendelssohn's *Wedding March* came to a screeching halt. Damn! Why do all the good ones have HIV, he wondered for the thousandth time since the plague had leapt from a chimpanzee to a human host.

"How is that going for you?" Josh asked.

"It's going well. I was feeling crook as Rookwood for a couple years, but I'm on some new meds and they seem to help."

Just then Oscar carried in a birthday cake flaming with forty candles and placed it in front of his partner, Ralph. The men sang *Happy Birthday* and then the toasts began, followed by presents and photos. The two men didn't have a chance to talk again until the end of the evening.

"Do you date men who are positive?" Mark asked.

"Yes," Josh lied.

"Then, here's my number. Call me if you want. Let's have coffee. You can tell me about your new book."

For the next week, Josh couldn't stop thinking about the hot Tasmanian dancer. He carried Mark's number around in his pocket, intending to call him, but hesitating. He hated to admit it, but he was half hoping he would lose interest. The only thing stopping him from making the call was the invisible bug living inside Mark's beautiful body. Since he had broken up with his last boyfriend, Josh had been with a number of men. He had always presumed his partners might be HIV positive and took precautions. He knew he could have safe sex with Mark if it came to that, but he already knew that Mark would be more than a one night stand. And Josh didn't know if he was ready for that. He'd heard too many stories about mixed couples, one positive and one negative, who had broken up because the virus ultimately had become too big of a barrier in the bedroom. "It's a buzz kill," one friend had told him. "We could never cut loose and just do it. I was always holding back, watching myself like the pool lifeguard. 'Hey, there, stop that.'"

At the end of the week, on a Sunday morning, Josh was sitting in his kitchen, sweaty from his morning run, drinking orange juice and trying to read the newspaper. He couldn't concentrate. Opening the arts section, he saw an ad for The Australian Ballet Company. A sinewy young man held his dainty female partner aloft in a hyper-romanticized pose. They would never show two men together, Josh thought. In that moment, he decided he would never forgive himself if he let this one get away. His heart was pounding as he picked up his mobile phone.

"Hey, Mark. It's Josh."

"Hey, Josh. How's your head?" Mark asked.

"Great. I haven't had a drink since I saw you. You inspired me."

"Bloody hell! That's the first time that's happened. I usually drive men to drink."

"Well, you've been driving me crazy all week, thinking about you." Josh immediately began banging his fist against his forehead, cringing. He sounded like an infatuated school girl.

Mark laughed. "You've been driving me crazy, too. I got your number from Oscar and I was debating whether I should call you."

They made plans to meet for coffee that afternoon, to celebrate Josh's seven days of sobriety. After three hours in a sidewalk café and too much coffee, they strolled down the avenue to an Italian restaurant for dinner and talked for another three hours.

After the waiter brought their tiramisu and espressos, Mark asked, "Have you ever tried to find your biological parents?"

"No. When I was a kid, I always wanted to know who they were, but now, I'm afraid of what I'll find."

"Still, it might give you some peace."

"Then I wouldn't have an excuse to drink."

"You don't need an excuse. You had your last drink at the party."

"What makes you say that?"

"Because you made a decision, and I'm going to help you keep it."

Josh smiled. He ran his fingertips across Mark's knuckles. "How are you going to do that?"

"I'm taking you to AA with me."

"I've been to those meetings. They don't help."

"But you haven't gone to meetings with me. When you reach your three month mark, I'll let you kiss me. And again at six months. And nine months. When you get your one year coin, I'll let you sleep with me."

Josh placed his hand over Mark's. "But I want to sleep with you tonight. I don't think I can wait that long."

"I'll be waiting, too, and it'll be hard for me. It's part of getting sober. You have to focus on yourself for the next year. A sexual relationship will only mess you up right now."

Josh squeezed Mark's hand. "That's a lot to ask, don't you think? After one date?"

"It's your choice. But I won't date you unless you're sober."

"So if I choose you, our next date is an AA meeting?"

"And the next one and the next one. As many times a week as you want, but we start with a meeting and we finish with a hug. That's it."

"Jesus, Mark, you better be one hell of a lay."

June 1998

"Good-bye Chicago!" Georgia Jones declared, as she and her brother, Jonathan Jones, crept across the Illinois border into Indiana in the Friday afternoon rush hour traffic.

"I think you're happier about this move than I am," Jonathan said, smiling. He was sitting in the front passenger seat with his bare feet on the dashboard. His window was open to the clamor of diesel engines and the industrial brew of refineries and steel mills. It was early summer, and the brown pall over Lake Michigan was thicker than usual.

"I had to get out of that town," Georgia said. "There are too many ex-girlfriends back there telling lies about me." She was wearing a bright yellow sundress and leather sandals. Her tight orange afro almost touched the roof of the old Subaru. She was not pretty in a conventional way, but she was striking. "Jonathan in drag," one ex had described her. And she filled a room with her personality.

Jonathan laughed. At forty, he had relaxed into middle age with thick glasses and a small paunch. He was wearing khaki cargo shorts and a Hawaiian flower print shirt, a going away gift from one of his parishioners. After three years at the Chicago Theological Seminary and five more years at a big south side church as an associate minister, he was going home to Detroit to save the Church of the Inner Light from extinction. Once a grand old house of worship, it had fallen on hard times as the city itself had decayed.

"I still don't understand why you want this church," Georgia said, as she blasted her horn at a silver Mercedes convertible, edging its way in front of her on its way to a weekend cottage in the dunes. "Momma says it's a bunch of dried up old ladies and drunks looking for a quiet place to sleep."

"That's about right. I think I've met the entire congregation, at least the ones who care enough to put money in the plate."

"And?"

"They're ancient. Two of them have passed away since I accepted the job. It's going to be a challenge. But I'm looking forward to it. I was getting bored with the South Shore crowd. Rich black folk can be just as pompous and petty as rich white folk."

"Uh-huh. I hear that. But still, Momma says these folks can barely keep the lights on, let alone pay you."

"I admit it's a leap of faith, but I hope to turn things around. That neighborhood needs that church. At least I've got a job."

She looked over at him and raised an eyebrow. "Don't worry about me. I'll have a job before you lose another old lady."

"Planned Parenthood again?"

"No, I'm thinking of hooking up with an AIDS outreach program for the brothers. Try to teach them to practice safe sex and stop infecting our sisters."

Jonathan shook his head. "Good luck with that. I'll fill my church before you convince one of them to wear a rubber."

Georgia and Jonathan settled into the old parsonage with her two cats, Letitia and Leslie, and his dog, Zeke, a big mutt with long black fur and a tail that knocked over plant stands and small children. They hadn't lived under the same roof since childhood, and their mother predicted they wouldn't last a week. But after a few heated moments over music and menu preferences, they managed to negotiate reasonable terms of co-existence.

The Church of the Inner Light was a former synagogue that had been recycled by a splinter group of disaffected black Baptists in the 1950's. They had grown tired of the shenanigans of their minister who had spent the congregation's hard earned tithes on Cadillacs and fur coats for his mistress. Their goal had been to reach back to the original message of Jesus Christ, stripped free of theatrics and bling. An activist church, they had opened a soup kitchen and homeless shelter and sent scores of volunteers south for the civil rights marches in the 1960's. Some of those who had marched in Selma, Alabama with Dr. King in 1965 were still in the pews every Sunday morning, praying for a miracle to save the church from the wrecker's ball.

When the neighborhood was still vibrant and the congregation still prosperous, the church had bought an old gray stone manse nearby for the young firebrand minister and his family. After he was shot dead in the sanctuary one Saturday morning in 1985, trying to convince two teenagers not to steal the silver-plated communion service, his widow moved out, and the church limped along with a string of pastors, most of whom chose not to live in the parsonage for safety's sake. A determined crew of septuagenarians and octogenarians had cleaned the old home and trimmed back the bushes in the days before Jonathan and Georgia arrived.

Within a month, Georgia had talked her way into a job with an AIDS service agency that didn't know they needed her until she convinced them she could save lives and find funding to cover her salary. Her old friends held a small homecoming party for her, and that night she met Cecily Ferguson, an engineer with General Motors. "That girl had me tongue-tied," she told Jonathan the next morning at breakfast. "Sweet, sexy, black as midnight and all woman. Hmmmm."

"When do I get to meet her?" he asked.

"Tonight. She's coming over for dinner. Can you make your lasagna and let me take credit?"

"What did you tell her?"

"I might have said something about how good I was in the kitchen."

"Georgia, this never ends well. Just tell her the truth. She won't care that you can't cook."

"I'm sorry. I couldn't stop myself. It's her passion, and I wanted her to like me, so..."

Jonathan looked at his watch. "I've got to go. My first official board meeting. I'll pick up the ingredients and help you make it, so you don't have to lie."

"Thanks, Johnny. Now, we've got to find you a man."

He laughed as he headed for the front door. "Don't waste your time."

Jonathan had dated discreetly in divinity school, but after he graduated and started work, he had become celibate. To him, it seemed the only option. He couldn't be openly gay and keep his job, and he hated the dishonesty of hiding his love life. At first, he had found it hard to give up sexual intimacy, but as time passed, he had found abstinence truly allowed him to focus his spiritual energy on his work. He took some solace in the writings of St. Augustine, who had converted to Christianity and taken up celibacy after the man he had loved died suddenly. As the youth minister, Jonathan had started several athletic and academic clubs for the children and doubled and then tripled participation. The pied piper of the South Shore, the board president had called him. Revenues had risen accordingly as happy parents rewarded the church for keeping their children busy. When Jonathan announced he was leaving, the senior minister had told him he was making a grave mistake. "You have a great future here. In ten years, you could have my job. Wife or no wife. You would be a power broker in this city. All the politicians would seek your support." That was all Jonathan needed to hear to know he'd made the right decision.

December 1, 1999

"How do I look?" Jerry Boston asked his wife, Diane. Truth be told, at thirty-seven, Jerry looked like he was fifty. A combination of bad genes and high stress had taken its toll. With a body shaped like a pillow, hunched shoulders and sagging jowls, he looked more like his father with each passing year.

"You look great, Jerry." A native of southern California, Diane knew how to make the best of limited physical assets. She had selected a charcoal gray Brooks Brothers suit for him and had it tailored to shape and slenderize him as much as possible. She'd had the local cobbler add half inch heels to his new wingtips. He was wearing a perfectly tailored French blue shirt. "It matches your eyes," she had said. With two trips to the local tanning salon, he had taken on just the right glow of prosperity. His flashy watch had been replaced with an understated model. She'd even given him speech lessons to wash out some of the worst New York slang and mangled pronunciations.

"I feel like a fraud," he said, looking at himself in the front hall mirror.

"You look like a million bucks, and you're going to knock them dead. Show them the same confidence you show me, and they'll be begging you to work for them." Diane was as slim and attractive as the day he had met her at a campaign fundraiser in Los Angeles. She worked hard to keep her figure with frequent trips to the health club, her only time away from their two kids.

After years of working miracles behind the scenes for other political consultants, Jerry had started his own firm and stunned the cognoscenti of both parties by masterminding the come-from-behind victory of a conservative Republican over a moderate Democratic incumbent U.S. Senator in Illinois. The triumph had launched Jerry into the stratosphere of political consulting, and he had been flooded with new business, but he still had not landed the client he could sell to the American public as President of the United States, savior of the free world and defender of American family values.

The Bostons were members of the Arlington Fairfax Jewish Congregation, a Conservative synagogue. Both of them had been raised in the Reform tradition, but it suited Jerry to reject his parents' High Holidays' pretense and hone closer to the faith of his immigrant great-grandfather, Nathan Boskowitz. Nevertheless, Jerry's sense of God was more racial than mystical, tied more to the struggles of the tribe than it was to the God of Abraham.

Jerry had recognized the common interests of conservative Jews and evangelical Christians long before other Republicans and figured he was doing Jehovah's work, even if it were more and more dressed in the trappings of born again Christianity. For this reason, he had been hounding Congressman Bob Hamilton's office for an appointment. Finally, after six months of delays and excuses, he had been granted a thirty minute breakfast meeting with the rising star and his elderly father, who happened to be in town for a veterans' convention.

Diane had suggested that he feed them at the stately Willard Hotel. "It reeks of Washington's power elite, and you want to be perceived as part of that clique."

"I'll make a reservation right now," he had said.

"And don't order a bagel," she had instructed. "Too ethnic. Get scrambled eggs and an English muffin, buttered. It's simple to eat and hard to spill. Drink your coffee black. Alpha dogs drink their coffee black. Order breakfast even if the Congressman doesn't. The old man will be grateful. He looks like he eats several times a day."

Bob Hamilton had won each successive House race by ever wider margins. "We're shooting for eighty percent next year," he said at breakfast, with the confidence of an heir to the throne.

"I'm sure you'll succeed," Jerry responded. "But when you run for the Senate, you'll have to appeal to a wider population."

Robert Hamilton III shook his head. "We Georgians are all pretty much the same, Mr. Boston. Rednecks, at heart. Bobby doesn't have to change his message." Robert III smiled as he jammed a piece of bacon in his mouth.

"Maybe so," Jerry said. "But, if you want to win the presidency, you have to run a Senate campaign that will position you for a national race. I can help you with that."

Bob was taking notes. "That sounds interesting. Maybe you could pitch some ideas to my staff. Give us a chance to evaluate your thinking."

"Now, don't get in such a hurry, Bobby," Robert III said as he swabbed up his egg yolk with a corner of white toast. "The Senate race is still three years off." Robert III grabbed his cane and stood, oblivious to the grape jelly on his tie. "Thank you for your time, Mr. Boston."

The meeting had lasted barely twenty minutes. Bob and Robert III shook hands with Jerry in the lobby of the Willard. "I'd be glad to speak to you or your staff any time," Jerry said. "The party needs you, Congressman. The country needs you. And I'd like to help in any way I can."

"Good-bye, Mr. Boston," Robert III said, with a smile that was beginning to fade.

In the limousine, Bob asked his father, "What did you think?"

"For Christ's sake, Bobby. He's a fucking Jew. We'd be a laughingstock back home if we hired a kike from New York. I can't believe you agreed to meet with him in the first place."

"I don't know. He's got quite a reputation. He's a funny looking little guy, but he seems very smart. And you know what they say. They know how to fight dirty."

Robert III shook his head as he watched Jerry Boston trudge down the sidewalk with his briefcase. "Bobby, Bobby, Bobby. Haven't I taught you anything? We can't trust a Jew with such an important position. They're only out for themselves. I don't even play golf with them. You can't trust their scores."

"Dad, your country club doesn't accept Jews."

"Exactly my point. And that's the way I like it."

June 2000

"Congressman, I need five minutes of your time." Jerry Boston tugged gently at Bob Hamilton's suit sleeve as he was coming out of a sub-committee hearing.

Bob glanced at his watch. "Hi Jerry. I've got three minutes. Talk fast."

Jerry had been peppering Bob's office with proposals and suggestions for the Senate race for six months. He'd been allowed to meet with Bob's chief of staff, Rory Dugan, twice, but he hadn't been allowed another audience with the Congressman himself. Dugan had urged Bob to hire him, but Bob had resisted.

"Great," Jerry said. "Let's step over here for some privacy." He steered Bob to a quiet corner of the hallway. "I've just got word that Senator Holmes is going to march in the gay pride parade in Atlanta next week."

"No kidding. Why would he do that?"

"Who knows? Probably some gay cousin came screaming out of the closet. He obviously feels he can take some heat on this and still get re-elected."

"He's going to be hard to beat, that's for sure."

"With your permission, this is what I'd like to do." Jerry leaned closer to whisper and Bob bent down to hear him.

The smile on Bob's face grew and grew until he started chuckling. "I like the way you think, Jerry. If you can pull this off, you're hired."

"Thank you, Congressman. You won't be disappointed."

On a hot Sunday afternoon in late June, United States Senator Jed Holmes wiped his brow with his handkerchief as he walked down the parade route of Atlanta's gay pride festival amongst a string of local officials. At sixty-five, the white-haired Holmes was four years into his second six-year term. He was a folksy, good old boy from rural Georgia in the grand tradition of Deep South politics. A Democrat, he was a moderate by Georgia standards and a conservative by blue state standards. A man with national aspirations, he had taken the advice of one of his consultants, a slick, fast-talking dude from California, who had told him he needed to widen his base to include gays and other traditional elements of the progressive coalition.

Midway along the route, a very tall, very manly transvestite in lavender taffeta that, even by gay pride standards, was flamboyant, stood at the edge of the crowd. In a long blonde wig that did little to hide his five o'clock shadow, he waved at the senator with his hot pink feather boa. "Over here, Senator. Come over here," he squealed in falsetto. Holmes didn't hear him or pretended not to. He waved stiffly from the center of the street surrounded by young staffers waving his placards. The lady in lavender swore under her breath, shifted her weight on her white leather pumps and then edged her way past a heavy-set Atlanta cop looking very unhappy with his assignment. Just as Holmes approached his position, the he/she bolted past the policeman and rushed headlong into the senator's arms. There, she embraced the old man and planted a big, wet lipstick stained kiss on his left cheek, making sure not to block a clear view of Holmes' reaction. In campaign mode, Holmes had been walking the route with a frozen, what-am-I-doing-here smile that remained for the pictures taken with a camera with a telephoto lens from a second floor window fifty feet in front of Holmes.

After the kiss, the lavender fan disappeared into the crowd and stepped into the back of a white van a block away. There, he threw down his wig and slapped a high five with another Jerry Boston operative. The ex-Marine had lost the coin toss for the job of van driver. The booby prize was the job of Senator-kissing transvestite. The dejected Marine had been promised an extra bonus in his paycheck to keep him happy and quiet. He also kept quiet about his happy discovery that nylon stockings felt really sexy on his big hairy legs. Holmes finished the parade and immediately chewed out his chief of staff who was busy scrubbing the lipstick smear off the senator's cheek. "No more queer parades," Holmes declared. But the damage had been done.

The resulting photos were priceless. Most showed Holmes' bewildered discomfort, but one in particular caught him in a split second when his reflexive grin seemed to show that he had actually enjoyed the transvestite's attention. The photo processing expert heightened the lurid hues of that image to enhance the ex-Marine's ensemble, matching makeup and baby blue eyes. Jerry Boston stored the negatives and prints in a safety deposit box, to be held until they were needed.

Chapter 7

August 12, 2001

Pat McCormack and his sister, Bridget McCormack, were walking the length of the Vietnam Veterans War Memorial wall inscribed with the names of over 58,000 dead and missing American soldiers. Despite the muggy late summer heat in the nation's capital, Pat was wearing a dark business suit, white shirt and tie. "Why are you all dressed up on such a hot day?" Bridget asked. She was in her civvies, as she called them, jeans and a T-shirt. In class, back at St. Gabriel School, on Chicago's south side, she wore a dark skirt, white blouse and black veil. Her students called it her holy hat. It was optional in her order, but she preferred to wear it, as a sign of her vows.

"I don't feel comfortable out of a suit in public," Pat answered. "I don't get this whole business casual thing. Can you imagine James Bond in jeans?" He was a slight man of medium height with nondescript features and dull brown hair, the kind of man who could fade into a crowd and not be remembered. Pat McCormack was the perfect spy.

"I thought Bond preferred not to wear any clothes at all." Bridget kept her brown hair short and straight, parted on the side. With sensible shoes, a thick waist and no make-up, she looked very much like the lesbian she was not.

"Speaking of going naked, how's your love life?" he asked with a smile.

"Every bit as good as yours, I suspect."

"Someday, Bridget, I'm going to have you meet one of the many women I have slept with."

"I won't hold my breath." Bridget stopped to study the names. "We should be more respectful. Let's see if we can find Uncle Joe's name. He should be along here somewhere. There he is." She stepped forward and touched the letters carved into the stone, Joseph P. McCormack. "Oh, my goodness. I'm going to cry."

Pat stood back, watching a young redhead twenty paces ahead of them. "Didn't Dad say he was fragged by his troops?"

"No, he didn't. Don't ruin this for me, Paddy." She placed a sheet of paper over Uncle Joe's name and ran a lead pencil across it to make the impression she wanted to show her third graders that fall on

Veterans Day. Folding the paper carefully so as not to crease the name, she placed it in her small black purse. "Okay, I'm done. Let's go get some ice cream. You've made me wait long enough. Tell me your big news."

Pat looked around at the crowd and then motioned her onto the grass. "Let's cut across the mall. I don't know who's listening."

She ambled after him. "I thought you had retired. Why the secrecy?"

Pat lowered his voice. "You never really leave the agency. I'm carrying around twenty years of secrets, so I need to be careful what I say."

"Well, don't tell me anything you shouldn't."

"I can trust you. You're a nun. It's like going to confession." With that, Pat lit into a summary of the murder and mayhem he had wrought on behalf of the American taxpayers.

When they reached the National Air and Space Museum, Bridget found the ladies room and prayed for her brother's soul as she urinated. In the museum's Wright Place Food Court, Bridget ordered her chocolate cone with sprinkles. Pat continued his tale after checking to make sure the nearby tables were empty. "After I blew up the bus station in Kinshasa, I got promoted. They decided I was too valuable to be out in the field, so they brought me home and trained me to hack into computers. I've become quite a high-tech geek. And I was also planting listening devices, tapping phones, intercepting mail, breaking into document storage facilities. You name it, I did it. I can find out anything I want to know about any human being on earth, alive or dead. I'm going to make millions."

"How?"

Pat snorted. "I'm going into private consulting. A group of my buddies from the agency and I are starting our own firm. Harris Security International."

"Why not McCormack Security International?"

"I could have added my name, but I don't want the limelight. Too many years being a spook, I guess. I'll just take the big paychecks."

"Who's going to hire you?"

"Politicians, lobbyists, corporations, rich people. We will be the best because we were the smartest and toughest sons of bitches that ever worked for the agency. We're going to charge three times the going rate, and we'll get it, no questions asked."

Bridget licked that last bit of sprinkles away. "But how will they know you're so tough if everything you did was secret?"

Pat smiled. "Let's just say some people very high up in this administration have already spread the word. They know our work."

"I thought you hated politicians."

Pat nodded. "I do. They're all scum. In the last twenty years, I've learned they can all be bought and sold. With the right amount of money or power or sex. Kinky motherfuckers, some of them. But I don't have to like them to take their money."

Bridget crunched into her cone. "I'd like to go to mass tomorrow. Will you join me?"

Pat rolled his eyes. "I'll drop you off and pick you up, but I'm not stepping foot inside a church again unless it's to do a job."

• • •

In Langley, Virginia at the headquarters of the Central Intelligence Agency, a gray haired gentleman and a shapely blonde were holding a short meeting. The blonde, Angela Patterson, was studying a recent photo of Patrick Allen McCormack on top of a thick folder. "Not much of a looker, is he?" she commented.

Her boss, Phinneas Graves, smirked. "Actually, he fancies himself quite a ladies' man. Hopefully, you won't have to find out first hand. For now, all I want you to do is review his file and get familiar with his background."

Angela glanced at an old photo of Pat with an exotic-looking Eurasian woman. "May I ask why?"

"We brought him home ten years ago after a string of embarrassments. 'Rogue elephant on a rampage,' one section chief described him. He always got the job done, but he often made a mess, whether it was too much collateral damage or disappointed fiancés screaming at hotel staff. He'd woo them with the promise of American citizenship and then disappear when his assignment was finished. He's done a great job since then. With heavy supervision. But, you can see from his profile, he's not the most stable guy. It could be that he'll make his transition to civilian life smoothly, and you'll never meet him. I just don't know. We'll monitor him remotely, light surveillance from time to time. If anything serious crops up, I'll give you a call."

Angela had flipped to his psychological profile. "James Bond fantasies? You've got to be kidding."

Phinneas grimaced. "I know. It's embarrassing. All the way down to playing baccarat. He's quite a high stakes gambler. You may want to meet him just for the amusement."

She closed the folder and stood. "I'll take a pass. I have enough crazy men in my life."

"Really, but I thought you were —"

"I'm talking about my dad and my brothers. Real whack jobs. All of them."

"I know. I've read your file. That's why I picked you for this assignment."

October 2001

"So, this is our last session," Dr. Jacob Schuler said to his patient, Joshua Stein.

"Yes." Josh was sitting in a black leather Barcelona chair facing the avuncular therapist. Now a full professor in the University of Sydney's Department of English, Josh had grown a tight dark beard and trimmed his curls.

"How do you feel about that?" Jacob was sitting in a matching chair facing Josh in a sunlit office in Darlinghurst. With a shaved head, goatee and glasses, the psychologist looked the part, except for the tank top and shorts. Jacob was a favorite in the community. A gay man, himself, he had coaxed many a tweaker off the ceiling and into rehab. Over the years, he had counseled men dying of AIDS, offered grief therapy to their lovers, and helped men come out to their families, go through divorces with their wives and breakups with their boyfriends. Josh was one of his healthier patients. Mild depression. Part of the human condition.

"I feel great," Josh said. "Hell, it's been almost four years. It's about time, don't you think?" Josh uncrossed his legs and looked out the window at the blossoming crab apple tree. He, too, was dressed in a tank top and shorts. It was the season.

"You always forget," Jacob said. "I don't answer questions. And certainly not that one."

"If you could answer, you'd probably say I should have quit two years ago. I'm just wasting your time. But you're not going to answer and now I have to defend why I just said that. Like what am I doing here if I think I should have quit two years ago? And maybe it's just because I like talking to myself in your nice office with you taking notes and nodding. But we both know that's not true. Because two years ago, I still wasn't ready to say I wanted to spend the rest of my life with Mark. And now I know I do, and…I forgot the point I was trying to make."

"This is your last session," Jacob reminded him.

"Ah, yes. Sometimes I think I might have arrived at the same place at the same time without you. Mark has changed my life in so many ways. All of them good. When I met him, I was drinking hard. No one else understood. I had perfect parents. Kind, loving, accepting. For years, I had been fine with that. I'm Jewish, I told myself. I'm proud of my heritage. I love my parents. But, then I would say to myself I have another set of parents, the woman who gave me away and the man who fucked her. They haunted me. I sometimes imagined I had a parallel life with them. I dreamt up different versions, and none of them was happy. Sometimes life can be too perfect, I thought. Almost artificial. Sometimes, I felt like I didn't deserve the life I was handed."

Jacob nodded. He'd heard it all before.

"But then I met Mark. He got me to stop drinking. He introduced me to Zen Buddhism. I reexamined my life. My priorities. As he says, 'Nothing gets your attention like the prospect of dying.' And it transformed him. Before he got the new meds. Living in the now. That's the only way to truly enjoy life, isn't it?"

Jacob looked up from his note pad and stared blankly at Josh.

"Or it could just be a normal part of getting older. I'm forty-three, and I'm in great shape. But, still, I'm forty-three. I'll never be twenty-three again, or thirty-three. Well, maybe I look thirty-three, but I'm gay. That's to be expected. And my doctor says I'm healthy, but who knows what's in my genetic mix. For all I know, my people fall over dead of heart disease in their forties. And I've given up trying to find them. My mother keeps digging, but the trail disappears in a cardboard box on a desk in a sad little room in the Dublin airport, with me screaming at the top of my lungs."

The room went silent, and then a kookaburra kingfisher in the crab apple tree made its presence known.

Josh stood and went to the window to look for the bird. "See. Even the kookaburra is laughing at me. He's saying, 'Stein, you fool, get your thumb out of your ass and come join me in the sun. Stop kvetching about your life and start living it.'" The bird flew away, and Josh turned to face his therapist. "I'm done talking."

Jacob smiled and rose to shake his hand. "Congratulations, Josh."

That night in bed, after making love, Josh asked Mark, "Are you scared?"

"Of what?" Mark asked back. He was curled up next to Josh with his head on Josh's shoulder.

"Of standing up in front of all those people and telling them that you love me and you want to live with me for the rest of your life."

"No, I can't wait."

"I'm scared."

"Why?"

"Because I think that's the most profound statement one human being can make to another. I pick you and you only."

"Why is that scary if you know you picked the right guy?"

"Because I want us to go on forever and ever. I can't imagine life without you."

"And you figure I'm going first?"

"Well, you are five years older."

Mark pinched Josh's nipple. Josh yelped and tried to reach one of Mark's nipples. The two men wrestled until they both realized they were hard again. And then they kissed.

October 2002

The glossy brochure featuring Senator Jed Holmes' Kodak moment with the lavender drag queen was produced and mailed by a little known Georgia-based family values organization called Dads, Moms and Kids. Jerry Boston had covertly set up the non-profit group at the time the photo was taken. No contributions to Dads, Moms and Kids came directly from the Bob Hamilton for Senate campaign. Rather, several wealthy individual donors sympathetic to the Hamilton cause had underwritten the cost of the brochure and its mailing. Emblazoned across the bottom of the eight by ten photo in rose pink all caps bold italic lettering was the simple message, "*HOLMES LOVES GAYS!*" The crude wording was intentional. Dads, Moms and Kids was not a sophisticated organization, and it was wise not to show too much creativity in the piece. Besides, the photo spoke a thousand words, none of them kind in the minds of the targeted voters. The brochure was mailed to conservative and independent voters a week before the election. Jed's approval ratings plummeted twenty points in two days and never recovered. In response to press inquiries, the Hamilton campaign officially disavowed any involvement in the brochure.

By contrast, in the same polling, a significant majority of Georgia voters rated Bob Hamilton as "highly likeable." People simply "felt good" about him and his beautiful wife and lovely children. The positive public opinion and press were all the result of an elaborate and expensive public relations campaign that had been launched by Jerry Boston two years before. He had outlined a step-by-step, year-by-year game plan to Robert III and Bob in their first official meeting shortly after the notorious photo was snapped. While Bob and his father were admiring "The Kiss," as it came to be called in the campaign, Jerry had made his pitch. "If we follow my strategy, I promise to put you in the White House before the end of your second Senate term." Even Robert III had been impressed.

Two weeks after the meeting, Robert III had suffered a mild heart attack. He was eighty-one. His doctor had discouraged surgery because of his age and tests that showed very little damage had been done. Robert III had soon resumed his regular routine of golfing and drinking. But he was scared. He had very much wanted to live to see his son become president and to see his grandchildren grow up and marry. When his son announced for the U.S. Senate, he had re-doubled his efforts at fundraising. The work had exhausted him. Bob tried to get him to slow down, but he would have none of it.

The second heart attack had been much more severe, damaging a large portion of his heart and landing him in intensive care the weekend before Election Day. In great pain and heavily sedated, Robert III had revised his life goals. He simply wanted to see his son sworn in as a U.S. Senator. He was in Atlanta's best hospital, and his son had cancelled all campaign activities to be at his bedside. On his second night, Robert III was alone at three in the morning. His wife, Martha, had left at midnight to get some rest at a nearby hotel. He had been resting comfortably, so Bob had slipped out to grab a cup of coffee in the hospital cafeteria. In the fifteen minutes his son was gone, a nurse entered the room to check his vital signs.

Coming out of his narcotic haze, Robert III could see a black figure hovering above him, but, without his glasses, he couldn't see the smile on Darcel Mulberry's face.

"Where's Bobby?" Robert III demanded, his whole body tensing.

Darcel kept smiling and spoke with a soothing baritone. "Your son will be right back. He just stepped out for some coffee."

Now he could vaguely discern Darcel's smile, but it seemed

menacing. His breathing was shallow and labored. The pain in his chest was intensifying. Darcel leaned forward to insert a thermometer. "Time to take your temperature."

Darcel's face finally came into focus, but by then Robert III was too panicked to see clearly. The face before him was not Darcel's, but that of a nameless young black man who had nailed him with a curse at the end of a rope on a court house lawn when he was nine. The same young black man who had begun to haunt his dreams in recent weeks. He didn't see Darcel's smile, but a twisted grotesque death mask cackling at him. Robert III spat in Darcel's face, and then he raised his arms to bat him away, screaming, "Git away from me, nigger. I didn't kill you. Where's Bobby?"

The smile left Darcel's face as he tried to restrain Robert III. The final heart attack hit with such force that he collapsed in unbearable pain. He grabbed his chest and gasped for air. Darcel waited perhaps fifteen seconds, humming "Swing Low, Sweet Chariot," and then pushed the button for a Code Blue emergency. The last thing Robert III saw and heard was Darcel smiling again, six inches from his face, as he whispered, "So long, motherfucker. See you in hell."

Bob returned to find an emergency crew trying to revive his father. Darcel led him away, saying, "They're doing all they can, but it doesn't look good."

December 2003

On December 13, 2003, American military forces captured Iraq's deposed leader, Saddam Hussein, on a farm near Tikrit, Iraq in Operation Red Dawn. The action was Major Billy Short's last official task as a member of the U.S. Army Special Forces. Although his unit had tracked down and pinpointed the location of the despot, as with many other missions, they were not allowed to take credit for their success. While colonels and generals spoke to the press in Baghdad about the amazing feat, Billy and his crew were on a plane headed for Germany en route to Fort Bragg. He had completed twenty years of service the prior August, but he had stayed on to bag the dictator.

"What if you don't catch him?" his wife, June, had asked.

Billy had laughed. "Then, you should be praying he turns himself in, because I'm not quitting 'til I catch the bastard."

After traveling from base to base with Billy for too many years, June and their sons, Jimmy and Joe Bob, had moved to Savannah,

Georgia to be closer to her parents. Billy arrived home on Christmas Eve. After dinner, the boys, twelve and fourteen, had headed to the basement to play video games. Billy and June were sitting on the sofa, stuffed, staring at the Christmas tree and listening to Christmas carols.

"Now what?" she asked. The big hair was gone, replaced by a short relaxed perm. She was a busy mom, raising two boys and selling real estate full time.

"Now we have sex every night and twice on Sundays," he said with a grin and put his arm around her.

"I already know that," June said. "But what are you going to do during the day?"

"I was thinking I'd open my own detective agency."

"How do you expect to keep busy? There's not that much crime around here?"

"I'm not going to investigate crimes. I'll get work from lawyers, businesses, suspicious spouses, that sort of thing. I'll do private security work, too. Help folks protect their computers and confidential information, prevent corporate espionage. It's very lucrative."

She reared back her head and looked at him. "You think there's a lot of secret stuff in Savannah that needs protecting?"

"Well, I don't plan on working full time. At least not at first. Until I build up my reputation. I figure I'll teach the boys how to hunt. I want to spend some time sailing. And then there's all the sex I'll be having with you." He started kissing her neck.

"Hey, get a room," Jimmy called out from the kitchen where he had a clear view of the sofa as he opened the fridge.

"Excuse me," Billy said to June and headed toward the kitchen. "Don't you talk like that to your parents, you hear me. You show some respect. Things are going to change now that I'm home. You understand."

"Yes, Dad." Jimmy grabbed a can of soda and took off down the stairs.

Billy returned to the sofa. "Now where were we?"

"Welcome to the war zone," June said. "Those two have been testing me ever since their hormones kicked in. Speaking of which, will you talk to them about the birds and the bees?"

"First, give me a refresher course," he said, smiling.

April-May 2005

After Rosa Parks Gibson graduated from the University of Maryland with a degree in journalism, she landed a job at the *Washington Post*. The first thing she learned was that cub reporters write stories about garden shows and traffic accidents. After eight years, she had moved up to covering the local political scene, but she hungered for the big time. The Capitol Hill beat or the White House. For the time being, she had to be satisfied with city councilmen taking bribes and mayors taking drugs.

Her love life had been uneven. Few women could tolerate her intensity. She was more often single than not, but she was never lonely. She traveled with a group of big brassy women who had a good time wherever they lit. But then, she met Natalie Jordan.

Rosie and her friend, Shaneetha Mims, had been nibbling appetizers at a lesbian breast cancer fundraiser, when Natalie entered the hotel ballroom. Natalie was wearing a bright blue strapless cocktail dress and looked very sexy in matching heels and cornrows. "Shaneetha, who's that little lipstick girl?" Rosie asked.

"I don't know, but I know the girl she's with. Alexis something."

"Come on. You're going to introduce me to Alexis and I'll take it from there." At twenty-nine, Rosie had grown into her frame nicely by big girl standards. She carried her weight well, her mother would say. "Voluptuous," was the term that Rosie used. Shaneetha and she were dressed in dark business pant suits. With their close-cropped hair, they looked like half the women at the party. "Hurry up, Shaneetha," Rosie said. "Before she draws a crowd. She's already got the whole room drooling over her."

After the introductions, Rosie turned to Natalie. "How come I haven't seen you at these affairs before?"

"Because I don't do these affairs. I came as a favor to Alexis."

"Thank God for Alexis."

Natalie smiled. "Actually I'm here because Alexis just broke up with her girlfriend. It was pretty nasty. She had an extra ticket. She didn't want to be alone tonight."

Rosie raised her wine glass. "Here's to nasty break-ups."

They clinked glasses, and then Natalie asked, "Where's your girlfriend?"

Rosie took a big gulp of white wine. "I don't have a girlfriend. I've been saving myself for you."

"Uh-huh. I bet you say that to all the girls."

Rosie gently touched Natalie's forearm. "Honey, don't trifle with my affections. I'm dead serious. We were meant to meet tonight. Don't you see?"

Still smiling, Natalie rested her glass against her cheek. "See what, Rosie?"

"Alexis and her girlfriend had a big old catfight and here you are. You're the rainbow after the storm. And I'm lucky enough to be in the right place to see this vision of loveliness."

Natalie blushed. "Thank you. That's very sweet."

Rosie didn't tell her about the other vision she had seen that night. The sleek African feline had perched briefly on the rail of the ballroom's mezzanine before leaping into the darkness.

Six weeks later, the two women rented a U-Haul truck and packed up Natalie's things. Rosie had called her sister, Althea, in Baltimore the night before. "This is it, girl. This is the real thing. She teaches first graders and sings in the church choir. A preacher's kid from Philly. She's so sweet and delicate. I can't believe it. I keep pinching myself. And she already has ideas for our apartment. She's such a nester."

Althea had just put her three children to bed. She giggled. "You have to admit your place could use some work."

"Hey, now. I have other talents. She says she wants to get a house someday with a yard and kids."

"I thought you were never having kids."

"I could be persuaded. Maybe. With Natalie."

"Damn. I gotta meet this girl. She's turned you inside out."

On the other side of the district, Natalie was talking to her friend, Alexis. "Are you sure you're doing the right thing?" Alexis asked. "Rosie's got a reputation."

"A reputation for what?"

"Well, actually it's more of a nickname. Sass Sister."

Natalie laughed. "She's sassy, all right. But nothing I can't handle. She melts around me. She calls me Princess. Just like my Dad."

The morning after Natalie moved in, she asked Rosie, "Would you like to come to church with me. I have a solo today." They were in bed together, Natalie nestled against Rosie's big breasts.

"Oh, Princess, I'd love to, but I don't do church. I've got a direct line to God twenty-four/seven, and every time I hear some old timey minister telling me what's right from wrong, I get interference on my line, and then, I have to pray twice as hard to get the connection back. Maybe you could give me a private recital."

September 11, 2007

"I want to stop my son from being re-elected to the Senate. I can't tell you why, but I have good reasons. Do you think you can help me?" Martha Hamilton asked Billy Short. Marion Randolph, Billy and she were sitting on the east veranda at Sea Haven, the baronial estate Martha had inherited from her parents. Since Robert III's death, Marion and she had spent more and more time at the home on the coast south of Savannah. It was a sultry afternoon, and Marion Randolph had just served big glasses of sweet iced tea with lemon.

"Well, Mrs. Hamilton—"

"Please, call me, Martha." She was sitting on a porch swing, holding Sassafras, a small calico kitten that Marion had given her for her eightieth birthday. Sassafras was playing with the buttons on her mint green cotton dress.

"Martha, if there's dirt on your son, I'll find it." Billy gulped down his iced tea. He was sitting opposite them in a wicker chair, looking uncomfortable in his coat and tie. His shirt was soaked.

"Great. I like your attitude. I hired a big Atlanta firm several years ago, and they didn't find a thing. I know my son's not that clean. Lawyer friends of mine say you're the best. I understand you're ex-military."

"Yes, ma'am. Twenty years, Army Special Forces."

"Check his taxes, donors, staff, sex life, whatever you can find. I don't want to destroy him. I just want him out of office."

"I'll do all that and more. What kind of budget are we talking about?"

Martha waved her hand dismissively. "Unlimited. And a big fat bonus if you can help me stop him."

Billy looked at Marion as if to ask, "Is she kidding?"

Marion smiled. "This matter is very important to Martha, but she trusts you to spend her money wisely."

"Thanks, Marion. I couldn't have said it better myself." Martha patted his knee. She turned to Billy. "And above all, the utmost discretion is required. I don't want Bob to know I've hired you."

"Don't worry about that. I cover my tracks."

Sassafras began to mew pitifully. Marion picked her up. "She's hungry. I'll get her some milk." He took her inside.

Martha smoothed out her dress. "I know you must think I'm a horrible mother. I love my son. But it's for his own good."

"I understand. I got a couple boys that need some strong guidance. We do what we can."

Martha smiled and touched his hand. "Thanks for understanding. You've got such warm brown eyes. I can tell you're a good man."

"Thank you kindly. I like to think I am. Is there anything else I need to know?"

She stood and he joined her. "No, that's all for now. And in the future, when we meet, please dress more comfortably for your own sake. You look very handsome in your suit and tie, but we don't stand on ceremony here."

"Thanks, again, ma'am. Duly noted."

By the time Marion came back, Billy had left. "He seems like he knows what he's doing," Marion said, as he sat down next to her.

"I agree. And I like him, too. He's such a man's man."

Marion laughed. "You big flirt. So if he's a man's man, what am I?"

Martha kissed his cheek. "You're my man." She sat back and looked out at the water. "You know, I've decided I don't want to go back to Atlanta. I'm going to give the house and land to Bob, if he wants it. I'd rather live here year round. Does that suit you?"

"It suits me fine."

"I'll feel guilty about Kathleen and the kids. We won't see them as much. I guess I'm a bad grandmother, too."

Marion put his arm around her. "Stop beating yourself up. This is our time. Finally. Let's enjoy it."

Chapter 8

March-April 2008

The members of White Australian Resistance, also known as WAR, were in Sydney for a secret meeting to discuss the Asian invasion of the continent and what actions they might take to discourage the influx. Also on the agenda was the ongoing menace of the Jews, aborigines and homosexuals. They met in the banquet room of a one star motel in Mt. Druitt, one of the grittier blue collar suburbs west of Sydney. After a long day of haggling over strategy and tactics, the leader announced, "It's a full moon tonight. Time for Romper Stomper." Dozens of the skinheads took off in carloads for a night of cracking heads in the city. They hit Darlinghurst about midnight, cruising down Oxford Street, searching for victims. Gay men were out in large numbers and exchanged taunts with the hooligans at stoplights.

Driving to the fringe of the district, one group of WARriors spied a lone man walking toward his car on a dark street. "What do you think, Quentin?" the driver asked a short man with bad teeth riding shotgun.

"Looks like one of them. What else would he be doing here?" Quentin responded. "Let's get him." Quentin and four other men jumped out of the car, while the driver stayed behind as lookout. When he heard their footsteps, Mark Cross turned to face them. They all stopped in their tracks.

"Can I help you?" he asked.

"We'll help ourselves, faggot," growled Quentin from the rear, and the men set upon Mark with their fists and brass knuckles.

"I've got AIDS, you bastards!" Mark roared back, at which point Quentin whacked him on the head with a truncheon.

Mark came to just as they tightened the noose around his neck. The skinheads had found just the right tree in a deserted section of Parramatta Park, west of the city. They had stripped him naked, tied his hands behind his back and, with a black marker, scrawled the words "Die Faggot" on his chest and swastikas on his buttocks.

Quentin smirked when Mark started to struggle. "If you weren't so sick, I'd cut off your dobber."

"Go to hell, you dizzy queen!" Mark bellowed and then spat in his face.

89

Quentin screamed, "Pull it tight," as he frantically tried to wipe Mark's saliva out of his eyes. With that, the other men yanked on the rope and hoisted Mark off the ground. With all his strength, Mark lifted his powerful legs and thrust them forward, clamping his feet around Quentin's neck. With one swift jerk, just before he passed out, Mark cracked Quentin's C4 vertebrae, shoving a sliver of bone into the little man's spinal cord and killing him instantly.

By the time the other men had secured the rope around a branch and realized Quentin was dead, police sirens were wailing in the distance. They dragged Quentin's body to the car and threw it in the trunk, leaving Mark's body still swaying in the silver moonlight.

Josh Stein was in Melbourne at an academic conference. At first, he had decided to skip it, then, he'd asked Mark to join him, but finally he'd decided to go alone, when Mark learned that an old friend from Hobart would be in Sydney for the weekend. "No, stay," he'd said to Mark. "Have fun with Rupert. I'll be stuck in meetings. I'll see you two for dinner Sunday night."

Mark and Rupert had gone to dinner in Darlinghurst and then headed to Rupert's favorite bar, The Midnight Shift, where Rupert had met Chase, a young American from California on holiday. Once he was sure that Rupert had found his entertainment for the evening, Mark gave his old friend a kiss and headed for his car, which he'd parked blocks away in what he called his "secret parking space."

When Josh couldn't reach Mark on his mobile phone early Sunday morning, he didn't worry because Mark often turned it off or forgot to recharge it. Nevertheless, he skipped out on the rest of the conference and grabbed an earlier flight, eager to get home. The two men had bought Josh's boyhood home in Bondi Beach after his mother had died the previous Passover. When he found the driveway empty and their dog, Lorenzo, whining at the back door, Josh called Rupert who had been trying to reach Mark all morning. The two of them went searching for Mark's car, and when they found it still parked in his favorite spot, Josh's heart started to race. Just feet from the car, Rupert found Mark's keys. That was when Josh panicked. He called his old boyfriend, Jeremy Logan, who had connections in the police force. "Have you caught the news?" Jeremy asked.

"No. What's happened?"

"There was a murder in Parramatta Park. The police are calling it a hate crime. They haven't identified the victim. I don't want to think the worst, but let me make some calls."

"Where's the body?" Josh asked.

"Let me find out."

Jeremy stood next to Josh when the morgue technician unzipped the bag. He held Josh while he sobbed over the body of his dead lover. The police vowed to find Mark's killers, but the skinheads had scattered to the four corners of the continent. Quentin's body had been buried deep in the soil of the Outback, a thousand miles from Sydney, where only kangaroos watched the grisly task. And his head, minus his bad teeth, had been burned and then sunk in a weighted canvas bag several miles off the coast of Perth.

Josh took a leave of absence for the balance of the school term. His friend, Vince Scavullo, had flown in for the service and accompanied him back to New York. Josh stayed with Vince and wandered the streets and parks of the city while Vince was teaching class at New York University. Vince had grown from a studly graduate student into a nebbishy professor. "It's something in the water here," he had explained to Josh.

A month later, the two men were standing on a subway platform at three in the morning headed home to Chelsea when four young thugs threatened them with knives, demanding their money. Without thinking, Josh sent all four of them sprawling with several well-placed kicks. The hoodlums were dazed and hurting. A woman called for the cops on an emergency phone, but before they arrived, Josh and Vince had hopped on the next train.

Vince was stunned at Josh's proficiency. "You kicked ass back there. I had no idea you were such a Jackie Chan."

"I can't believe I did it either. I've trained for years, but I never thought I'd use it."

Vince slapped him on the back. "You're my hero. My knees were shaking and you were stomping their butts. Jesus, I need a drink."

"I need one, too. Let's find a bar that serves them strong."

"Are you sure? I don't want to be the one who gets you started again."

"No, I'll be fine. I'm just having one. Bitch slap me if I try to order a second."

Vince laughed. "I'm not touching you after what I just saw."

The two men found a quiet neighborhood saloon and sat down at the bar. Josh breathed in the vapors of his gin martini and then set it down. "I could have killed them."

"Hey, take it easy. They deserved what they got."

"No, I mean I was that close to losing it. I should have been with Mark that night. Maybe he would still be alive."

"Maybe you'd be dead, too. Maybe there's a reason you're still here."

"What kind of god lets a man die like that? And lets me live to mourn him for the rest of my life?"

"I don't have an answer for you."

Josh pushed his glass away. "Take me home and make love to me."

The next morning at breakfast, Josh said to Vince. "I'm ready to go home."

"Are you sure? You're welcome to stay as long as you want."

"Thanks, but it's time for me to get on with my life. Mark is gone. I have to face that."

Two days later, Josh flew back to Sydney. He picked up Lorenzo at Jeremy Logan's house and hugged his old friend. "Now begins the hard part," he said.

June 7, 2008

After Piet Webber died from a heart attack in Cape Town during a carjacking, Elaine Webber Griffin called to tell her brother, Roger. High on a combination of marijuana and cheap red wine, he roared with laughter. When he finally calmed down, Elaine said, "I don't want to go to his funeral, but I feel like I have to."

"Why? He was a monster." The cannabis had heightened Roger's feeling of betrayal. He lay in bed, propped up with pillows, five pounds short of three hundred, naked and stoned.

"I know, but he was my father. And my children's grandfather. If I don't go, I'll have no relationship with my brothers. Claus, at least, is not so bad. And I love his wife, Gwen."

Roger started to cry uncontrollably. "I have no one. No one loves me."

"I love you, Roger. You know I do. And Mom loves you. And all your friends."

"I have no friends. They all hate me. Since I got fired."

"When did you get fired?"

"Last month. The bitch said I was unreliable."

Elaine rested her head against the wall in the master bedroom and sighed. She always called Roger behind closed doors. "I'm so sorry, Roger. What are you going to do?"

"There's nothing I can do. I've been blackballed. None of the theatres will hire me. They won't even talk to me. I'm persona non grata."

"What are you on?"

"Nothing. I'm completely sober."

"Roger," she said with a tinge of annoyance.

"Well, maybe a little weed."

"And?"

Roger drained his wine glass. "That's it. It was just a couple hits. I can't afford it any more."

"When I get back from Cape Town, I'll come see you, I promise."

"I would love that. Maybe you could help me look for a new flat. I'm going to downsize and simplify my life."

Elaine opened her purse and pulled out her check book. "I'd be glad to help."

June 30, 2008

When Billy Short pulled up the circular drive at Sea Haven in his Chevy Silverado truck, Yolanda Jackson, the cook/housekeeper, stepped out onto the east veranda drying her hands with a kitchen towel. "How you all doing?" she asked, smiling, as she came down the steps.

"I'm doing fine, Yolanda. How's Martha?"

"She's doing as well as can be expected. She's out by his grave."

Billy found Martha Hamilton on her knees tamping soil around a flowering gardenia plant. The scent was heavenly. He took a seat on a dark granite bench next to Marion Randolph's grave. It was at the edge of a stand of Georgia pine trees, just about to be flooded with the noonday sun. "Hey, Martha."

Red-faced from the heat, Martha looked up with a weary smile. She was barefoot, wearing a wide brimmed straw hat, gloves and a gardening apron over a bright blue cotton sundress. "Hey, Billy." She rose slowly and then sat down next to him.

"This is such a pretty spot," Billy said as he looked out over the trees and water.

Martha pulled off her gloves. "It was his favorite. He wasn't much for the beach, but he liked the view from here. He grew up dirt poor in pine woods, so these old trees always felt like home to him."

Billy patted her shoulder. "I'm sorry for your loss. It must be very hard for you."

Martha nodded. "He was the best. And I took him for granted. I figured since he was so much younger, he would always be here. And prostate cancer usually isn't fatal…"

There was a break in the conversation, and they listened to the wind in the trees and the roar of the surf. Billy broke the silence. "I'm afraid I still don't have a smoking gun." He handed her his latest report.

"Oh, dear. Really?" Martha read through the summary and then looked up. "What do you suggest?"

"I'll start with his staff problems, the former klansman, the mercenary, the ex-hooker and feed that to a couple bloggers. Give that a week or two to build and then dump the information about the donations from the Aryan nation members and the Chinese defense contractors. Let that stew for maybe three weeks and then give the *Times* and the *Post* the information about his tax shelters. That should keep him busy."

Martha flipped through the report. "Do you think he knew about any of this? He's not usually this careless."

"I doubt it. It's hard to keep track of every dollar donated. The hires were probably political favors. The tax shelters are over the edge, but not blatantly illegal."

"Is this enough to stop him?" Martha asked.

"It really depends on how he reacts. Most politicians stonewall and prevaricate. We'll just have to wait and see."

"Who's this gentleman?" she asked, pointing to a photo of a middle-aged black man, walking his dog.

"That's the Reverend Jonathan Jones. Pastor in Detroit. He was in Peru with Bob. They met at Duke on the cross country team, reconnected in New York and signed up for the Peace Corps together. Shared a hut in the jungle for two years. He's been profiled in the local press for saving the church, rebuilding the congregation, setting up a bunch of social services for the poor folk in the community."

"I always wondered who talked him into joining. If you believe Bob's campaign hype, you'd think the whole idea was his alone."

"I hired several people to try to get close to him. One joined his church and tried to get to know him. Another one played your son's biographer and asked for an interview. As far as your son is concerned, Jones is not talking. I even had a couple others try to hit on him. See where he comes out sexually. Nothing took. He lives like a monk with his sister. Very small circle of friends, mostly hers. Seems content to do God's work and walk his dog."

"What did he ever see in Bob? They couldn't be more different." She closed the folder and looked up. "I like your strategy, Billy. Go for it."

"Will do, Ma'am."

November 2008

On November 4, 2008, Bob Hamilton was re-elected to the U.S. Senate with eighty-two percent of the vote, an unheard-of plurality in modern politics. He had beaten former Senator Jed Holmes' son, Seth, who had vowed to bring down the man who had ruined his father's career. And, at one point in the campaign, it seemed he might have his vengeance when Billy Short's well-placed stories began to tarnish Bob's sterling image. But Seth Holmes' staff was no match for Jerry Boston, who soon had the voters believing Seth, himself, had planted the employees from the hell on Bob's staff and solicited the dirty money from the racists and the Communists. In the shuffle, the sketchy tax shelters didn't even make page one, looking, at that point, like another Holmes' concoction.

Just as Bob was celebrating his most glorious victory, his party's presidential ticket was going down in flames. An unpopular war and a bad economy had doomed the GOP's chances. The turn of events was a godsend for Bob. It would have been hard to challenge a sitting president from his own party in the next election. And the Democratic victory gave him the force of darkness he needed to energize his supporters and launch his four-year crusade to save America.

The American Family First Foundation had strongly supported Bob's candidacy in both senatorial campaigns and had given him a ninety-nine percent family friendly rating for his Congressional voting record. Since her husband's death, Emily McIntyre had become the single most powerful spokesperson for the religious right. The Foundation's improving fortunes were due in part to financial and sex scandals embroiling two of its competitors. But mostly, its unquestioned preeminence was due to the iron-willed determination of Emily herself. Bob had met Emily several times at party functions, but he'd never had an in-depth conversation with her. The day after the election, she called to ask for a one-on-one meeting.

They met at the Foundation's executive headquarters. A thin, somber matron escorted Bob into Emily's office. It was a gray November afternoon, and the room's only artificial light was a brass desk lamp with an opaque charcoal shade. Emily was dressed in a severe black suit. There were white roses in a crystal vase on her desk. Bob felt as if he had joined her at a wake.

She got right down to business. "As you can imagine, we are extremely disturbed with the election results."

"I, too, am extremely disturbed. With a better campaign, we could have avoided this loss." In the fading light, Bob could barely see Emily's face.

"Exactly. Incompetents." Emily's disembodied voice was controlled, but angry. "They backed off when they should have attacked. We offered our staff and consulting agency to the campaign, but they ignored us."

"I'm very sorry to hear that. They were fools." Bob, in fact, had known about the presidential campaign's decision to turn down the Foundation's offer at the time it was made, six months before. One of Jerry's moles had passed along the information. Jerry and Bob had agreed that it was a fatal mistake, but they also had agreed not to press the campaign to reconsider.

"They'll pay in hell for it." Emily snarled as she lunged forward into the light, her hands gripping the edge of her desk, her face contorted in rage.

Bob was stunned by her anger, but, without losing a beat, he leaned forward and responded sympathetically, "God willing, Emily. It's a tragedy."

"It's a catastrophe!" she exclaimed as she rose and began to pace. "Babies will die by the thousands because of their arrogance. Faggot-lovers will infiltrate the judiciary. Christendom will be under siege. All we have worked for will be lost if we do not win the next election." Her voice raised, Emily was seething at this point.

Bob stood, too. "I agree. The stakes are very high. We have to do everything humanly possible to get back in power."

Emily had stopped pacing. For a long moment, she stood motionless before she turned toward him. Her face was flushed, but the fire in her eyes had dimmed. She spoke this time in a reverential tone. "It will take more than that, Senator. It will take God's grace. We are in a battle with the devil for the soul of this country. If we lose,

God will wreak his vengeance on all of us. We cannot fail."

"We will not fail. I promise you that," Bob solemnly replied as he stepped forward to touch her shoulder.

Emily sobbed and pulled him to her in a tight embrace, her head resting on his chest. "Thank you, Bob. Oh, I wish Larry were here. This is so hard for me to do without him."

Bob froze for a second and then gently patted Emily on her back. This was not what he had expected, but he was delighted. He was glad to be the surrogate male in Emily's life as long as it stopped with hugs. "I wish he were here, too, Emily. He was a great man. We all miss him. Just know that he is with us still, and he will help us win this fight."

He could feel her tears dampen his shirt, and he continued to hold her until she sniffled and dropped her arms to her side. Embarrassed, she turned her back on him and plucked a tissue from the box on her desk. "Thanks for coming, Bob. We'll talk more later," she said, her voice barely louder than a whisper.

June 17, 2010

"We're going to announce in six months and I don't want any surprises," Jerry Boston said to Pat McCormack. They were sitting in Jerry's office at Boston & Associates in Washington, D.C.

"Don't worry. There won't be any surprises," Pat said with a confident smile. He was slouched in his chair taking notes. It was their first meeting. He loved working for presidential campaigns. The higher the stakes, the better. In the ten years since the founding of Harris Security International, Pat's reputation had soared. He was the go to guy for the toughest jobs.

"The bloggers keep throwing crap at Bob, and I spend all my time cleaning it up," Jerry continued. "I want to know everything there is to know about him before we start the campaign so that I can neutralize it upfront."

"Is there anything I should know before I start?"

"No. I've spent almost ten years with this guy, and he's the cleanest politician I've ever met."

Pat smirked. "That's an oxymoron, isn't it?"

Jerry grimaced. "You'll learn that I don't have much of a sense of humor about my work. And one more thing. Find out who's digging up all this shit on Bob."

Pat closed his briefcase and stood. "Consider it done."

June 24, 2010

Since he had left the CIA, Pat McCormack had not intentionally killed anyone. There had been one shot, intended to cause a flesh wound, that had been fatal. His eyes were not as good as they used to be. The client, an emir from one of the Persian Gulf states, had been satisfied, nevertheless. Rather than scare off an undesirable suitor for his eldest daughter, Pat had simply provided a permanent solution. The emir happily had paid him a bonus. It was shortly after that misadventure that Angela Patterson had come into his life. She'd met him at the grocery store, one of the few places he frequented in his private life. He was a workaholic and lived on frozen dinners and carry out. He had no close friends, no social circle and no extracurricular activities, except for the occasional hooker. Pat couldn't believe his good luck when the shapely blonde walked off with his cart by mistake. She had apologized and offered to buy him coffee in the grocery café. He'd gained a little weight and lost some hair in recent years, but he had concluded that his mojo must still be working.

A week after Jerry Boston hired Pat, Angela had a meeting at CIA headquarters with her boss, Phinneas Graves. "How's it going?" he asked.

She shifted in her chair. "Do you want the professional response or the personal one?"

"Both."

"Professionally, it's going well. As you can see in my report, I finally gained access to his home this week. It's a fortress. Like a super-secure mini-mansion. He designed it himself. We've got the blueprints, standard stuff, for the most part, if you're in the mob or the drug trade. Twelve foot high wrought iron fence around the property, topped with barbed wire, all of it electrified with the flip of a switch. Illegal, but not unusual. High wattage, motion sensitive outdoor lighting protected by bullet proof glass. The walls and roof are eighteen inch reinforced concrete. The windows are small, high and bomb proof. There are cameras and motion sensors everywhere. After he passed out, I took a closer look. He's installed anti-bugging devices in most rooms. He's got security control panels with monitors in his bedroom, kitchen and basement. And then there are Doctor No and Odd Job, his two Rottweilers. He told me they're trained to protect him, so I was not to make any false moves. I put them down for a few hours with some special candy.

"He drives a heavily armored late model Mercedes with bomb

proof glass. But his treasure is the Aston Martin convertible that Sean Connery drove in *Goldfinger*. He told me he seldom takes the car out of the garage, though he pulls it onto the driveway from time to time if the weather is good and sits in the car, fantasizing about Pussy Galore next to him as he drives recklessly down mountain roads, pursued by Goldfinger's thugs."

Phinneas leaned forward. "Really?"

"I made up the last part, but I bet I'm not far off. He asked me to sit in the car with him when he was giving me the tour. Then, with a remote, he turned on the music. The *Goldfinger* theme song. Blaring out of speakers all over the house, the garage, the entire property. It was bizarre."

"Why do you think he wants that level of protection?"

"I think he's afraid somebody might want to get back at him for one of his hits. And now he can afford to feed his paranoia."

"Any indication that might be true?"

"None that we can detect. I think he's done it to himself. Living with the ghosts of all his victims."

"Remorse would be unusual for him."

"More likely projection. It's what he would do if someone tried to kill him. Hunt down his enemy and take him out."

"That's a pathetic existence."

"Not as pathetic as his sex fantasies."

Phinneas leaned even closer. "Yes?"

"Let's just say he likes to play rough."

"I hope he didn't hurt you."

"You know that'll never happen. He drinks too much to do much harm. And it's short lived. Short in every meaning of the word. Oh, yes, and he calls his penis Sean. Isn't that charming?"

Phinneas chuckled. "I'm sorry you have to do this for your country."

"Not sorry enough to do it yourself if you could."

Phinneas smiled. "I'm afraid my seduction days are over, although I've done my share of undercover work. On a serious note, my director wants to increase surveillance. McCormack just got hired by the Hamilton people. We know they play hard ball, and we don't want one of our alums embarrassing the agency. If he thinks he can kill an Arab prince without repercussions, who knows what he'll do next."

Angela crossed her legs. "So more playtime with Sean you're saying?"

Phinneas nodded. "I'm afraid so. I'll put in a recommendation for high risk pay for you. Retroactive, of course."

"I've planted our bugs. They trump his technology, but we haven't learned anything yet, except the way he talks to Doctor No and Odd Job when he's alone." She rolled her eyes.

Phinneas shook his head. "Fascinating character."

June 19, 2011

Martha Hamilton was sitting on the bench by Marion Randolph's grave at Sea Haven. It was the third anniversary of his death, Juneteenth, African American Emancipation Day, the kind of June day he loved. She could hear him repeat his grandma's saying. "Hot enough to stupefy the crackers and give us niggers a break." The shade and sea breeze offered little relief. She sat on the bench and talked to him as sweat ran down her back.

"Marion, dear, I hope you can hear me. I need your advice. You always know what to do. And without you, I feel increasingly lost. It's no laundry list this time. Just the one problem. But it's the big one. Should I tell Bob? Don't shake your head at me. I know we've been round and round about it. And each time, I've dug my hole deeper. The answer is obvious, of course. I should. The truth is always the right answer, even if it is late in coming. As much as I don't want him to be president, I do love him, and I'd rather he hear it from me. What he does with the information is his choice. I know. You don't need to hear any more. It's time, isn't it? All right, I'll shut up and let you rest."

In the next instant, a blood vessel burst in Martha's brain, and she knew something was wrong. "Yolanda," she screamed before she slumped off the bench and fell on to Marion's grave.

Chapter 9

October 31, 2011

The black limousine slowly turned the corner in the gridlocked noonday traffic of the nation's capital. Heavy rain from the remnants of Hurricane Ruth pelted the gray windows. Thunder cracked sharply overhead as the Cadillac forded the small curbside river and glided up the embankment to the hotel's entrance. Under the large forest green canopy, the vehicle came to a pause.

The door behind the driver opened and Jerry Boston emerged. Hunched against the wet autumn chill, he buttoned his suit coat and shuddered at a second thunder clap. Scurrying around the back of the car, he opened the door for the other passenger. Out stepped Senator Robert David Hamilton IV, looking very elegant in a dark Armani suit and power red tie. His thick black hair had a touch of gray at the temples. Instinctively, he smiled at the random huddle of guests and hotel staff perched on the edge of the driveway and followed his new chief of staff toward the lobby.

Rosie Gibson was running late. Her editor had asked her to cover the luncheon at the last minute. She said a short prayer as she paid the cab driver. Stuffing her pocket book into her purse, she looked up and exhaled, "Thank God!" Twenty paces in front of her, at the hotel entrance, the main speaker, Bob Hamilton, was bending over to kiss the powdered cheek of a middle-aged lady in lavender.

Rosie was a presence. She carried her large frame with the regal gait of an African empress. Her hair was close-cropped and natural. Dressed in an emerald green pant suit with matching pumps and large gold hoop earrings, she took her time now and studied the pair as she passed them.

They seemed totally at ease, more than just casual acquaintances. Bob Hamilton was the rising star in the conservative firmament, and Emily McIntyre was the queen of family values. An unholy alliance, if Rosie had ever seen one. The next thunderclap was deafening. Everyone froze for a second, wondering if lightning had struck the hotel. The rain intensified and hail began to pound the hotel canopy. Rosie locked eyes with the jungle cat, growling in the bushes just beyond the driveway apron. She said another prayer and hurried inside.

Just as Rosie found her table near the front of the hall, the room went dark, and a spotlight hit a large American flag behind the dais. After the national anthem, the pledge of allegiance and a long fiery invocation calling for the salvation of the homeland, the lights went up. Rosie opened her program as a children's choir began to sing "Faith of Our Fathers." She caught the title of the senator's address and shook her head: "Onward Christian Soldiers, Marching as to War."

• • •

"And so, in conclusion, ladies and gentlemen, I want to thank again Mrs. McIntyre and the American Family First Foundation for the opportunity to speak to you about a subject that is close to your hearts and mine. We stand together to preserve the American family against a wholesale assault on its values. I, like you, believe our nation's strength and greatness for the last two centuries have been fostered by a deep faith in God, our Creator. With your help and support, I will fight to ensure that no unborn child is denied a right to life. Further, I will battle those forces who would destroy our sacred institution of marriage by allowing homosexuals to be joined in unholy unions. Thank you and God bless you all!"

In unison, a thousand diners in pinstripes and pastels rose to their feet, cheering and applauding. The senator turned to Emily, who was seated next to him on the dais in the Imperial Ballroom. Emily rose, subtly straightening her Oscar de la Renta suit. She beamed at Bob and presented him to her loyal followers with an extended arm, her diamond earrings glittering in the bright stage lighting. Bob hugged her gingerly and then turned to face the camera with a perfect smile. The applause escalated as the pair waved to the crowd, drowning out the thunder that had continued to boom throughout the meal. A photo of the pair would be posted on the Foundation's website within two hours, with a note that the Foundation's Platinum Heaven Club had raised a million dollars that afternoon to preserve the American family.

Five hundred signed copies of the senator's book, *With God's Help*, stood in neat stacks at the back of the ballroom on tables draped in American flag bunting. An hour later, Bob was shaking the hand of the last grateful purchaser, the president of the Virginia chapter of the American Family First Foundation, Mrs. John (Maxine) Swale. She had purposely held back to have a few extra moments with the senator. A buxom lady in pink, Swale pulled back strands of her freshly dyed red hair. She was surprised at how young he looked in person. Why, he could pass for forty, she thought.

"Senator, I look forward to the day when I can call you Mr. President." Maxine's breasts seemed to swell as she nervously took a deep breath. Bob firmly grasped Maxine's right hand with both of his and held her eyes with his deeply sincere gaze, the one that made most humans believe that he was profoundly moved by what they had just said.

"Maxine, dear, thank you for your confidence. And thank you for your hard work for the Foundation. With your help and God's, I'm sure we'll win." He held her hand a moment longer in silence, meaningful silence, Maxine thought. It was as if the two of them were alone in the room and they had shared a silent prayer together. Maxine imagined herself standing next to Bob as he took the oath of office, January snow gently falling on his perfect tresses, anointing him for the coming battle. She shivered as he said good-bye and drifted across the ballroom, her panties dampened.

"Thank you, Bob," Emily whispered, as the Maxine's heels clicked toward the ballroom exit. "Today was a big step forward. We should be able to raise another million selling copies of today's program."

"Thank you, Emily." Bob scaled back the charm. Emily was a partner, not an acolyte. "I can't do this without you. I look forward to dinner with the executive committee next week."

Emily patted Bob on the back. "Everyone's on board. The last hold-out was Stevens. He and Jensen were law school classmates, but I've convinced him that Jensen is not our man. Too unreliable."

"I like Howard a great deal. He's a good man," Bob replied as they headed out of the ballroom. "But I know what you mean. Some of his votes have been, well . . . puzzling." Bob searched for a word to convey agreement without appearing overly zealous to attack his Senate colleague.

"Jensen's an ass!" Emily's face reddened into a contemptuous scowl. "He's too willing to compromise to broaden his base. He doesn't realize he will have no base by the time he's done caving in. We certainly won't be there for him."

Bob nodded in appropriate sadness at Jensen's lack of wisdom. He caught a whiff of Emily's lavender scented deodorant, working hard to counteract her heat. A flicker of a smile crossed his face. He was glad Emily was on his side.

"Bob, we gotta go." Jerry Boston was huffing as he half-jogged toward them. Emily wondered why Bob had hired this little Jewish gnome of a man.

"Emily, you know Jerry, my chief of staff." Bob was peeved. The Foundation was more important than a Commerce subcommittee meeting. He gave Jerry a look.

Jerry ignored the look and gently pulled on Bob's elbow. "Of course. Excuse me, Emily. Sorry, we have to hustle. We're running behind."

Emily waved them off, contented that the next president of the United States was willing to be late for an important meeting in order to pay her homage. "Go on, Bob. We'll touch base later this week."

• • •

"What the fuck was that about?" Bob glared at Jerry as he loosened his tie.

The rain had stopped, and sunlight was breaking through clouds in the west, but inside the limousine, the world was permanently tinted gray. Jerry was still agitated and out of breath as the driver eased into mid-afternoon traffic. He grimaced at Bob's profanity. In eleven years, Jerry had turned the pretty boy into one of the most powerful men in Washington. Without him, Bob still would be just another me-too vote in the House of Representatives, cutting ribbons on the weekends in Alpharetta, Georgia. He, Jerry Boston, had just done the pompous prince a great service, and for this, he was getting abuse.

Jerry flicked a button to raise the privacy window, closing them off from the chauffeur. "We have a problem. Your background check has turned up something odd."

Bob snorted. "Like what? We went through this before. In the Senate races. I'm clean."

"It's not your taxes this time. It has to do with your mother's medical records. We need to talk to her. Soon."

Bob's throat tightened. "What? Some sort of genetic disorder?"

"No." Jerry studied Bob's face as he spoke his next words. "When your mother was sixteen, she got pregnant. She was in Switzerland at a boarding school. The medical records show she had an abortion. It went badly. She ended up in the hospital. Supposedly it rendered her infertile."

• • •

Rosie Gibson read through her story one more time and then pushed the "send" button. The Platinum Heaven Club luncheon had put her in one of those moods. She'd written the truth, rather than just who, what, when, where and why. She knew exactly which words her editor, Max Sherman, would strike. Max had spoken to her several times when she went off the reservation like this. She was no longer writing satire for the campus paper, he had told her. Still, Rosie smiled at her description of Emily McIntyre's queenly presentation of her new prince to the assembled nobility. This was reality as she saw it. Not a satire. These white folk were the aliens, the ones out of touch with a merciful God. She was the working girl on a tight budget in an expensive town. Her reality was a diabetic mother without health insurance, a sister raising three kids alone and a gay brother living with HIV. Not exactly the poster family for the American Family First Foundation.

Rosie tore open a bag of chips, her reward for completing the article. Her cell phone rang.

"Hey girl, whatcha doing?" Natalie Jordan asked. She was driving home from her school in Bethesda, Maryland in a ten-year-old Volvo station wagon.

Natalie's high-pitched voice made Rosie smile. "Getting in trouble with my boss. What about you, honey?"

Natalie purred, "Sitting in traffic thinking about you. What did you do now?"

"Told the truth." Rosie popped a chip in her mouth.

Natalie laughed. "Rosie, you know better."

Rosie took a swig of diet soda. "I couldn't help myself. I had to listen to a bunch of rich white folk carrying on about saving babies until they find out their little darlings are gay. All in the name of Jeeee-sus."

"Your favorite crowd. No wonder they got you going. You tell 'em, Rosie!"

"Yeah, I did. And someday, I'm going to get my sorry black ass fired."

An email notice flashed on Rosie's screen. "Oh, shit. Gotta run, babe. I'll be home around seven."

Max's cover message was short: "Brilliant and completely inappropriate. Keep it up and you'll be writing obituaries."

• • •

Martha Hamilton stared into the flames of the large stone fireplace in the living room at Sea Haven, her rheumy eyes searching. Draped over her bony shoulders was an old black wool shawl, handmade by Marion Randolph's grandmother. A young nurse in a crisp white pantsuit sat nearby in a matching leather wing chair, reading a romance novel by the light of the fire. She glanced up occasionally to check on her charge. Martha paid her no attention. Strains of Mozart were barely audible over the crackle of the fire and the crash of the sea. A full moon shone through ten foot high French doors open to the water.

Sassafras sat at her feet, purring contentedly in the heat of the fire. Her tail stirred, grazing Martha's leg. She looked down at the fat calico cat and a half-smile curved up the left side of her face. "Sassy," she whispered. The nurse looked up and checked her watch. "Another fifteen minutes, and then I'll take you up to bed. It's almost nine." Martha seemed not to hear as she studied her pet. Her son, Bob, had insisted on hiring the nursing service, and Martha had been too weak to object.

In another wing of the house, the cook/housekeeper, Yolanda Jackson, had already gone to bed. The chauffeur/gardener, Jim Pike, was sitting naked in front of his computer masturbating at the image of a large breasted woman fingering herself. Just as he was about to ejaculate, the lights flickered off and on and his screen went black. "Fuck!" He couldn't stop the stream of semen spurting onto his chest.

A quarter mile west, outside the security gate, a man in coveralls jumped a short distance to the ground from a utility pole wrapped in kudzu and crawled inside the back of a black van. The driver started the engine, pulled the vehicle onto the private road and headed toward the highway, its headlights off. The man in coveralls was sitting on the floor of the van in front of a bank of audio equipment, video monitors, and computer screens. He put on a pair of headphones and began making adjustments. Several screens blinked on. "All right," he chortled, looking up at one of the screens. Pike had reconnected to the porn site. When he reached the main road, the driver lit a cigarette and switched on the headlights. He turned right onto the two lane state highway and then right again a half mile north. At the end of a gravel road, he pulled into the garage of a large vacation home surrounded by pine trees.

"Bedtime, Martha," the nurse rolled the motorized wheelchair next to Martha's chair. Sassy hissed in protest, lumbered away and resettled closer to the fire. Martha didn't move as she watched Sassy's escape. The nurse stood in front of Martha and held out her hands. Still no response. Finally, the nurse bent over and gently lifted the frail eighty-seven-year-old from her arm chair.

In her bedroom, Martha waited until she heard the elevator motor taking the nurse back to the first floor. Picking up a remote control, she flicked through the television channels, stopping when she saw a couple waving to an adoring crowd. Emily McIntyre's lavender outfit registered a garish violet on the color screen. Martha grimaced as she studied the image of her smiling son. An ad came on. She turned off the set and pulled back the bedcovers. Swinging her spindly legs over the side of the bed, she pressed against the mattress with her hands as she slowly rose to her feet. Then, using the wheelchair as a walker, she carefully shuffled her way to a large window and opened the drapes, letting the moonlight flood the room. She struggled to raise the heavy casement window doing most of the work with her left hand and breathed deeply as the sea breeze wafted over her.

Returning to bed, she set her alarm for five o'clock to wake herself in time to close the window and drapes. In the kitchen, Jim Pike didn't notice the floor creak above him as he ate a cold piece of fried chicken in his boxer shorts. It was an old house full of strange sounds, and he had learned to ignore them. A half mile away in the back of the black van, a computer tracking the television set in the master bedroom recorded the news story of the American Family First Foundation luncheon and sent a report.

November 1, 2011

The three men were sitting at a small conference table in the senator's office under the glare of fluorescent lighting. It was well after midnight. The cleaning lady had been shooed away and the door had been locked again. Cable news readers mumbled, barely audible, on two televisions nearby. Bob Hamilton was poring over photocopies of documents typed in German, as if he might be able to decipher them if he concentrated. Jerry Boston stood to take a call on his cell phone, walked to the far corner of the room and looked out at the brightly lit Capitol Building. The third man, Herman Baumgartner, had arrived at Dulles airport from Zurich three hours before. He was red-eyed and hungry. The Americans had ordered pizza for him, but he was lactose intolerant. He sipped cold coffee and chewed on breath mints.

Bob had no appetite. His head was throbbing, and he'd had three bouts of diarrhea since he'd heard Jerry's news. Everything he knew to be true about his identity and his family was now in question. He had been mulling over his childhood memories for hours, searching for a telltale clue that would somehow confirm he was, indeed, the child of the people he thought to be his parents. If only his dad were still alive. A dozen times, he had pulled out his cell phone to call his mother, but each time he had stopped himself. What would he say to her? Teenage pregnancy, abortion, infertility, secret adoption? She was a proud woman, and she could be unpredictable, especially since her stroke. Besides, it might not be necessary. After all, the investigation was ongoing.

And then, there was the matter of her will. His mother had always been very vague about her estate planning. He'd tried to be a dutiful, attentive son, but they had never been close, not like he and his father had been. Maybe that's the reason, he thought. I'm not her flesh and blood. He shivered. Making a note to call his lawyer the next morning, he wondered what the legal standard for mental incompetence was in Georgia.

Bob looked up from the documents, bleary-eyed, and studied Herman Baumgartner. Tall, lean, blonde, blue-eyed, Teutonic – he reminded Bob of an SS officer out of central casting. Only the dark business suit broke the spell. "How did you get these records? Jesus Christ, it's been seventy years."

Once an agent with Germany's Federal Intelligence Service, the BND, Herman spoke impeccable English. "I cannot disclose our methods. That information might put Mr. Boston and you at risk." Herman was polite and patient despite his fatigue. He was paid well to be polite and patient by Harris Security Systems, Ltd., a British subsidiary of Harris Security International.

"Why go after my mother? I thought you were supposed to be investigating me." Herman's implacable demeanor only made Bob more irritable.

"It's standard policy on a search of this nature to look into the backgrounds of parents, spouses, children, in-laws, aunts, uncles, cousins, nieces, nephews. We look at least one generation up and one generation down." Herman eyed the pizza, tempted.

"So you're telling me you have files on my kids?" Bob slammed the sheath of papers on the table. Jerry glanced over his shoulder as he continued talking on his cell phone.

Herman gathered up the papers, putting them back in order. "We do have files, but only because each child is over the age of five. Under five, we simply note the name, birth date, school, if any, blood type, and a DNA sample, if that's an issue."

Bob jumped to his feet and leaned over the table. "Have you taken DNA samples from my children?"

"I'll call you back." Jerry shut his cell phone and sprinted across the room.

Herman, still seated, still calm, placed the papers in his folder. "No, is there any reason why we should, Senator?"

Bob knocked over his chair as he stepped around the table toward Herman. "Fuck, no, asshole! Stay away from my kids!"

"Bob, calm down." Jerry put up his hands and stepped between the two men. Herman's face had reddened, but he had not moved.

"Herman's only doing the job we pay him to do." Jerry gently pushed Bob back a step. "If he doesn't dig it up, your opponents will. He's done us a favor. At least, now we know, and we can deal with it."

Herman was standing now, almost at attention, one hand behind his back. "I did not mean to upset you, Senator Hamilton. There is much we can do to address this matter."

"How about destroying the fucking records for starters?" Bob, embarrassed at himself, had turned his back on Herman and was pouring himself a whisky.

"That's already been done. This is the only remaining copy of your mother's medical files in Zurich." Herman handed the file to Jerry.

Bob took a big gulp of scotch, exhaled deeply, and turned to face Herman. "I'm sorry for what I just said. You have to appreciate this is quite a shock for me. If these records are accurate, I don't know who my parents are. The woman I called my mother for fifty-three years got knocked up when she was sixteen, had a abortion and couldn't have conceived me if she had tried. I'm in the middle of a race for the presidency of the United States, and I don't even know if I'm native born to this country."

Herman closed his briefcase. "I understand the issue, Senator. We have several agents searching and reviewing your mother's medical records in this country. My colleague, Pat McCormack, will have a status report for you shortly."

"Can I get you something stronger to drink?" Jerry was pouring himself a rare vodka on the rocks.

Herman shook his head. "Any more questions, gentlemen?"

"Yeah, any idea what McCormack's people have found so far?" Bob asked.

"As I understand it, there is very little and nothing out of the ordinary. Nothing to confirm the Swiss records."

Bob saw Herman to the door. As the German stepped into the darkened hallway, he heard the buzz of a paper shredder. Herman paused as the door was being locked behind him. He heard Jerry's muffled voice. "That was the pollster on the phone. Very good news, Bobby."

November 11, 2011

"The Hamiltons are not your parents, Senator." Pat McCormack said, as he handed a one page summary of his team's findings to Bob Hamilton and Jerry Boston. The three men were sitting around a conference table in Pat's office at Harris Security International headquarters, a one story white stone building, perched on top of a hill overlooking the late fall foliage of a northern Virginia forest. It was a bunker like facility, protected by a state of the art security system, guarding information that could destroy a thousand reputations.

Pat continued, "We've been able to collect DNA samples directly from Mrs. Hamilton and from the personal items you provided from Mr. Hamilton. They are not a match with your DNA. For reasons not yet apparent, they concocted an elaborate ruse to convince the world that you were their child."

Bob was dumbstruck. Sitting back in his leather chair, he looked out over the tops of the trees to the horizon and wondered again who the hell he was. Pat McCormack was droning on about paper trails and witnesses, but he had stopped listening. He was imagining toothless Appalachian hillbillies showing up as his inauguration, claiming to be his parents.

"We believe no one else has this information," Pat was saying. "And we can find no other documents or witnesses that would challenge the Hamiltons' story."

"Except for his mother," Jerry said.

"We'll get to Mrs. Hamilton in a moment. Let's just look at what your opponents would find in the unlikely event they went looking. Mr. Hamilton was something of a hypochondriac. He saw dozens of doctors. In his medical records, we found no complaints of impotence even late in life. He reported his sexual health as 'good' and intercourse as 'fairly frequent' to more than one doctor. Although, I understand they had separate bedrooms in the latter half of their marriage, is that correct?"

Bob's face reddened. "Dad always said it was because he snored so loudly that Mom couldn't sleep. He gave me the impression that they were still having sex. With more detail than I wanted."

Pat looked down at his notes. "There's not much of a paper trail on Mrs. Hamilton. Before her stroke, she hardly ever saw a doctor. You told us that Mr. Hamilton's friend, Dr. Ronald Potter, delivered you. As you know, he died of testicular cancer five years after you were born, and we have found no trace of his records. Your birth certificate states that you were born at Beauregard Memorial Hospital, a private hospital outside Atlanta. Beauregard Memorial closed in 1968. Its records were in storage at a warehouse until they were shredded thirty years later. Without those records, we are as yet unable to reconstruct who else on the hospital staff might have been present for your birth."

"What about health insurance records?" Jerry interrupted.

"The Hamiltons had no major medical coverage. They paid cash. We've also found nothing in the records of nearby adoption agencies, hospitals or doctors to suggest that another woman was your birth mother, Senator."

"What about friends and relatives?" Jerry asked. "Has anyone interviewed them about Bob's birth?"

"Mr. Hamilton had no siblings and only one cousin, now deceased. Mrs. Hamilton had one sister and several cousins, all now deceased, too. The sister died in World War II. The children of the cousins were either not yet born or too young at the time to have been aware of the sham pregnancy. Many of the friends are gone. What we have learned from those still alive is that Mrs. Hamilton took to her bed five months before you were born. The story the Hamiltons put out was that she was having a difficult pregnancy. No one alive recalls seeing her during that period."

"So where are we?" Jerry took off his glasses and stroked his forehead. He was getting a headache.

Bob sat up, exasperated. "Why don't I just talk to my mother and get it over with?"

Pat smiled for the first time. "You don't want to do that. At least not yet. Maybe never. Mrs. Hamilton has lived the last seventy years with the secret of her pregnancy and abortion. She's kept your adoption a secret for over fifty years. Psychologically, she's obviously very heavily defended about all this. A woman of her era no doubt would feel an intense amount of shame and guilt. Apparently, the last thing she wants is for you, or worse yet, the whole world to know. She wants those secrets to die with her."

"Moreover, she is in a weakened mental and physical condition. Our review of her recent medical records show that she has lost her ability to walk, she has trouble talking, limited bladder control and impaired mental capacity. It's not clear your mother could carry on a lucid conversation, let alone remember much about the past. Her prognosis is that she could stroke out at any time. It's better to let nature take its course."

"Christ, Pat, we're talking about the woman he calls his mother," Jerry snapped.

"I'm sorry, Senator. Old habits." Pat stifled a second smile.

"Don't apologize." Bob waved his hand dismissively. "Let's talk about another scenario. What if she takes a turn for the better? What if she wants to clear her conscience before she dies? What if she simply starts talking one day?"

Pat paused before answering. "We're monitoring that internally. We'll know if there's any improvement in Mrs. Hamilton's health."

Bob felt his stomach flip. He had hired this cretin to spy on his mother. And he had asked his lawyer to prepare papers to declare her mentally incompetent. It has come to this, he admitted.

"One final question." Jerry handed the summary back to Pat. "What if some old couple comes out of the woodwork and claims to be Bob's parents? Maybe they demand DNA tests, all that."

"That is certainly a risk. We are continuing to look for his birth parents. My guess is that we will never find them. Martha Hamilton went to a lot of the trouble to create the pretense of a pregnancy and birth. I'm sure she took the same care to protect her identity from the birth parents. She was with the agency for years, so she knew what she was doing."

"What do you mean?" Bob asked. "All she ever told me was that she did some clerical work for the O.S.S. during the war."

Pat laughed. "Mrs. Hamilton was a spook. And a good one. Where do you think she got all the material for her spy novels. She retired six months before you were born."

Bob's head was spinning. "You're wrong. She worked for the

Red Cross after the war."

Pat smirked. "That was her cover. She was a Cold Warrior. Cracking East German spy rings."

Still not comprehending, Bob said, "Dad would have told me."

"Mr. Hamilton was in the dark. I'm sure he thought she was doing good works. Rebuilding Europe."

"Jesus Christ. Who am I?" Bob asked, speaking to himself.

Pat exchanged glances with Jerry. "That's what we're going to find out, Senator."

November 18, 2011

"I don't think I have the stomach for this," Bob Hamilton groaned. He was meeting with his personal lawyer, Alison Sterling, over lunch in the private penthouse dining room reserved for partners and their clients at Alison's law firm, Boudreau, Mintz, McDonald and Sterling. Their table overlooked downtown Atlanta, a maze of interstate highways, unremarkable architecture and dozens of streets named in honor of the peach tree. Bob had ordered a chicken Caesar salad, but was only picking at it as Alison drilled through the steps she would take to have Martha Hamilton declared mentally incompetent to manage her own affairs.

Alison had been the law firm's first female partner, and she had a reputation for being its most ruthless. She was the quintessential junk yard dog litigator that so many clients crave when they want to win at all costs. Her scorched earth discovery and courtroom tactics had won her the enmity and begrudging admiration of hundreds of lawyers. In her mid-forties, she wore her highlighted blonde hair in a bun by day and loose by night. Never married, she had an active, but discreet social life. Yoga, limited exposure to the sun and organic foods had kept her youthful she had told her two sisters, who had long since succumbed to middle-aged spread in suburbia. She worked hard and played hard, often with powerful men who were willing to heel. Alison liked to dominate.

She gently touched the senator's hand, flashing a diamond encrusted white gold band on her wedding finger. She had told Bob she wore it to ward off unwanted suitors. "I understand how you feel, Bob. It's not easy suing your mother. I've done this several times for clients, and they all have the same reluctance. But, it's always for the best in the end. Your mother's a very wealthy woman. She's a sitting duck for scam artists. Her own staff might be taking advantage of her, and you wouldn't find out until it was too late."

Alison was not making him feel better. He put down his fork and took a drink of mineral water. He had dreaded this meeting, and it was worse than he had expected. The reality of it, reading through the petition with his mother's name in the caption, was hellish. He had done battle with many adversaries on the campaign trail and in Congress, but none of those confrontations had prepared him for this. Facing down his own mother. To take control of her life.

Jerry Boston and he had weighed the pros and cons, and they had agreed that he had to be prepared to file the competency petition on short notice if there was any possibility that his mother might start babbling about his true identity. He had not told Alison about Harris Security, the Swiss medical records or anything related to his questionable origins. As far as Alison knew, he was genuinely concerned about his mother's mental capacity and the preservation of her assets. She didn't know that he would use the lawsuit to isolate Martha Hamilton from the press and put her in restricted care, probably under sedation, so that her secrets could be kept secret. The small comfort he took was that she very well might need protection, that she might ultimately forgive him and that it was, after all, for the good of the country to get him elected president and reinstall family values in the White House.

There was a significant downside. The competency petition could be a big black eye for the campaign if his opponents or the press portrayed him as the ungrateful son suing his mother to take control of her money. His mother's lawyers could make him look bad unless the situation was contained quickly. Alison had promised him she could get a ruling in his favor within a week. Jerry and he had agreed that if they had to file suit, the sooner the better, in light of the impending caucuses and primaries. The pressure was on Harris Security to come up with answers about his birth parents by whatever means. Jerry had given Pat McCormack a deadline, the end of the year, six weeks away. The first presidential contest, the Iowa caucuses, would be held in January. The prospect of suing his mother over the holidays was chilling.

As the bile rose in his throat, Bob took another drink of mineral water and sighed. "I know you're right, Allison. It's for the best. These papers look fine. Get everything ready to go and wait until you hear from me. We may need to file before the end of the year. I'll keep you posted."

Alison absolutely gleamed. She lived for conflict and conquest, and this fight would be one of her most challenging. Wresting several billion dollars away from a future president's mother would be a major triumph, another notch on her gun. She would celebrate with Juan tonight, she decided. If she couldn't abuse a captain of industry, she'd settle for a well-endowed young man. Juan was a personal trainer at her health club. He was a twenty-one-year-old Adonis from Mexico, and he loved older women, especially blondes. As soon as she left the meeting, she would give him a call and tell him to be at her place at nine, dressed like a jock who needed to pass her class in order to play football. Juan would have to submit to her to make the team. He knew the drill.

Alison reached across the table and shook Bob's hand, still fantasizing about spanking Juan's sweet ass. "You've made the right decision, Bob. I'll make sure you don't regret it."

Chapter 10

November 30, 2011

Martha Hamilton had nodded off after lunch on the screened porch adjacent to her bedroom at Sea Haven. Sassafras was asleep on her lap. They were nestled together on a Victorian cane couch with chintz cushions surrounded by Boston ferns gently swaying in pots hanging from the ceiling. It was unusually muggy for late autumn. The nurse was on break. Yolanda Jackson paused at the door, wondering for a second if Martha were still breathing. When she saw Martha's chest lift almost imperceptibly, Yolanda heaved a sigh of relief and tip-toed onto the porch.

"Martha," she murmured. Sassy continued to purr undisturbed, but Martha slowly opened her eyes and registered a crooked smile. Yolanda continued, "I'm sorry to disturb you, but Father Bingham, the new priest from St. Paul's, is here."

Martha knitted her brow. She hardly qualified as an active parishioner. Indeed, she had never been a believer. The last time she had set foot inside Booneville's small Episcopal church was her mother's funeral. She shrugged and nodded to Yolanda. A minute later, Yolanda escorted the Anglican priest onto the porch and offered him lemonade. Eric Bingham was dressed in an ill-fitting black suit and clerical collar. He was a handsome young man in his early thirties with a square jaw, short red hair and light blue eyes.

Dabbing his forehead with his handkerchief, he drawled deeply, "Thank you for asking, Miss Jackson, but I'm fine for now." Rivulets of sweat ran down the side of his face as he settled into a cane chair opposite Martha. Sassafras hissed at Eric, jumped down and followed Yolanda off the porch.

"I apologize for barging in unannounced, but when I start in a new parish, I always make it a point to visit the shut-ins in the community." Eric tugged on his collar and gave her a big "God loves you" smile. There was an awkward silence, filled only by the whine of locusts in a hackberry tree nearby.

Eric leaned forward, his elbows on his knees, his hands clasped prayerfully. "Mrs. Hamilton, I understand you're not much of organized religion. And I can understand that. I was pretty wild in my youth. Nothing wrong with a healthy bit of skepticism when it comes to matters of faith. But what with your stroke and all, I figured you've had some time to think. I suspect you've even said a few prayers for your own recovery. No atheists in foxholes, and all that. So I wanted to reach out to you. Let you know I'm here for you. And that you're in my prayers."

Martha nodded she understood.

Eric leaned closer as he lowered his voice. "If there's anything you would like to share with me now. Anything you want to get off your chest. Confession, if you will. I call it a conversation, really. But totally confidential. Just between you and me. Then, just let me know." His smile tightened.

The hair on the back of Martha's neck lifted like a cat's, and she looked away from her visitor, her mind racing. The locusts sang louder as a fresh blast of humid air blew across the porch. Eric dabbed his entire face this time. Martha looked back at her guest and deep into his eyes. The priest held her gaze, not blinking, smile unbroken. For the first time, she felt the heat. Her pulse quickened, and she wet her diaper. Her hand began to shake as if she were palsied, and she hoped he did not detect her fear. She shook her head.

Eric nodded. "I understand. You barely know me. If you change your mind, Ms. Jackson knows where to reach me. Is there anything else I can do for you?"

Martha shook her head again.

Eric stood, lingered for a second and then bent over to touch her hand. Giving it a firm squeeze, he said, "It was nice meeting you, Martha. Take care." She smelled garlic and mouthwash on his breath and consciously fought not to flinch when he touched her.

After the parish Buick passed the security camera, Yolanda pushed the button to close the gate as she watched the old sedan disappear on the monitor in the pantry. When she turned, she let out a small yelp. Martha had been standing behind her watching the screen intently.

"Martha, you scared me," Yolanda exclaimed.

Martha shushed her with a finger to her mouth and then motioned her to a kitchen chair. Slumping back into her wheel chair, Martha adroitly guided the machine with the hand lever, rolling it up next to Yolanda.

Martha whispered with perfect enunciation, "Send the nurse home. Then come back here. We need to talk."

December 7, 2011

Emily McIntyre stepped out of her black Mercedes coupe, clasping her Bible and her Louis Vuitton purse. It was a crisp morning in the hilly Maryland countryside beyond the suburban sprawl of Washington, D.C. The sun was shining and the sky was blue, but Emily was solemn. Her weekly trips to visit her son, Frankie, always put her in a reflective mood. She walked up the steps of the main building, a sterile glass and steel structure. The grounds of Bedford Manor looked more like a college campus than a private residential facility for adults with mental limitations. She signed in at the front desk, pinned on her security badge and was buzzed through the metal door. The interior lobby was an award-winning space filled with natural light, plants and a water sculpture that provided a soothing white noise, occasionally interrupted by the voices of residents and staff. Generally, Bedford Manor was a happy place, as it was planned to be, although there were moments, from time to time, when a resident's frustration with his or her neurological parameters or limits of freedom or isolation from family broke out into the open. But mostly, there was calm and, if need be, medication.

Frankie was waiting for her behind a large, leafy tropical plant near the front of the lobby. It was their routine. He would jump out and say "Boo," and she would act surprised. The first time, he really had scared her, but now she knew how to play along. She didn't like the game. Her mother-in-law, Trudy McIntyre, had given extra attention to Frankie's needs. After she had passed, her husband, Larry, had taken primary responsibility for Frankie and they had developed a special bond in the years before Larry had died. Emily especially missed Larry when she made these visits. Much more than she missed sleeping with him. It was here that she felt utterly alone. Frankie's three brothers all lived in other parts of the country. She was everything and everyone to Frankie. It frightened her. She hated how she felt, but she wished that Frankie were normal, or that Frankie....had never been. And that made her feel very guilty and very un-Christian.

Frankie was a gift, she told herself...her cross to bear. She had to be an example to all the women who considered aborting their babies when they learned that the fetus had Down syndrome or some other problem. She, of all people, could not have doubts.

"Boo!" Frankie shouted in her ear.

Emily jumped, scared again. "Frankie, stop that, damn it!" she snapped and jerked away from him. Tears welled up in his eyes, and he started to cry. This big bear of a man, twenty-two years old, was bawling in front of her like a little boy. She hadn't seen him cry since they had talked about his father, some months back. She had sworn she would never make that mistake again. When he cried, she felt helpless and angry.

"Nurse!" she called frantically. Out of nowhere appeared a pleasant looking young black man in street clothes with a staff badge that read, Rodney Martin. He smiled at her, but he headed straight for Frankie.

"Hey, Frankie. What's the problem?" Rodney gave Frankie a big hug and held him until he quieted down.

"She yelled at me," he sobbed. "Mommy used a swear." Frankie looked over Rodney's shoulder at Emily, fear in his eyes.

Emily was struck again by how much Frankie was her son. The other boys all took after Larry's side of the family. All of them tall with blonde hair and blue eyes. Frankie was so like her father. Naturally muscular, jet black hair, brown eyes, ruddy cheeks. What a handsome man he could have been, she thought.

Rodney stepped back from Frankie, hands on his shoulders. "Did you try to scare your mom again?"

Frankie grinned, "Yeah. I yelled 'Boo' at her from behind the tree."

"Maybe you should try a different game with your mom next time." Rodney turned to face Emily and smiled. "Hey, Mrs. McIntyre, are you all right?"

Emily tightened her hold on her Bible. "Yes, thank you. Now I am. I'm sorry. I know Frankie's game. It's just that today I was distracted, and…"

"No problem. Call for me if you need me." Rodney headed down a hallway and they had the room to themselves. Emily purposely picked Wednesday mornings to avoid other visitors and residents. She wasn't comfortable watching them interact. Most of them were so close and huggy, joking and laughing. It made her feel like a bad mother. Frankie and she had a nice enough time, but it was quiet and subdued. She didn't like it when he got too excited.

But today it would be okay if he got excited. She had pictures of him. They sat down on a leather sofa facing the water sculpture. After a prayer for salvation from their sins and a Bible story about an angel telling Mary she was pregnant with the Son of God, she opened her purse. Inside, she had an envelope with proofs from a professional photographer. Frankie had come home for Thanksgiving for the first time in three years, and all of his brothers and their families had been there, too. It was a command performance. They had all stayed at her palatial estate in northern Virginia. The Clinton and Bush-Cheney years had been very good for Emily and the American Family First Foundation. The Clinton scandals and Bush Bible-thumping had energized evangelicals, many of whom had become involved in politics for the first time. For the last two decades, those folks had been writing checks to change the moral climate of the country. Some of that money had paid for Emily's grand residence, her six figure Mercedes and lifetime care for Frankie at the exclusive Bedford Manor.

Emily spread out the photos on the glass coffee table in front of them. There were color proofs of the entire McIntyre clan in matching McIntyre plaid outfits, all with Emily and Frankie front and center, her arm around him. One of them had been selected for the Christmas card that was being mass-mailed that week to Foundation members and several thousand government, church and corporate officials. Then, there were the black and white photos of just Emily and Frankie, Frankie in a business suit, his first, and Emily in a conservative dark dress. In each, he was seated in an arm chair by the fireplace, and she was standing next to him with a hand on his shoulder, smiling, her head tilted slightly toward him, as instructed by the photographer. These would be for the Foundation's website, brochures and annual report. "Don't touch the pictures, Frankie. Just look."

• • •

Billy Short walked the perimeter security fence at Sea Haven, looking for anything out of the ordinary. His two sons, Jimmy, twenty-two, and Joe Bob, twenty, were walking the fence in the other direction. Billy's hunting cap covered his close-cropped graying hair. He'd picked up twenty pounds in the eight years since he'd left the army, and he was breathing heavily by the time he returned to his Chevy Silverado truck. His sons were waiting for him, both of them leaning against the tailgate smoking cigarettes.

He looked at the young men with their thick blonde mops. How could they be his, he wondered. Indolent airheads, both of them. The boys had taken a few courses at the community college, but neither one had any ambition. Jimmy was assistant night manager at the Subway franchise, and Joe Bob worked part time at the Home Depot. They liked to go hunting with their dad, and they were crack shots, but they had no interest in the armed forces or law enforcement. Military buzz cuts and boot camp would be just the thing for both of them, he thought. Make them into men. "Did you give your section a thorough going over?"

"Yeah, Daddy. We didn't see nothing," Joe Bob said.

"Christ all mighty," Billy muttered and spat tobacco juice at their feet. He'd walk their section after he met with Martha Hamilton. He glanced up again at the utility pole by the gate and snapped another shot with his old Army reconnaissance camera.

"Whadja see up there?" Jimmy asked as he lit another cigarette.

"Never mind," he spat again. His wife, June had made him hire the boys for this job. Martha Hamilton paid full rates. The boys could at least carry his equipment, she argued. They could learn his trade by observation. He shook his head at nothing in particular and hefted himself into the driver's seat. "Pick up your cigarette butts and git in." The boys obliged and jumped in the back of the truck.

He asked the boys to circle the house and then go down to the beach and search for signs of intrusion. He knew they'd be worthless at the task. They'd spend their time picking up seashells and wading in the surf. But he had to keep them busy while he spoke with his client.

"Hey Martha, old girl, how you all doing?" Billy sat down next to Martha and Sassy on the sofa in the library and kissed Martha on the cheek. He stroked the cat's back until she began to purr. The door was closed and they were alone. He set a small black box on the coffee table next to the silver coffee service and flicked a switch. "We can talk here. I've checked this room for bugs. And this little gadget will scramble any signal if I missed one. All they'll hear is static. Got it on loan from one of my old army buddies."

She patted his hand. "I'm good, Billy. How are you and the family?" Martha was wearing a cobalt blue Chanel suit, one of her old favorites. Yolanda Jackson had helped her with her hair and make-up. She sat erect and felt very much alert and alive.

"Everybody's fine. When Yolanda brought me your letter, she said you'd been hiding your progress. I'm glad you're up and about."

Martha nodded. "Me too. The nurses Bob hired didn't want me to move, and I knew I wasn't going to get well if I paid attention to them. I've never been much for the medical profession."

"Me neither. I always suspected they could have done a better job with my shoulder. I'm sure it wasn't easy for you, fighting to regain control. You're tough."

"I'm not so tough. And now I'm scared. What do you know?"

"Well, Martha. I don't believe you're scared of anything, but we do have a situation here. Somebody's watching you. That's for sure. They have the whole house under electronic surveillance, probably phones, online computers, cable TV, the works. I saw the hook-up just outside the front gate. They coulda been more careful about it, but I'm sure they didn't think you'd be snooping back at them."

Billy scratched Sassy's head. "Your employees, Jackson and Pike, check out, but it's good you canned the nursing service. They're easy to infiltrate. The minister's a doozy. He gave very authentic looking credentials and recommendation letters to the church board. The references check out on one level. When you call those numbers, you get an answering machine for the person listed, but the actual identities of those references are all fake. A small town church board's not going to second guess the authenticity of Professor so-and-so or Bishop hump-de-dump two states away when they heap praise on young Eric Bingham or whatever his name is. Somebody went to a lot of trouble to plant him on the hope that you'd pour your heart out. I suspect he's doing double duty while he's in town, reviewing surveillance tapes, et cetera. I'd say these guys are ex-CIA, FBI or military. They know what they're doing and they're spending a lot of money doing it."

Martha thought back on her visit with the young priest. Some sixth sense had told her that he did not ring true. She remembered how he had stared her down with his cold charm. "Now tell me again why I shouldn't be afraid, Billy."

Billy turned serious. "You tell me Martha. What do you have that they want?"

There was a long silence. A grandfather clock in the hallway struck the hour. "It would help to know who *they* are first," she said.

Billy shifted his position, not completely comfortable with this subject. "Well, if I'd venture a guess, I'd say it's either your son or one of his adversaries. And I'm not sure it makes a difference who it is. You son is running for president. The stakes are high. This has become an ugly business."

"My son plays to win." Martha leaned over and, with one hand, poured herself a cup of chicory coffee, added cream and settled the china cup and saucer in her lap.

Billy poured himself coffee black and grabbed a couple of homemade shortbread cookies. "I know it's none of my business, but I've always wanted to ask. Why are you trying to sabotage your son's career?"

"Let's just say it's better if he stays out of the public eye."

"Excuse me? The man's a United States senator. I'd say the horse has left the barn." Billy could hear his sons' laughter as they headed toward the house in the gathering dusk.

"Yes, but the presidency is exponentially worse. He'll be on a world stage. I can't say anymore just now."

They could hear the boys in the hallway. Yolanda was trying to quiet them down and coax them back onto the veranda with the promise of soft drinks.

Billy shrugged. "No problem. Sorry for asking. Here's what I suggest short term. Leave all the bugging and wiretapping in place and just be careful what you say and do. When you want to reach me, come in here, turn on this device and call me on Yolanda's cell phone. That way we don't tip them off and we have more freedom to develop a counter-strategy once we know more. I'll try to find out who's paying for all this."

Martha was always comforted by Billy's no-nonsense decisiveness. She also loved the fact that he didn't kowtow to her. She enjoyed her time with him even though the business was unpleasant. Feeling his body heat, she wished that she were younger and that she still had a man in her life. Martha touched his knee. "I've got a couple more things for you."

"What can I do?" Billy swallowed the shortbread and finished his coffee.

"Find out what you can about Emily McIntyre and her American Family whatever Foundation. Specifically, how she's connected to my son. When I watch her on TV, she makes my skin crawl. Underneath, I think she's a very angry lady."

Billy took some notes. "Will do, what else?"

Martha took a deep breath, held it and slowly exhaled. "There's someone I want you to find. An old friend."

Chapter 11

December 24, 2011

"The guy walks away from his big money job in Manhattan so that he can dig wells and build septic tanks for the Peace Corps in some bum fuck part of Peru," Rosie Gibson said, as she headed down the entrance ramp to the interstate. She checked her rearview mirror before taking another big bite of her glazed doughnut.

"And what's your point? Lots of people have left good paying jobs to join the Peace Corps." Natalie Jordan took a small sip of her hazelnut flavored coffee. It was still too hot to drink.

"Yes, and every one of them has a story. I'm simply trying to figure out Hamilton's." She licked the icing off her fingers and wiped her lips with a napkin.

Rosie and Natalie were driving their Volvo station wagon north from Washington, D.C. to Baltimore to pick up Rosie's mother, Eulalia, her sister, Althea, and Althea's three kids on their way to Natalie's parents in Philadelphia. The Christmas Eve weather report was not good, six to ten inches of blowing snow. But, even with bad roads, they expected to reach Philly in plenty of time for the children's service that evening at Natalie's father's church.

Rosie finished the doughnut. "Ever since Max gave me this assignment, I've wondered what motivated Hamilton to take off for Peru and what turned him into such a religious zealot while he was there. The rest of the story's pretty boring. It tells itself."

"Why do you care? Max just wants a biography, right? Not a psychoanalysis. Is anyone else doing this much work on their candidate's profile?" Natalie broke off a small piece of her blueberry scone.

"No, no, you're right, but I'm assigned to Hamilton for the entire campaign, not just for this article. I'm going to be spending a lot of time with him over the next year if he makes it past the primaries." Rosie looked down at the box of pastries and picked a chocolate frosted cake doughnut. "From everything I've read, he was a pampered little rich boy with parents who cared more about golf and horses than the meaning of life. He was a frat boy at Duke. After business school at Wharton, he plunges into the belly of the capitalist beast on Wall Street, makes a ton of money and cashes out for Peru."

"So maybe that's white man's guilt. How else they gonna fill the ranks of the Peace Corps." Natalie took another sip of coffee. She loved the smell of hazelnut.

"OK, I'll buy that as a general proposition, but Hamilton doesn't fit the profile. There's nothing granola liberal about his past. Those are the kids who sign up for the Peace Corps. Not the trust fund babies from the plantations. But, let's say you're right. Let's say he got a wild hair up his ass and joined, maybe even to spite Colonel Sanders back home. What happened to him in Peru that sent him back a born-again Bible beater who's compelled to save brown babies from being aborted? What Heart of Darkness Passage to India experience did he have that made him see the light? Unlike every other come-to-Jesus politician, Hamilton never tells us." Rosie braked hard as a semi-trailer truck barreled on to the highway directly in front of them.

Natalie lurched forward, spilling some of her coffee on her jeans. "Pay attention to the road, Rosie. The snow is beginning to stick. Do you want me to drive?"

"No, I'll switch with you at Mom's." Rosie wondered why she ever discussed her work with Natalie. Her partner wasn't much for politics.

Natalie felt the tension. "Why don't you just ask Hamilton?"

Rosie smiled at Natalie's naiveté. "I'll do that, but I'll get some bullshit non-answer. He's already decided what he wants the world to know. I need to talk to people who knew him back in the day. I just don't have time for that now." She plucked a vanilla frosted long john from the box. "Anyway, honey, what are you getting me for Christmas?"

Natalie stared down at the empty box between them. "How about some stock in Dunkin Donuts?"

· · ·

Emily McIntyre took her seat early in the front row of the sanctuary of the Church of the New Faith in Upper St. Clair, Pennsylvania. It was her favorite service of the year. Candlelight and carols on Christmas Eve. The church had continued to prosper since Larry and she had moved to Washington to set up the American Family First Foundation. The edifice was a gleaming cathedral of gold, glass, limestone and richly burnished wood filled with an overflow crowd of well-heeled believers.

She looked up, admiring the heavy evergreen boughs and

twinkling white lights that draped the rafters. She loved the smell of pine. Squeals of laughter came from the rear as the children's choir assembled in red and green robes for their march down the aisle. Soon they would lead the congregation in *"O Come All Ye Faithful."* Returning here always rejuvenated her and reminded her of the early days with Larry beside her, building their dream.

She was alone. Three of her sons were visiting their wives' families around the country. Frankie was staying with a friend's family near Bedford Manor. The friend, Lily Roach, was Frankie's age and also had Down syndrome. Emily was relieved when Lily's parents offered to take Frankie home for the holiday. She would have felt guilty if he'd had to stay at the home with the handful of others who had no place to go for Christmas. She promised herself she would call Frankie after the service before dinner at the senior minister's home. The ministry team had planned a special celebratory meal that night to honor her work for the church.

She looked over her shoulder and smiled at the thousands of faces of young couples, fathers, mothers, children and grandparents, all assembled behind her. These were her people. God-fearing people. People who wrote checks to the Foundation because they believed in her and what she was doing to save the country. Turning back, she bowed her head, closed her eyes and folded her hands just as the organist began to play *"The First Noel"* as a prelude to the choir's grand entrance.

Silently, she prayed, "O Lord, on this most holy of nights, I ask for a special gift from you, not for me, but for all of America. Please, in your wisdom, see clear to guide Senator Hamilton in his bid for the presidency and help him to defeat his enemies. Bless him with the words and persuasive power to convince the voters of the righteousness of his path. Lift him above all others so that he may lead us out of the darkness and back into the light. He alone is the perfect candidate to do Thy work on this earth. He alone has the faith and the courage to do battle with the baby killers and sodomites. He alone will protect the American family from the corruption of our culture. Watch over him and protect him from harm. Keep him pure and strong. Keep him true to the cause. In Jesus name, I pray. Amen."

Later that night, as the peppermint ice cream and coffee were being served at the minister's home, Emily realized she had forgotten to call Frankie. It was too late. He would be in bed asleep. She would call him on Christmas morning. Frankie was in bed, but he was not asleep. Lily had joined him after her parents turned in. She had tiptoed down the hallway in her Winnie the Pooh flannel nightgown and ever so quietly opened and closed his door. He had been waiting for her naked under the covers, tumescent. Pulling back the down comforter, she hiked her nightgown above her waist and climbed onto the bed. Straddling him, she encircled his penis with her fingers and slowly guided him into her. In the darkness, they gently rocked together. Bending over to kiss him, Lily whispered, "Merry Christmas, Frankie." Giving her a big hug, he replied, "Merry Christmas to you too, Lily. I love you."

• • •

As Lily Roach crawled off of Frankie McIntyre and headed back to her bedroom, Bob Hamilton left his sleeping wife and went down to the kitchen of Mary O'Malley's rambling old home in Winnetka, a wealthy lakefront suburb north of Chicago. He was in search of milk and Christmas cookies. He couldn't sleep. He was not looking forward to seeing his mother the next day. Sliding into the booth in the breakfast nook, he opened the *Chicago Tribune* to the editorial page and sipped his milk. Just as he took a bite out of a star-shaped sugar cookie, his brother-in-law, Jack O'Malley, stomped through the back door covered in snow. A cold blast of air followed him into the kitchen.

Over fifty, Jack wore his graying hair in a spiky urban style that screamed gay to Bob. Despite the sub-freezing temperature, Jack was wearing only a brightly colored knit scarf over his turtle neck sweater. His nose and cheeks were bright red. His blue eyes were bloodshot.

"What were you doing out there?" Bob asked. He never knew what to say to Jack.

"Going for a walk. Trying to sober up." Jack replied as he unwound his scarf with a theatrical flourish. Jack was a Broadway scenic designer.

"You *were* throwing them back tonight."

"Ah. You noticed. Family gatherings require more alcohol than usual, and Christmas tops the list." Jack grabbed a couple of sugar cookies, a Christmas tree and a bell, and slid into the booth across from Bob.

Bob froze. He'd always managed to keep his distance from Jack, always suspecting he had HIV. He still had half a glass of milk and three cookies. There was no quick way to exit.

Jack leaned forward into the circle of light from the overhead lamp, his knees touching Bob's. "So, I understand you're running for president."

Bob moved his legs and forced a smile. "Yes. That's the plan."

Bob could smell the alcohol on his breath, the alcohol and the virus, he thought. Bob instinctively leaned back to avoid contagion. He didn't believe the science. Semen and blood, but not saliva. Why not saliva? Jack was a spitter when he talked.

"And my big sister, Kathleen, would be First Lady. Hard to believe." Jack seemed to lean even closer.

Bob rested his head against the back of the booth, as far as he could retreat. "Yeah. She's not real excited about that."

"I know. She's told me." Jack bit the top off the Christmas tree. "So, Bob, what are you going to do about the homosexual problem once you're elected?" Jack had tilted the hanging lamp so that it illuminated Bob's face.

"What do you mean?"

"Oh, come on, Mr. President. What's your Christmas wish for all the homosexuals of the world?"

"Jack, I'm sorry if I –"

Jack let go of the lamp and let it swing between them. "Oh, don't be sorry. It's not your fault. It's our fault, really. After all, we chose this dangerous life style, right?"

"If you say so," Bob said. He was getting pissed.

"I don't say so. It wasn't my choice. I've been queer since I can remember." Raising one eyebrow, Jack reached out and tapped Bob's wedding ring. "What's your story?"

Bob jerked his hand away and lurched out of the booth, jamming his thigh against the table in the tiny space. "Go to bed. Jack. You've had too much to drink."

"You're right. I'm drunk. Pay no attention to the drunken faggot in the corner booth.. Check, please!"

"Good night, Jack," Bob said, as he left the kitchen.

"Good night, Mr. President."

December 25, 2011

Martha Hamilton kept her son waiting for a half hour after he had arrived at Sea Haven on Christmas afternoon. He'd called on

Christmas Eve to see if she would be feeling well enough for a visit. Yolanda Jackson had relayed the message to Martha, and she had assented. It had been three months since he'd last been to Sea Haven. In the interim, there had been several calls to the house, which Yolanda had answered. He had always asked about Martha's health, but hadn't asked to speak with her, saying he didn't want to bother her. "Doesn't want to bother his own mother?" Martha questioned Yolanda. "As if I were in a coma," she harrumphed.

Bob had flown to Savannah from Chicago in a private jet and rented a car to drive south an hour an a half to Sea Haven. He'd paid the pilot triple time to fly on Christmas and agreed to return to the airport within four hours. He'd have time for only a brief conversation with his mother. The briefer, the better, he had thought. His family had stayed behind in Chicago with Kathleen's mother and brothers. In mid-December, a Senate page had spent the better part of a week researching various gift ideas for him. He always found it nearly impossible to buy for her. What do you get for an eighty-seven old invalid billionaire? She had everything she wanted. Finally, they had settled on a family photo, hastily shot at an Atlanta studio. Professionally matted and framed on an expedited basis, it was a very handsome gift, he thought, as he waited next to the roaring fire in the library.

Yolanda had mailed Martha's gifts to Kathleen's mother's home two weeks before, all carefully chosen and wrapped with Yolanda's help. Books for the children. Family heirloom jewelry for Kathleen. And a two foot tall bronze rendering of Prince in full gallop for Bob. Very much in a Frederic Remington style. A beautiful black stallion, Prince had been Bob's horse, a birthday gift from his parents. He'd died of old age when Bob was in Peru. It was a remarkably thoughtful and beautiful gift, Kathleen had said that morning as he held it up for everyone to see. Bob had felt both touched and guilty. When he heard the elevator motor announce Martha's imminent arrival, he panicked. Since he had been sworn in as a U.S. Senator, he had hardly ever been alone. He almost always was accompanied by staff. At Sea Haven, his grandmother's home without his grandmother, he felt very much a child again and very much alone. The framed family photo seemed a wholly inadequate gift at that moment.

"Merry Christmas, Bob." Martha was sitting in her wheelchair no more than a foot from him. He was startled not only by her presence, but by the clarity of her speech. Her smile was still somewhat twisted by paralysis, but his mother's voice rang true and strong. She looked amazingly well, much better than she had three months before. She had gained weight, and the color was back in her cheeks. Her white hair was full and perfectly coiffed. Sitting confidently upright, she looked absolutely regal in her royal blue suit and pearls. He was speechless.

Martha placed her hand on his. "How was your flight?"

"Fine, Mother, fine," he managed to mumble. "You look great. You sound great."

"Thank you. It's been rough, but I've been through worse." She hated to admit it, but she was enjoying her son's shocked reaction. She figured he had presumed she was fast approaching a vegetative state. That was certainly how he had treated her since the stroke, as if she had already been consigned to a hospice. It made her wonder if he wanted her dead or if he was simply uncomfortable with her paralysis. Then, it made her sad because she feared she was correct on both counts.

As he updated her on the grandchildren, she studied him as if he were the stranger that he had become in the last ten years. She wished that she could suspend judgment for once and simply love him unconditionally, like mothers were supposed to do. But she could not. She saw her son objectively, and what she saw frightened her. He used everyone to advance his interests at every turn. Just as he had gone to Herculean efforts to spend a few minutes with her on this special day. He didn't want to connect with her so much as show face, guard his flank on the inheritance and check up first hand on her health.

"Thank you for the statue of Prince. I cried when I unwrapped it."

"I'm glad you liked it. He was a magnificent animal." Martha had purchased Prince for Bob for his eleventh birthday, but Robert III had taken credit, sneaking out to the stable with Bob during his birthday party. When Marion Randolph reported the secret visit to Martha, she had exclaimed, "That man. He's always trying to be the hero."

Picking up the gold foil wrapped picture frame, Bob asked, "Would you like me to open your present?"

"No, no, I should be able to manage." He placed the package on her lap and watched in amazement as she deftly ripped the paper and held up the photo for examination with one hand. "Thank you, Bobby. This is priceless. Your family is beautiful. You are so lucky. I shall have this hung in my bedroom so that I can look at your family every morning and evening. Thank you." A lone tear made its way down her left cheek. She didn't bother to wipe it away.

As they munched on cranberry pecan bread and sipped hot tea, she sensed a new layer of anxiety in him. He was unusually complimentary and attentive. There was a subtle tension in his body language that no one but a mother could detect. "I can't tell you how happy I am to see you doing so well," he said. "You're an amazing woman."

"Nonsense. There are no prizes for growing old. I'm still here because my genes have pre-ordained it. I wish I could claim the credit, but all I do is open my eyes every morning."

"I wish Dad had been given the same gift." Bob looked into the fire, his eyes moistened.

"I know you miss him, Bobby. You loved him so, and he loved you."

"Oh, yes," he sighed. He was showing the first real emotion of the visit, she realized. And he would never feel the same way about her.

"The best way to remember him is to love your children as much as he loved you. And I know you do. That's his gift to you." It galled Martha to admit it, but Robert III had trumped her with Bob even in death.

"Thank you. That's very sweet of you to say. I do try very hard to be as good a father as he was to me." He looked down at Sassafras who had entered the room and was meowing for attention at his feet. "And as good a parent as you have been, too."

The afterthought didn't even hurt anymore. She knew why it had taken him a couple beats to recover and mention her. Still, she wished he hadn't bothered to come. His presence only reminded her of her biggest failure in life. Before she could offer a perfunctory thank you for his weak endorsement, he stood abruptly, scaring the cat, who leapt onto the coffee table, nearly tipping over the teapot. Martha's quick one-handed reach to catch the china pot astonished him.

"Do you have to go so soon?" she asked as she settled back in her chair. She was conflicted, feeling guilty that she had wanted the visit over, wondering if they would ever have a real moment of love before she died.

"Yes, I'm afraid so. I promised the pilot he could see his family tonight. I'm running late as it is. Next time, I'll bring Kathleen and the kids for a weekend if you think you can take three teenagers in the house."

It had been years since Bob had joined his family for a visit. Bob had used a series of excuses. She had stopped asking. Bob had his reasons, and she wasn't going to force a visit that wasn't wanted. His offer caught her off guard. Maybe there was hope. Maybe she had misread him after all.

"I would love that. Come any time." She rose from her wheelchair.

"Mother, be careful," he exclaimed as he reached out to steady her.

"I'm fine, really. I've been shuffling around for some weeks now, short distances, to and from the bathroom." She used the moment to hold him close to her. She couldn't remember the last time they had hugged. "Thanks for coming," she said, this time meaning it.

December 31, 2011

Edward Brock, also known as Reverend Eric Bingham, yawned and stretched as he leaned back in his chair. It was almost five o'clock, and the Booneville library would be closing soon. The building had originally been the in-town home of a wealthy rice plantation owner. The planter had gone bankrupt when the market for Georgia rice had collapsed in the late nineteenth century, and the town of Booneville had bought the mansion. With large white Corinthian columns supporting a broad portico, it was a grand facility for such a small town. Ed, however, was holed up in a dank corner of the basement in a small windowless room set aside for viewing microfiche. The cool damp air smelled of mildew and old books. He had spent the week between Christmas and New Year's poring through old copies of county newspapers on brittle microfiche film and found nothing of note. Swigging the last dregs of cold vending machine coffee, he grimaced and pitched the Styrofoam cup into a wastebasket. He hadn't had a cigarette since noon, and the lack of nicotine was making him edgy.

Staring at the ceiling tiles, stained brown from ancient leaks, he resolved that this would be his last day in this room. Like the courthouse records, the newspaper files had been a bust. His boss, Pat McCormack, would not be happy. He had demanded a report twice a day for the last two weeks on the status of Ed's search. "We've got a 31

December deadline with the client. I don't want excuses. I want answers," Pat had said repeatedly, each time with increasing ferocity. Ed was sleep deprived. In the preceding week, he had spent his days searching court house records and his evenings conducting or attending various Christmas programs and services at St. Paul's Episcopal Church. This week, he had carried home from the library each evening county and family histories, staying up until two or three each night, searching for something, anything that might help answer the puzzle. His work had been made more frustrating by gaps in the newspaper records and misdated microfiche reels. The seventy something librarian, Loretta Heaton, seemed barely competent and inordinately suspicious of his interest in the old records. He wasn't sure he could trust her to retrieve the reels he requested. And he was afraid that, in some passive-aggressive way, the old maid was holding out on him simply because he was a pushy young man new to town. The old Baptist had sniffed, unimpressed, when he told her he had replaced Father Dolan at St. Paul's.

In a few minutes, he would be able to step outside and take a big drag on a Marlboro. In three hours, after he had filed his daily report with McCormack, he would be checking in to an airport hotel near Savannah. Ed had scheduled an evening with Mary Jo Hampton. With blonde hair, blue eyes and 36 double D's, Mary Jo was a county fair queen gone bad. She'd been charging the men of Savannah for her services since her junior year in high school. All three judges in the county fair contest had been her clients. Ed had managed two brief sessions with her since he'd started this assignment, and he was looking forward to New Year's Eve with those big tits.

"The library will be closing in fifteen minutes. Happy New Year to everyone. See you next year," Loretta announced over the loudspeaker.

"Bitch!" Ed answered back to the ceiling speaker as he sat forward. Fantasizing about Mary Jo had given him a hard on, and he was debating skipping the last reel in favor of a smoke. Then he thought about McCormack's angry red face, and his penis went soft. Rubbing his eyes, he picked up the last box. The label read, "Booneville Democrat Message - July-September 1945," but the reel inside was dated April-June 1945. "Fuck yeah. Here you are." Ed had been searching for local accounts of the Boone-Hamilton wedding all week to no avail. Other papers along the east coast, including *The New York Times*, had carried brief accounts of the society union, but none with any detail.

Threading the tape into the machine, he noticed the stain of pre-cum on his Anglican black trousers and smiled. Humming to himself, he cranked the machine rapidly through the early copies until he came to Monday, May 7, 1945. "Boone-Hamilton Nuptials" was the bold headline on page one. Ed was familiar with the poorly written, wordy articles by Doris Kendrick, daughter of the newspaper's owner and society editor from 1934 to 1952. Her stories were gossipy tripe, but they were thorough. Scanning through the long piece, Ed drummed the table nervously with the fingers of his free hand. "Come on, Doris, don't disappoint me. Cough it up."

The lights flicked off and on, killing the power to the microfiche machine temporarily. "Reverend Bingham, it's time to go. Some of us have parties tonight." Loretta had opened the door and stood over him with a prim smile and a hand on the light switch. Ed was in too good of a mood to tell her to fuck off. Instead, he pulled out his wallet, handed her a fifty dollar bill, and said, "Miss Heaton, give me ten more minutes, if you would please. Here's a contribution to the First Baptist building fund."

Ignoring her, he turned back to the machine. She protested, but he kept reading. Deciding the bribe was adequate, she finally said, "Well then, that's very generous, Reverend Bingham. Thank you very kindly. I'll be at the front desk." Just as Loretta reached the bottom of the stairs, she heard him hit the table with his fist and shout, "Hot damn!" Shaking her head, she folded the fifty and headed up the stairs. She knew just the outfits she was going buy for her sister's new twin granddaughters, Courtney and Kimberly, at the Kids Kottage on Main Street.

• • •

The Hamiltons had bought a home in the Georgetown after Bob was elected to the Senate. It was huge by Georgetown standards, but absolutely necessary to wine and dine Washington's movers and shakers. Still, one hundred fifty guests on New Year's Eve managed to fill every public room to overflowing. Jerry Boston heard his cell phone ring only because he was in the first floor powder room.

Answering, he said, "You're cutting it close, McCormack. Another couple hours and you'd be a pumpkin. Let me call you back. I need to step outside to hear you."

Jerry waited until he was in the backyard gazebo fifty feet from the house before he called back. "Make this fast. I'm freezing out here."

Pat McCormack loved playing for high stakes. His favorite assignments for the CIA had been causing mayhem that toppled governments or triggered wars. He had been like a kid with lethal firecrackers. In his civilian life, he was no longer allowed to blow up buildings, so his new heroin had become helping decide who rules the last remaining super power. He desperately did not want to lose his source of heroin. Pat was still in his office, surrounded by five team leaders on the Hamilton project. They had been working eighteen hour days non-stop for six weeks. There had been no Christmas, Hanukkah or Kwanza celebrations for them or their teams. Thirty staff members charging by the hour had run up more than a million dollars in fees. But all of it would be for naught if Pat couldn't deliver on his promise to Bob Hamilton to find his biological parents.

"Happy New Year to you, too, Jerry. I'll be quick. I have very good news. Just this evening, we have located his parents' wedding guest list. That list will lead us to the senator's biological parents."

"No, no, no. That's not good enough. You were going to have the answer by midnight tonight. Not a list of guests who attended a wedding in the middle of the last century." Steam was rising from Jerry's head in the cold night air. He hardly ever drank alcohol, but, on this night, he had downed three vodka tonics in fast succession. He had left four messages for Pat throughout the day, none of which had been returned. He was pissed and tipsy.

"Jerry, I hear you, but this list *is* the answer. It is only a matter of time until we find who we're looking for. I am so confident I'm taking the whole team off the meter until we find them. However long it takes."

"That's bullshit. The Iowa caucuses are a week away, and you don't have an answer for me." Jerry leaned against a pillar on the back of the gazebo facing away from the house. He had to pee again. Damned prostate. As he let fly on the Hamiltons' holly, he was half listening to McCormack's blather.

Interrupting, Jerry declared, "No more crap. Your job is to make this problem go away. Find them. You understand?"

Pat smiled. He had bought himself time and expanded the scope of his mission. This job was too easy sometimes. "I understand completely, Jerry. Consider it done. Give the senator my best."

• • •

Alison Sterling was in heaven. This was her best New Year's Eve ever. She had just won a multi-million dollar jury verdict for the firm's biggest corporate client against one of her most hated opponents in the Atlanta bar. It was the largest award in the history of her firm, and it would go a long way toward supporting her drive for the biggest share of partner profits in the coming year. During the six week trial, she had forced herself to maintain her diet and yoga program, allowing her to end the year five pounds lighter than when she had started it. She looked fabulous and she felt fabulous.

Her Christmas present to herself was a New Year's weekend in a luxury suite at the Trump International Hotel in New York City. And the bow on her present was strapped naked, spread eagled and blindfolded on the satin sheets of her king size bed overlooking Central Park. The young man, Adam, was one of her favorites. He was sleeping, spent, next to her as she made a design with his semen on his rock hard tummy. When she was done, she licked her finger. His semen was the sweetest she'd ever tasted. Adam was a working class kid who had done well at Northwestern University on a theatre scholarship. He wanted to be an actor, but alas, he was not as good an actor as he was a waiter. Hence, his present predicament, trussed to the four corners of Alison's bed. She kissed one of his pink nipples until both of them came to life. Even in his slumber, his cock began to stiffen in response to her attention.

Reaching between his legs, she adjusted the nine inch dildo she had gently worked past his anal sphincter earlier that evening. She didn't want it slipping out just yet. Her fingers grazed the rose tattoo above his pubic area, one that she had designed for him. It was her mark on him for the rest of his life. Stroking his inner thighs, she smiled at the reddened areas, where she had lashed him with her cat-o-nine-tails, just enough to cause momentary pain, but not enough to reduce his excitement. It was a wonder she paid him. He had as much fun as she did.

She slipped off his blindfold so that she could admire his beauty. He'd had his thick black hair buzzed short for a small part in an off-off-off Broadway production. And let his dark beard grow to a three day stubble just for her. She wiped away a bit of spittle at the edge of his lower lip. At her climax, she had told him to open his mouth and then spat into it repeatedly with each wave of her orgasm. Asleep, he seemed so innocent. Like the first time she had met him. Before he had learned to follow her orders. He was a gorgeous hunk of man, and he was all hers for the rest of the night.

The only thing that would have made her triumph more delicious would have been to have a man of power in bondage. Adam was great fun, but Adam was there because he needed the money. When the clock ran out, he would go home to his girlfriend or boyfriend or whatever and resume his life at the bottom rung of New York theatre. What really made Alison moist was a man in a business suit or a military uniform or even religious vestments. She loved stripping off the clothes that defined the man and taking control. They all looked the same in their birthday suits. Same equipment. Same pleasure spots. Same needs. Her current fantasy man was Senator Robert Hamilton. He would be the ideal hunk for submission. She touched herself as she thought about their conversation earlier that week. He had started by saying, "I called to tell you we've got to put the petition against my mother on hold."

"Shit," Alison had said to herself as she snapped a pencil. "Sure, Bob. Have you had a change of heart?"

"No, no, nothing like that. It's just that I don't think we could prove her incompetent at this point. I met with her on Christmas Day. She's more lucid than ever. It's almost like she never had a stroke."

"Are you sure it's not just the holidays working on you? You know. Over the river and through the woods. We all idealize our family at this time of year."

"I wish I could say that, but that's not the case. I even suggested that I bring the whole family to her place for a weekend. She's that much better."

"Oh, Bob. You sound discouraged. I suspect this is only a temporary episode of clarity. With her medical history, I can assure you that it's only a matter of time. In addition to the stroke, she's also no doubt begun to experience a series of mini-strokes that take their toll day by day and week by week. As I say, I've been through this before with other clients. If need be, we can get a court order for an MRI. I'm sure we'd find enough white spots to convince a judge that she shouldn't be overseeing her own affairs and the billions of dollars that rightfully belong to you and your children."

She had heard him sigh. "I don't know, Alison. As much as I think it's the right thing to do, it also kills me. She's my mom after all. It was amazing when I saw her. It was almost like old times."

Alison had realized she'd said enough, maybe too much. It was time to shut up and let him stew. She had planted the seed. She would let it grow for a couple of weeks. He'd be back. "Maybe you're right, Bob. That's great about your mom. I hope she has a complete recovery."

"Thanks for understanding, Alison. I don't know what I'd do without you. You're great. Maybe we should talk sometime about a role for you in Washington. Maybe Attorney General when I get elected."

"I'd love that, Bob. Maybe we could talk over dinner sometime. I'd be glad to come to D.C. if necessary. I've never seen your office."

"Great. Let's make plans after the New Year."

Alison was close to another orgasm as she imagined herself alone with Bob, after a romantic dinner at his home in Georgetown, the wife back in Atlanta with the kids. Better yet, she fantasized about a liaison on the night of his inauguration. Everyone would be fast asleep and she'd have the President of the United States of America, Commander in Chief of the armed forces, gagged and whimpering beneath her in the Lincoln Bedroom. The New Year would be a very good year, indeed.

After she came, Adam began to stir. As he awoke, he found her straddling him with scissors clipping away at his pubic hair. "Hey, don't do that. I like my bush," he said. He tried to struggle free as she had trained him to do.

Holding his hardening penis in one hand and her scissors in the other, she smiled, saying, "Careful, boy. We wouldn't want to have an accident, would we?"

Chapter 12

February 11, 2012

On a cold Saturday morning, Rosie Gibson was standing outside the Church of the Inner Light in Detroit, shivering, waiting for someone, anyone, to answer the bell. She was excited, but also nervous. She had been trying to set up an interview with Reverend Jonathan Jones for a month, and, the day before, he had finally returned her call. "I'll give you one hour tomorrow. That's all I can spare. I'm preparing my sermon," he had said.

Working long hours, she had tracked down the names of Peace Corps volunteers who were in Peru at the same time as Bob Hamilton. She had already spoken with two of them. They had met him at the time, but they had not worked with him. Both had said to look up Jones. Her pretext for each interview had been a fifty-year retrospective look at the Peace Corps mission in Latin America. From that stepping off point, she had gradually worked the conversation around to fellow volunteers in Peru, and then expressed mild interest that Bob Hamilton had been there at the same time, probing for as much as they could remember about him.

Finally, the church door opened, and there stood a tall handsome, middle-aged black man, with a shaved head and horn rimmed glasses, looking fit in bright blue running clothes. Jonathan Jones smiled and said, "Sorry to keep you waiting. Would you like to get some coffee? There's a little shop down the street."

"God, I would love some coffee, Reverend. And a doughnut, too. I skipped breakfast." Rosie had dressed for the Russian steppes, in a red wool pant suit, boots and a heavy wool houndstooth overcoat. It was one of the outfits she had bought to follow Bob Hamilton around Iowa and New Hampshire.

"Call me Jonathan. They have the best cinnamon rolls in Detroit. They bake them right there and slather them with frosting." Jonathan tugged on his hooded jacket. I have to keep running just so I can indulge."

"Sounds perfect." A connoisseur of pastry, Rosie thought. She liked him already.

Snow was beginning to fall as they reached the little corner shop. It was an old storefront that lesbian friends of Georgia Jones had renovated into a black bohemian answer to the corporate coffee chains.

"Take two. They're small. My treat," he said as she eyed the selection. They were not small. They were huge, scrumptious looking creations. The minister was definitely a man after her own heart.

They settled into a booth in a back corner of the shop, away from the regulars reading their papers and checking their emails. She took a big bite of one of her vanilla frosted cinnamon rolls. "Hmmm," she purred and nodded approvingly. "Thanks for seeing me, Jonathan. As I said, I'm doing a retrospective article on the Peace Corps."

Jonathan stirred the cream into his coffee and then looked up at her. "Rosie, I subscribe to your paper online. I've read your articles on Bob Hamilton. You may be doing a story on the Peace Corps, but you're not here to talk about that, are you?"

His voice was so soothing and his manner was so gentle. She looked out the window at the swirling snow. The big spotted cat was lounging on a row of newspaper boxes, watching the two of them, switching her tail as the snow thickened. She was closer to Rosie than she had ever been.

"Oh, Christ," she sighed. "You're right. I'm sorry for not being upfront. It's just that I thought you might not talk to me or maybe you'd call the senator first. I'm trying to fill in the holes on the senator's background, and he doesn't have much to say about his time in Peru. I was so excited to learn from the others that you're the man to talk to. You must hate me for using you like this."

Jonathan blew on his coffee and then took a small sip. "I don't hate you, Rosie. I knew from your first call what you wanted. I wasn't sure until yesterday that I wanted to talk to you. But now, I'm ready. So fire away."

Jonathan told her how Bob Hamilton and he had met on the cross country team at Duke, how they had reconnected in New York in Central Park at a training session for the marathon. He had grown weary of working non-stop for a big New York law firm and Bob had grown dissatisfied with the drudgery of investment banking. At first Bob had been skeptical about Jonathan's suggestion to join the Peace Corps, but then had changed his mind. Jonathan described their living conditions, the work they had done, and the people they had met. He talked about their frustrations and triumphs, the rice and beans, the insects and snakes, the trips to the market town for supplies and the Pisco sours they used to drink in excess.

"That's fascinating," Rosie said as she switched tapes in her recorder. "I'm really curious about the senator's spiritual awakening.

From what you tell me, the Peace Corps was not exactly a calling for him. Yet, he came back and set up New Life to save all those babies and he claims to be born again, himself. Was there some 'come to Jesus' moment for him down there? It seems to have changed you. You came back and went to divinity school."

It was noon, but it looked more like early evening. The snow storm had turned into a blizzard, and the steamy windows of the shop were rattling as the wind buffeted them. Jonathan looked at his watch. "Wow. We've been here almost two hours."

Rosie's heart sank. Just one more question, she prayed. "I'm sorry for taking so much of your time. Can we just cover this subject and I'll be on my way."

Jonathan gazed out the window at the stalled traffic. He could barely see across the street. "I don't think you'll be flying out today. This storm's supposed to drop ten to twelve inches. I've got to go home and walk a very old dog. Do you want to join me? The parsonage is close by."

"I would love to join you."

They walked out the door of the shop into the snowy maelstrom. As they headed toward the parsonage, Rosie asked, "So what do you think? Is Hamilton for real? Did he really get right with God?"

"You remind me of my sister, Georgia," Jonathan said. "Would you like to meet her?"

February 15, 2012

"I found her," Billy Short sang in Martha Hamilton's ear as he leaned over and clasped her shoulders from behind. She was sitting on the bench by Marion Randolph's grave. It was sunny and warm. She had kicked off her shoes and was enjoying the feel of the new grass between her toes. The garden had already come to life with early spring blossoms. Yolanda Jackson had helped her walk the short distance to the bench from the end of the wheel chair ramp. Two weeks before, a local contractor had installed three ramps descending from both sides of the east veranda and off the back porch, each leading to a different garden.

Billy gave her a smooch on the cheek and then danced a jig around the bench as he waved his ball cap overhead and hummed the tune of a drinking song he had learned in the army.

Martha cheered, tapping her foot as he danced. Then, she patted the place next to her on the bench. "Sit down, Billy. I know the words to that song. You should be ashamed of yourself." They both laughed, and Billy sat down beside her, giving her a slight shove with his shoulder. She shoved back with more force than he would have expected.

"God, it's good to see you sitting out here," he exclaimed. "You look so much stronger than you did at our last meeting."

"I continue to amaze myself. I love this season. I want to spend as much time in my gardens as possible. It makes me feel so alive."

"Well, your friend is still very much alive." Billy picked up a folder he had set on the ground next to the bench. He opened it and handed it to Martha.

Martha gasped. Looking over her shoulder, Billy said, "She's an attractive woman. Almost as good looking as you, Martha."

Martha studied the color photo, still speechless. Lizzie Hoffmeier was simply dressed in a heavy black overcoat. Her bobbed hair was tinted orange. The stone cottage behind her looked small, but quaint. Finally, she said, "Oh, Lizzie, it's been such a long time."

Billy pulled out his handkerchief and handed it to her as she began to tear up. "It wasn't easy finding her. She's fallen off the grid," he said.

Martha continued to study the photo, entranced. "Where did you find her?"

"Living in a small village in the Scottish highlands under an assumed name. She doesn't leave her house much. Crappy weather. I froze my tail off. She finally came outside to refill her bird feeders."

Martha smiled. "Lizzie always loved birds. It makes me so sad. Over fifty years."

"From what I can piece together, she's calmed down a bit since she wrote you."

"I'm glad to hear it," Martha said. "She was always in trouble, and I had no hope that she would ever change her ways. She was such a free spirit."

Billy took off his ball cap and scratched his head. "That's one way of putting it. She's still on the lam from her last job in 1999. There are several outstanding warrants for her arrest. Grand larceny. And those are just the ones I found in the U.K."

"Oh, dear," Martha sighed. "She would have been..."

"I know. Seventy-five. Amazing, isn't it? Like I say. She's still striking. She lives simply. She has no help and keeps to herself. From what I can tell, she doesn't travel. She has a gentleman caller. A local widower."

"Good for her. Did you learn if she has any children?" Martha asked.

Billy mulled over her question for a moment and then he said. "You tell me."

Martha reddened. "What do you mean?"

Billy shifted on the bench so that he could face her. He took her hand. "Martha, you hired me because I'm good at what I do. Very good. You also hired me because you trust me. It's time to trust me with this. Shortly after you learn that someone's digging into your private life, most probably because your son is running for president, you send me to find your old friend. A friend you haven't seen for over fifty years. Senator Hamilton is fifty-three years old. Shall we talk about the secret between Lizzie and you?"

February 27, 2012

"I don't understand what you're saying," Emily McIntyre said, agitated. She was sitting in the starkly modern executive suite of Bedford Manor's director, Percival Winston. It was a cold winter morning. A whitetail deer nonchalantly meandered past the tinted window wall. Its vaporous breath was illuminated by the first rays of the sun cresting the woods to the east. The doe was foraging for food in a stand of birches near the building, pushing aside the barren leaf cover. Not finding what she wanted, she looked up and stared at the two humans behind the plate glass.

Percival generally was a happy man. He had a cushy job with a beautiful office. He worked for a well-endowed facility, which paid him a substantially above-market salary with good benefits. The staff was top notch, and the residents were, for the most part, docile. Everyone paid their bills on time in full. There were no charity cases at Bedford Manor. At forty-eight, he was coasting toward a comfortable retirement in Florida with his second wife, a woman twenty years younger than his first wife. Percival was a vain man, proud of his moderately puffy six foot frame and his hair plugs, which he actually believed no one noticed. Clearing his throat, he looked up and saw the deer. "Oh, she's back. Beautiful animals, aren't they?" he asked, not expecting an answer. His leather desk chair squeaked.

Emily hissed, "Tell me again what you just said."

Percival cleared his throat again and folded his hands together on top of his immense Italian-designed black marble desk. He leaned forward as if Emily could not hear well. "I said that we have reason to believe your son has impregnated Lily Roach."

"That's not possible!" she declared.

Percival felt a headache coming on. "That was my first reaction, too. We were equally shocked. But the tests are conclusive. It looks like she's about two months along."

"She may be pregnant, but there's no way my Frankie could be the father. I've done my research. Down syndrome males are sterile. Frankie will never be a father."

"We know the odds. It's very, very rare, but there is at least one documented case in the literature. Your son is one in a million."

"How could this happen?" she snapped. Her blood pressure had elevated steeply, and she was feeling sick to her stomach.

Percival's chair squeaked again, a couple of times. He was squirming like a pinned bug. "We suspect it happened over the holidays at the Roaches, although…"

"Although what?" she growled.

"Your son and Lily say that they have continued to have sexual relations since they returned to Bedford."

"This is outrageous," she steamed. "I'm paying you thirty thousand a month to make sure that shit like this does *not* happen."

Percival's face reddened. Emily was his most difficult parent. He knew she'd go nuclear, but he still was not prepared for her ferocity. "I completely understand how you feel, Emily, but part of what you pay for is Bedford's philosophy of empowerment and growth. Our job is to allow your son to develop to his maximum potential. That involves a certain amount of freedom of movement on the premises. We do not watch our residents twenty four/seven. We respect their privacy to a certain degree. It's all set forth in the contract."

"How many times has this happened before?"

"Never."

"How do you know it's Frankie? If she says she's slept with him, she could have slept with half the residents here, and the staff, too, for all I know." Emily could not allow herself to process this information. It was unacceptable. She had long since reconciled herself to Frankie's condition and the pain that went with it. She was not about to go through that trauma again. If it were true, she knew her grandchild would very likely have Down syndrome, too.

"We've given lie detector tests to our staff and interviewed the other residents. The staff is in the clear. They had no idea that Frankie and Lily were that close. It seems that some of the residents were aware of the relationship, but they kept it secret at the couple's request."

"You did all that without talking to me first? It's a wonder I haven't read about it in the newspapers. What about my son's privacy rights? What about mine? What's to prevent someone from telling the press? Don't you realize who I am? There'll be a feeding frenzy if this scandal gets out."

"The staff is obligated by law to preserve Frankie's privacy. And I can't imagine any of our residents talking to the press. We were simply trying to confirm your son's story, one that you seem to doubt." Percival was getting his balls back. By this point in the conversation, he had decided that Bedford Manor might be better off without Frankie McIntyre and his mother. He didn't need this kind of static. "There is no scandal here. Down syndrome adults are capable of forming loving relationships. You should know that Frankie and Lily are talking about getting married, finding employment and living together to raise the baby. I would have thought that your foundation would support couples like them."

Emily was beside herself. Next Christmas' family photo flashed in front of her, including Frankie, Lily and their new special baby, all in McIntyre plaid. Wailing like a banshee, she picked up the nearest object on Percival's desk, a rare Tiffany paperweight, and hurled it at the deer, still watching the humans in their glass zoo. With a solid thud, the safety plate absorbed the blow and then cracked into a mosaic of a hundred crooked spokes radiating outward from the point of impact. The doe was unfazed, but Percival was apoplectic. His favorite paperweight lay in pieces on the floor.

March 2012

"Hello."

"Yes, I'm calling to ask a survey question. Would you hold it against Senator Howard Jensen if you learned that he took part in circle jerks when he was a Boy Scout?"

"No. I mean yes. What?"

"Thank you. I'll put that down as a maybe." Click.

The operator, one of two hundred Young Republicans from

conservative college campuses, screened for their loyalty to the Hamilton campaign, was sitting in a large windowless room in an empty strip mall on the outskirts of Corpus Christi, Texas, repeating a script crafted by Jerry Boston after painstaking market research. The kids worked every evening in their temporary cubicles for five hours, tracking the time zones from east to west, calling key voting districts in states holding their primaries the following week.

For their efforts, the students' airfare, hotel, meals and expenses were paid by a political action committee, Tell the Truth, Jensen, Inc. The collegians were on spring break, and after the calls were made, the PAC hosted a party each night with open bars and music. There were day trips to beaches, water parks and sporting events. Each student signed a loyalty oath, promising to keep secret their work on the survey under penalty of banishment from the party. All of them dutifully recorded the respondents' answers, which were promptly shredded the next morning. None of them knew that a push poll was intended to smear a candidate, not collect valid data.

Senator Jensen, from Minnesota, was giving Bob Hamilton a horse race in the Republican primaries, more than Jerry Boston had expected. Jensen was winning in the Northeast and West coast, losing in the South and mountain states and breaking even in the Midwest. More than half the delegates had already been selected in February, and the numbers were evenly split. Bob had a slight lead, but many of the primaries yet to be held were toss-ups. Jerry had to dig deep in his bag of dirty tricks to poison the electorate, keep Jensen supporters home, motivate Hamilton voters and turn off undecideds to the whole process.

There was a glimmer of truth in the survey question. One member of Jensen's scout troop had gone on to play professional baseball and had come out of the closet after he had retired. He had just published a book, ghost written by one of Jerry's operatives, and funded by yet another obscure PAC, claiming, among other things, that members of his troop took part regularly in circle jerks on campouts at Lake Minnesaukenauk when the boys were eleven and twelve. Named as one of his fellow troop members, but not specifically labeled as a participant in the jack-off fests, was the senior senator from Minnesota, Howard Jensen, an Eagle Scout and a member of the esteemed Order of the Arrow.

Reports of the scandal first hit the internet bloggers and then swept like wildfire through Fox News, the radio screamers and the late night talk show monologues. Soon, there were child psychologists debating the pros and cons of group masturbation by prepubescent boys on National Public Radio programs. One caller told the therapists he remembered that the Boy Scout handbook at that time discussed nocturnal emissions at page 702, wondering perhaps if the paramilitary organization was subliminally endorsing what he thought was a fairly common scouting phenomenon. "The National Jamborees were amazing!" he said. "Twenty thousand boys in tents for a week. Things were bound to happen."

The news cycle lasted six days before Senator Jensen appeared on the Sunday morning talk shows with the ex-baseball star, next to him, admitting that he could not remember the senator being present at even one of the contests to see who could ejaculate first into the bonfire. Unfortunately for Jensen, other troop members, held in reserve by Tell the Truth, Jensen, Inc., appeared on *Sixty Minutes* that night confirming shamefully that they took part in some of the self abuse tournaments and that Jensen most certainly was present and perhaps even a ring leader. Innocent photos of the troop members frolicking in the lake, wearing little more than skimpy bathing trunks, were soon making their way across the internet. Grainy footage of half naked boys singing Kum Ba Yah My Lord around a campfire, their arms wrapped over one another's shoulders, smiling and giggling, as if they were keeping a secret from the scoutmaster filming them, was posted on YouTube the next day. Viewers saw what they wanted. Young boys enjoying their innocent camaraderie on a warm night during 1967's Summer of Love. Or over-sexed young men swaying side to side in some homoerotic ritualistic prelude to a night of debauchery. "Orgiastic Saturnalia!!!" one scandal sheet screamed on its cover page, with an enhanced close-up of twelve-year-old Howard Jensen, seemingly leering at the crotch of one of his fellow onanists. Copies of the gossip rag, sat prominently, dog-eared from repeated readings, on ten million racks next to the checkout lines of Wal-Mart, Costco, CVS and dozens of other grocery and drug store chains.

By the following Tuesday, every American above the age of six not in a coma had heard the story. The Hamilton for President Campaign disavowed any connection to Tell the Truth, Jensen, Inc., and Bob Hamilton personally condemned the tactics used by TTTJ, though he was careful not to challenge the truth of the story, and he declined to answer questions about his own juvenile participation in communal wanking festivals as an inappropriate subject for his family values campaign. Later that night, at campaign headquarters in Washington, D.C., Jerry Boston walked out of a huddle of his exit pollsters and strode into Bob's office with a big smile on his face. Bob was sitting on his sofa in his shirtsleeves, watching Fox News coverage of the primary results. He was alone, as he preferred to be on election nights since Robert III's death.

"We've done it, Bobby! We just took Texas. That gives us a majority of the convention delegates." Jerry looked at his watch. "I'd say give it forty-five minutes to let the networks catch up with our exit polls, another fifteen minutes for Jensen to concede and then you can go out and make your victory statement."

Bob jumped up smiling and gave Jerry a bear hug. "Thanks, Jerry. You're amazing. I wish I could name you my vice-president."

Jerry snorted. "No, thanks. I'll stick with Chief of Staff. We've got to find a new running mate, though. I thought you could tap Jensen, but he's too dirty now. I'll come up with a list tomorrow."

"Whoever we pick, we need to pass him by McIntyre this time. She was pissed that we were going to go with Jensen."

Jerry managed to keep from sneering. "She's got to understand we need to balance the ticket. We can't pick your clone. Jensen would have been perfect. A moderate Midwesterner. Now we've got to find someone with his profile."

"She's the reason we won tonight. Or at least she thinks she is. What if she turns against us? Or tells her people to stay home?"

"Bob, she has no other horse to ride at this point. She's picked you. She's stuck with you. Especially after tonight. We'll be nice about it, but we're not giving her a veto. She's not running this campaign. Not yet, anyway."

March 26, 2012

"Just don't answer any questions about our sex life," Bob Hamilton said to his wife, Kathleen, on his cell phone. He was in his hotel room in Beverly Hills, preparing for a day of fundraising with Hollywood's conservative elite, an older, mostly male crowd. Chuck Norris was hosting a $2500 a seat luncheon for him in a couple hours at the Beverly Wilshire Hotel.

Back in Druid Hills, Kathleen was not happy. "This is the last interview I'm doing for you. I don't know why I agreed."

Bob smiled. "I think it's because you lost a bet. You said I couldn't make you cum three times. You were complaining about menopause, blah, blah, blah. We rang the bell four times, as I remember."

Kathleen was standing in the kitchen watching Rosie Gibson sniffing the lilacs in the back yard. Rosie was wearing a loose fitting pink jersey sleeveless dress. She'd taken her shoes off and left them at the edge of the terrace with her purse and notebook. "I remember, but you tricked me. We've always paid back those bets with more sex. This is not fair. I should tell her why I'm doing the interview. Then, the whole country will realize I'm your sex slave."

Bob was studying the face book of the wealthy fading stars he would be meeting at the luncheon. "If you do that, be sure to mention you're over fifty and that you came four times. I'll have every woman over thirty voting for me."

"Very funny. Why don't you want to talk to her?"

"Because she's a radical black lesbian. The *Post* is out to get me. That's the only reason they assigned her to me. All she wants to do is make me look bad. I'll have to give her an interview eventually, but for now, she's willing to take you."

"So I'm the sacrificial lamb, huh?"

"I'm sorry. I'll make it up to you when I get home. We'll go for five this time."

An hour later, the two women were sitting on the terrace in the shade, drinking iced tea and laughing at stories about the children in their lives, Kathleen's kids and Rosie's nephews and niece.

"And then Rob said he was going to be Robert the Last," Kathleen said. "Poor little boy. He was only five. He couldn't understand why we couldn't think up a different name. For the next six months, he insisted we call him David. His middle name. But when he realized it was his father's and grandfather's middle name, too, he gave up."

"I sympathize," Rosie said. "I wasn't happy being named for Rosa Parks for the first twenty years of my life. Finally, in my African American history class in college, it dawned on me what an incredible honor it was to bear her name. Maybe your son will appreciate his name when he gets older."

"We'll see. He'll be twenty this year. He says he's not having kids."

Rosie took a sip of her tea. "I've got one last area to cover. What can you tell me about Jonathan Jones?"

"Who?"

"Reverend Jonathan Jones. He has a church in Detroit. He was in the Peace Corps with your husband."

"Hmmm. Bob's never mentioned him. He told me all about his work in Peru. Maybe he mentioned him once. When we first met. But they must not have been very close, or I would have heard more about him."

Rosie shrugged. "Probably so. I'll ask the senator when I get a chance."

That night, while she was dining on Chinese carry out with Natalie Jordan at their kitchen table, Rosie asked, "Don't you think it's odd? That he'd spend two years living cheek to jowl with the man and never mention him to his wife? And never contact him, not even once in over twenty years?" Their cats, fluffy black Latifah and fluffy white Henrietta, were perched on empty chairs at the table, watching the women intently, hoping that some of the cashew chicken and catfish stir fry would make it into their bowls.

"Maybe they didn't get along. Maybe he's a racist like his daddy." Natalie picked through her rice with her chop sticks, looking for morsels of catfish.

"No, Jones says they got along. He only has nice things to say about Hamilton. Though he was no help on his spiritual awakening. He says Hamilton was very private about his faith."

"Maybe they got along too well." Natalie continued to search.

Rosie sipped her chardonnay and smiled. "Nah, the world would be too perfect if that were true."

Chapter 13

March 2012

Roger Webber cashed his government welfare check at the currency exchange and then dropped by the corner bar to pick up a pack of Marlboro Lights and a draft of Miller Lite. "Hello handsome," he said as he batted his eyes at Kenny Pickett. Roger slid onto the barstool closest to the cash register, where Kenny posted himself unless a customer needed him. The bar was empty. The lunch crowd had left, and the afternoon drunks weren't due for another hour.

"How's my boyfriend?" Kenny asked, smiling. He was a young man who had fled Canada's Northwest Territories after high school for the big city of Toronto. Half Inuit, half white, he had the sloped brow and straight black hair of his mother and the blue eyes of his father. Roger thought he was "the most beautiful racial mix on earth." The compliment had been good for a free beer the first time Roger had proclaimed it, and a little extra attention after that. Kenny was unwaveringly heterosexual, and the bar itself, Coughlin's Tap, was not particularly gay friendly. But Roger still favored it because Kenny would flirt with him, privately, just for fun. Roger thought there was a slim, slim chance Kenny was curious. Kenny was simply bored with his job and amused at the specter of this obese older man thinking that he might someday get lucky.

"Never better," Roger answered. "Life is a cabaret. I leave for Paris in the morning."

Kenny set the beer and cigarettes in front of Roger. "Oh, yeah? You gonna bring back a souvenir for me?"

"Why yes. What would you like? Wine? Cheese? How about a fancy suit? I'd have to measure you for that. We'll start with your inseam. Do you hang right or left?"

Kenny gave Roger his change. "How about a beret? I think I'd look good in a beret."

"You would look marvelous in a beret. But it should be a bright color to set off your hair. Maybe a cherry red."

"Get me a black one."

Roger sipped his beer. "No, I think cherry red. It would bring out your pouty red lips." Just then, the door opened and in walked a burly man in a black leather bomber jacket and ripped jeans. "Who's that?" Roger asked. The gentleman had a brown mullet and a red beard. He sat down two stools over from Roger, smelling like old leather and gasoline.

"Beats me," Kenny said and went to take his order.

After Kenny served him a Guinness Stout, Roger lifted his glass and said, "Cheers."

The man looked over at Roger as if he were seeing him for the first time and nodded before he chugged his beer. Then, he slid his glass toward Kenny for a refill.

"You're not from these parts, are you, stranger?" Roger asked in his best John Wayne.

It turned out that the man in the leather coat was Clem Mitchell from Manitoba. He'd just arrived in Toronto after riding his Harley-Davidson cross country for three days. Hoping to find work, he had made plans to stay with a friend, but his friend's shift wouldn't end until five, so he was killing time. He was more talkative than Roger would have guessed and was soon regaling Roger and Kenny with stories of riding herd out west on a cattle ranch.

"So you're a real cowboy?" Roger asked. "I've never met a real cowboy. How exciting!"

Clem smiled. "I'm the genuine article." Kenny went to take an order from the first of the afternoon drunks, and Clem leaned toward Roger and asked, "Would you like to find out how a real cowboy does it?"

Roger wasn't sure he'd heard right. It had been years since he'd been propositioned. "Excuse me?"

"I'd ride you hard and put you up wet. Would you like that?" Clem winked at him and stroked his crotch, which, Roger had already noticed. It was a very full basket.

"I'm not sure. It's been awhile. You might have to start out slow. Break me in again."

Clem stood and lightly slapped Roger's ample rump. "What's the matter? Your cherry grown back?" Clem placed his palm on Roger's back and left it there, as if he were one of Roger's oldest friends.

Roger made a barely audible moan. It had been a very, very long time since any man had done that. Touched him in a familiar way. Without being paid. Roger reached down and grabbed Clem. He wasn't hard, but he was packing a python. "I'm afraid it has grown back," Roger said. "I'm not sure I could handle all that. How big are you?"

Clem massaged Roger's shoulders with both hands as he leaned forward and whispered in his ear. "Nine inches. Thick as a beer can." He pressed his crotch against Roger's butt crack.

"Well, I can't say no to that, can I?" Roger climbed off his bar stool, and the two men turned to head out the door, Clem's hand on Roger's shoulder.

"Roger, you forgot your change," Kenny called.

"Keep it, Kenny. See you tomorrow."

Roger didn't see Kenny for a month. Just inside the door of Roger's dingy little studio apartment, Clem flattened Roger with a sucker punch. Then, he kicked Roger in his groin and face until he was sure the fat man was in too much pain to move. After yanking Roger's wallet from his back pocket, he pulled out every drawer of his bureau and dressing table. He lifted his mattress and tore through his shoe boxes. All he could find was Roger's stash of pot. "Where's your money," he growled at Roger.

"You've got it all," Roger whimpered. "Please don't take it. That's all I have." He had curled into a fetal position in a puddle of his own urine.

Clem picked up Roger's jewelry box and dumped the contents on the floor by Roger's head. Dropping to his knees, he pulled on Roger's ear hard. "Is any of this shit worth anything?"

"No," Roger cried. "It's cheap costume stuff."

"What else you got?"

"Nothing!" Roger screamed.

Clem whacked Roger's head with the wooden jewelry box and then pummeled him with his fists. Finally, exhausted by his efforts, he let up. Standing, Clem gave Roger one more kick in his ribs and snarled, "Keep your mouth shut, faggot, or I'll come back and kill you, you hear me?"

Barely conscious, Roger nodded as blood dribbled out of his mouth and shit filled his drawers. An hour later, Roger came to. He was in agony, and he couldn't lift his head without the pain becoming unbearable. Scooting on his back to the door, he managed to reach the knob and unlatch it before he passed out again. When his neighbor, Florence Wort, came home from work, she saw the door ajar and caught a whiff of Roger's feces. Putting down her grocery bags, she tiptoed across the hall and peered through the crack in the door. Roger was an unpleasant sort, and she was afraid he would accuse her of spying if he caught her. When she saw the blood on the floor, she gasped and jumped back from the door. Twenty minutes later, as her butter brickle ice cream melted, she watched four beefy paramedics struggling to heft Roger's body onto a stretcher. Police officers held back her murmuring neighbors who had gathered for the show, as a handsome young detective asked her, "Did Mr. Webber have a habit of bringing home rough trade, ma'am?"

Roger had a broken jaw, broken nose, two broken front teeth, two black eyes, a concussion, three cracked ribs, a ruptured spleen, a badly bruised scrotum and a badly bruised ego to boot. When he got out of the hospital, he papered over his dressing table and bathroom mirrors with male centerfolds. He couldn't stand to look at what he had become. With his two front teeth missing, and a six month wait under the Canadian health care system for a dental appointment to get measured for a bridge, he stopped going to Manhole on Saturday nights. He'd long since given up nursing even one overpriced drink, but he had cherished still the illusion of a nightlife, as he stood in a dark corner and lusted after the beautiful young men parading past him.

His mother, Bernice, had come for his hospital stay, and his sister, Elaine, had come to help out for the first week of his convalescence at home. Elaine didn't mention his moving to Vancouver because she wasn't sure anymore that she wanted him living close by. She had given up hope that Roger would ever climb back out of his abyss. When she left to go home, he cried. Sitting at his dressing table, he looked up at his old London photo, now outflanked by Lance and Rourke, tanned California boys smiling on a white sand beach without a stitch of clothing or a care in the world. He threw himself a kiss, too humiliated to hear himself speak without his incisors. Lowering the shades, he took a Vicodin, crawled into bed and pulled the covers over his head.

April 1, 2012

As Roger Webber was falling asleep, Josh Stein was sitting on his sun porch in Bondi Beach, his feet propped up on a second chair, flipping through the Sunday edition of *Sydney Morning Herald*. He smiled when he came to an article entitled, *"Four men attacked in Darlinghurst."* The article read:

> In what appears to have been an unprovoked attack late Saturday night, four men, ranging in age from twenty-two to thirty-six, were beaten unconscious and then stripped of their

clothing in an alley just meters from the busy Oxford Street night life at the heart of Sydney's gay community. Carved on each victim's forehead, right pectoral and left buttock was a crude X. All four victims were admitted to St. Vincent's Hospital. Two are in critical but stable condition and two are in fair condition. At least one of the victims is a member of the White Australian Resistance, wanted for questioning in the 2006 hate crime murder of Bondi Beach resident, Mark Cross. Despite the throngs of locals and tourists present in the neighborhood at the time of the attack, police have been unable to find any witnesses. Names of the victims are being withheld pending contact of their next of kin.

Josh took a sip of his coffee, winced slightly as he shifted the ice bag on his right foot and turned to the books section.

April 6-8, 2012

"Hey Grandma, how are you doing?" Robert Hamilton V asked. Martha Hamilton was sitting by Marion Randolph's grave. It was Good Friday, and the rest of the family had gone to the three o'clock service at the First Baptist Church in Booneville. Robert V had begged off, claiming he had a headache.

"I'm doing fine, Rob. How's your headache?"

"It's much better." He sat down next to her. "Do you miss him a lot?" Robert V was a tall athletic young man with his father's dark curly hair and his mother's blue eyes.

Martha nodded. "Yes, but not so much since the stroke. I feel like we're closer now. It won't be long." Shoeless, she was wearing a simple pale blue smock.

"Don't talk like that. We still need you here. Marion will understand."

Martha put her arm around his broad shoulders. "Well, when you put it that way, I guess I could stick around for a little longer."

Robert V was finishing up his second year at Duke with straight A's in a pre-med curriculum. He had been back-up quarterback for the football team the first two seasons, but, with the starting quarterback graduating, Robert V was slated to take his spot in the fall. He had just finished spring practice and was still sore from the hits he had taken the week before. In shorts, tank top and sandals, he looked like an MTV version of Rodin's The Thinker as he leaned forward, elbow on his knee, his chin resting on his knuckles. Martha knew this mood. Her grandson had something to say, but he wasn't quite ready to say it.

"So I hear Martha's going to Berkeley," Martha said to take off the pressure.

"Yeah, she wants to get as far away as possible."

"Why is that, do you think?"

"She can't stand Dad's politics, and she's tired of being part of the perfect American family. She's always arguing with Dad. She told him she thought he was a big fake."

Martha smiled. "So, he's got two Marthas hounding him." She loved all of her grandchildren, but she particularly liked Martha's spirit. A pretty brunette, the younger Martha refused to wear makeup or conform to Southern female conventions. She was a rabid feminist, environmentalist and anti-capitalist who planned to study political science so that she could run for office and oppose her father's policies. She had enjoyed casual sex with a couple boys in high school, but she wasn't particularly enamored with the institution of marriage. She thought it was anachronistic, and she didn't like what it had done to her mother, Kathleen.

"Don't get me wrong," Robert V said. "She's not out to hurt Dad or anything. She just wants out."

Martha nodded. "She wants to create her own identity. I remember. I was the same way."

"Yeah, and she thinks Mary's clueless because she sucks up to Dad so much."

"How is Mary? She told me all about her little sports car, but not much else."

"Yeah, she got her way with Dad on that one. She wanted a convertible for her birthday and Mom said no, but when she and Dad came home from the dealer, she had her rag top."

"A bright red BMW, I think she told me."

"Yeah, she wanted a baby blue Ferrari, but Dad wouldn't pop for the extra twenty grand. Martha didn't want a car when she turned sixteen. She goes everywhere on a bike or bus. So, I think Dad wanted to indulge Mary."

"What else is she up to?"

"She's playing tennis for Lovett this season. And I hear she's been dating some of the football players. Mom's been riding her to study more and party less. Martha's convinced she'll get knocked up before she gets out of high school."

"Oh, my. That would be a headline." Martha tried hard to stifle a laugh.

Still hunched forward, Robert V was gently rocking up and down on the balls of his feet. He was just about ready, Martha thought.

"I've been reading through your novels again this week," he said.

"Really? I'm flattered. Do they improve or get worse on a second reading?"

"I'm older now, so I'm enjoying them more. I missed a lot of stuff the first time. I didn't realize how many gay characters were in your books."

"Ah, yes, when I first started writing, it was necessary to be more subtle when alluding to certain sexual orientations."

"Why did you write about so many gay characters?"

"Well, because they're part of life. They've been part of my life."

Robert V sat back and looked at her. "Really? Like who?"

"Like my sister, for one. Your grandfather's mother. My best friend in Washington. Countless others."

"You're kidding. Dad's never said anything about any of them."

"That figures. I tried to teach your father to be open-minded, but your grandfather had more influence on that issue, I'm afraid."

"Yeah, he gets pissed off when Mom talks about Uncle Jack. Like we're not supposed to know he's gay. I think it's partly because Mom is so fond of him."

"Well, it doesn't fit very neatly with his political agenda."

"I know. Tell me about your sister and the others."

"Well, I'll start with your great-grandmother, Lillian Clay Hamilton. She was from a genteel Virginia family that had lost its wealth in the Civil War. She gave the Hamilton fortune class and taught Robert Jr. how to behave like a gentleman. He was a gregarious, hard-working, womanizing man. But, Lillian didn't mind his indiscretions because she preferred the company of women. She traveled to rural North Carolina twice a year to visit a childhood friend who had never married, Beryl Riggins. When Lillian's Parkinson's disease became advanced, your grandfather moved her into a home. He refused to believe his mother was a lesbian and tried to keep Beryl from visiting, but I arranged for visits and even sleepovers behind his back. She was there when Lillian died."

"And your sister?" Robert V asked.

"Ah, Charlotte. Your great aunt was the sweetest human being I've ever known. She was the good girl and I was the bad girl growing up. I couldn't be like her, so I was the anti-Charlotte for many years. We weren't close until I came back from boarding school in Switzerland. My parents had banished me to St. Gert's, hoping I would reform."

"What had you done?"

Martha smiled. "Let's just say I was too friendly with too many boys. I thought it was the perfect way to get back at Mother. But enough about me. Charlotte became my hero when she dropped out of Bryn Mawr to go to nursing school. We weren't in the war yet, but they needed nurses in England, and she wanted to help out. My mother was beside herself. Nursing was too pedestrian for her perfect daughter. Bedpans and sponge baths and all that. To make matters worse, by the time Charlotte graduated in forty-two, we were in the war, and she joined the Women's Army Auxiliary. In those days, many people thought women who joined the military had loose morals, preying on the husbands and boyfriends of the virtuous women back home."

"I'd always heard a lot of them were lesbians," Robert V offered, with a smile.

"Little did we know at the time. Apparently, my sister died in the arms of her lover, a nice Jewish girl from Des Moines, named Darla, when a German bomber crashed near their encampment. The impact of the explosion toppled an old tree which fell on their tent as they slept. In northern Italy. I didn't know about Charlotte and Darla until after the memorial service when I received a letter from my sister. She'd written it the day before she had died. She was so happy. Darla and she had made plans to move to California after the war. I was destroyed by Charlotte's death, but knowing that she had fallen in love made the pain somewhat more bearable."

"I can't imagine losing Martha or Mary," Robert V said, staring at the ground.

"What made it worse for me was that I was still grieving the loss of my best friend at the OSS. Ramsey McAllister. I fell in love with him the first day on the job. He brought me a dozen pink roses. I had just graduated from Wellesley, and Daddy had wangled me a job with the spy agency because I could read and write German. Ramsey was the most gorgeous man. Forty and unmarried. I should have known."

Robert V looked up. "Known what?"

"That he was gay. I figured it out. Intuitively, I guess. He admitted it, finally, and then it was our secret. We carried on like a couple. It gave him cover and it kept my mother off my back. She was pushing your grandfather at me, urging me to marry him, worried there wouldn't be any men left by the end of the war. Our fathers were best friends. Old southern families, same social circles. So Mother was scandalized when I told her I was dating Ramsey. He was twice my age."

"What happened to him?" Robert V was staring at the ground again.

Martha's eyes moistened. She sighed. "Poor Ramsey. He took me to his cabin on Maryland's eastern shore for Labor Day weekend. It was 1944. On the way there, he told me a friend would be joining us. Tucker Lawrence. An old school chum from Yale. They were on the rowing team and later roommates and then lovers. After school, they saw each other barely once a year at their parents' summer homes. Ramsey told me they had broken up a dozen times over the years, but Tuck had always come back, hoping Ramsey would someday choose him over his career."

"Why couldn't they be together?"

"In those days, being gay in the government, especially in a job like Ramsey's was grounds for immediate dismissal. The thinking was homosexuals were subject to blackmail by foreign agents. They would betray their country to keep their secret. And so, that weekend, at Ramsey's cabin, some of Hoover's men were in the bushes, snapping photos of Ramsey and Tuck kissing on the porch swing. What Hoover didn't know was that Ramsey had a friend at the FBI who told him about the photos. He didn't wait for the agents to arrest him. He put a gun in his mouth and pulled the trigger."

Robert V stood up and shoved his hands in his pockets. "God, that's horrible!"

"It was horrible," Martha said as she looked up at her grandson. "He was such a sweet man. I was devastated. To make it worse, I had to sit through several hours of grilling by the FBI. They wanted to know every nasty detail about Ramsey and Tuck. I lied. I told them that Ramsey and I had been sleeping together." Martha smiled. "Hoover was furious. I'm sure he kept a file on me until the day he died."

Robert V sat down. The two of them looked out at the water in silence, the frail old woman and the college athlete. Then, Robert very calmly said, "Grandma, I'm gay."

She patted him on his knee. "Thank you for telling me, Rob. I'm happy for you."

"Why? It's my father's nightmare. And mine too, playing football. You can't be gay and play college football."

"I'm happy that at your young age, you can say out loud who you really are. My sister, my mother-in-law, my friend, Ramsey. They didn't think they could."

"Well, I'm not exactly out. To anybody. Except for you. And one guy I talk to online. We haven't met yet. I'm scared to meet him actually. If it ever gets out, I'm dead at Duke. They'll find some way to kick me off the team."

"A senator's son? I doubt that."

"What if Dad wins the election? I was thinking I'd come out after I left Duke, but how do I do that if he's the family values president? I wish he wasn't in politics."

"Me, too. Well, maybe he won't win. Have you told your mother?"

"No, not yet. I'm afraid if I tell her, she'll tell Dad, and I'm not ready for that."

"Why don't we talk to her together? I'm sure I could convince her to hold off telling your father."

The next evening, Bob and Kathleen Hamilton drove into Booneville for dinner at the old Booneville Hotel. It recently had been refurbished for the growing number of tourists coming to town to see the Old South. Bob had reserved a private room for a romantic meal of what passed for haute cuisine south of Savannah. Back at Sea Haven, the kids were busy making pizzas with Yolanda Jackson, Jim Pike and Martha. It was Saturday pizza night, the kids' favorite meal at Grandma's house.

"How can you ruin a sirloin steak?" Bob asked his wife as he tried to cut his meat.

"I told you to get the fish. It's delicious. I'm surprised. I expected everything on the menu to be deep fried. Here. Have some of mine. Why don't you send it back?"

He sipped his pinot noir and made a face. "I can't complain. Whatever I say will be on the internet before we finish dessert, and I'll be painted as the boorish millionaire whose tastes are too highfalutin for the people."

"But you are a boorish millionaire with highfalutin tastes."

"George Bush ruined it for the rest of us. We all have to act like we love barbeque and potato salad."

"Well, you can always drop out of the race. Then, you can eat whatever you want. And send back overcooked steak anytime you want."

"Don't kid, Kathleen. I've come too far. I want this. Very much."

"I'm not kidding. I know this is what you want, but it's no life for me. I never see you anymore. And, I can't even listen when you start talking about gays like they're perverts. My brother is not a pervert."

"Your brother is a piece of work, gay or straight."

"There's nothing wrong with my brother. Kathleen took a sip of her pinot grigio. Her face was red and she was close to tears. "Bob, I can't do it. I don't want to be the First Lady. I don't want our kids to have to live in the White House. I'm afraid if you win, I'll have to get a divorce."

Bob stopped chewing his tough meat and swallowed it whole. "This is Mother's doing, isn't it? She's put you up to this?"

"No, this has nothing to do with your mother."

"Kathleen, why now? Why wait until after I've clenched the nomination to pull this on me?"

"I've always felt this way, but I've reached my breaking point."

Bob sat back and scratched his forehead. "All right, all right. Let's take a deep breath. The president is very popular. The chances of my winning in November are less than fifty-fifty. Let's make a deal. If I win, you divorce me. If I lose, I will drop out of politics altogether. It will kill me because the two things I want most, I can't have together. But I love you. And I don't want you to stay with me if you're unhappy."

"Really, you would do that? Give up politics?"

"Yes. If I can't be president, I don't want to stay in the Senate."

"If that's the deal, I'll take it. But you know who I'll be voting for."

Bob sighed and pushed away his plate with a weak smile. "Of course, I wouldn't expect you to change now."

As they were driving home, Kathleen said, "I keep forgetting to ask you. That reporter was interested in some guy named Jones from your Peace Corps days. He's a minister in Detroit now. How come you've never mentioned him?"

"Oh, I don't know. We didn't have much in common. By the end of two years, we were barely speaking. I haven't thought about him in years."

The next morning, Easter Sunday, Martha was on the east veranda in her night gown, wrapped in a shawl, watching the sun rise over the Atlantic. She was proud of herself for having made the entire trip unassisted from her bedroom with her walker. She was stroking Sassy and nuzzling against her soft head when Bob walked out the door in his slippers and bathrobe.

"Mom, how long have you been up?" He sat down beside her on the wicker settee.

"Oh, not long, maybe a half hour. When you get older, you can't sleep as well. Watch, I'll need a nap after lunch. What's your excuse?"

"I couldn't sleep. Dinner wasn't very pleasant last night. Kathleen's pretty upset with me."

"That's what I hear. And?"

"We've made a compromise, but I'd rather not discuss it."

"Fair enough. Is there anything else you would like to talk about? Anything at all?"

A nearly undetectable flash of uncertainty crossed his face. He broke eye contact briefly. To prepare the lie, she suspected. And then, the smile. It was the same as his first smile as an infant. Broad and engaging. Except that it was no longer innocent. It now carried an invitation to false intimacy. "No, Mother, I can't think of anything. Is there something you want to tell me?"

Billy Short had told Martha that the Hamilton campaign had hired Harris Security International and that it was Harris who had bugged her house, tapped her phones and hired the odious Reverend Bingham to pry a confession out of her. Martha patted his knee, "No, just that I love you."

April 25, 2012

"How would you like to go on holiday?" Lizzie Hoffmeier asked her boyfriend, Andrew McClintock.

"I'd like that very much. Where should we go? Edinburgh? London?" The couple was canoodling after making love in Lizzie's cottage. They were nestled under a down comforter in Lizzie's bed on a brisk evening. Outside her cottage, her bird feeders were swaying in the strong breeze, and waves were lapping the shore of Lochbroom in the tiny fishing village of Ullapool, Scotland.

"I was thinking Spain. On the Costa del Sol." Lizzie's face had been nipped and tucked a couple times, but underneath her flannel nightie, she was drooping in the usual places for a woman soon to be eighty-eight.

"Sounds lovely, but it's a might pricey for a poor fisherman." At seventy-seven, Andrew was still strong and lean from years at sea. He'd retired ten years before and given his fishing boat to his two sons, but he still went out on occasion when they were short-handed.

"This would be my treat. I have a home in Marbella. All you'd have to do is cook for me." She was running her fingers through the hair on his chest as she nibbled on his earlobe.

"Hen, how many homes do you have?" His salt and pepper hair was an unruly thatch, made more so by their lovemaking.

"Just the two," she answered. "I haven't been down there since we met, and I'd like for you to come with me."

They'd bumped into each other at the village library two years before. He had been looking for history and she had been looking for a Martha Boone novel. He'd lost his wife, Anna, five years before and he'd been in mourning ever since. His older son, Leif, had worried about him losing weight and losing interest in life in general. Anna had been the love of his life, and both sons had been surprised, but delighted when he had taken up with Lizzie.

"You've been keeping secrets from me," he said as he tickled her chin.

"Oh, there's a lot you don't know about me." She reached down and caressed his flaccid member.

"You're a lady of mystery, that's for sure."

"That's the way you like it. I keep things interesting." She was slowly stroking him, thankful for the wonders of the little blue pill.

She had stalked Andrew for months. There was something about his manner, his sad soul that had touched her. At the library, she had practically knocked him over to get his attention. "I'm so sorry. Are you all right?" she had asked. When he had reassured her that he was fine, she had asked, "May I buy you a cup of tea?"

He had smiled, flattered. "You're not from here, are you?"

April 28, 2012

"Hamilton called me today," Jonathan Jones announced to his sister, Georgia. They were walking his dog, Zeke, on a warm spring night in Detroit.

"No kidding. What did he want?"

"He was very nice, apologized for not staying in touch, asked what I'd been up to. Then he said I may be getting calls from the press because he's running for president, says he's sorry for the inconvenience, and then he asked if anyone had contacted me."

"What did you tell him?"

"I told him I'd talked to Rosie Gibson."

"What did he say to that?"

Jonathan shook his head and chuckled. Zeke stopped to sniff a locust tree and lift his leg. "He got very nervous. What did she want to know? What did we talk about?"

Georgia put her hands on her hips. "What did you say?"

"I said he didn't need to worry. I would never discuss the nights we used to go drinking."

"Jonathan Jones, I can't understand why you want to help him. At least let him sweat for being stupid enough to call you."

"I know. I felt like shit afterward."

"What did he say then?"

"Oh, he was very appreciative. 'Thank you so much, Jonathan. I can't tell you how much I'm indebted to you. I won't forget this.'"

Georgia shook her head. "I'm blaming you if that man becomes president."

April 30, 2012

"I tried the new drug on him last night," Angela Patterson reported to her boss, Phinneas Graves. The two of them were sitting in Phinneas' office at CIA headquarters in Langley, Virginia. It was her weekly briefing about Pat McCormack.

"Oh, yes? How did that go?"

"I asked him about the Hamilton campaign. It's the only project he's working on these days. It was pretty garbled. He's very upset because Harris has been losing so much money on the assignment. Some kind of promise he made to Jerry Boston. It has to do with a woman named Elizabeth Hoffmeier, a friend of Hamilton's mother. Apparently, Hoffmeier was the maid of honor at his parents' wedding in 1945, and McCormack has been trying to locate her."

"That name rings a bell." Phinneas flipped through a file on his desk. "I thought so. Martha Hamilton used the agency to track down

Hoffmeier several times in the fifties." Phinneas licked his lips. "Do you suppose they were lovers?"

Angela giggled. "You're too much, Phinneas. You're so old school."

Phinneas blushed. "How do you mean?"

"You're always looking for lavender love. Like that's the biggest secret anyone could ever have. It's cute, actually."

Phinneas twiddled his wedding ring and cleared his throat. "It's strictly a professional curiosity. When I started out, it *was* the biggest secret."

"Well, I don't think that's what McCormack is looking for. As I say, he wasn't completely clear. He was very guarded about it even under the drug. That's his agency training. The drug must not be as good as the contractor promised."

"That wouldn't be the first time. Remember their amnesia drug? What a bust."

"I think it's much bigger than a lesbian love affair," Angela continued. "And I don't peg Martha Hamilton for a dyke. We know her marriage was a cover for her work with the agency, but I'll bet she was doing the black guy. The stable boy. They were very close."

Phinneas smiled as he stroked his chin. "Really? That must have been hot."

Chapter 14

May 1, 2012

They had just finished lunch when Billy Short said, "They know you're not his mother."

The words hit Martha Hamilton like bullets. It was as if a half century of motherhood had been repealed. She had been exposed as a fraud. "How do you know?" she asked. They were sitting in lounge chairs on the beach at Sea Haven under a big blue and white striped umbrella. She'd installed a motorized chair lift on the stairs to the beach, and Billy had carried her to the umbrella. It was a sunny day and the sea was calm. Perfect for a picnic by the water.

"They've been searching hospital records, adoption agency records, birth certificate files. They're focusing on 1958, the year the senator was born."

"They won't find anything. I made sure of that." Martha's mind was racing, wondering where she had slipped up.

"They met with a guy who flew in from Zurich, ex-German intelligence."

"Oh, dear." She remembered Franz's devilish smile.

"What?"

"Somehow they found out about my abortion." The stains on Dr. Klein's vest came to her, and then the pain. "What a shock for Bob. He must hate me for lying to him all these years." She remembered holding him for the first time. "I feel terrible. I wanted to tell him myself."

Billy flipped a page in his notes. "They've been looking at old newspaper files at the Booneville library, focusing on the 1940's."

"What could that be about?" A hermit crab scuttling across the wet sand stopped to check them out and then hurried on its way.

"Finally, they've put out feelers to find your friend, Lizzie Hoffmeier. Here and in Europe."

"Damn, I thought I'd been so careful. How did they know?" She remembered the last time she'd seen her old friend. She'd kissed her good-bye at the farmhouse near Hamilton Oaks.

Billy shrugged. "They may not know. They may just be running down leads. They're still trying to track down your friends from Miss Porter's and Wellesley."

"There's not many of them left."

"But we've got a problem. If I can find Lizzie, so can they. And they're also going to find out about her arrest warrants. These guys are blunt instruments. They want information and they don't care how they get it."

"You think they might threaten her?" She remembered the fear in Lizzie's voice when she'd called to tell Martha she was pregnant. Two seagulls started squawking over a dead fish at the edge of the surf.

"It wouldn't take much to scare her. She didn't pick Ullapool for the weather. She's hiding from the law. From what you tell me, she's excitable. She's not young any more. I think we need to tell her what's going on."

"She'll disappear again, won't she?"

"Probably. I could tell her what this is all about and that if he doesn't win the election, they'll lose interest, and I could help her get a new passport and find her a safe place to stay for the time being. Maybe you could cover her expenses for a few months."

"Of course. I wish she could come stay with me. I miss her so."

"That would be nice. Maybe after the election. Presuming he loses."

"Heaven help us if he wins."

"I better get going. I need to pack for Ullapool. Godforsaken little town. It's actually got a tourist trade. Go figure."

He handed her the picnic basket, picked her up and headed toward the stairs. "Oh, I almost forgot to mention," he said as he carried her. "I'm still digging on Emily McIntyre. She's a very lonely woman. Her kids can't stand her. No sex life. She's got her hooks into your son. They meet on a regular basis. I'm sure you've heard about the big rally they've planned in Washington next week."

Martha grimaced. "Yes, it's all over the news. She reminds me of a hateful old nun in boarding school. Sister Marlisa Magda. Mad Dog, we called her."

May 2, 2012

"I found her," Ed Brock said. He was talking on a cell phone just outside Edinburgh Castle. He had rushed up to Scotland from London without packing for what passed for spring above the fifty-fifth parallel. A cold wind was blowing inland from the North Sea, and it was threatening to rain. He was shivering in a light jacket as he circled away from a group of Japanese tourists and tried to keep his signal.

"Where is she?" Pat McCormack asked. He was sitting in his office, going through the unbilled time on the Hamilton account. His unhappy partners were sitting in the conference room next door, waiting for a status report.

"She's in a piss ant town in northern Scotland. Ullapool. The police are looking for her. Apparently, she has a taste for fine art. She's stolen enough to fill a museum."

"Jesus Christ." Pat closed his eyes and stroked his forehead.

"She's living under the name of Edith Hampstead," Ed said. "Can you believe it? She goes to all that trouble to take cover and then she uses the same fucking initials."

"Yeah? It still took you four months to find her. I'm sucking gas here big time. I want you to find out what she knows and then say good-bye. Clean it up. Do a thorough search. I don't want any reference to the client left behind."

"What if she's not his mother?"

"What do you mean what if she's not his mother? You're the one who told me you'd found the fucking Holy Grail when you dug her up."

Ed took a long drag on his Marlboro. "You know it was never more than an educated guess. You had to tell the client something that night. I gave it to you."

Pat was starting to steam. The running total on the Hamilton account since New Year's Eve was $2,459,601.37, none of which he could charge to the client because of his macho promise. "Between you and me, she's his mother. Nobody else has found anything. So she's the designated mother. Find out what you can and then get back to me."

"You still want me to say good-bye even if she's not his mother?" Ed asked.

"Well, you can't very well interrogate her and then kiss her on the cheek, can you? The client said our job was to make this problem go away. That gives us leeway. Now, stop biting your nails like a school girl and go do your job."

May 3, 2012

Billy Short could tell from a block away that something was wrong. It was below freezing and there was no smoke coming from the chimney of Lizzie Hoffmeier's cottage. He knew she liked to keep a fire going in her hearth until bedtime, and it was barely noon. The front door was locked and no one answered his knock. The back door had been forced open and stood ajar. Inside, he found the place had been ransacked. Drawers had been upturned, pillows and cushions had been shredded, plants had been ripped from their pots, food containers had been emptied.

A raccoon scurried past him as he made his way to the bedroom. Billy sniffed the air, checking for death, but picked up nothing more offensive than raccoon urine and stale cigarette smoke. In the bathroom, he saw blood spatter on the wall under the sink. Just a drop or two. Dried to a reddish brown. As he reached down to scrape the blood into a plastic sandwich bag he had retrieved from the kitchen, he saw a cigarette butt behind the toilet and dropped it into another bag.

On a second go through, he found blood specks on the floor by the back door. A patch of the tile floor nearby had been scrubbed clean. He scraped up those specimens as best he could, left the house and headed for the library. In the local newspapers and on the internet, there was no news about Lizzie or her friend, Andrew McClintock. It was dusk by the time he left the library and walked past McClintock's small home. It also was dark and smokeless. Finally, he checked the harbor. The McClintock boat, the Anna Mae, was missing from its slip. He figured the sons were still out to sea and hadn't discovered their father's absence.

When he called Martha, she was hysterical. "This is my fault," she said. "I should have sent you sooner, but I didn't want to scare her needlessly. I was afraid she'd panic and take off again."

"Now, don't get upset yet. We don't know what happened."

"What about the police?"

"I can't go to the police without blowing Lizzie's cover. Let me sniff around here and see what I can find out."

"It's Bob's people again, isn't it? They must know. But why would they want to hurt her?"

"We don't know who did what or why yet."

"Billy, I'm scared. Lizzie and I are the only ones still alive who know the truth about Bob. And now Lizzie...." Martha started to sob and then she stopped. "If they have Lizzie, they know about . . . ."

"About what?"

Martha's mind was racing. "I can't say. Not now. Not over the phone. Just find Lizzie."

"I'll do my best. I'll have the blood analyzed. I'm sending my boys over to guard your house. Don't admit any strangers. Don't accept any deliveries. Don't talk to your son. At least not about this. We don't want to tip him off. I know it's hard, but you need to stay calm."

"All right, Billy. I'll do my best."

Billy cleared his throat. "I apologize in advance for my sons. They're a little rough around the edges, but they're good kids and they'll do what I tell them."

May 5, 2012

It was Emily Schmidt's finest hour. The American Family First Foundation had organized the largest march in the nation's history. Two million men, women and children flooded the nation's capital and filled the National Mall to overflowing. Chanting "Families First," "Death to Choice," and "Save the Flag, Burn the Fags," the multitudes jubilantly shouted down protestors held back by police and National Guard troops. The Democratic president left town for Camp David, abandoning the seat of government to the zeal of a restless tribe of jingoistic nativists hell bent on imposing their brand of faith on the nation.

After a string of speeches by lesser lights in the movement, Emily McIntyre took the podium. She was dressed in a cream white Givenchy suit with a lavender rose pinned to her lapel and a matching cream white hat with a lavender ribbon. The crowd went quiet as they saw her image projected on eight JumboTron screens positioned along the length of the Mall. She was not smiling. This was a war rally. The crowd had been whipped into a take no prisoners fever, and she was not going to disappoint.

Her arms raised toward the heavens, she began, "My fellow Christians, we are a Christian people. We are a Christian nation. We are a Christian army!!"

The roar of applause and cheers was thunderous and undulated in waves as the screen flashed images of a blonde Caucasian Christ on the cross, the Foundation's Holy Youth Brigade marching goose step in navy uniforms with gold crosses emblazoned across their chests and resolute expressions fixed on their faces, and, finally, live shots of Emily, arms aloft, victorious.

"There is only one nation under God. We are that nation. There is no separation of Church and State in the eyes of God. We serve but one God, and our God rules all the earth. Our God rules the White House. Our God rules the Congress. Our God rules the Supreme Court. Under God, we rule!!!"

The mammoth throng burst into a holy frenzy of adulation, a seething tempest of righteousness, a furious cacophony of Amens and Hallelujahs. The JumboTrons flashed scenes of the assembled masses, close-ups of faces twisted in angry rapture, mid-range shots of the surging hordes waving their signs and shaking their fists and aerial shots of the teeming flock from the Goodyear blimp.

She continued to deliver her call to battle in the measured cadence of an imperious archangel of the Lord. It was a monumental triumph for the Foundation and most especially for Emily McIntyre. Thousands of evangelical churches across the nation were filled with true believers following her every word on a special feed from the Foundation's broadcasting studio.

"How will we take back our nation?" she asked.

"How?" her followers asked back in a deafening roar that reverberated off the marble walls of the buildings and monuments that lined the Mall.

"By taking back the White House!" she bellowed.

The crowd exploded into a sustained hurrah that swelled to an ear-piercing howl when cannons by the reflecting pool began to boom one after another in succession, closer and closer in time until they all erupted at once causing a concussion of sound that rippled outward across the concourse, so powerful that it knocked over small children and shook the internal organs of anyone within three hundred yards.

"Fellow Christians," Emily proclaimed. "I present to you the next president of the United States of America, Robert David Hamilton!!"

Bob Hamilton rose from his chair on the stage, clasped Emily's hand and thrust it skyward in exultation. The Holy Youth Brigade Band, a thousand strong, broke into *The Battle Hymn of the Republic*. The lyrics of the anthem scrolled down the giant screens so that two million souls could sing the inspiring call to action in unison, "Mine eyes have seen the glory of the coming of the Lord."

At the conclusion of six verses, the crowd once again burst into resounding applause, whistles and hoots and then just as quickly went mute when Emily raised her hands for silence. As Bob Hamilton took the podium, she stepped to the side, but stayed in the Foundation's camera frame. She was to be portrayed as his mentor, or more accurately, his proctor.

"Fellow Christians," he began. "We stand today at a precipice. We have two choices. We can go higher and ascend into the heavens or we can turn back and go home, to the safety of our churches and houses of worship. If we go higher, the path will grow steeper and more arduous. The risks will increase, and the dangers will abound. But, those of us who reach the summit, the peak of power and glory, will bask in the love of our Lord. If we lose faith and go back down the mountain, we may think we are safe, but the path will fall away beneath us and we will plunge from the precipice into the crevasse. Because of our indifference and disillusionment four years ago, we tumbled into that deep hell hole, where we watched the pillars of the temple fall around us.

"Everything that we had worked so hard to build together, all the mighty battles we had fought, all the victories we had won in the courts and all the constitutional amendments we had passed have been for naught. In four short years, the enemy has rolled back the path to the kingdom and torn down our monuments and hurled insults in our faces, while the abortion mills dump their bloody fetuses in the garbage, and secularists feed smut to our children and sodomites soil Christ's altar with their false promises of unnatural and abominable love.

"These four years in the wilderness are not unlike the forty years the Hebrews wandered in the desert. The Lord has banished us from the high place as he did the Israelites because we were unworthy. The chalice was within our reach, but was lost because we became lazy and greedy and too comfortable. We took our power for granted. We were corrupted by it and we were cast out. It has been a time of great sorrow. The skies have grown increasingly darker these past four years as the forces of evil have grown stronger. Many of us have despaired and walked away from the fight. Many of us have given up on God. How could He have allowed this terrible wind to blow across the land and strike us down, we have lamented.

"But, fellow Christians, all is not lost. There is always redemption in Christ. There is always hope. There is always a new beginning. We can be born again and purified through the fire and blood of holy conflict. And that is where we are today. About to do battle. About to charge up the hill in God's holy war paint. About to reclaim our legacy. About to fulfill our destiny. About to be lifted up on the wings of angels and hurled into the white hot furnace of combat. This is our time. This is our crusade. This is our divine right. Will you join me in this struggle?"

"Yes, we will!!!!" two million voices answered.

"Will you gird yourself and enter the fray and smite our foes and lay waste to their lands and march with me back into the temple?"

"Yes, we will!!!!"

"Will you never forget the pain we have suffered from our sins, and stand resolute by my side as we press onward and upward, never stopping, never giving quarter, until we have total victory?"

"Yes, we will!!!!"

"Then, I say to you the Lord will bless our conquest, and He will give us dominion over the land and He will subjugate our enemies before us. And our prayers will be answered. And the prophecy will be fulfilled. Let us pray."

Bob and Emily, the other dignitaries and the assemblage all dropped to their knees, clasped their hands and closed their eyes. Reverend Homer Throckmorton from the Church of the New Faith, the mother church, began The Lord's Prayer.

Rosie Gibson had been watching the spectacle from the vantage point of the press box. She was remembering the story her mother, Eulalia, had so often told about the March on Washington almost fifty years before on the same piece of ground. She was recalling the footage she had watched innumerable times of Dr. Martin Luther King Jr.'s famous words as he set forth his dream for America. She, herself, was praying for the words she would need to describe the travesty that she had just witnessed, for words that would compellingly dissect and eviscerate this religious hoax, for words that would pull the sheets off these charlatans and condemn them for invoking hatred and violence in the name of faith.

As the preacher said "Amen," she raised her head and breathed a sigh of relief. There, high above the crowd at the very peak of a ten story gleaming cross of gold stood her sign that all was well, that the words would come, that the truth would out. The great cat roared and snarled as she looked down on the impostors beneath her. Rosie looked back at the senator and the queen of family values and smiled. The words had come to her. Bob Hamilton was the Prince of the Pharisees, and she would fight her editor, Max Sherman, with every ounce of her conviction to get those words into print.

• • •

Martha Hamilton turned off the television as soon as Reverend Throckmorton began the Lord's Prayer. She took Sassy off her lap and set her on the floor. Standing, she grabbed her walker and headed out of the library to the east veranda. There, she slowly paced back and forth, trying to calm herself. Her outrage at her son, her anger at herself, her fear for Lizzie and her worry about Robert V all racked her soul. She felt helpless for the first time in her life.

Torn about what to do, she headed back into the house to call Billy Short. She knew he would tell her to sit tight, but she had to vent, she had to talk to someone. Billy didn't answer his cell phone. She headed into the kitchen where she found Yolanda Jackson boiling water. They sat at the kitchen table, drinking green tea and eating homemade lemon cookies, both of them railing on about Bob Hamilton, Emily McIntyre and the other pontificating hypocrites at the rally.

"What would you do if you had a son like mine, Yolanda?"

Yolanda shook her head. She was Marion Randolph's younger cousin and Martha's long time friend. A woman in her fifties, she had raised seven children, all of them college graduates. Martha had paid their tuition. She worked for Martha more for the companionship than the money. "It's hard to say. We all love our children, but, sometimes, we have to go against them in order to help them."

"I agree with you completely, Yolanda. Thank you. That's what I needed to hear."

Martha tried Billy's cell phone three more times. As far as she knew, he was still in Scotland. When Jimmy and Joe Bob Short came in from their rounds of the property, she asked, "Have you boys talked to your father recently?"

"No, ma'am," Jimmy said. "Not since yesterday."

"Thanks. Yolanda has dinner waiting for you in the kitchen." Martha headed into the library, closed the door and tried Billy one more time. When she got no answer, she said a little prayer to Marion. "Give me strength and help me to do the right thing."

She called Bob Hamilton's cell phone and reached him just as he was leaving a reception for political and religious leaders celebrating the success of the Foundation's rally. Jerry Boston had stayed behind to conduct a strategy session with the campaign's state chairmen, and Bob had told the limo driver to take him to his Georgetown home. He was looking forward to some peace and quiet.

"Bob, this is your mother. We need to talk."

"Sure, Mom. What's up?" He knew better than to ask if she'd listened to his speech. He'd get a short, harsh critique of his twisted values.

"Are you alone?"

"Yes, are you okay?" Bob's stomach flipped.

"I'm healthy, but I'm very upset. I hate to do this over the phone, but I've got to say it while I have my nerve."

"Sure, go ahead." Bob's heart started to race. His mother and his wife were the only two humans who could rattle him with their tone of voice.

"Apparently, you already know this. Bob, your father and I adopted you. Your biological father is dead. Your biological mother is Elizabeth Hoffmeier. She's an old school friend of mine. She was living a quiet life the last few years in Scotland, but she and her friend disappeared from her home a few days ago, and it looks like foul play. Her house was torn apart, and there was blood. I haven't been able to sleep I've been so worried about her. I have every reason to believe that the people you hired, Harris Security, had something to do with Lizzie's disappearance. I want to know what you know about it, and I want you to do whatever's necessary to ensure the safety of her and her friend."

"Jesus, Mom. I have no idea what you're talking about. This is all news to me. I can't believe you're telling me I'm adopted — "

"Oh, save the crap for your commercials," Martha shouted. "I know what your people have been doing, digging into hospital records, adoption files, spying on me, hiring some creep to impersonate the new priest at St. Paul's. I'm not some ditzy twit you can cast your spell on. I'm your mother. Or at least I'm the woman who raised you. Though not very well, I'm afraid. I have your number, Robert Hamilton. And if you don't produce Lizzie and her friend safe and sound, I'll go to the police and the press, and whoever else will listen to me, and I'll tell them the truth about holier than thou, Bob Hamilton. Do you understand?"

Martha never heard Bob's answer because yet another artery had burst in her cerebrum, her blood pressure having shot well past normal. The telephone receiver hit the old oak floor with a clatter, and Martha's head flopped back on the sofa. Yolanda was listening outside and immediately opened the door when she heard the noise. She picked up the receiver and heard Bob ask, "Mother, are you there?"

"Your mother's collapsed, Bob," Yolanda said through her tears. "I'm calling 911."

May 6, 2012

"You can't stop them, Mother," Larry McIntyre Jr. said.

"Oh, yes, I can. And I will," Emily McIntyre responded.

Larry Jr. had flown in from St. Louis and arrived at Emily's Virginia estate early Sunday morning. He was waiting on her front portico when she arrived home from church.

"Why, Larry, what a pleasant surprise," she had said, not at all happy to see her eldest son. She knew why he was there. The week before, Emily had filed a motion for a preliminary injunction in Maryland state court to prohibit Lily Roach from marrying her youngest son, Francis, and to prohibit any Maryland state or county official from granting a wedding license, on the basis that Frankie was mentally incompetent, incapable of knowing the ramifications of marriage and, therefore, incapable of entering into the contract of marriage with the requisite intent. Since Larry's death, she had served as Frankie's legal guardian and conservator, and she had been shocked to learn that she needed to take such extreme action to prevent what seemed to her an impossible union. "What did you think of our rally yesterday?" she had asked her son as she walked up the steps to the portico.

"I don't want to talk about your rally. I want to talk about Frankie. And Lily," he had responded. And they had taken the argument into what she called her drawing room. She closed the doors so that the staff couldn't hear.

Forty-year-old Larry Jr. looked very much like his father, and he carried himself and talked very much like his father. Tall, blonde and handsome, he was a successful corporate executive with a lovely wife, three talented children and a beautiful home in the upscale suburb of Clayton, Missouri. What he was not was a religious nut, like his mother, nor were any of his brothers.

"Mother, we're going to fight you on this."

"What do you mean, 'we'?" She was wearing a lavender Pierre Cardin ensemble and was unpinning her matching hat so that she could check her hair in the mirror above the mantle.

"Joe, Luke and I. We've hired lawyers to represent Frankie and we're going to challenge your right to be his guardian. We've talked to Frankie and he has agreed to seek his emancipation from you."

She turned to face him. "Oh, *now* you all swoop in and want to help. Where have all of you been the last twenty years? Do you think, all of the sudden, you know what's best for Frankie? I'm the one who visits him once a week. I'm the one who has to calm him down for his dental visits. I'm the one who has to listen to his endless stories. I'm the one—"

"Stop. I've heard you carry on for years about what a burden Frankie has been for you. The truth is you packed him away to Bedford as fast as you could. What was he? Twelve? When you locked him up. Just because the hormones were kicking in and he wasn't docile enough for you."

She sat down on what her sons called her throne. An original Louis the Sixteenth gold lacquered arm chair. "Larry, he was tearing the house apart. He was getting so big and strong and out of control. I couldn't reason with him."

Larry Jr. stood over her, his arms crossed. "He broke a lamp. Any one of the rest of us did way more damage to your precious furniture than he did. You were looking for any excuse to get him out of the house. He's been at Bedford for half his life. He's a great kid if you'd ever take a moment to get to know him."

"That's just it. He's a kid. He's not an adult, and he's not capable of making his own decisions. Especially about something as important as marriage."

"He's ready to be a man now. He understands the significance of what he's done. He knows that he's going to be a father, and he's excited about starting a new life with Lily and their baby. The rest of us are happy for them. Why can't you be happy?"

She gripped the arms of her chair and clenched her buttocks. "You're telling a fairy tale, Larry. They're not going to live happily ever after. They'll be children trying to raise another child. Most likely another child just like them. Am I the only one who's willing to say out loud that Frankie is mentally deficient? That he has the mind of a ten-year-old?"

"Our lawyers will subpoena the files at Bedford, and we'll have him tested for intelligence. I'm sure we'll find that with a little supervision of his finances, he'll do just fine. If he makes mistakes, well then, haven't we all?"

"You'll lose and you know it."

"Mother, I'm prepared to cream you in the press if you don't withdraw your petition and sign these papers." Larry Jr. handed her a folder. "You won't look very family friendly by the time this is over."

Emily rose from her chair and walked away from him. "Larry, I'm your mother. How can you do this to me?"

"I'm not doing anything to you. I'm protecting my brother. Your son. I think if Dad were alive, he would be disgusted with what you're doing to Frankie."

Emily started to cry. Larry Jr. stepped over and put his hand on her shoulder. She jerked away. "Leave me alone," she snarled. "I'll sign your damn papers. Just leave me alone."

Chapter 15

May 7, 2012

Jerry Boston climbed into bed as quietly as he could so as not to wake his wife, Diane. As soon as he settled in, she rolled over and gave him a hug. "That was a long meeting," she said with her sleepy voice.

"There was a lot to talk about."

"Like what?" She stroked his cheek.

"You don't want to know."

"That bad?"

"Let's just say the rich are different."

She curled her leg around his leg. "Now you've got my attention. Dish. And don't leave anything out."

Jerry sighed. "Well, when we left the Hamiltons in our last episode, Martha Hamilton had just stroked out after spilling the beans about Bob's real parents. The real mother's gone missing, and Martha has accused Bob of doing her in, spying, bugging phones, et cetera, et cetera. We still don't know how Martha found out about McCormack's crew. But, she's a wealthy lady, ex-spy herself, so she's resourceful.

"We take all this to McCormack today and ask, 'What have you done with Bob's mom?' He gets all defensive, more worried that we know he's fucked up than he is about the fuck-up itself. Turns out his man goes to the mom's house in some podunk village in Scotland and gets whacked on the back of the head by the mom. Mind you now, McCormack's guy is supposed to be the best, ex-CIA, blah, blah, blah and this old broad is almost ninety. She gets the jump on him, and when he comes to, she and her boyfriend are gone."

"She's got a boyfriend? At ninety?"

"Go figure. I thought Wasps gave up sex after fifty. So we have no idea where mom is now. After months of tracking her down. Turns out she's American, which is good. Bob's not barred from being president. But she's wanted in a dozen jurisdictions."

"For what?"

"Grand larceny. That's all we need. For her to get arrested. We were better off not finding her. And whoever followed McCormack's guy to the mom's house found traces of blood from our guy getting whacked and tells Bob's mom —"

"Which mom?"

"Martha. That it looks like the Scottish mom has been hurt or worse. Martha blows a gasket and has another stroke threatening to go public with Bob's nefarious deeds. Thank God for small miracles."

"Jerry, don't say that. She's been through a lot."

"She's a pain in the ass. She could sink us if she ever comes to. Anyway, the icing on the cake is that Bob's son is a fruit."

"You're mixing your metaphors."

"He's gay. And he's not only gay, he's doing it with a black kid going to North Carolina State, down the road from Duke. McCormack's people have been reading their emails and tailing them. So to speak."

"Omigod, what did Bob say?"

Jerry chuckled. "I shouldn't laugh. He's my guy. I picked him and I made him what he is today, but I got a certain amount of satisfaction watching him melt down in front of McCormack and me. He turned beet red and started yammering about how they must have the wrong kid because his quarterback son couldn't possibly be gay. Then, McCormack hands him the photos they took of his son making out in his Jeep with the black kid. McCormack was enjoying the moment, too. I could tell."

"That poor boy. What's Bob going to do?"

"Absolutely nothing. Bob's son has been emailing the black kid for nine months and has only met him the one time. We figure we can scare Bob's son back into his hole with a couple of anonymous phone calls and then remove the temptation. The black kid smokes weed. So we'll get him busted and kicked out of school. Send him back to Red Dirt Woods or wherever he comes from and break up the happy couple. Maybe buy us a year before Bob's son tries it again. By then, Bob will be in the White House."

"Oh, that's horrible."

"That, my dear, is politics. It's a contact sport."

"Speaking of which, our son has been playing more than sports."

"Nathan? Why, what's he been up to?"

"More like who he's been up to. Some girl named Dakota with big breasts and a half-buttoned blouse was coming out of his bedroom when I got home from the market. She just smiled and walked out the door. Nathan says they were studying for a history exam, but he was lying. I could smell sex when I walked in his room."

Jerry chortled. "Damn, he's ballsy. I could never have pulled that off at his age."

"That's because your parents would have killed you if you'd tried. He's sixteen, and it's only going to get worse from here on out. We've got to have a discussion with him about safe sex."

"You're right. I'll talk to him."

"Thanks."

"So she was hot? This Dakota girl?"

May 8, 2012

"Thanks to you, I got my ass chewed out yesterday," Pat McCormack snarled.

Edward Brock was sitting in Pat's office, slunk low in his chair. He had taken a Vicodin two hours earlier, but he was still feeling the pain. The stitches were on the back of his head, but his entire skull was throbbing. Even his teeth hurt. "I told you, I'll fix it. I'll find her."

"We don't have time for that. I'm going to make her come to us."

"How are you going to do that?"

Pat smirked. This was why he was a partner and Ed would always be a contract employee. "I've had the senator's press office release the news that his mother has just suffered a second stroke, that she's almost completely paralyzed and that the senator asks for the nation's prayers."

"Is she that bad?"

"Who knows? I made sure the story got picked up by all the wire services and cable networks. It should be news in most of the major dailies around the world. I figure Ms. Hoffmeier will try to come see her old friend on her death bed. We've got his mother's place under surveillance. So when she shows up, we can take care of her."

"Do you want me to go down there?" Ed scratched the back of his head. His stitches were beginning to itch. "I'd like to be in on that."

"No. I don't want to jinx it. Remember? At the agency, we never sent in the same guy twice. Besides, somebody might recognize you. Nothing like getting arrested with a whore to blow your cover as a priest."

"I still say I was set up. How did the cops know I was at the hotel?"

May 25, 2012

"Your honor, it's a matter of conducting a couple of simple tests," Alison Sterling said. "To determine how much brain damage Mrs. Hamilton has suffered. Once we know the results of those tests, we can address who should have control of her medical care and financial affairs." Alison was dressed to kill in her navy blue suit with a hemline several inches above mid-thigh, three inch patent leather heels and a white blouse opened one too many buttons. She was wearing her shoulder length hair down for maximum effect. Local Booneville counsel had told her that Judge Quentin Knobloch was particularly susceptible to the legal arguments of an attractive blonde.

Judge Knobloch smiled down on her. He was a heavy-set gentleman with watery blue eyes and an ill-fitting, sandy brown toupee that didn't match his graying sideburns. "Thank you, Ms. Sterling." Five days before, Alison had filed Bob Hamilton's lawsuit in Booneville seeking to declare his mother mentally incompetent and to have himself appointed as guardian and conservator of her estate. Dropping his smile, Judge Knobloch turned to Martha's counsel and said, "Ms. Grimm, do you have any further rebuttal?"

The hearing had dragged on for a day and a half in the grand oak-paneled courtroom. The 1872 limestone courthouse, at the center of Booneville's town square, was the pride of the community. It was a monument to the thrift and industry of the good citizens of the county. The old courthouse had survived the War of Northern Aggression only to be destroyed by lightning one hot summer night in 1869. Air conditioning in the old building was problematic. At three in the afternoon on the Friday before the Memorial Day weekend with the full sun burning through the south windows, it seemed to be non-existent. The ceiling fans did little more than stir the dust and mold in the packed courtroom.

Dressed in a charcoal gray pant suit, Atlanta lawyer, Penelope Grimm, rose and approached the podium. She was a middle-aged spinster who had devoted her life to the law and her prize Pekinese pooches. At least that was the image she had portrayed to the outside world. In truth, she shared a duplex with her lover of many years, Daphne Lambeau, a New Orleans native who cooked the most amazing Cajun and Creole dishes. Penelope was wearing some of that fine cuisine on her hips and thighs, but, on balance, she struck the local gentry as an attractive gal, smart looking with a friendly smile. Not one for make-up, she'd let Daphne teach her how to apply just enough to look feminine by Booneville standards. Her graying hair was short and business-like. No one in Booneville, except the court reporter, Charity Wheeler, had the slightest idea that she was a daughter of Sappho.

"May it please the court," Penelope began. "Ms. Sterling has presented no evidence that Mrs. Hamilton is mentally incompetent. Nor has she shown that Mrs. Hamilton has no chance of improving from her current condition. Mrs. Hamilton is, as her doctor explained, making a slow recovery. She is conscious and she is able to communicate. She is making decisions about her care, her finances and even her defense in this action. With her medical history, she knew that another stroke was a possibility and she has provided for that eventuality by giving me power of attorney over her financial affairs and by appointing her old friend, Yolanda Jackson, as her guardian and the person primarily responsible for decisions about her medical care. Ms. Jackson has lived at Sea Haven for many years and assisted Mrs. Hamilton with her recovery from her first stroke. She is intimately familiar with her care and daily routine."

"Yolanda's her housekeeper, right?" the judge asked.

"Yes, Ms. Jackson is on staff at Sea Haven, but she is much more than the housekeeper."

"Yeah, she's also the cook," his honor added with a smile. The courtroom tittered at his remark.

"She also maintains the household accounts, pays the bills, makes all purchases for the estate, hires and oversees service personnel, acts as a personal secretary for Mrs. Hamilton—"

"And she also cleans the toilets, changes the sheets, folds the laundry and does the dishes."

"She does all that, too."

"She sounds like my wife," the judge cracked, and the gallery laughed more heartily this time.

"Unfortunately, Mrs. Hamilton does not have a spouse. She was widowed some years ago. Her arrangement with Ms. Jackson has been more than satisfactory. Mrs. Hamilton is a very wealthy woman, and she could have chosen to hire any number of professionals to do what Ms. Jackson does, but she chose Ms. Jackson, and her choice is legally binding."

"Well, that's for me to decide, isn't it Miss Grimm?" Judge Knobloch asked, no longer smiling.

"That's correct, your honor. To apply the law to the facts. But we have heard nothing in the last two days from Ms. Sterling that would support reversing Mrs. Hamilton's wishes and allowing her son to step in and take control of her affairs. She expressly chose not to give him any power."

"Didn't he hire a nursing service for Mrs. Hamilton after her first stroke?"

"He did, but it was without his mother's authorization, and she fired the service because it was incompetent. Their records show that Mrs. Hamilton was an invalid, incapable of walking, speaking or feeding herself, when in fact, Mrs. Hamilton regained all of her faculties without and in spite of the nurses her son hired."

"I understand Mr. Hamilton has not been allowed to visit his mother," the judge said as he stood to pace behind the bench.

"That is correct. Mrs. Hamilton does not wish to meet with her son at this time. They've had a falling out, and she is not ready to consider reconciliation."

"And she's able to tell you all this by blinking her eyes."

"Yes, your honor, although she has begun to show some movement in her left hand and foot."

"You're going to have to do better than that, Ms. Grimm. I find it very hard to believe that Mrs. Hamilton said all that by blinking her eyes." He stopped pacing and grabbed the back of his chair. "What is she doing? The Morse code?" Judge Knobloch began blinking dots and dashes at her. Now, everyone in the courtroom, but Penelope, Yolanda Jackson, Billy Short and Charity, the court reporter, broke out in laughter. The judge let it ride for several seconds and then pounded his gavel for silence.

"Actually, your honor, Mrs. Hamilton knows the Morse code and several other codes. She used to work for the OSS. She's only had to use the Morse code on rare occasions. It's exhausting for her to use it extensively. We're able to communicate mostly with questions calling for yes or no answers."

"So you're asking her leading questions. Questions of your own choosing. Have you ever asked her if she wants to see her son?"

"At least once a day, your honor. Sometimes twice a day. The answer is always in the negative."

"For all I know, Yolanda and you have poisoned her against her son since her stroke."

"You could only make that finding if you determined that Ms. Jackson had lied under oath and that I had breached my fiduciary duty and my responsibility as an officer of the court. And neither one of us has given you any cause to come to that conclusion."

The judge's face reddened. Sweat was dripping from under his rug. He pointed at Penelope with a thick stubby finger. "You keep telling me what I'm supposed to decide, Ms. Grimm. That may be the way you big city lawyers talk up in Atlanta, but down here in Booneville, we still let the judges make the decisions." He sat down abruptly. "I've heard enough. I'm granting Mr. Hamilton's motion to require his mother to undergo the diagnostic tests, as specified. Depending upon the outcome of those tests, I will make a final ruling on guardianship and control of Mrs. Hamilton's estate." He rapped his gavel. "This hearing is over. Court adjourned."

Billy drove Yolanda and Penelope back to Sea Haven to report to Martha. Yolanda was weeping quietly next to Billy. "I don't know what I could have done differently," Penelope said from the back seat.

"You did a great job. The fix was in on this one," Billy said. "Sterling's probably on her knees right now in the judge's chambers."

"I've heard a lot of stories about Alison, but I can't believe she would stoop to that," Penelope said.

"I've done some research on Ms. Sterling, and I can tell you she's done that and more to win a case. Let me worry about her. For now, we've got to protect Martha. I don't want her staying overnight in the hospital. Penelope, I want you and Martha's doctor with her from the moment she leaves the house to the moment she arrives back home. I'll hire the ambulance service. No one, and I mean no one, is to have access to her with the exception of the examining doctor. Once you get the names of the medical experts Sterling proposes, let me know and I'll run a background check. It's very important that you follow my instructions. I'll be at the hospital, but you won't see me."

"They're going to kill her. I just know it," Yolanda sobbed.

"No, they're not, Yolanda," Billy said, as he patted her shoulder. "Not if we all do our part."

June 5, 2012

"Hey, handsome, look at you," Kenny Pickett said, smiling. He was polishing beer glasses at Coughlin's Tap when Roger Webber walked in the door.

Roger smiled broadly. He was sporting his new front teeth. His sister, Elaine, had paid for him to go to a private dentist and get the bridge. He was also twenty pounds lighter. Elaine had signed him up with a handsome trainer/nutritionist, and Roger was working hard to please him. Dressed in jeans and a loose fitting dress shirt, Roger was still an XXXL, but in his mind he was already down to an XL.

"Hey, boyfriend, what do you think?" Roger asked, as he twirled for the full effect. He patted his butt. "There's less junk in this trunk."

"You look great, Roger. The usual?"

"Nope. It's the new me. Diet Coke and no smokes." Roger sat down on his stool. "I've got a new job. Well, it's not a paying job, but still it's in my line of work. Costume design. It's for a community theatre troupe. They perform in a church basement and they're doing 'Hello Dolly.' How could I not help out with that show? It's one of my favorites. So many feathers. So many sequins."

Kenny set down the Diet Coke. "Good for you. How did you hook up with them?"

"Oh, I'm going to a counselor at the church. And she suggested it. She thinks it will help me get my mind off of the attack. Maybe I'll sleep better. Not so many nightmares."

Roger glanced up at the television above the bar. It was tuned to ESPN, but the sound was muted. It was evening, and the bar was about half full. The Toronto Blue Jays were trailing the Chicago White Sox, two to seven in the top of the eighth. Another so-so season for the Jays. Roger knew nothing about baseball, but he loved baseball players, especially the rookie pitcher, a beefy boy from Arkansas, and the Latin guy at shortstop, Jose something. When the game cut to a commercial, Roger was about to look away to check out the clientele when he saw himself on the screen. Or at least a photo of someone who looked exactly like him when he was much younger.

The ad continued with a montage of photos of his look-alike growing older, with a beautiful wife and three cute kids, shaking hands with presidents and world leaders. Roger was transfixed. He stood to get a closer look. "Kenny, Kenny, turn up the sound quick."

Kenny hit the remote button just as the ad ended with a shot of the handsome man saying, "I'm Senator Robert Hamilton, and I approved this ad."

"Kenny, who is that guy?"

"Beats me. Some political hack running for president in the States, I guess."

"Oh, it's too good to be true," Roger said as he sat down again.

"What?"

"I'm afraid to say it out loud."

"Why?"

"I've hoped for so long."

Now Kenny was intrigued. "Go ahead. Say it. You won't spoil it."

"Since I was a little boy, I've always wanted to have a brother."

"I thought you had two brothers."

Roger frowned. "I was adopted, remember? They weren't really my brothers. I always thought somewhere in the world I had a real brother. Someone who would love me for who I am."

Kenny put a refill in front of Roger. "Your sister loves you."

"Yes, and I love her, but it's not the same. I've always wanted to believe that I had family. Someone besides the parents who gave me away."

Kenny was pouring a draft of beer from the tap. "Family's not all it's cracked up to be. Every time I go home, it seems all we do is fight."

"Yes, but my fantasy brother and I never fight. We agree on everything."

Kenny slid the glass down the bar. "That is a fantasy. Nobody will agree with you all the time. Unless maybe he's your clone."

"That's it," Roger shouted. The patrons of the sleepy bar all looked up.

"What?"

"He's my twin!"

"How could he be your twin?"

"How could he not? He looks just like me. Or at least how I used to look. Too many years ago."

Kenny leaned back against the counter. "You think?" He'd never seen Roger like this sober.

"I don't just think. I know! And you're the one who helped me figure it out. Thank you, Kenny. Come here. Let me kiss you. For good luck."

Kenny smiled, leaned over the bar and let Roger plant his lips on his cheek. Several in the bar groaned.

Roger jumped off his bar stool. "I'm off."

"Where you going?"

"To find my twin."

June 8, 2012

Jeffrey Jones and his boyfriend, Ernest Rhodes, were walking Zeke late on a warm Friday night. Jonathan Jones, and his sister, Georgia, had taken their nephew, Jeffrey, into their home when he was fourteen. His mother had kicked him out when he told her he was gay. Jeffrey and Ernest had just graduated from Wayne State University, and they had invited friends to come to the parsonage for a barbeque. Georgia had invited a few of her friends, too, and one, Bethany Armstrong, had brought her brother, Lincoln. Most of the guests had left. A few had crashed in the attic, Jeffrey's old room.

"So what do you think? Is your uncle gay?" Ernest asked Jeffrey.

"I don't know."

"Have you ever asked him?"

"Yeah. He says it doesn't matter what he is. What matters is that he is cool with me."

"I think he's gay. I saw him with Lincoln tonight. They were cleaning up in the kitchen. I walked through to go to the bathroom. There was something going on."

"Maybe they were just drunk."

"Yeah. Gay drunk. I swear I almost caught Lincoln grabbing your uncle's butt."

"No shit? Saint Jonathan?" Jeffrey shook his head and smiled.

Early the next morning, just before sunrise, Jonathan woke up to see Lincoln pulling up his briefs. Lincoln was a thirty-eight-year-old website designer with the body of a boxer and the sensibility of an artist.

"Hey, where are you going?" Jonathan asked in a whisper.

Lincoln was sitting on the edge of the bed pulling up his socks. He looked back at Jonathan, smiled and whispered back. "I'm sneaking out of the preacher's house before the neighbor ladies wake up."

Jonathan reached out and touched his shoulder. "You don't have to go because of me."

"Oh, yes I do. You can't have the whole church gossiping about Pastor Jones having a sleepover. All it takes is one busybody."

Jonathan sat up and wrapped his arm around Lincoln's waist. "I don't care about the busybodies. Come back to bed."

Lincoln lay back in Jonathan's arms. "This is a big step for you. You need to take this slowly. Don't do anything rash."

Jonathan kissed the back of his neck. "I'm too old to take things slowly. I want to see you again. Soon."

Lincoln reached back and rubbed Jonathan's head. "Me, too. Maybe you can come up to my cabin with me."

"I'd love that." Jonathan squeezed him tight. They could hear voices in the attic above them. Lincoln sat up and Jonathan released him. As Lincoln dressed, Jonathan pulled on some gym shorts and a shirt and followed him down the stairs. They kissed and hugged at the back door just as the sky began to lighten.

"I had fun, Jonathan. You're a very sexy man," Lincoln said.

Before Jonathan could answer, Lincoln had taken off at a trot toward his car.

"Uh-huh," Georgia said. She had just entered the kitchen and witnessed the good-bye kiss.

Jonathan turned around with a sheepish grin on his face.

"Nice choice," Georgia said, as she pulled the coffee can out of the refrigerator.

"He's amazing," Jonathan said as he sat down at the table.

"See what you've been missing all these years."

"I'm glad I waited. Last night was perfect."

"You deserve it. I'm glad you two got together. Bethany and I were hoping you'd click." She finished pouring the water into the coffee machine and sat down next to him.

"It just felt so right. So easy with him. I don't want to hide any more. I don't care what anyone says."

"It's about time."

"But he's telling me to take it slow. He's worried about me. How about that?"

"Listen to him. Just let it unfold. Enjoy each step."

"I intend to."

June 11, 2012

"Jerry, there's some crank on the line," Lorraine Whitson said as Jerry Boston rushed past her into his office at Hamilton campaign headquarters in Washington, D.C. "He says he's Bob's twin brother. He's called a dozen times. He's got a funny accent. British maybe?" Lorraine had been with Jerry since he'd opened his own firm, and she knew to keep the crazies away. So when she made an exception, Jerry listened. This one in particular caught his attention.

"Put him through," he said, closing his door.

"Hello, Mr. Boston?"

"Yes, speaking."

"I'm Roger Webber, and I live in Toronto. I saw Bob Hamilton's ad on TV up here, and I think he's my twin brother."

"Why do you think that?" Jerry was starting to get a migraine. Roger sounded effeminate and sure of himself.

"Well, I saw the ad with the photos of him when he was younger, and I was shocked because they looked just like me when I was in my twenties. I was adopted. I grew up in Cape Town, but my mother says she went to Dublin to get me. I've always thought I had a twin brother."

"When were you born?"

"The man in Dublin told my mother I was born on July 4, 1958."

"You could get the senator's birthday off the internet. How do I know you're for real?"

"Because I have photos of myself from my youth, and we look like twins. A DNA test would confirm it. I'm very excited. Imagine. Brother of a United States Senator."

"Are you looking for money?"

"Heavens, no. I want to meet my brother. I want us to be family."

Jerry reached into his desk drawer for his migraine medication. "Okay, Mr. Webber. I've got your number. Let me do some checking and call you back."

"You promise to call me back? Your secretary said she would, but she never did. I was about to go to *The New York Times* to tell my story."

"No, no. Don't do that. I promise to get back to you. If you go to the press, I can guarantee you will never meet the senator. So, hold tight. Okay?"

"Okay," Roger said musically. "I'll be waiting to hear from you, Jerry."

Chapter 16

June 18, 2012

Emily McIntyre steered her black Mercedes coupe into the last spot at the far end of the rest stop parking lot at Mile 108 of Interstate 95 in Caroline County, Virginia, sixty odd miles south of Washington, D.C. The tourist season was in full bloom. The picnic tables were full, and the minivans and SUV's were lined up one after another unloading large Americans waddling off to urinate before they continued their voyages south to Richmond or Williamsburg or beyond, deeper into the old Confederacy.

Emily read her temperature gauge. It was ninety degrees Fahrenheit outside. She was glad she had insisted that the meeting take place in her car. She was not about to dress like a vagabond and rendezvous in the heat behind some tree amongst the dog shit, horseflies and used condoms.

She had been waiting fifteen minutes when Pat McCormack tapped on her passenger side window. Once inside, he said, "I'm sorry I'm late. I was waiting for a final report on our boy in Toronto." He was sweating like a pig, Emily thought. She was worried that he would drip on her leather interior. He smelled like bad cologne. It reminded her of the musky Jade East the boys in high school had worn.

"What do you have?" she asked. She wanted to keep the meeting as short as possible. Pat McCormack was such a disagreeable man on so many levels she could barely tolerate their association.

Pat opened his folder and handed her photos of an obese middle-aged man coming out of Coughlin's Tap. "This is the guy. From appearances, as you can see, he hardly looks like he could be even a distant relative of Hamilton. But much of his story holds up. He grew up in Cape Town. His parents told school officials they adopted him locally through a church agency, but there's no birth certificate. All the school records show his birthday is the same as Hamilton's. Webber told schoolmates his parents picked him up at the Dublin airport. He went to Cambridge University, lived in London briefly, and then moved to Toronto. We found some high school and college photos of him." Pat handed copies to Emily. "Obviously, he wasn't so tubby back then."

Emily gritted her teeth and clinched her buttocks. She was staring at Bob Hamilton. She could see it in the eyes, the nose, the chin, the dark curly hair. "And you're sure he's a homosexual?" Emily sniffed. "I thought they were all steroided-up body builders."

Pat snorted. "He's as queer as they get. Theater major. Costume designer. He performed drag for years in fag bars all over Canada. He lives in the gay ghetto. Rents gay porn. Talks like a pansy. His drag name was Mercedes Bends." Pat smirked and slapped his knee. "Get it?" He bent forward to give her a visual clue.

Emily grimaced, deciding on the spot her next car would be a BMW. "Yes, I get it. What's he do?"

"He doesn't do much of anything. He's on the dole. Does some volunteer work for some theatre group. Spends a lot of his time in this dive." Pat pointed at the Coughlin Tap photo. "He used drugs in the past, but he can't afford the habit much these days. Little pot here and there."

"Does he have any family or friends?"

"His mother and sister are in Vancouver. The father's dead. He's estranged from his brothers in Cape Town. Talks with his sister every couple of days. His mother once a week. No real friends to speak of. Has to hire his sex. Got roughed up by some cowboy, told the cops he wasn't a prostitute, but they didn't believe him. Sees a therapist once a week. Her notes are pretty scary. He's an unhappy old drag queen."

"Have you told Boston any of this?"

"No, I came straight to you."

"This guy's not going away?"

"No. And from what Boston says, we won't be able to keep him quiet even if we humor him. He wants a reunion with Bob, and then I'm sure he'll want to stay at the White House. He'll be a hundred times worse than Billy Carter."

Pat's cell phone rang. "Excuse me. I gotta take this." Pat listened briefly and then said good-bye. "That was our lab. We collected some hair from his apartment when he was out. We've got a DNA match. He's Hamilton's twin, all right."

Emily hit her steering wheel with both fists. "God damn it! This can't be happening!"

Pat smirked. "So much for the perfect candidate, huh?"

"Mr. McCormack, I pay you too much for you to make fun of me," Emily sneered. "Bob Hamilton *is* the perfect candidate, and he will be the perfect president. Don't tell Boston any of this. Tell him Webber's a kook and you scared him away. Then, get someone up there quickly and put him to sleep. Make it look like he overdosed. I don't want the police sniffing around."

Pat had received many orders to terminate human life, and he had never felt the least bit squeamish. He would never acknowledge it to his conscious brain, but something in his lower brain missed the killing. It had awakened in him a certain primal bloodlust. Ten years behind a desk in suburban Virginia had given him a nervous twitch that only disappeared when he was out of the office on assignment. He loved the easy lifestyle that came with the money at Harris Security, but most days he had regretted taking early retirement from the agency.

Yet, there was something about Emily McIntyre's cold-hearted words, putting a hit on Roger Webber, as if he were an old dog who'd lost control of his bladder, that gave him goose bumps. Her instruction made perfect sense to him, but hearing it come from her thin, dry lips, sitting there in her fancy car with a gold cross hanging around her neck, struck him, for the first time, as evil, a concept that he had long ago decided was an invention of the Roman church to wring money out of the hapless dolts who feared going to hell.

He smiled to himself. He'd give this job to Ed Brock. He could picture him having to cozy up to the fat old queer. "Consider it done. I'll send you a message. Check Craigslist in the usual spot in a couple days.

She rolled her eyes. "Isn't there a better category than casual encounters? There's so much filth on that site. When Bob's president, we're going to clean up the internet."

"Well, until then, let's stick with it. It's discreet. All you have to do is search for the key words and read my message."

"Couldn't you pick other words?"

"What's wrong with Madonna and whore?"

June 19, 2012

"Hello, Edna." Billy Short smiled down at the retiree sipping her Bloody Mary under the beach umbrella. He was wearing a white polo shirt, khaki slacks, a ball cap and sunglasses.

Edna Roberts looked up at him quizzically through Vera Wang pink tinted sunglasses. She was wearing a black Versace one piece swimsuit. Through the marvels of liposuction, plastic surgery and breast implants, she had transformed herself into the vamp of Sanibel Island, Florida. At fifty-two, with her L'Oreal Feria Hot Toffee hair in a chic little cut, compliments of Sebastian of the Sanibel Day Spa, she was a living legend among the AARP set for her many conquests and insatiable libido. "I think there's been some mistake. I asked for Jorge," she said.

It was a brilliant summer morning with a cloudless azure sky, a gentle surf washing up fresh treasures for the shell hunters and a chorus of song birds trilling in a nearby grove of Australian pines. Edna was sitting on a private beach facing the Gulf of Mexico, the property of her condominium association, Whispering Palms. It was a gated community with guards, cameras and dogs. Each of the fifty owners had a luxury appointed two or three bedroom waterfront casita. From her screened lanai, Edna could see schools of dolphins leaping out of the water, manatees surfacing for air and pelicans swooping low for a breakfast of fish. With palm trees, hibiscus and bougainvillea, it was a manicured paradise.

With his best "aw shucks" Georgia drawl, Billy said, "Sorry to intrude, Ms. Roberts, but I need to talk to you about your relationship with Larry McIntyre."

Edna lost her composure, and she looked away. After an awkward moment, she turned back to face Billy. "Who are you and how did you get past security?"

Billy sat down on the sand next to her lounge chair. In the shade of her umbrella, he took off his sunglasses so that she could see his "warm brown eyes," as Martha Hamilton called them. "I'm Billy Short, and I flashed a badge I use. Don't blame your security guy. It's very authentic looking. I'm working for a friend of mine who's concerned about Emily McIntyre's influence over the presidential election. I thought you might share my friend's concern."

"I really don't want to get involved. That's all in the past for me."

"Did you hear Frankie McIntyre's getting married?"

Edna broke into a smile. "Little Frankie? Oh, I used to love it when he came to visit his dad at the office. He was such a sweetheart."

"Yeah, his momma has had him locked up for the last ten years, but he met a nice girl at the home and they fell in love. They're expecting a child."

Edna giggled. "Oh, that little devil. He was always such a pistol. She must be something to catch him." Then, she stopped herself. "That witch locked him up? For ten years?"

"Oh, she found a fancy enough place. It's where rich people put kids like Frankie when they want to hide them, I guess."

"That's just criminal. He was such a good boy. And he loved his father."

"That's what I hear. His momma filed a lawsuit to keep him from getting married, but she withdrew it a few days later. I guess her boys must have talked sense into her."

"Why that's outrageous! She should never have been a mother. I don't know how Larry put up with her for so many years."

"It's kind of ironic, isn't it? Her parading around like she's Mother of the Year."

"She puts on a good show. Fools most people. But the boys suffered. And Larry, too."

Billy shifted on the sand and took off his sandals. "That's where you came in, right?"

"I don't know what you mean."

"I mean Larry needed a friend. And you were there for him."

She drained her Bloody Mary, checked her watch and looked over her shoulder toward the pool. "I have an appointment for a massage, and I should be going."

Billy smiled. "I'm sorry. Jorge will be back in an hour. I left him an envelope at the security gate with a message and some cash. I paid him for five more sessions. Don't let him tell you different. I hope you don't mind. My friend and I think Emily McIntyre is a danger to the country. We need your help."

Edna pursed her thick, pouty lips. "You're very sneaky with your badge and bribery. Just so you know, Jorge is a legitimate massage therapist."

"I'm sure he is. And a very handsome young man, from the looks of his ad."

"Well, I suppose it wouldn't hurt to talk some more." She rose from her chair and bent over to get her towel. Billy appreciated the view. With the exception of a few dimples of cellulite at the top of her thighs, there was very little left of the church secretary. "Let's get out of the sun," she said. "Would you like some fresh squeezed orange juice, Billy? I made some this morning after my power walk."

June 22, 2012

Ed Brock picked up two vodka tonics at the main bar of the Manhole and carried them to the dark corner where Roger Webber was installed for the evening. Roger was wearing a shiny purple satin long sleeve shirt and black jeans. He was convinced the outfit was slimming. Ed was wearing a sleeveless tight black T-shirt and even tighter jeans. He had grown designer stubble and left his briefs at home. The tattoos on Ed's big biceps were what first caught Roger's eye. One was a skull and the other was the head of a handsome smiling devil. Definitely a leather pig, Roger had figured.

They'd been checking each other out for a half hour, each of them leaning up against the wall, pretending to look at the porn on the overhead screens. Then, the more sustained eye locks had begun, and then, Roger could have sworn, there was a brief smile. After that, things had progressed quickly. Ed had introduced himself as Clint. Then, he had said, "I was hoping you'd be here tonight."

"Why? I've never seen you before." Roger had inched closer so that they were almost touching.

"Oh, I've been around. I've seen you, but I've been too shy to say hello." Ed had smiled and leaned into Roger's purple satin shoulder. He was a solid six foot, but next to Roger, he had looked almost diminutive.

"That's hard to believe," Roger had said, getting all fluttery. "You look like the kind of guy who takes what you want."

Ed had reached behind Roger, stroked his butt and said smiling, "This is what I want."

"Why me? With all the hot men you could choose from tonight."

Ed had looked around the room as he continued to stroke Roger's butt more assertively. "They're all too skinny for me. I like a man with some meat on his bones." He had squeezed Roger's butt hard and then given it a firm pat. That was when he had offered to get Roger a drink.

Four vodka tonics later, Roger was very tipsy and very giddy. "How about we head back to your place," Ed said, smiling. He was facing Roger, and he had his hand inside Roger's pants encircling his semi-erect penis. Roger was grateful he had managed to rise to the occasion despite the alcohol. Ed tightened his grip on Roger and kissed him, thrusting his tongue past Roger's partial plate, almost dislodging it. Thank God for the fixative, Roger thought.

When Roger hesitated, Ed kissed him again and pulled Roger's hand down to his own crotch, where, with a good deal of pocket pool stimulation, he had been able to get an erection. It was not nearly as big as Roger's but it was a show of good faith.

"Hmmm, I'd love to get my mouth around that," Roger said. "But I've made a new rule with my therapist. No hook ups on first meeting. Maybe we could do lunch tomorrow."

Ed kept smiling. "I can't wait that long. I need some now." He leaned closer and spoke into Roger's ear, "Would you like to *fuck* me, Roger?"

"Oh, God, would I!" Roger was as stiff as granite now and deliriously horny.

"Then, let's go back to your place so you can *fuck* me. I like it hard, Roger. Can you give it to me hard?" Ed was spraying his words in Roger's face. "I want to be your bitch boy tonight. Take me home, spank my ass and then pound me hard."

It was "bitch boy" that closed the deal for Roger. Ed was everything butch that he had never been. Ed was his father and his brothers all rolled into one rock hard, tattooed stud begging to service him. It was his ultimate fantasy.

Back in Roger's apartment, Ed produced a pint of vodka and poured them each a glass. While Roger was in the bathroom, Ed poured the latest generation knock-out drug into Roger's drink. Eli Lilly had developed it for the federal government and had promised it was completely untraceable. Unfortunately for Ed, given Roger's weight, it took longer than expected to take effect. After they tore off each other's clothes, Roger decided Ed's butt was too perfect not to spank. His ass red, Ed began sucking Roger's penis for what seemed an interminable amount of time. Roger gave him rave reviews, even though Ed gagged at several points. And then they moved on. Roger was in the process of rimming and fingering Ed's anus, and Ed, in spite of his revulsion, had begun leaking pre-cum, when the drug finally, finally began to slow Roger down.

"I'm not feeling so good," Roger said. "I think I had too much to drink." Seconds later, Roger collapsed forward onto Ed with two fingers two knuckles deep in Ed's rectum.

Ed strained his neck getting out from under Roger and rolling him onto his back. With a syringe, he administered the lethal dose of speed into a vein in Roger's left arm, wrapped Roger's fingers around the syringe and then set it on the bedside table. Ed quickly dressed, donned a pair of rubber gloves and searched the apartment, checking Roger's pulse every so often. The big man's heart raced faster and faster. At one point, Roger moaned. Ed could have sworn he called out, "Clint." Then, there was a small cry, more like a whimper, and it was done. Roger Webber had been put out of his misery. Ed checked Roger's pulse three more times a minute apart, just to be sure.

He took a photo of Roger's corpse with his camera phone, as requested by his boss, Pat McCormack, the king of ghouls. And then he left, vowing to get out of his line of work as soon as he could afford it. As lethal as the evening had been for Roger, it had been disturbing, deeply disturbing, for Ed. Roger's perfect fantasy had been unfolding just as Ed's worst nightmare had been unlocked. Fellating Roger's member had broken loose a flood of long forgotten memories. Memories of detention after school at Saint Athanasius Academy in Father Willoughby's office. Ed had been an unruly kid with undiagnosed attention deficit disorder. He had wound up in the priest's office once or twice a week through most of second grade, just before his family had fled Buffalo for the suburbs to get away from the encroaching Negro. Just seven, Ed had been curious and sexually precocious. Of all the boys that Willoughby had molested over his long tenure at Saint A's, Ed had been his favorite.

• • •

Just as Roger Webber took his last breath, Josh Stein, put his arm around his sister's shoulder. Sarah and he were taking a walk in the moonlight along the beach in Malibu, California.

"How's it going?" she asked. There had been such a flurry of activity since he'd arrived from Sydney that afternoon that they had not had a chance to really talk. Sarah and her husband, Cliff, a screenwriter, had hosted dinner for Josh, their two sons, daughters-in-law and grandchildren at their home overlooking the Pacific.

"It's going well," Josh said. "I think I'm coasting into middle age with more grace than most gay men."

"Ha! You look better than half the surfer boys here." At fifty-eight, Sarah had not succumbed to the southern California ethos, requiring her to starve and sweat her way to a size six. She was a generous size twelve and happy with herself. A redhead, she had kept out of the sun and preserved her skin. That accomplishment alone was a remarkable distinction in the land of tan.

Josh kissed the top of her head. "Thanks for saying that. You always were my favorite sister." They walked on in silence. Josh breathed in the ocean air. "You've got a great life here. Would you change anything if you could?"

"Like real world change or fairy godmother change?" she asked.

"Either or both." They were walking barefoot at the edge of the surf.

"I'd have you living close by so that I could see you more often, and then I'd find you a husband."

"Oh, so fairy godmother change. Finding me a husband would take some magic."

"Why are you so hard on yourself? You're a catch." A cruise ship out for the evening glided by, lit up like a Christmas tree. They could hear faint strains of a new Madonna release. Just a few weeks younger than Josh, she was still going strong at fifty-three.

"Catch or no catch, it's more a problem of demographics. Most of the men my age are partnered up, fucked up, overweight or dead."

Sarah laughed. "It's the same with straight men. You should date younger men, then. Widen your net. You're one hot daddy."

Josh smiled and squeezed her tight. "What do you know about hot daddies?"

"You forget. Cliff's surrounded by all these closeted gay men in the business. I swear they make up half of Hollywood. I've met most of them at parties. The younger man is always along as a business associate or body guard. Sometimes, there are two of them."

"So, you're suggesting I pay for a younger companion?" Josh steered Sarah deeper into the surf to torture her with the cold water.

Sarah laughed again and kicked water on him. "No, silly. I'm just saying I'm aware of the phenomenon. Younger men who want someone older and wiser."

"Someone who can take care of me in my dotage?"

"Someone who can keep up with you. Someone who can keep you from contemplating your navel so much."

"Someone who can help me forget Mark?"

"No. You should never forget Mark. But life is for the living. Mark would kick your butt if he knew you were still single. It's been six years."

"I know, I know. You're right. It's not as if I don't try. God, I've met so many men on the internet. We meet for coffee, lunch, dinner. Sometimes sex. I call them interviews. It always turns out that the ones I like don't like me and vice versa."

"What about Vince?"

"Who? Vince Scavullo?" Josh chuckled. "He's a cutie, but we live at opposite ends of the planet."

"Well? It's time for a change. If you were in New York, I'd consider my wish granted."

"God, I don't know. New York? I love Sydney."

"Single in Sydney. Sounds like a bad movie title. Just consider the possibility. When you're visiting him next month, think how it would be. You might surprise yourself."

"All right, I'll do that. But enough about me. Let's talk about you."

"Okay. What do you want to know?"

"So are Cliff and you still doing it?"

She gave him a shove and knocked him off balance. He fell into the surf laughing.

Sarah stepped back to avoid retaliation. As Josh walked out coughing and dripping, she said, "It's none of your business. And yes we are, thank you very much. Like minks."

June 25, 2012

Martha Hamilton was propped up with pillows on a portable hospital bed that Yolanda Jackson had wheeled onto the screened porch next to Martha's bedroom at Sea Haven. She had regained some use of her left arm and leg, but she was still speechless. Only garbled sound came out when she attempted to speak. The words were there, but they got jumbled on the way from her brain to her vocal chords. Her comprehension was high and coming back fast. She loved to have Yolanda talk and read to her. Television seemed more of a wasteland than ever, but she still dearly loved to listen to public radio. And there was always Mozart.

It was early morning, and the warm moist air was laden with the scent of jasmine and four o'clocks. The blossoms of the morning glory vines that had latched onto the old screens were just beginning to open. Martha was watching and listening to a couple of cardinals in the hackberry tree nearby. Sassy was curled up next to her, and Martha was lightly stroking the thick fur on her neck. Rather than focus on what she could not do, she had chosen to celebrate what freedom she still had and what pleasure she could still experience.

Trapped inside her body yet again, she was no longer fearful of the unknown. She had been fighting for whatever progress her brain managed to restore and left the rest to her memories. It had been seven weeks since her stroke, and she knew she would never walk again, not even with a walker. Her dream was to make it down the ramp in her wheel chair to Marion Randolph's grave by the end of the summer. A photo of the two of them, embracing, sat unabashedly front and center on her bedside tray. She wanted him in her line of vision at all times, and she thanked God that Yolanda could read her mind.

In the last seven weeks, she had come to a grudging compromise with God or Whatever had set things up and put them in motion. She had agreed to open a conversation. She would search through her life for the moments of grace she had witnessed, most of them shared with loved ones, and she would acknowledge that those brief episodes were transcendent glimpses of what some might attempt to describe as heaven on earth. In return, she had asked for one final show stopping wonderment. She had a long list of wishes, but she would settle for one. After that, she had decided she was ready to let go. What she had found, after cutting that deal with the Divine, was that every moment had become more intense. Her senses had been heightened, and her emotions had flooded to the surface, unrestrained by the strictures of fear, shame or guilt. And every contact with another living being, including Sassy, had become precious.

"Hey, Martha," Billy Short said as he knocked lightly on the door frame to announce himself. He kissed her forehead, gently squeezed her hand and gave Sassy a couple of long strokes on her back.

Martha's smiled with her eyes and winked at him. She slowly lifted her arm and patted the back of his hand.

"Whoa, look at you," Billy said, smiling. "Every time I come by, you're getting stronger and prettier." Billy sat down next to her bed and took off his Special Forces ball cap. He was wearing jeans, a blue dress shirt and boots. "I've got good news for you. We don't have to worry about your son's lawsuit any more. It seems Bob's lawyer, Alison Sterling, not only plays rough, but she likes to watch herself afterward. She pissed off some kid when he found out she had a camera in the bedroom recording some heavy discipline. He broke into her house, with a little help from me, and raided her DVD collection. I made a deal with him. He could keep his sessions, but I got the rest."

Martha lifted her eyebrows in amusement and made a fist.

Billy shook his head. "Lordy, Lordy. I thought I'd seen everything, but she even made me blush. There was one time with the Chief Justice of the Georgia Supreme Court, where she ripped off his robe." Billy chuckled. "I can't say much more without embarrassing myself. Let's just say justice did not triumph. The things she made him do."

"Ha!" Martha blurted out, surprising herself.

"I figured you'd enjoy this moment. Well, I gave her a call, duly recording every word, and told her what I had. She started shrieking at me, threatening all sorts of legal actions, accusing me of blackmail. And then, she shut up. And I waited. And then she asked, 'What do you want?'"

Martha pounded her mattress with her fist as hard as she could.

"So what will happen is Miss Sterling will pull her punches at the hearing this afternoon, enough to guarantee your son loses and you win. Your medical tests weren't helpful to her, but that judge wouldn't have cared. He's been panting for a whole month, waiting for Alison to grace his chambers again. I told her she needs to lose and lose bad. Insult the judge, make fun of Booneville, dress conservatively. I'll give her back the DVD's but she'll never know if I copied them, so I figure we own her at this point."

Martha's eyes were moist as she beckoned him to come to her. He stood and leaned over so that she could kiss him on the cheek.

"Thank you, dear," he said. "That means a lot to me." With a tissue, he wiped tears from her eyes and then his. "The not so good news is we have to increase security here. I think your son was using the lawsuit to keep you quiet. Now that we've shut that down, he'll try some other way. I told you earlier that the saliva on the cigarette butt and the blood at Lizzie's place came from a male. The most likely candidate is a former agent named Ed Brock. He's got a troubled history with the CIA, and he's been free lancing for Harris Security. Rough character."

Billy pulled a fax out of his back pocket, unfolded it and showed Martha a blow up of a grainy driver's license photo. "Is this your Reverend Bingham?"

Ed Brock's cold blue eyes stared out at her. She closed her eyes and nodded. Her heart started to race and her breathing became labored. Billy folded up the photo and put it away. "I'm sorry. I didn't mean to upset you, Martha. I promise. You'll be safe. I'm bringing in a couple of old army buddies of mine. They'll be here soon. I won't leave for court 'til they show up. Jimmy and Joe Bob will be here, too."

Standing up, he took her hand. "I wouldn't tell you all this if you weren't so smart. And tough. You'd know if I was holding something back."

Martha nodded.

"I haven't had time to look for Lizzie. I figure she and the boyfriend got a ride on his boys' fishing boat. They probably got dropped off somewhere on the continent. After everything settles down, I'll go find her for you."

Martha tried to smile. She would have to renegotiate her deal with God.

Chapter 17

June 29, 2012

Elaine Webber Griffin was sitting at Roger Webber's dressing table, going through his jewelry box. She was smiling as she remembered the times she'd seen her brother up on stage wearing the gaudy pieces of plastic and glass. There were boxes on the floor. She was packing up Roger's few possessions. Most would go to a resale shop run by a local AIDS service agency. It had been just a week since his death. The autopsy and coroner's report had delayed his funeral. Roger had left no instructions about burial. She had figured he would have been embarrassed by an oversized casket, so her mother, Bernice, and she had decided to have him cremated. He would finally be moving to Vancouver. She planned to bury his urn in a flower garden in her backyard. He would be surrounded by pansies and petunias.

The police report had indicated a probable drug overdose, and the coroner had confirmed it. Very little had shocked her about her brother over the years, but this news had disturbed her. In recent weeks, Roger had carried on to her about how happy he was with his new teeth and his weight loss. He had been ecstatic about his community theatre work, and he had sung the praises of his therapist. "I want you to meet her," Roger had said to Elaine. "She's a gay man in a straight woman's body. She totally gets me, and she won't take any crap from me. If I get all hissy, she just gives me this look, and I start laughing, and then she starts laughing. God, I love her."

He'd also been very proud of staying sober. She'd attended his three month sobriety ceremony at a Narcotics Anonymous meeting in a nearby church basement just a week before he died. On the day of his death, he had told her that he was going to the Manhole that night to prove to himself he could enjoy the evening without booze or drugs.

And then there had been Roger's most recent excitement about finding his twin brother. "He's model gorgeous," Roger had said. "I would look just like him if I lost a hundred pounds." Elaine hadn't had the heart to ask him how he could possibly know. But then, he had said, "I've seen pictures of him when he was in his twenties and thirties. And they took my breath away. It was like looking in the mirror. He's really famous and powerful, too. But I'm not going to tell you who he is until I speak to him. You're going to be so surprised."

Her brother had been many things, bitchy, narcissistic, lazy, cynical, creative, quick-witted and gluttonous. But, he had never been delusional. As much as he had carried on about his acting career and his many diets, she had known that he had known, in his heart of hearts, that they were lost causes. She had known about his brother fantasy for years, but never before had he ever hinted that a sibling might actually exist. Maybe he'd reached the man he called his twin and he'd been rejected. Maybe that was why he'd juiced up that night. She'd probably never know. She checked her watch. She would have to finish up quickly if she were going to make her plane that evening.

Placing Roger's jewelry in the box to be shipped to Vancouver, she stood and realized that something was radically wrong. When she'd been in town for his sobriety ceremony, she'd help him take down the centerfolds that had covered his mirrors. With his new false teeth, he had finally been willing to look at himself again. What was missing from the upper left hand corner of the mirror was Roger's eight by ten glossy from his salad days in London. For as long as he had owned the table, he'd kept the photo in that place of honor. It had been a shrine to his youth. It had held the promise that he might still some day regain his beauty.

When she couldn't find the old photo behind the dressing table or in the drawers, she started searching through a box of loose snapshots he had kept in his closet. She hadn't really bothered to look through them, thinking she'd take her time once she was back home. Halfway through the pile, she realized something else was radically wrong. None of Roger's childhood pictures were in the box. She flipped through them faster, thinking maybe he'd organized them in chronological order. But when she reached the last photo, one of Mike and her at her wedding, she realized that half the wedding photos she'd given him were missing. The thirty-year-old picture of Roger and her in London's Trafalgar Square, one of his favorites, was gone. There was no photo of her brother from the twentieth century.

Elaine looked around the tiny studio apartment and realized for the first time that she was at a crime scene. Her police training and her gut told her that Roger had not been alone the night of his death, and that his prattle about a twin brother had something to do with his passing. The thought made her angry and scared. She was angry that Roger had died just as he was beginning to help himself, and she was scared for herself and her family. Abandoning the boxes, she left Roger's apartment and headed for the church where he'd spent so much time.

An hour later, she was sitting down with Roger's therapist, Gillian Sorrell, in her cubbyhole office at the First Unitarian Church. Gillian seemed young to Elaine, too young to be the amazing counselor Roger had described. She was petite, pierced and punked out with a bleached blaze moussed at a forty-five degree angle above her chestnut brown shock of hair.

"Roger told me so much about you, and I barely had a chance to say hello at the funeral," Gillian said. "What can I do for you?"

"I'll get right to it, Gillian. I think my brother was murdered and I think it has to do with the man he presumed was his twin. He never identified him to me, but I was hoping he'd told you."

Gillian lost her sympathetic consoling smile. "When I heard that he had died, I thought there must be some mistake. And then I went back and checked my notes, looking for what I had missed. I couldn't find any warning signs. I was so hopeful for Roger. What makes you think he was murdered?"

"Somebody's stolen every photo of Roger before he hit three hundred pounds. I think they were trying to destroy any record that would confirm his resemblance to this mystery twin."

Gillian sucked in a long breath past the silver stud below her lower lip. "If it's the guy Roger told me about, he'd have his reasons to keep Roger quiet. I never thought they'd take him seriously." She opened a drawer in her credenza and lifted out a thick file. Leafing through it, she pulled out several pages and handed them to Elaine. "He printed these off the senator's campaign website at the library. Roger claimed he looked just like this guy when he was younger and slimmer."

Elaine studied the blurry printouts of Bob Hamilton's smiling face at Duke and on his wedding day. The shot with his wife and their first child was the one that stopped her cold. The young father, at thirty four, bore an uncanny resemblance to her brother, before he'd begun to pack on the pounds. "May I borrow these?" she asked.

"You can keep them. Just let me know what you find out." Gillian handed Elaine her card. "Your brother was a sweet, sad man. I hope his next time around, he gets a gentler path."

Elaine smiled weakly. "Didn't he tell you? The only way he's coming back is with Judy's voice, Marilyn's body and Oprah's money."

July 7, 2012

Larry McIntyre Jr. was straightening Frankie McIntyre's bow tie. They and their brothers, Joe and Luke, were nervously waiting in the anteroom just off the front of the sanctuary at the United Church of Christ in Bethesda, Maryland.

"Do you have the rings?" Frankie asked. He felt uncomfortable in his formal morning suit.

Larry Jr. smiled. "Yes, I have the rings."

"Show me," Frankie said.

Larry pulled them out of his pants pocket and presented them for Frankie's inspection. "See. I promise. I won't lose them."

"How do I look?"

"You look great."

Frankie turned to examine himself in the full length mirror by the door to the sanctuary. They could hear a Bach oratorio on the pipe organ. A trumpet trio chimed in with brassy clarity. "I don't look great," Frankie said with a frown.

Larry Jr. came up beside Frankie and looked in the mirror. "Of course you do. What do you mean?"

Frankie started to tear up. "Look at me. I'm ugly. Everybody's going to say, 'Look at the ugly groom.'"

Larry Jr. put his hand on Frankie's shoulder. "That's nonsense. You're young and handsome. I wish I was young, dark and handsome like you."

"You're just saying that because you're my brother." He stuck his tongue out at his image.

Larry Jr. stuck out his tongue and made a face.

"Stop making fun of me," Frankie said.

"I'll stop it when you stop feeling sorry for yourself. You are so lucky. You have a beautiful bride waiting to marry you. You're going to be a father soon. You've got a new home close by Lily's parents."

Frankie looked at himself one more time and then turned to face Larry Jr. "Is Mom coming?"

"You know Mom's not coming."

"She doesn't want me to get married. She's mad at me."

"Mom is Mom, Frankie. She's mad at me right now, too. And Joe and Luke."

"Because of me, right?"

"No, because for once we stood up to her. We should have done it a long time ago. Don't worry about Mom. She's got a disease that makes her angry all the time. It's nobody's fault. It just is. We can't fix her, but we don't have to be around her."

Frankie nodded. "She can't help herself?" The bridal procession music had begun.

"You're right. She can't help herself. I think she was born that way. Come on, let's line up. It's time to go."

"Like me."

"Huh?"

"I was born the way I am. She was born angry."

"You got it. Okay, let's get you married."

July 10, 2012

"How do you pick these places?" Emily McIntyre asked Pat McCormack with considerable irritation in her voice. He had just scooted into her Mercedes in the parking lot of the Groveton Confederate Cemetery in the middle of Manassas National Battle Park, west of Washington, D.C. In spite of the July heat, he was dryer this time. And fresher, too. The musk was missing.

Pat smirked. "I've told you. We can never meet in the same place twice. Did you take the route I gave you?"

"Yes."

"And did anyone follow you?"

"No."

"This is standard agency procedure. If you want to keep our meetings secret, you need to follow my directions. I know what I'm doing."

Emily bit her lip. She'd managed to eat most of her lipstick since she'd arrived. She swore he made her wait. And there was no apology this time. "What's so important?" she asked.

"The black guy. Jones. Hamilton's Peace Corps buddy."

"What about him?"

"He's found himself a boyfriend."

"Why is that a problem? I thought you suspected he was a homosexual?"

"The problem is not what he is, but why he decided all of the sudden to open the closet door. We know he's been following Gibson's stories in the *Post*, we know he's met with her, we know his sister and nephew are gay, and we know about the hinky phone call from Hamilton."

"I listened to that conversation. What was that all about?"

Pat winked at her. "Oh, come on, Emily. You can figure that one out. Two guys stuck in the jungle for months on end. Men have their needs. Jones probably gave Hamilton a blowjob or two."

Emily winced. She hated that word. She could still hear her husband, Larry, wheedling through the bathroom door, trying to coax her to submit to his wishes. "That's disgusting. This is why we should have them all locked up. They prey on the rest of us like vultures."

Pat shrugged. "Well, when you put it that way…."

"I still don't see what the big deal is. Jones hasn't peeped for all these years. He refused to give Gibson any dirt. Why do we care?"

"Because of what it signifies. Our psychiatric expert thinks Jones is starting to unravel. He's gone without any sexual contact for decades. Now, not only has he broken the seal, but he's seeing just one guy. He's risking his career, his reputation, everything."

"Sounds like a midlife crisis to me."

"Our doctor says it's something like that, but it's more critical. It's like a personality break. Hamilton's call may have precipitated it. There's no telling what he might do."

Emily felt nauseous. "What are you saying?"

"I'm saying he might pop off at any moment. He's a loose cannon."

"There's nothing to tell, is there?" Emily already knew the answer and could see headlines screaming scandal just days before the convention.

"It doesn't make any difference if he's telling the truth. Jones is no bimbo or crack head whore. He's a minister. And he's black. You don't want him on the *Today* show the morning Hamilton is nominated."

Emily suddenly opened the door of her Mercedes. A blast of heat filled the car. She vomited her breakfast onto the asphalt, splattering the side of her door with bits of poached egg and white bread toast in the process. Just as quickly, she slammed the door shut, locked it and reached for a tissue in her purse to wipe her lips.

"Are you okay?" Pat asked. He was delighted with her reaction. He had her right where he wanted her.

Emily was beet red with humiliation. She took a swig of her bottled water. "I'm fine. I think I've got a touch of food poisoning."

"So you can see what the problem is."

Emily looked out across the cemetery at the rows and rows of white headstones. So many souls dying for their country. The ultimate sacrifice. She closed her eyes and prayed silently. "Lord, give me strength to wield your sword for righteousness sake. Absolve me of this act for I do it to save the babies and the nation."

"Emily, are you all right?" Pat asked as he checked his watch. "I've got to leave soon. I'm picking up my sister at the airport."

She opened her eyes and glared at him. "Never, ever, talk to me while I'm praying."

"I'm sorry, it's just that—"

"I don't care about your sister. Why the hell is she coming to town? The convention's next week. If I can skip my own son's wedding, you can tell your sister to stay home."

"Listen, Bridget is no problem. She's been visiting me for years. She pretty much takes care of herself. She's a nun, for God's sake. She's easily amused."

Emily gripped her steering wheel. She wanted to scream. This creep was asking her to hurry up and approve Jones' murder so that he could meet his sister's plane."

"Do it!" she shouted.

"Do what?" He was recording her. He didn't want any misunderstanding later.

"Get rid of Jones," she said with a deep, guttural voice.

He could smell her vomit breath. The sulfurous odor almost made him gag. No woman had ever scared Pat. In his world, they were inherently inferior to men. They were meant to serve and please. He'd avoided female bosses at the CIA for that reason. But he couldn't avoid Emily McIntyre. She had offered him twice his annual compensation at Harris to work on the side for her. It had seemed too easy at first. All he had done was feed her information. But their roles had evolved. She had begun giving orders, and he knew they had to be followed. She had no limits, and he understood that. She would do whatever was necessary, regardless of the cost in human life. No one in the Hamilton campaign had her zeal. They were political amateurs by comparison. She played for keeps. And so did he.

July 12, 2012

Rosie Gibson was sitting in the third row from the back in the Washington National Cathedral. She'd never been in the huge gothic structure. The building seemed oddly out of place to her. A monument to the medieval Roman church built by anti-papist Anglicans in the heart of a black city. It was a hot Sunday in mid-July, but the nave was cool. Limestone walls rose from the marble floor into the darkness of the vaulted ceiling ten stories above her. She marveled at the intricacy and beauty of the stained glass windows. The late afternoon evensong service had just begun with the Great Choir singing some ethereal Latin chant. This wasn't so bad, she decided. She closed her eyes and started to dial up. The nub of her discussion was her relationship with Natalie. They were going through a rough spot. Rosie had become obsessed with cracking Bob Hamilton, and she hadn't been home much. For the first time in many years, Natalie was taking the summer off. She wasn't teaching. She wasn't taking courses. She was enjoying the season. And she wanted to share at least part of it with Rosie.

"Why did you pick an election year?" Rosie had asked when Natalie complained.

"Because I don't think in terms of politics. I think in terms of us. We need time for us. Now," Natalie had said. They had been standing in the small kitchen of their condo at midnight. Rosie had just arrived home from work and was dipping herself a big bowl of Cherry Garcia ice cream. Natalie had walked into the room, grumpy from having her sleep disturbed, dressed in a school T-shirt and panties, shielding her eyes from the overhead light.

"Well, I care about us, too," Rosie had responded as she put the nearly empty pint carton back in the freezer. "But I can't just walk away from this assignment. This man is dangerous."

Natalie had slumped into a chair at the kitchen table. "I know. I've read every article. You've been tearing him to shreds. But you've gone off the deep end. Give it a break this weekend."

Rosie had put down her spoon. She couldn't enjoy her Ben & Jerry's if Natalie was going to nag through every bite. "Honey, the convention's next week. I can't lay off now. I promise you after the convention, we'll go away. Just the two of us and relax."

Natalie had flounced out of the kitchen without a word, and they hadn't spoken since.

Rosie wasn't getting any Dear Abby answers from the Almighty at the cathedral, so she decided to sit back and enjoy the music. She'd just begun to nod off when someone sat down next to her and asked, "Are you Rosie?"

Rosie opened her eyes, sat up quickly and yelped, "Yes," before she remembered where she was. Several parishioners glared over their shoulders at her.

Sitting next to her was Elaine Webber Griffin. She was dressed in a prim black dress, her sign of mourning in a house of worship. Rosie was dressed in a canary yellow two piece suit, her sign that it was summer in the city. It had been two weeks since Elaine had spoken with her brother's therapist, Gillian Sorrell. She no longer knew anyone on the Toronto police force and no one would listen to her story about her brother's death being suspicious, especially after she had mentioned that she thought he might be Bob Hamilton's twin. And her husband, Mike, had been no more sympathetic. He'd suffered in silence with Roger's many dramas over the years, and he was not about to let the last one play out after his death on such a grand scale.

"Your brother was fucked up, Elaine," he'd said after listening to her crime theory. They were in their backyard. Mike had been digging a hole with a spade for Roger's urn, and she had been planting more petunias. A successful lawyer who spent too much time flying back and forth across the Pacific, he had grown pudgy and pasty.

"I know he was a mess," Elaine had said. "But he didn't make this up. I see the resemblance in those photos. It's uncanny. And what happened after he opened his mouth? He ends up dead and his prints have been stolen."

"Your brother had more bad luck than anyone I know, but that doesn't mean somebody murdered him. And certainly not some rich American politician who could care less what Roger Webber thought."

"Mike, they've removed all those photos and campaign videos from the website."

Mike had stopped digging and wiped his brow. "Let's say you're right for the sake of argument. Who do you go to with your story? The police in Toronto don't believe you. No one in American law enforcement is going to pay attention. If you're right, all you'll be doing is painting a bull's eye on your back and mine and the kids' and your mother's. Is that what you want?"

Elaine knew Mike wasn't really concerned about their safety because he thought it was all bullshit, but she was scared stiff and she was mad as hell. After a week of research online, she had decided the most sympathetic ear she could find belonged to Rosie Gibson. In their first call, Rosie had been rushed. She had been on deadline. "I've got photos of my brother, Ms. Gibson," Elaine had said. "Photos that prove he's Senator Hamilton's twin brother."

That remark had riveted Rosie's attention. "Can you come to Washington?" she had asked.

Elaine had made hard copies of snapshots of Roger from her own collection and scanned them all onto two duplicate computer disks. She'd left one set in the safe in their bedroom with a note to her husband, in the event something happened to her, and then scheduled her flight to coincide with his departure for Hong Kong. Her mother would care for her teenaged children. Her story was she was heading back to Toronto to finish packing up Roger's apartment.

Touching Elaine's hand, Rosie smiled and said, "Hi Elaine. Let's take a walk." They headed toward the altar and then out the south entrance. Rosie pointed toward a flagstone walkway. "Let's take a stroll through the gardens. Shall we?"

The two women found a bench with some shade. They were surrounded by lavender and poppies. "Thanks for seeing me, Rosie," Elaine said with a sigh. "I had no one else to turn to."

"I'm glad I can help."

Elaine opened a large canvas shoulder bag and pulled out a manila envelope. She handed it to Rosie. "These are photos of my brother. When he was younger."

Rosie emptied the envelope onto her lap. On top of the pile was a copy of Roger's favorite, his professional headshot, the one that he'd stuck on his dressing table mirror. He'd given it to Elaine when she'd visited him in London, and she'd framed it and hung it with other photos in the family room in Vancouver.

"He was so excited to have found his brother," Elaine said. "I checked his cell phone bill. It came in the mail after he died. He'd called one number in Washington several times, each for just a minute or two, but the last call lasted several minutes. I called the number. It was Jerry Boston's office at the Hamilton campaign. His secretary answered, and I said I had the wrong number."

"I know who Jerry Boston is," Rosie broke in. "He's the little weasel who created Hamilton. Nothing happens without his say so. He doesn't have the title, but he runs the campaign. And he's Hamilton's chief of staff."

"The last call was a week before his death. His therapist said he was waiting for them to call him back."

"You said you had some other evidence?"

"I had his bed sheets analyzed for DNA," Elaine said. "I used to be a cop. The lab found samples of semen and saliva from someone besides Roger. I'm convinced that man killed Roger"

"How do you know Roger didn't have company earlier?"

"Because I know Roger. He was a slob about everything but sex. He changed the sheets while his dates were getting dressed. It was major point of hygiene for him. 'Fresh bed linen is the mark of a true gentleman,' he always said. I was the first and only person Roger called after he'd been with someone. He always told me way more than I wanted to know, but I was always happy for him. That he had some joy in his life. There hadn't been any joy in Roger's life for many years, so if he had sex with another man, and I didn't hear about it, it's because that man murdered Roger before he had a chance to call me."

Rosie clasped Elaine's hand. "You must have been very close to your brother. I can't imagine my brother, James, being so intimate with me."

Elaine smiled to herself. "I was his only friend, and I feel like I failed him."

Rosie picked up the scent of the animal first. It was a pungent, feral odor. When she looked up, there, not ten feet away, the big cat paced, watching Rosie steadily, never breaking her gaze, as she circled back and forth.

Rosie nodded at the beast and then turned to Elaine. "Don't you worry. I'll find a way to tell your story."

July 16, 2012

Monday mornings were slow at the Church of the Inner Light in Detroit. There were no services or committee meetings or counseling sessions. It was usually Jonathan Jones' day off. Typically, he dropped by to pick up the receipts from the Sunday offering plate, deposited them at the local branch bank and went home. He had just unlocked the cash drawer in his desk when he heard the noise in the hallway. His office door was open. Not even the smallest child could approach without the ancient oak planks creaking. Relocking the drawer, he called out, "Who's there?"

When he didn't hear pounding footsteps retreating down the hallway, he knew he had a problem. It was not a teenage punk looking for a quick grab and go. Opening another drawer as loudly as he could, he pulled out his Bible and yelled, "I have a gun!"

Still no response. Maybe he had imagined it. It could have been a rat. Or the old building sagging. Or his tinnitus. His heart racing, he said a quick prayer for protection and walked cautiously toward the doorway. When he reached the hallway, he found it empty. Feeling somewhat more confident, he exhaled and walked down the hall toward the sanctuary.

With each step, Jonathan felt more certain that nothing was amiss. It was, after all, a glorious July morning, and, in a couple hours, he was leaving with Lincoln Armstrong to head north to Lincoln's cabin on a quiet little lake surrounded by pine trees and other well-appointed cottages. It was an enclave for Detroit's gay Baby Boomers. He was thinking about long sunny days, lazing in a row boat, pretending to fish, long evenings reading by a crackling fire, drinking a glass of wine, and long nights making love to Lincoln.

Jonathan's mind had left the building and traveled one hundred fifty miles north, only to come smashing back to inner city Detroit with a heavy blow to the right side of his head. His brain bounced violently back and forth inside his cracked skull, bruising severely at the point of impact. He collapsed in a heap, banging his head on the floor, causing yet another concussion.

Standing over Jonathan with the heavy brass cross from the altar, was Ed Brock, playing church thief, dressed all in black, from his leather gloves to the extra support panty hose pulled over his head. His assignment was to make the robbery look drug-crazed and spontaneous. The likely suspect should be a "coked up gang banger from the hood" Pat McCormack had instructed. He was not to use a gun, nor was he to use his lethal martial arts training. Professionally administered death blows to the nose or throat would not have been consistent with a homie crackhead's assault. He was to take the money, and, most importantly, take out Jonathan Jones.

Just as Ed raised the cross to whack Jonathan several more times for good measure, he was tackled from behind by Jeffrey Jones. The two men tussled, cursing and whaling away, as they rolled past Jonathan's inert body. When Lincoln Armstrong came running down the hallway, yelling, "Get the fuck off him, you motherfucker," Ed realized he had to abort. L'eggs or no L'eggs, his cover had been blown. He was not dressed like a brutha, and his white Irish skin was exposed where Jeffrey had pulled on his ears and torn his stocking.

Neutralizing Jeffrey with one elbow to his gut, he leapt to his feet just as Lincoln threw his first punch. Ed ducked and then flattened Lincoln with a blow to the back of his neck. Leaving his three victims sprawled on the floor, he sprinted to the door, pulling off his shredded hosiery, and launching himself down the steps. Thirty seconds later, he was burning rubber out of a nearby alley in his rental car and racing to the airport.

Still groaning with pain, Jeffrey crawled over to Jonathan, asking, "Are you all right, Uncle Jonathan?" He lowered his head to listen for breathing and put his finger on Jonathan's carotid artery. Jonathan's breathing was short and fast, and his pulse was pounding. As Lincoln slowly sat up, holding his neck, Jeffrey called 911 on his cell phone. A pool of blood was forming under Jonathan's head. Just as the operator answered, Jonathan stopped breathing. Jeffrey started screaming in the phone for help, crying uncontrollably as he pumped up and down on Jonathan's sternum.

Lincoln grabbed the phone from Jeffrey and yelled out the street address of the church. "Hurry, fast, please," Lincoln wailed. "We can't let him die!"

Chapter 18

July 16, 2012

"Whatever happened to the guy who claimed he was my twin?" Bob Hamilton asked Jerry Boston. They were riding in the back of a limousine from New York's LaGuardia International Airport to the presidential campaign's headquarters hotel, the Waldorf Astoria. It was Monday, the first day of the Republican National Convention, which was being held at Madison Square Garden. They were flanked by secret service agents in black SUV's front and back.

"McCormack shooed him away. He's a crackpot. McCormack said he doesn't look a thing like you. Very heavy." Jerry smiled.

"What? Why are you smiling? I could have a twin. At this point, nothing would surprise me," Bob said

"Apparently he's some old drag queen."

Bob's gut tightened. He looked out the window as the limo crossed the East River. "Have you talked to Alma today?"

"No, I left a message with her office. They were supposed to send a revised draft of her speech last night."

"God, I can't believe we're stuck with her."

"You're the one who caved in to Emily."

"I did not cave in. She was on our short list, too. She's good on paper. Hispanic, Roman Catholic, female, conservative, governor of a western state."

"Bitchy, crazy, ruthless, and dumb as a post," Jerry shot back.

"She passes all the litmus tests, abortion, gays, guns, death penalty. Israel, Jerry. She's very strong on Israel."

"That's because she's one of those rapture folks. When the Iranians finally blow up Jerusalem, she expects to fly up to heaven."

"She's never admitted to that."

"What? Flying? You better pray to God, you never need surgery once you're in the White House. She'd push the button herself if she thought she could see Jesus."

"You're pulling my leg. She doesn't get the football while I'm under. Does she?"

For the rest of the trip they grumbled about Arizona Governor Alma Cruz, Emily McIntyre's pick for Bob's vice president. At first they had resisted her selection, but polling showed they needed an ethnic female to counter the other party's ticket.

The limo pulled up in front of the Waldorf, and a Secret Service agent opened Bob's door. Twenty feet away, Josh Stein and his friend, Vince Scavullo, were making their way through the noonday throngs with bags from Barney's and Bloomingdales. Neither of them could afford Barney's, but both had found a hidden treasure on the bargain rack. They were in their gay summer uniforms, black slacks, tight pastel tops, leather sandals and Ray Ban sunglasses. In the midst of a heat wave, the New York streets were bleeding oil, and the air was fermenting with a combination of smog, garbage and Chanel. A bank sign down the avenue read one hundred one degrees Fahrenheit.

Bob and Jerry were marching toward the hotel's revolving door surrounded by a phalanx of security just as Josh and Vince reached the line of federal agents who were blocking their path. Josh pulled off his sunglasses to rub his eyes. The acrid air was making them burn. He had just begun to ask Vince, "What's this all about?" when his eyes locked with Bob's.

Bob Hamilton and Josh Stein were slightly taller than the men in black. Josh immediately put his hand on Vince's shoulder and stood on his tiptoes. Bob continued to walk forward, but he was craning his neck, looking back over his shoulder at Josh, his eyes wide open, as if he'd seen a ghost.

"Watch your step," Jerry said just as Bob caught his shoe on the edge of the carpet at the hotel entrance. Bob fell forward against Agent Brady, who immediately assumed Bob had been shot. Brady whipped around, pulling his gun, throwing Bob further off balance. He fell against Jerry, knocking him to the ground and banging his head against the rim of the revolving door.

Agent Brady yelled, "He's down!" Twenty young men in suits pulled their guns and searched in every direction. Another twenty agents stepped out of the crowd, one of them shouting, "Everybody on the ground! Now!"

Everyone but Josh hit the pavement. He hadn't heard the command. He was too focused on the tall guy who'd tripped. Vince jerked on Josh's arm. "Get down, Josh," he screamed in a panic.

Just then, Agent Wilson aimed his gun at Josh and said, "Put your hands up and drop to your knees!"

By then the agents had hustled Bob and the bleeding, cussing Jerry inside the hotel, and Josh regained his senses. Slowly, he raised his hands and knelt, dumbfounded by what he had just seen.

Agent Wilson was aiming at Josh's forehead, and three other

agents had circled him, each of them aiming at a different quadrant of his skull. What bothered them was that Josh was not screaming, "Don't shoot." Something they would expect from an innocent civilian. With a muscular build, a flat tummy, close-cropped dark hair, a graying goatee, aboriginal-designed tattoos crawling around his bulging biceps and a diamond stud in his left earlobe, he looked definitively un-American.

Just as Agent Maxwell was about to kick Josh to the ground from the rear, Agent Brady stepped outside and yelled, "The senator's fine. He tripped."

The agents holstered their guns, and Wilson announced, "All clear. You can get up now."

Everyone else stood, but Josh stayed on his knees. He was replaying in his mind the brief moments that had occurred before the senator went down.

"Josh, what's wrong with you?" Vince asked, jiggling his shoulder. "Come on. Get up. Let's get out of here before somebody shoots you."

They walked two blocks with Vince doing all the talking and Josh grunting responses, all of it about their close call with a security meltdown. "I can't believe it. They were about to blow your head off," Vince was saying.

"Who was that guy?" Josh asked.

"Bob Hamilton. He's a Jesus freak running for president."

Josh stopped Vince in the middle of the sidewalk and said, "Look at me. Do you think I look anything like that guy? Hamilton."

Vince squinted as he considered the possibility. "Seriously, Josh. I know you'd love to find your family. But you don't want to be related to that guy. He's a big time gay basher."

"I don't care about his politics. Just look at me objectively. What do you think?"

Vince steered Josh to the curb to avoid angry comments from New Yorkers trying to grab lunch and get back to the office in thirty minutes. "Listen, maybe you do. I don't know. I try not to look at the man any more than I have to. I switch channels when his ads come on."

"I understand you hate his guts. Just tell me what you think."

Vince studied Josh's face. "I guess. Maybe in the facial structure and the eyes. And the eyebrows. And hairline. Smile for me."

Josh dutifully smiled his toothiest politician's smile.

"You've definitely got the same smile, except I don't trust his. You're better looking."

"No, I'm not. The rest of it is superficial. I look Australian gay. He looks mainstream America."

"No, he looks very wealthy, cob up his ass, America."

"You won't let yourself see it, will you? He and I looked into each other's eyes, and we both freaked. I could tell. I spooked him."

"Are you telling me he's gay?"

"No, I'm telling you we were both thinking the same thing."

Back at Vince's apartment in Chelsea, while Vince jumped into the shower, Josh went online to learn what he could about Bob Hamilton. Wikipedia told him they shared the same birthday and they were the same height. He copied the page with Bob's official Senate photograph. Maybe they were distant cousins who, by some quirk of fate and genes, had been born on the same day with near identical looks four thousand miles apart. Or maybe, just maybe, they were twins tragically separated at birth. Or maybe it was all wishful thinking, fueled by the fumes of Manhattan on broil.

In his suite at the Waldorf, Bob Hamilton had cancelled meetings with state delegations and gone into seclusion. The excuse was a stomach bug, but the truth was dysphoria. "What was the story on the guy in Toronto again?" Bob asked Jerry Boston. Bob was sitting on a couch trying to control his nervous bowels, and Jerry was pacing, sporting six stitches above his left eye, worried about Bob's peculiar behavior.

"Why do you care? He's a nut."

"Because I saw a guy on the sidewalk who looked just like me. It was like somebody hired one of those celebrity doubles. Maybe the other side knows about the adoption and the crank calls, and they're trying to get me rattled."

"Oh, please. What did he look like?"

"Well, he was tall, good looking, tanned, very short hair, my age, I'd say. Oh, yeah, he had a goatee and a diamond in his ear."

"That sounds like half of New York. Don't you think if they went to all that trouble, they'd make him shave, get rid of the ear ring and dress him up in a suit?"

"No, this was much more disturbing. It was like it was me, but from a parallel universe."

Jerry sat down on the coffee table and looked Bob in the eyes. "Are you cracking up on me?"

"I'm not crazy, and, now that I think about it, he wasn't a plant. He was as surprised as I was."

"Bob, it was a random serendipitous coincidence. Let's not forget why we're here. We've worked too hard. Let's not screw it up now. Do you have your speech?"

"Yes."

"Then, let me hear it from the top. And no more twin talk. Okay?"

"Okay."

July 17, 2012

"Why do I have to go?" eighteen-year-old Martha Hamilton asked. She was standing in her parents' bedroom in Druid Hills, Atlanta, early Tuesday morning, the week of the Republican Convention.

"We've been through this. You know why," Kathleen Hamilton said. She was closing one of her suitcases.

Martha clenched her teeth. "This is the last time I will ever appear in front of a camera with him."

"It will be my last time, too, dear. In a weak moment, I promised your father if he won the nomination, we'd join him one last time."

"Since when do you have weak moments? I thought you'd given him an ultimatum."

"I'd rather not discuss it. Let's just say I lost a bet. Now go tell Lulu your bags are ready."

"I can carry my own bags downstairs."

As Martha stomped out, sixteen-year-old Mary Hamilton bounded into the room. She was wearing an incredibly short black skirt and a tight lime green sleeveless top with a plunging V neckline. "Mom, can I ask you something?"

Kathleen was deep in her closet, making her final shoe selection. "What is it, Mary?"

Mary stood at the door to the closet, leaning against the frame, striking her best wheedling pose, with her arms behind her back. "Can Boo come with us?"

"Who is Boo? And the answer is 'No' unless Boo is a small stuffed animal."

"Mother, how could you not know who Boo is? I've been talking about him forever. He's my boyfriend. Boo Boynton. He's captain of the football team. Or at least he will be this fall. He can bunk with Rob."

Kathleen was even deeper into the huge closet. "The answer is still 'No'. What happened to Brett or Bud?"

"Oh, God, mother, I broke up with Baird last month."

"Well, I'm sorry if I can't keep up, Mary, but you go through boyfriends like some women go through stockings."

"Mother! That's so mean. I love Boo!"

"I'm sure you do, dear. As much you loved Baird and all the rest of them."

Mary pretended to cry. "You just say that because you didn't have boyfriends in high school."

Kathleen smiled to herself. "You're right, but then I married your father, didn't I? Think about it. Quality over quantity."

"What are you saying? That I'm a tramp?" Mary had given up on trying to manufacture tears.

Kathleen turned toward her daughter, her arms full of shoes. She took one glance at her daughter's outfit and said, "From the way you're dressed, I'd say you pegged it yourself. Go change. Right now. Or I'll come pack for you."

Mary ran out of the room shrieking. Kathleen dropped the shoes into her second suit case, and called out, "Rob, are you ready? We need to leave for the airport soon." When there was no response, she headed down the hall to his room. The door was closed. She knocked and heard a faint "Yes."

Inside, she found her son sitting on the edge of his bed, his bag next to him. The shades were drawn and the room was dark. "Are you okay?" she asked.

"Yeah, I'm fine."

She sat down next to him and put her arm around him. "What's wrong?"

"You know what's wrong. Kamal won't speak to me. I think he blames me for getting kicked out of school."

"He shouldn't do that. It wasn't your fault he was smoking pot."

"Yeah, but I told him about the calls I got. Somebody knew about us."

"Wait a minute. What calls are you talking about?"

"Anonymous calls. In the middle of the night. Some guy with a gruff voice."

"What did he say?"

"Things like, 'Hey Robbie boy. We know you're a faggot. Break it off with the black kid or we'll call your coach."

"Oh, no. Rob. That's horrible. You should have told me sooner."

"You've got enough to worry about without me whining."

"Nonsense. You're my son. I don't want anyone threatening you. Listen, I know you don't want to go to this convention either. None of us do. Except for Mary."

"And Boo." Rob smiled.

"So, you heard the drama?"

"I'm surprised she waited to do Boo last. She's dated the rest of the team. Now, she's got a complete set."

Kathleen laughed and hugged him. "I just pray she doesn't get pregnant. Anyway, what I was saying was, as soon as we get home, I want the three of us, you, your dad and I, to talk. About you. And Kamal. He needs to know."

Rob shook his head. "It'll kill him."

"No, it won't. He wants you to be happy, just like I do."

"Are we talking about the same guy? He wants us to be poster children for his career."

"I know he may seem that way, but he does love you."

Mary called from the bottom of the stairs. "The car's packed. Dallas says we need to go, or we'll miss the plane."

Kathleen gave Rob one more squeeze and jumped up. "See you downstairs." She hurried back to her room. Her luggage was gone. Lulu, the maid, had lugged the bags down to the car, where Dallas, the chauffeur, had loaded them into the Cadillac Escalade. Kathleen looked around the room one more time to make sure she hadn't forgotten anything. The phone rang, and she wasn't thinking when she answered. She had learned long ago to let Lulu screen calls on the land line.

"Hello, is this Mrs. Hamilton?"

The distinctly Australian accent threw her off. "Yes."

"My name is Joshua Stein. I've been trying to reach your husband with no success. I gather he's very busy this week. So I wanted to leave a message for him."

"Listen, can you call back in two minutes and the maid will take your message? I'm running out the door."

"I'm sorry. I'll be quick. I just saw your husband outside his hotel here in New York, and I think we're related. I was adopted and I wondered if he were adopted. We share the same birthday and we look alike. I know this sounds crazy, but I'm very sane. I'm a retired university professor from Sydney in New York on holiday. Here's my number."

Exasperated, she pretended to take down his number. "Goodbye, Mr. Stein." Shaking her head, she hurried down the stairs. The whack jobs were coming out of the woodwork. She couldn't wait for the election to be over.

• • •

"We're not running that story, and that's final," Max Sherman shouted into his receiver. He was in his office at the *Washington Post*, and Rosie was at the Republican National Convention's media center, set up in rented space across the street from Madison Square Garden. She was standing in the tiny cubicle assigned to her, staring down at her laptop screen. It was late Tuesday afternoon, and the deadline for filing her story was fast approaching. She had written two stories. The first was the conventional convention story, summarizing Bob Hamilton's meteoric rise to the top of the party's elite, his consolidation of power, his fence mending with defeated foes, his shaping of the party's platform, his alliance with Emily McIntyre and his family's preparations to join him for his evening of triumph. The second story was the shockingly nasty tale of the death of Roger Webber after he had contacted the Hamilton campaign, claiming to be Bob's twin brother, complete with side by side photos of Roger and Bob when they were young men. The most striking pairing was Roger's London headshot and Bob's senior picture at Duke University.

"They look exactly alike," Rosie had proclaimed to Max earlier that day.

"They look like the biggest lawsuit we could ever buy," Max had replied.

"I can't believe it's come to this," Rosie had sputtered. "Hamilton threatens to sue and we back down from the biggest story of the year. If Watergate were to happen today, the break-in would never make it past our lawyers"

Max had guffawed. "Rosie, this is no Watergate, and you're no Woodward. This story is full of holes. The police and coroner's reports are lock tight. The deceased is a loony. The body's been cremated. A stranger's semen on a gay man's sheets is not news. The campaign flatly denies it ever received calls from anyone claiming to be

Hamilton's twin. And the sister's story that photos are missing proves nothing. She didn't even file a police report that they were stolen, and she used to be a cop. It's all innuendo and conspiracy theory. We're not the *National Enquirer*. At least not yet."

Rosie had stewed all day as she dug deeper into the Webber story. She was in touch with Elaine Webber Griffin who was interviewing the staff at the Manhole bar about Roger's last night. She was quizzing Bernice, Roger's mother, about the circumstances of his adoption. And, she was checking with researchers who were trying to find specimens of Bob Hamilton's DNA. She didn't have any additional information when she called Max to make one more pitch. It was a short, blunt discussion.

"You're going to regret this, Max," she said as she hung up on him, still staring at the two photos on her computer screen. She pushed send on the conventional convention story and went searching for the gourmet cookies the Republican Party had supplied to the press corps. As much as they hated journalists, the Republicans always catered better food.

Making her way through the warren of cubicles filled with reporters from all over the country and around the world, she didn't hear her cell phone until the last ring. Flipping it open, she saw a number she didn't recognize. "Hello," she said.

"Ms. Gibson, is that you?" Georgia Jones asked.

Rosie could tell that the caller was upset. "Yes, who's calling?" She had reached the refreshment table and found only crumbs remaining.

"It's Georgia Jones, Jonathan's sister. Something terrible has happened. Jonathan's been hurt."

Rosie went weak in the knees. She sat down in the nearest cubicle. The Kuwaiti television reporter was at prayers and would never know what transpired in his chair. "Please tell me he's okay," Rosie said.

"He's in bad shape. Someone attacked him at the church yesterday morning. He's had brain trauma. I guess that's the word for a really severe concussion. He's on a ventilator to keep him breathing, and he's in a coma. The doctors are going to keep him in the coma until the swelling in his brain goes down."

"Oh, I'm so sorry, Georgia. I wish there was something I could do."

There was a pause on the line, and then Georgia said, more

calmly now, "There is. My nephew and Jonathan's boyfriend fought off the attacker. Jonathan was alone, just dropping by to get the Sunday offering. Somebody must have known his routine. They were waiting for him. Jeffrey ran over to the church to tell him that Lincoln had come by early to pick him up for their vacation."

"I didn't know Jonathan had a boyfriend," Rosie said, dabbing away tears.

"Yeah, they've only known each other a short time, but they're in love. I was so happy for Jonathan. He'd played it safe for so many years. He was finally beginning to live his life."

"What can I do?"

"Jeffrey said the man who attacked Jonathan was a white guy. He wore all black and a woman's nylon hose over his face. He knew what he was doing. He was no thief. He was there to kill Jonathan, and he would have if Jeffrey and Lincoln hadn't shown up."

"Oh, that's horrible." Tears were streaming down Rosie's cheeks. "He's such a good man. Who would do such a thing?"

There was another pause on the line. "I think Bob Hamilton put out a contract on my brother because they were lovers in the Peace Corps, and he wanted to make sure Jonathan never talked. Hamilton called Jonathan a while back, after your visit, to make sure he had kept his mouth shut, and Jonathan told him not to worry. But I think Hamilton decided to shut him up anyway."

Rosie got a sickening feeling, the kind she got when she saw photos of lynchings or Holocaust survivors or torture victims. She had always wanted to look away, but she had always forced herself to look back, to remember that as much hope as she had for humankind, there was still a grotesque, twisted slice of her species who would rape and murder as long as no one stopped them. It helped her remember that part of her job was to shed light on the dark corners and tell the world who was responsible.

"Georgia, I'm going to call you right back. I've got a story I have to file. Please know that I'm praying for Jonathan."

While she was on the phone, the large cat had crept into the cubicle and leapt up onto the desk. She was sitting not three feet from Rosie, her eyes lidded, her demeanor subdued. There was a tranquility about the animal this time that Rosie had never witnessed. Without thinking, she reached out and gently touched the cat's head. The contact was ever so brief, but the impact was powerful. All of Rosie's sadness and anger and fear dissolved into an overwhelming sense of peace and calm.

Within five minutes, five thousand journalists on all ten floors of the media center had an email message flashing on their screen. It was Rosie's story about Roger Webber, under her *Washington Post* byline. The article was entitled: "Hamilton's Alleged Identical Twin Brother Dies Mysterious Death, Prince of the Pharisees Refused to Meet with Possible Pauper Kin."

• • •

"Hey Natalie, it's Rosie."

"Rosie who?" Natalie Jordan answered. She was sitting on the back porch of their condo with the cats, Latifah and Henrietta, reading a lesbian romance novel and sipping a glass of white wine.

"Rosie who loves you more than life itself, Rosie."

"I don't know anyone by that name. Good-bye."

"Don't hang up, please. This is important. I just did something very dangerous, and I need for you to take the cats and go to your parents right now."

Natalie closed her book and sat up. "What's wrong?"

"Turn on CNN in about fifteen minutes and you'll see. I dropped a bomb on Hamilton, and there's going to be a lot of angry white men running around, looking for me. I want you some place safe. I'm sorry. I'll make it up to you. I've got to go."

• • •

The Hamilton for President Campaign Committee issued a press release thirty minutes after Rosie's story exploded onto the cable networks and blogosphere. It stated:

> Senator Robert Hamilton categorically denies each and every statement made by Rosa Parks Gibson in her screed about the unfortunate death of a Canadian citizen named Roger Webber. Ms. Gibson has conducted a one woman campaign to destroy the senator's reputation pursuant to her ultra left-wing radical homosexual agenda. Her employer, *The Washington Post*, has summarily terminated Ms. Gibson and apologized to Senator Hamilton for her unauthorized and unlawful use of her position to issue a knowingly false

story. The senator will seek damages against Ms. Gibson and the *Post* and is asking law enforcement authorities to determine if Ms. Gibson has committed a crime.

Chapter 19

July 18, 2012

Emily McIntyre had just finished praying over her oatmeal and strawberries and was about to take her first bite when the telephone rang. She was sitting in her suite at The Ritz Carlton Hotel in Manhattan, overlooking Central Park, early Wednesday morning. The room was full of congratulatory bouquets from Foundation chapters across the country. All of them delighted that she would be speaking that night at the Republican National Convention. Hers would be the last speech before Bob Hamilton's name was placed in nomination.

"Hello," she said.

"Emily, it's McCormack."

"I told you never to call me."

"I had no choice. We've got a problem and I have to run it by you before I take action."

"I thought everything was under control. Has Jones come out of his coma?"

"No, we're okay there for now. This is a new problem. Yesterday morning, a guy name Joshua Stein called the Hamilton residence. The senator's wife answered. Stein claims he's Hamilton's twin, too. And he made no mention of Webber. He told her he was a college professor from Australia and he wants to talk to Hamilton."

"Jesus, was there a whole litter?"

"It gets worse. We checked him out. He is who he says he is, and he's gay. He's written several queer novels. We called him on behalf of the Hamilton campaign and got his address in New York. And we have him under surveillance. He's a dead ringer for Hamilton. Same birthday. He's waiting to hear back from the campaign. We could schedule a meeting and take him out."

"How do you know he's not a copycat? With all the hullabaloo about Webber."

"Because he couldn't have known about Webber before he made the call. We don't have time for DNA samples. It looks like there were triplets. If not more."

Emily looked around the room at the hundreds of roses. A petal fell from one and then another. They all appeared to be wilting as the morning sun streamed into her room. If Hamilton even hinted that he accepted his gay brother, she knew that she would be ruined as a kingmaker. She would be a laughingstock among the God-fearing faithful. More important, the White House, along with Christendom, would be lost.

"Wait a second while I pray," she told Pat. She put the receiver down and knelt beside her bed. Burying her head in a pillow, she screamed like a banshee. When she was done, she took her head out of the pillow and whispered, "Amen."

Standing, she took the receiver. "All right, take care of it, but get somebody else to do it. I'm sick and tired of your guy botching everything. First, he lets the mother get away, and then he bungles the Jones job."

"I can't bring anyone else in on this operation. He'll be all right. I sent him up to New York as soon as I learned about the call. He's been watching Stein since last evening."

Emily gritted her teeth. "All right, but no more screw-ups. You're the one I hired, and you're the one I expect to carry out my orders." She hung up before he could answer.

Sitting down to eat her breakfast, she turned on Fox News. Just as she finished her oatmeal, the talking head said, "We have a developing news story coming to us live from Fort Myers, Florida."

Edna Roberts's face flashed onto the screen, but Emily didn't recognize her. Edna was standing in front of a bank of microphones, looking particularly vivacious in a tight low-cut black Dolce & Gabbana top. She was wearing a diamond necklace identical to the one Larry had given Emily. Emily switched channels to CNN, but Edna was still on the screen. She kept changing channels, but all the morning news shows had video feeds from Edna's press conference. Emily was headed to the bathroom to brush her teeth when she heard Edna's familiar sing-song voice.

"Ladies and gentlemen of the press, my fellow Americans, and most particularly, Emily McIntyre, I am here to confess my sins and ask forgiveness from Mrs. McIntyre. I am Edna Roberts and for most of my working life, I was Larry McIntyre's personal secretary, most recently at the American Family First Foundation. Shortly after Larry returned home from Vietnam, he and I began an affair that lasted until he died at his desk while I was having oral sex with him. I am not ashamed to admit that I gave pleasure to this good man that he could not find at home, but I am ashamed that I was a party to adultery, which I consider to be a mortal sin. In recent years, I have returned to the faith of my youth, Roman Catholicism, and I therefore confess my sins and seek absolution to avoid condemnation of my soul to the fires of Hell. Please forgive me Emily. Now, I'll take questions."

"Is it true that you've signed a book deal?"

"I'm in negotiation with several publishers, but I haven't finalized a deal yet," Edna responded. "Apparently there is quite a bit of interest in my story of secret love and redemption."

"Are you saying that Larry McIntyre and you were in love?"

Edna smiled and lightly touched her necklace. "We were and he was a very generous man and a wonderful father. I convinced him to stay in his marriage for the children's sake."

Emily McIntyre had been sitting on the bed, watching the broadcast stone-faced. She turned off the television and picked up the framed photo of her husband from the bedside table. After extracting the print, she walked into the bathroom and stood over the toilet, meticulously tearing it into tiny bits. Before she could flush, she grabbed her stomach in pain. Bent in half, she made an unearthly howl as oatmeal and strawberries cascaded out of her mouth and onto the soggy remnants of her one and only hero.

• • •

Pat McCormack was sitting on the toilet in his bathroom at home when he got the call. It was Harris Security's Herman Baumgartner, calling from Madrid. "She just got on a plane for Atlanta, with a connecting flight to Savannah. She's reserved a rental car at the airport. She's traveling under the name Erma Holt, and she should be arriving in Savannah at 7:00 p.m. on American Airlines Flight 1645."

Pat scribbled the information across the breasts of the Playboy centerfold he was examining. "Thanks, I'll take care of it."

• • •

Bob Hamilton was just walking out of his press conference at the Waldorf Astoria Hotel when Jerry Boston pulled him aside. Bob had spent the last hour denouncing Rosie Gibson's slanderous story that he had something to do with the near fatal attack on Reverend Jonathan Jones and that they had been lovers while they were stationed in Peru during their Peace Corps assignment. He'd finished by saying, "Consider the source. Ms. Gibson has been on a witch hunt to destroy me for the last six months. When she couldn't find any dirt, she started making it up. *The Washington Post* has denounced her for violating the ethics of her trade. The only reason, she's got press credentials is because the *Advocate*, a radical gay rag, hired her this morning. I'm sure it was all orchestrated for maximum damage to me and my campaign to restore family values to their rightful place in this country."

"I've cancelled your lunch with the Platinum Heaven Club," Jerry said. "I need you to come with me."

"Emily is going to be furious."

"Fuck Emily. We're through with her. We may be through, period."

They went back to Jerry and Diane's suite. Their families were having lunch with the spouses and children of other party luminaries. Jerry refused to explain until they were safely inside the room, and the door was bolted.

"I got this by messenger an hour ago." Jerry pulled a small tape recorder out of the room's safe and set it up on a table by the window overlooking Park Avenue. "It came in this box." Printed neatly across the top of the box was the message, "From your friends, Emily McIntyre and Pat McCormack." Billy Short had never mastered cursive.

"I don't understand," Bob said.

"You will. Soon enough." Jerry turned on the machine, and the two men stood over the table listening to a crystal clear recording of the telephone conversation between Emily McIntyre and Pat McCormack that morning. They could even hear Emily's muffled scream.

"Maybe it's been doctored up," Bob said. "They could do almost anything with the new technology." Bob looked down at the noonday traffic. "I can't believe they would bug my house."

Jerry shook his head. "I'm afraid it's genuine. I have a confession to make. McCormack may have misunderstood my orders."

Bob pivoted and glared at Jerry. "What orders?"

Jerry looked at the floor. "I got pissed off with his stalling. I'd had a few cocktails at your New Year's Eve party. The Iowa caucuses were just around the corner. McCormack gave me some bullshit that he'd met my deadline because he'd found your parents' wedding guest list. I lost my temper. I told him that it was his job to make the problem go away. When I heard about Webber, it crossed my mind that, well, McCormack might have thought he had approval to...."

"Approval to what?" Bob shouted. "Commit murder?" Bob's face had turned bright red. He'd already soaked his shirt during the recording, and Jerry's revelation had begun to make the room spin. He started to faint when Jerry caught him and landed him in a chair by the table. After a glass of water and some slow breathing with his head between his knees, Bob sat up and looked at Jerry, who was seated across the table from him.

"You're fired," Bob said.

"I understand how you feel, Bob, but you can't go through this alone. I didn't know anything about McCormack and McIntyre working together."

"I know, but you're still fired. The guy you hired to protect my ass is on a killing spree because you lost your temper."

Jerry shook his head. "Listen, Bob. When Gibson's story came out, I was as shocked as anyone. I feared the worst, but I couldn't believe McCormack would do such a thing on his own. And then I listened to this recording, and it all made sense."

"Shit!" Bob hit the table with his fist. "That's the guy who called my house, Jerry. The guy who freaked me out when we arrived. He thinks he's my brother. And because of you, he may be dead by now!"

Jerry was biting the inside of his mouth so hard, it had started to bleed. His migraine headache was ferocious. He squinted at the arrogant asshole who was trying to dump the entire pile of shit in his lap. He stood and buttoned his suit coat. "You son of a bitch! You don't have to fire me, because I quit. You listened to the same recording I did, but you've already selectively forgotten who ordered who to do what. McCormack has been taking orders from your dear friend, Emily McIntyre. She's the puppet master here. It's not my family that's fucked up with queers coming out of every corner of the globe to profess that they're my brother. It's not my old buddy who's claiming he sucked my dick in the jungle. Or was it the other way around?"

Bob sat back and covered his face with his hands. He wanted to cry, but he couldn't. "Actually, it was a little bit of both."

• • •

Pat McCormack was rushing down the stairs toward the front door of his home. He was headed to the airport, and he was excited. Eighty-eight-year-old Elizabeth Hoffmeier was his mark. It had been a long time. Just as he reached the bottom step, his sister, Bridget, stepped in front of the door.

"Hey, Bridge, sorry about this. I won't be gone long. I should be back later tonight."

Bridget didn't move. She stood with her hands behind her back and said. "You're not going, Pat. You're going to stay here with me and pray for your salvation."

Pat smiled. "You never give up, do you? I tell you what. You pray while I'm gone, and I'll go to mass with you tomorrow. Now move out of the way. I'm in a hurry."

Bridget pulled a gun out from behind her back and aimed it at Pat's heart. It was his favorite. The Walther PPK, the gun that Ian Fleming had made famous in his James Bond novels. "Sit down on the steps, Pat. We're going to talk."

"What's this all about?"

"Sit!" she snapped with all the authority of a third grade teacher.

Pat sat. "Spit it out. I've got a plane to catch."

"I heard your phone call this morning. The one with someone named Emily. I was listening at your bedroom door. And I've been watching the news. I know what you've been doing, Pat. And I can't let you continue hurting people."

Pat smirked. "You completely misunderstood that call. I've haven't hurt a flea since I left the agency. I'm a civilian now, Bridge. Let me go, and we can talk when I get back." He started to get up.

"Sit," she said, as she fired a shot over his head into the stairway carpet.

Pat lost his smile and sat down quickly. "Odd Job! Dr. No!"

"I let your dogs out. They're not going to help you. You were going to sic them on me, weren't you, Paddy? What were they going to do? Tear my throat out? Is this what you've become? You'd kill your own sister?"

Pat sneered at her. "Listen, you chose your path in life and I chose mine. I don't judge you and you shouldn't judge me. I've always been good to you. Why did you decide today of all days to stop me?"

"It's bad enough what you did for the government, but I can't let you keep killing innocent people for whoever pays you the most money. Don't you see how wrong that is?"

"What do you know about what is wrong? What's wrong is the Catholic Church killing all the Jews before each crusade, or standing by while Hitler murdered six million more or letting half of Africa die from AIDS because it preaches against condoms. Those are the pricks you work for. A bunch of faggoty old men in Armani robes diddling young boys when they're not telling the rest of us what to do."

"The church is not Christ, Paddy. It's run by humans, faggoty old men, if you will, but that's doesn't take away from the original message of do unto others as you would have them do unto you. Now, will you agree to pray with me?"

"What can I say? You've got the gun. Let's go in the other room where we can be more comfortable." Watching his sister, Pat rose slowly from his seat. "Come on. Put down the gun. How can I pray with a gun aimed at me?"

Bridget had never held a gun before. She was nervous. The noise and power of the bullet she had fired had rattled her even more. She wanted to believe her brother was capable of redemption. He smiled at her, holding out his arms. She smiled, hopeful, relieved. The tremor in her arm and the momentary drop in the angle of the gun barrel were all he needed to see. Lunging toward her, he hoped to surprise her, he hoped she would freeze, too scared that she would harm her brother, he hoped to grab her wrist and break it with one quick snap.

The bullet entered his brain right between his eyes and tore through the gray matter on its way out the back of his skull, splintering the newel post before it lodged deep in the sub-flooring of the entryway. The power of the bullet was enough to stop Pat's forward momentum. He landed on his knees, looking up at his sister in amazement. He couldn't believe Bridget had actually pulled the trigger. As blood poured out of his brain and into his open mouth, he tried to speak, attempting to mouth one final "Fuck you." But Bridget chose to hear "Father, forgive me."

Crying, she grabbed Pat's shoulders and gently laid him down on a pale Persian rug, now stained deep red with his blood. His eyes remained open, but his heart had stopped. For the next thirty seconds, he could still hear her as she started to pray, "Hail Mary, full of grace, the Lord is with Thee...."

• • •

"Hey, Momma, surprise! I'd like you to meet my wife, Lily." Frankie McIntyre and his bride were all smiles, standing in the doorway to Emily's McIntyre's suite at The Plaza Hotel. A foot shorter than Frankie, Lily was a cute redhead with freckles and a gap-toothed smile. At seven months, her swollen belly stretched her bright pink maternity dress to the last thread. Frankie was dressed for touring, in blue plaid shorts, a pink polo shirt and running shoes.

Emily had answered the door expecting room service. She had ordered lobster bisque and grilled asparagus, a light supper that would settle easily before she gave her speech at the convention. "Frankie, Lily, what are you doing here?"

"We're on our honeymoon," Frankie said as Lily and he stepped past Emily. "We're here with Lily's parents." He went to the window to look at the view of Central Park at sunset. "We've been to the Statue of Liberty and the Empire State Building, and now, we've come to see you. Our room doesn't face the park. You've got the best room, Momma."

Emily stayed at the door, hoping to keep the visit short. "Where are your parents, Lily?"

"They're taking a nap. We're staying here, too."

"Oh, how nice. Well, I hope to meet your parents, Lily. Maybe tomorrow morning for breakfast. Right now, I have to get ready for my speech. It's a very important speech. The most important one of my life. I need to be alone right now so I can practice it."

Just then room service arrived and the phone rang. It was Bob Hamilton. "Frankie, this is an important call from Mr. Hamilton, the man who is running for president. How about I call you tomorrow morning?"

The waiter retreated without a tip, and Frankie and Lily continued to stare out the window, pointing out the sights.

"Emily, I listened to a recording of a very disturbing phone call between Pat McCormack and you this morning," Bob said.

"Why, I don't know what you're talking about, Bob." Emily frantically motioned for Frankie and Lily to leave, but they were giggling at a pair of pigeons crawling along the ledge just outside the window. The male was all puffed up, trying to impress the female. He was trying to mount her, but she was having none of it.

"Don't bullshit me, Emily. Jerry told me about the call from Webber. He referred it to McCormack and McCormack went to you. It's all in the recording. Jones, too. Now, you're trying to kill my other brother. I've spent the afternoon trying to get hold of McCormack. His partners don't know where he is and they claim not to know about any of this. So I want you to order McCormack to call it off. Now, before it's too late."

"I don't even know who this McCormack is. It sounds like

somebody's gone to a lot of trouble trying to sound like me. This has to be the work of our enemies, Bob." Emily had stretched the phone cord its maximum length and was tugging on Frankie's shirt, but he shook his head and brushed her hand away.

"I'm withdrawing my name as a candidate for the presidency tonight, and I'm turning this recording over to the police. It will go better for you if you do what you can to save my brother's life."

"This is madness. None of this is true," Emily said. "You can't believe I would do any of these things. Bob, you can't give up now. You're so close. We've both worked so hard for this. This is your one chance to change the world. To make history. You're the anointed one. I've prayed too long and hard for you to throw it all away over a couple of homosexuals."

"Well, guess what, Emily? I'm one, too. And I can't tell you how disgusted I am at myself for the crimes that have been committed in my name."

Emily slammed the receiver into its cradle. "You little faggot!" she shrieked. "You are not stopping me." She tried to call Pat McCormack on his cell phone, and when he did not answer, she left a message, "McCormack, Hamilton knows everything. He's going to turn us both in. Get your guy to shut him up."

It was then that she realized that Frankie and Lily were still in the room. Lily was hugging Frankie. She had been crying. "Frankie, Momma's got to take care of some business," Emily said, patting his shoulder. "I'm sorry if I upset Lily. Sometimes, I get angry at the people I work with. Run along and I'll call you tomorrow morning."

An hour later on the tenth try to McCormack with no answer, Emily threw her cell phone against the wall. "Jesus Christ. I'm going to have to take care of this myself." She rummaged through her luggage until she found the small plastic handgun. She carried it for protection against the crazies. It was a Christmas present from the National Rifle Association and completely undetectable in the checked luggage security scans at the airports.

• • •

Josh Stein headed out of Vince Scavullo's apartment building into the warm summer night. He had a smile on his face and a bounce in his step. He was about to meet his brother. The Hamilton campaign representative had told him to come to Madison Square Garden's VIP gate and he would be escorted to a private audience with Bob Hamilton.

At last, he thought, his dream of finding his family had become a reality. He was full of questions that he hoped Bob could answer about their parents and birthplace and siblings. He wasn't at all put off by Vince's scathing comments about Bob's politics. "I'm sure once he gets to know me, I'll be able to change his mind," Josh had responded.

"But look what he did to this other guy who said he was his brother," Vince had pleaded. "This Webber guy. Poor schmoe. And the minister in Detroit. He's half dead."

"Vince, he says he wants to see me. Why would he say that if he'd done these other things? He's denied those stories. You know politics. Look what they did to your guy, John Kerry, a few years back. All lies, but that didn't stop them. Now, lay off. I'm in too good of a mood."

Josh figured he'd catch a cab on Sixth Avenue, and he was almost to the corner when he got hit from behind. Ed Brock threw him against the plywood wall surrounding a construction site and then shoved him through an open gate with a broken lock. Josh fell to the ground stunned, but conscious. His eyes focused just as Ed finished screwing the silencer onto his gun.

"Oh, no you don't," Josh yelled as he rolled behind a portable cement mixer. He heard thuds as two bullets hit the ground behind him in quick succession. Crouching, he waited as Ed approached.

In the thin file that Ed was given on Joshua Stein, there was no mention of his many years of martial arts training. So he was not prepared for what next occurred. Josh stood and kicked simultaneously, striking Ed's hand and sending his gun sailing fifty feet through the air. With two more quick kicks, Ed had been thrown back against the gate, which swung open. He landed on his ass in the middle of the sidewalk.

Now, Ed was pissed. Taking out a middle-aged queer wasn't supposed to be this hard. He had figured a couple quick chops, three bullets, and he'd be catching a cab to the airport. He was going to wrap this up before a crowd gathered. This was his last job for McCormack. He was moving to Arizona to sell Humvees for his brother.

Growling, he jumped to his feet before Josh could reach him, and landed his heel on Josh's chin. Josh stumbled back against the fence, but he managed to duck fast enough to miss the kick that would have crushed his larynx and stopped him from breathing. With all his strength, Josh thrust his head into Ed's belly and propelled him into the street onto the hood of a double-parked car. Both men were bleeding and wheezing in the heat, but Ed was twenty years younger. He absorbed the hit and punched both of Josh's kidneys so hard that Josh released his hold and fell back, staggering. He deflected Ed's next kick to his ribs, but he only managed to reduce the power of the impact. The pain of his ribs cracking was excruciating. He felt paralyzed and defenseless.

Ed smiled. He had been here many times before. His prey was wounded and waiting for death. It was that moment when the hunter and hunted become one. He saw the look in Josh's eyes, the look of surrender. But just as he lifted his fist to shove Josh's nose into his brain, Ed saw a glint in Josh's eyes that was unfamiliar, almost other worldly. In that instant of hesitation, Ed lost just enough thrust to allow Josh to deliver a direct blow to his groin. It was not so much the pain as it was the bewilderment that made Ed lose his balance. He tried to get his feet underneath him, but his efforts only propelled him further into the street, tipping backward like a falling giant landing first on his butt and then his head. Ed had died of shock before the bus tire rolled over his cranium. He had seen a horrific vision of a magnificent beast launching itself off of Josh's shoulders and bearing down on him with a blood-curdling roar.

No one else had seen the jungle cat, though Josh had felt a weight lifted off of him just as the animal leapt toward Ed. He looked on, dumbfounded, as Ed skittered backward and then disappeared under the tires of the bus. Before Josh could catch his breath, a hand with a damp cloth clamped down like a vise over his mouth and nose, and everything went black.

Chapter 20

July 18, 2012

Lizzie Hoffmeier was driving slowly down a two lane highway in a rental Mini Cooper. It was an unlit road, and she had her headlamps on bright. She hadn't driven after dark in years. The old man at the gas station in Booneville had given her directions to Sea Haven, and she was making her way landmark by landmark, aided by the light of a full moon. When she passed the sign reading, "Lazy Shores Bed & Breakfast, Jim Dobson and Fred Limbaugh, Proprietors," she knew she was close. The entrance to the long private drive was unmarked, but the distinctive stone pillars told her she was almost there.

She couldn't find a radio station with anything other than country western or rock music, so she'd been traveling with the silence of her thoughts since she'd left the airport in Savannah. She'd last seen Martha when they were both thirty-four, both of them holding their babies. Her babies. She wondered for the millionth time how life might have gone if she had raised Henry.

She'd been thinking about her old friend, Martha. Her stalwart, loyal, loving friend. Lying near death, the news reports had said. She had always known that Martha was a phone call away, and knowing that had carried her through many rough times. Lizzie had composed hundreds of letters in her mind to her friend, pouring out her heart, seeking advice, commiserating about Martha's husband, reveling in stories of Bobby's accomplishments, sympathizing with the loss of loved ones, all of it richly imagined, but nevertheless, very real to her, very reassuring to her each time she had attempted to start a new life with a new name and fresh hope. It was as if Martha had always been with her.

So, even though more than a half century had passed, Lizzie did not have the sense that they would be strangers when they met. They would take up where they had left off, even if the only communication were touch and telepathy. With that happy thought she motored down the quiet road, humming a tune she recognized as the song the band had played for the last dance at Artur's on the Zurichsee, Cole Porter's *At Long Last Love*. The night Martha had met Franz. She couldn't wait to tell Martha about her love, Andrew McClintock.

When Pat McCormack didn't report back to Herman Baumgartner and didn't answer his cell phone, Herman presumed

Erma Holt, aka Elizabeth Hoffmeier, was still alive and heading south. He contacted Mick Townsend and Lucius McCoy, the Harris Security team staked out at the beach house north of Sea Haven, and ordered them to intercept and terminate Ms. Hoffmeier. They were surprised by the order. They had always understood that they were on a routine surveillance assignment. When they couldn't reach Pat McCormack to confirm the order, they tried to reach his partners. But they were all in the custody of the Federal Bureau of Investigation, answering questions about McCormack's laptop computer files. Bridget McCormack had contacted the FBI right after she had finished her Hail Mary. She hadn't known what crimes her brother had committed or what wickedness he was about to do, but she had figured the FBI could make sense of it faster than she could.

Harris Security had not issued Mick and Lucius weapons for their stakeout, so they were forced to rush out to the nearest gun store to buy rifles with night vision scopes and armor piercing ammo. By the time Lizzie turned onto the private drive, they had been sitting for an hour on either side of the road halfway between the highway and Sea Haven's security gate. Neither man was happy with his assignment. They were crouching in the thick underbrush of the live oak forest, slapping away mosquitoes and worrying about cottonmouth snakes. Neither man had fired a weapon in years. They were techies, not sharpshooters. But Lizzie would make an easy target. They had the description of her rental car from Baumgartner, and when Lucius spotted the familiar outline of the Mini Cooper, he alerted Mick with his cell phone. However, before either man could train his sight on the little car's windshield, he felt a gun barrel in his back and hot breath on his neck.

"Drop your weapon and put your hands in the air," Jimmy Short ordered Lucius. Joe Bob Short had issued a similar command to Mick. Neither man gave resistance. They were glad to be relieved of their murderous task. Lizzie drove right past them, humming away, oblivious to the calamity she had narrowly escaped.

When she reached the security gate, Billy Short's ex-army buddies, Rex Stout and Ronnie Mueller, fully armed, checked her identification and held her while they called Yolanda Jackson. Then, Rex joined her for the short ride to the house, while Jimmy and Joe Bob walked Mick and Lucius out of the woods and down the road to the gate.

"You got any cuffs for these mopes?" Jimmy asked.

"Who are these guys?" Ronnie asked, shining a flashlight in their charcoal-blackened faces.

"Couple of hot dogs who work for Harris Security," Joe Bob said. "They were out in the woods all Rambo-like, aiming to kill that little old lady."

"I thought I told you boys to take a break," Ronnie said.

"We only take orders from Daddy, and he told us to be on the lookout for Miss Hoffmeier tonight," Jimmy said.

"Thank God for that," Ronnie said as he cuffed Mick and Lucius. "He'll be mighty proud of you."

• • •

Emily McIntyre was waiting in line to pass through security at the VIP gate at Madison Square Garden. She was holding her breath and praying as her Louis Vuitton purse with its lethal load sailed through the X-ray machine. The guard was about to do a hand inspection when she tugged at the straps of her purse. "Could you spare me the embarrassment?" she asked the handsome young man. "It's my time of the month."

"Why certainly, Mrs. McIntyre. Go right ahead," the guard said with a smile. The security work for the VIP gate had been contracted out to God's Shield, a company with Christian values and Christian employees, run by Russell Throckmorton, brother to Reverend Homer Throckmorton of The Church of the New Faith. All of the guards revered the ground upon which Emily walked. It never occurred to the young man that the post-menopausal Mrs. McIntyre was well past the curse of her monthly menses.

Emily had spent an hour schooling Arizona Governor Alma Cruz on the events of recent weeks, the extreme measures that had been taken, and the extreme measures yet to be taken. In exchange for Emily throwing her support behind Alma for the presidential nomination, Alma had agreed that, one month after her inauguration, she would pardon Emily for any federal crimes she had committed or might commit in the next twenty-four hours. Alma would also use her very personal relationships with New York City's Roman Catholic cardinal and certain Roman Catholic politicians to pressure New York prosecutors to accept her plea of not guilty by reason of temporary insanity induced by the public humiliation of Edna Roberts' confession. Alma had also agreed to block any attempt by Canadian authorities to extradite Emily to prosecute her for Roger Webber's murder. Finally, Alma had promised to withhold all faith-based funding to churches in Detroit unless their ministers campaigned for mercy for Emily in the case of Jonathan Jones' attempted murder. Emily figured the revulsion among the black clergy for a homosexual in their midst in combination with the threatened cut-off of federal pork would be all she needed to keep her freedom.

With that deal in place, Emily could proceed with her plan to murder Bob Hamilton before he could make his speech. She had to kill the heir apparent before he gave up his crown and destroyed her leverage. Once he withdrew his candidacy, Alma would no longer need Emily's support.

Emily checked her watch. Bob had cancelled her speech, and scheduled his announcement in her time slot. She had fifteen minutes to push her way through the backstage crowd and reach him. When she approached him, he was talking to Jerry Boston in a hallway packed with politicians and their handlers.

"Bob," she said. "I'm sorry for hanging up on you earlier. And I'm sorry for everything that's happened. Can we speak privately? I would like to make a confession tonight clearing you of any responsibility for my actions."

"Don't you think you're a little late for confessions, Emily?" Bob asked. He looked tired and older. He looked his age for the first time in his adult life.

"Do you realize what you've done to this man?" Jerry sneered. "You've single-handedly destroyed him."

Emily was doing her best to appear contrite. "Yes, yes, I know. I'm ready to face the consequences for what I have done, but I was hoping to make this one last gesture. To tell the world that it was me and me alone who took these actions. Surely, you can see the value in that."

"Why should I trust you?" Bob asked.

"You have nothing to lose at this point and everything to gain. Let me do this. I need to make things right with God."

Bob and Jerry exchanged glances. "I'll give you three minutes to tell me what you would say," Bob said. "Let's step into this conference room."

Jerry opened the door to a small room and turned on the light. "Jerry," Emily said. "I'd rather meet with Bob alone, if you don't mind."

"That's not going to happen," Jerry said. "It's either both of us, or no deal."

"That's right, Emily. I want a witness," Bob said.

"Whatever you say," Emily said, thinking this would be a bonus. Getting rid of Jerry Boston would eliminate one more problem. As the men led the way, she unzipped her purse and reached inside for her gun. "In Jesus name," she whispered to herself as she pulled the gun out and stepped through the doorway.

The next thing Emily felt was extreme pain as the door was slammed against her body with all the force two FBI agents could muster. Two other agents leapt from behind the door and tackled her, throwing her to the floor violently. Still holding the gun, she pulled the trigger, blowing off one agent's kneecap. The other agent twisted her arm until she let go of the gun and then threw her onto her stomach.

"God damn you, Alma! You set me up!" Emily shrieked.

Bob crouched down as the agent was cuffing her. "It wasn't Alma, Emily. It was your dear sweet son, Frankie. He told the police that you were sick and you needed help."

As the agent pulled her to her feet, she scowled at Bob and Jerry and blasted them with a final curse. "You're both going to hell. I'm doing God's work. I am God's messenger. He has spoken to me. God damn you all."

•••

When Josh Stein came to, he was sitting in the front passenger seat of Billy Short's Chevy Silverado. He'd been patched up, cuffed and seat-belted. Billy was barreling down the interstate somewhere south of Philadelphia, whistling along to the latest Dixie Chicks' hit, *She's My God, Too, Damn It!* Before Josh opened his eyes, he became aware of a dull pain in his rib cage and a fuzzy, distant throbbing in his head.

When Josh groaned, Billy asked, "How you doing?"

Josh looked up and found Billy smiling at him. "Who are you?" Josh asked.

"I'm a friend, and I'm taking you to meet your momma. Here's the key to those the cuffs. Sorry about that. I didn't want you jumping out before I could explain things."

As Josh unlocked the cuffs, he said, "My mother's dead."

"I understand Mrs. Stein is dead, but this is the woman who gave birth to you."

"She's still alive?"

"Alive and kicking. She's very excited to meet you."

"I was supposed to meet my brother tonight. What happened back there?"

"Hamilton knows about you, but he didn't set up that meeting. That was a ruse to get you out the door, so they could jump you. I didn't know if our friend was alone and I didn't have time to sweet talk you into believing me, so I had to put you to sleep and get the hell out of town before somebody else took a swipe at you."

"He was trying to kill me. Why?" Josh asked.

"There are people who don't want the world to know Bob Hamilton's brother is gay. Religious nuts and their hired guns. But you don't have to worry about them. They're either dead or locked up by now. Everybody knows you're okay. I called your friend, Vince, and Hamilton's people."

"Are you sure I'm okay? I feel like I got run over by that bus."

"You'd feel a lot worse if I hadn't shot you up with painkiller. That was impressive work back there, defending yourself. You obviously didn't need my help. Pretty good for an old fart."

"Do you work for my mother? Tell me about her."

Billy got a little misty eyed. "No, I work for one of the finest ladies I've ever known. She's the reason you're still alive. I don't know much about your mother, but I'll tell you what I can. The three of you were born in Georgia. That's where we're headed."

"The three of us?"

"Sadly, now only two of you. The guy you threw under the bus killed your other brother. May he rest in peace."

Josh started to cry. "So it's true. One of my brothers killed the other."

"No. That's not what happened. Let's see if I can find a news radio. You can hear for yourself."

Billy found a station just as the announcer said, "And here is Senator Hamilton's bombshell announcement earlier this evening at the Republican National Convention at Madison Square Garden:"

"Good evening. I appear before you tonight to announce that I am quitting my campaign for the presidency."

There was a great roar of protest from the crowd that swelled into a long sustained, "NOOOOOO!!!!" Bob continued, saying, "Without my knowledge, individuals purporting to act on behalf of my campaign have killed one of my brothers and attempted to kill my other brother."

The hue and cry quickly died down, as Bob's voice broke. "These are brothers I only very recently learned I had. These same individuals also attempted to kill my dear friend, Reverend Jonathan Jones. Although I was not aware of these crimes, the basic facts alleged by Rosa Gibson in her stories are true. Including my relationship with Jonathan Jones while we served together in the Peace Corps. We were lovers."

The boos of the crowd swelled to an angry howl. Bob's voice could barely be heard over the furious catcalls from the shocked conservatives. "I pray that Jonathan fully recovers from his injuries and that he can forgive me for treating him so badly. I apologize to my wife, Kathleen, for causing her so much pain, especially tonight. I send my love to her, my children, my brother, wherever he may be, and to my adoptive mother, Martha Hamilton. Good night and God Bless."

The announcer came back on. "Senator Hamilton had to be escorted out of the building by a small army of New York policemen as delegates stormed the stage. The convention collapsed into pandemonium after the announcement. New York's chief of police, Mike Finnerty, ordered the hall closed and brought in riot squads to break up the unruly Republicans who were attempting to march on the senator's headquarters at the Waldorf Astoria Hotel. When red-faced politicians demanded they be allowed to proceed, the police were forced to arrest the most belligerent critics, many of them prominent senators, governors and congressmen, as well as some of the nation's leading evangelical ministers. Reverend Homer Throckmorton led a charge of delegates up Madison Avenue, forcing police to resort to water cannons and dogs to quell the red, white and blue festooned mob, many of whom were chanting, 'Homos go to hell. We go straight to heaven.'"

Billy turned down the volume. "Sounds like your brother has got some explaining to do."

"Do you think he'll be safe?" Josh asked.

"Oh, he'll be fine. New York is the gay capital of the world. They're not going to let one of their own get hurt by a bunch of rubes from the sticks. Now, his wife. She's another matter. I'd hate to be in his shoes for that conversation."

• • •

"Natalie, it's Rosie."

Natalie Jordan had fallen asleep on the sofa in her parents' Philadelphia home watching the convention coverage. She'd been trying to reach Rosie Gibson all night. "Rosie, where are you? Are you all right?"

Rosie smiled. She was sitting with a flute of champagne in a bubble bath in her hotel room in mid-town Manhattan. "I'm fine. I just got back to my room. I'm sorry I didn't call. I've been giving interviews all night. It's been crazy."

"Interviews?"

"Yes. Everyone wants to talk to the black dyke who brought down Bob Hamilton. I'm going to be on three talk shows tomorrow morning. I turned down Fox News just for spite."

"Rosie, that's wonderful. Do you think you'll get your job back?"

Rosie laughed. "Max's boss called me, and then his boss, and then the publisher. Each one of them offered me more money than the last."

"What did you say?"

"I kept turning them down until the top guy called. I told him I wanted a syndicated column, and twice the money he offered me. He said yes before I finished my sentence." Rosie laughed again and sipped her champagne.

"Good for you. You deserve it. Does this mean you'll be working more hours?"

"No, I'm going to have a staff and everything. I can make my own hours. We're going to buy that house with a yard you've always wanted. And then we can talk about kids, if you're ready."

"Really, Rosie? Do you mean it?"

"Absolutely."

"I've got good news, too. I called Georgia Jones, like you asked. She says Jonathan's brain scans have improved so much the doctors brought him out of his coma. It looks like he'll be okay. She even spoke to him. He sends you his love. The doctors say it's a miracle."

Rosie put down her glass and stroked the head of the big spotted cat lounging on the ledge by her tub. The leopard purred and licked her fingers. "I'm so glad he's okay," Rosie said. "Life is full of miracles."

Chapter 21

July 19, 2012

Martha Hamilton opened her eyes and wondered if she were still dreaming. Sitting next to her bed in an armchair with a blanket across her legs was her old friend, Lizzie Hoffmeier. She was asleep with her hands folded in her lap. Martha smiled. A "bad girl" most of her life, Lizzie looked delicate and angelic in her slumber. Like a child. Like the child she was before her father had stolen her innocence. Martha was touched that Lizzie had risked so much to come.

The room was gray with pre-dawn light. Sassy was at the foot of her bed, still asleep. Martha gave her a nudge with her foot. Sassy meowed and stretched, in a way that said, "Leave me alone. Go back to sleep."

Lizzie stirred and opened her eyes. "Martha, how are you?" Lizzie said, smiling as she pulled off her lap robe and stood. Straight off the beach at Marbella, she looked vibrant and healthy in white slacks and a light blue blouse that matched her eyes.

Martha had just begun stringing words together coherently. "Happy. Thanks." Frustrated, she wanted to say, "God, I'm so glad you're here. Thanks so much for coming."

Lizzie gently hugged Martha and kissed her on the forehead. She sat down on the side of the bed and took Martha's hand in hers. The two old women began to cry.

"Guess who's coming today?" Lizzie asked.

"Marion?"

Without missing a beat, Lizzie said, "No, dear, he can't make it today. My son is coming. His name is Joshua Stein. He's from Australia. He was in New York on holiday when your man found him. He should be here by lunchtime. I wonder if he's Henry or Brendan."

"Great." Martha said as she pushed a button to elevate her head.

"And Bob is coming, too. He'll be here for dinner."

Martha groaned. "Why?"

"He's given up politics. It's a long story. I think he finally got religion."

Martha nodded. She thought, "Hallelujah! I'm in heaven. Thank God for Billy Short. He told me not to worry." But all she could say was, "Billy!"

Lizzie giggled. "I met his sons. They're delicious."

"Andrew?" Martha asked.

"He's back in Spain. I didn't want him to get in trouble if I got arrested."

Martha squeezed Lizzie's hand. "Missed you."

"And I've missed you. I was thinking about my summer at the farmhouse. Those were such good times. Do you still have the pictures you took of us? With the boys?"

Martha nodded. "Safe. Bedroom." She scrawled the combination on a notepad she kept on her tray.

They were looking at the old photos when Yolanda Jackson rolled in a cart holding breakfast. "How are you feeling this morning, Martha?"

"Great." Martha winked at Yolanda. It was her shorthand gesture of boundless gratitude for her dear friend and caretaker.

Lizzie sighed. "One of these precious boys is gone. So sad."

Martha nodded. Yolanda had told her the news about Roger Webber. "My fault," she said, thinking she should have exposed Bob sooner.

"Now, Martha. We talked about this. It's not your fault," Yolanda chided.

Martha turned to Lizzie. "How long?"

"Martha wants to know how long you can stay?" Yolanda said.

"As long as you'll have me."

"Good. Meet Marion."

"I'd love to meet him," Lizzie said. "Yolanda has told me so many wonderful things about him."

Martha nodded, thinking, "He wants to meet you, too."

• • •

"So start at the beginning, Lizzie. How did you two meet?" Josh Stein asked. Josh and Billy Short had just sat down to lunch with Yolanda Jackson and Lizzie Hoffmeier on the east veranda at Sea Haven.

They had spent the last half hour gathered around Martha Hamilton's bed, making introductions, hugging, crying and laughing at Lizzie's stories. Billy had kissed Martha on the forehead when he entered her bedroom. "We're home free, old girl," he had said. Eyes moistened, she had hugged him tight with one arm, thinking, "Thanks, Billy, you're the best." When Martha began to nod off, Yolanda had shooed them out of the room to let her rest.

"Oh, dear," Lizzie sighed. "If I tell you the truth, you may wish I weren't your mother."

"I've waited a lifetime. Trust me. I want to know everything," Josh answered.

"We met at a girls' school in Switzerland. My parents shipped me there after they found out I'd been sleeping with the minister."

"How did they find out?" Josh asked.

"When I told them I was pregnant. They took me to the family doctor for an abortion and then packed me off."

"Why was Martha there?" Billy asked.

Yolanda got up. "I'm going to check on Martha. I've heard most of this from her."

Lizzie smiled. "Martha was a rebel, and her mother was a puritan. That's all I'll say."

"How old were you, two?" Josh asked.

"Barely fifteen. It was 1939, and war was about to break out. Martha's parents thought we were safe in Switzerland, and my parents didn't care."

"So how did Martha end up pregnant?" Josh asked.

"I'm afraid I'm mostly to blame. We were on holiday in Zurich. I told Martha I wasn't going back to the school and I convinced her to stay with me. We went dancing that first night and met some gentlemen. Franz asked Martha to dance, and she fell for him. He was dreamy. The next day, we went on a picnic with Franz and his friends, and after lunch Franz and Martha went for a walk."

Lizzie took a sip of water. "At the end of the day, Franz said he'd call on her. But he never did."

Yolanda came through the door, smiling, with a tray of homemade chocolate chip cookies. "She's doing fine. She says, 'Don't believe anything Lizzie tells you.'"

Everyone laughed. "What happened after Franz disappeared?" Josh asked.

"Martha tried to book passage home, but with the war on, safe travel was scarce. She was stuck in Zurich. When she discovered she was pregnant, she knew she couldn't keep the baby, so I went looking for a doctor. Unfortunately, the guy I found was a butcher. I'll never forgive myself. Martha nearly bled to death. We rushed her to the hospital. She was there for weeks. They told her that she wouldn't be able to have children."

"So who's my dad," Josh asked.

Lizzie grimaced. "Peter Titford. I was living in London. He was a member of Parliament and married to money." She patted Josh's knee. "My father molested me. As much as I hated him, I spent much of my youth looking for men just like him. When I told Titford I was pregnant, he insisted I get an abortion. When I refused, he nearly killed me, choking me to the point I passed out. When I came to, he gave me only one option. Leave the country and give my child away. He insisted there be no record of the birth or the adoption. That's when I called Martha. She wanted to go after Titford, but I wouldn't give her his name. I was scared to death."

• • •

"What are they going to do to Momma?" Frankie McIntyre asked his brother, Larry. They were sitting in Frankie and Lily's hotel room in New York.

"I don't know, Frankie. The judge will decide."

"Like Judge Judy?" Frankie asked.

Larry Jr. smiled. The image of Judge Judy giving their mother a tongue lashing was irresistible. "No, not Judge Judy. Not a TV judge. A real judge. In a real court. Our mother has done some bad things, and she's going to have a long trial."

Frankie wrapped his arms tightly around his waist. "It's my fault, isn't it?

"No, it's not your fault. You did the right thing. Mom needs help. She's sick. She needed to be stopped because she couldn't stop herself. If you hadn't told the police, she might have done more bad things and been in bigger trouble."

Frankie started rocking. "So they'll help her get better?"

"No. Mom is going to have to fix herself. She needs to do a lot of praying."

Frankie stopped rocking and clasped his hands together in his lap. "I'll pray for her."

Larry Jr. clasped his hands. "I'll pray for her, too, Frankie. We all will."

• • •

Lizzie had held court for two hours. The strong July sun was flooding the veranda by the time she had finished her story. Her audience was spellbound. With Martha's help, Lizzie had been whisked away to Dublin to stay in hiding with Martha's friend, Nora Moriarity, a retired British intelligence officer. The plan had been for Martha to fake a pregnancy and take the baby after Lizzie delivered in a private hospital outside Atlanta. Only Robert III knew Martha could not have children. For six months, Martha took to her bed and refused all visitors, except for her nosey mother and proud father. The delivering doctor was a friend of Robert III's. He would fix the hospital records and pay off the staff to keep them silent. There would be no trace of Lizzie's presence or the birth of her baby. The infant would be safe from Titford. When they learned there would be three babies, Nora and Lizzie decided they would each raise a child. With Martha's help, Lizzie would assume a new identity and build a new life. Lizzie had been dubious. "I was afraid I would be a terrible mother," she said.

Robert bought a small farm near Hamilton Oaks, where Lizzie, Nora, and Hank Ketchum, hired security, stayed for the last six weeks of her pregnancy. The babies were born on July 4, 1958, and, two weeks later, Lizzie, Nora, Hank and baby boys, Henry and Brendan, headed home to Dublin. Hank left the women to their mothering and returned to London.

"What about Titford?" Josh asked.

Lizzie made a face. "That snake. It all might have worked if Hank hadn't double-crossed us. I suspect he was working for Titford the whole time. A week after we got back, Nora's doctor friend came by to check on the boys. He suggested I get some fresh air. Nora stayed behind to watch the boys, and the doctor and I left for a short walk. We were a block from the cottage when we heard the shots."

Lizzie and the doctor found Nora lying dead in a pool of blood and the cribs empty. Lizzie was hysterical and scared to death. The doctor sedated her and drove her to the train station. She refused to go to the police. From that point forward, she devoted her life to romancing philandering plutocrats and stealing their money, artwork, fancy cars, whatever they prized most.

"My payback for a lost childhood and stolen children," Lizzie explained. "I was a born actress. And a mistress of disguise. I could assume any identity I wanted. It was the way I escaped reality as a child."

She fenced the valuables and gave it all to charities for battered women and runaway children. Always just one step ahead of the law, she finally decided at seventy-five, that, "I wasn't angry anymore." And she retired to Marbella, and later Ullapool.

"What happened to Titford?" Josh asked.

Lizzie smirked. "He died a lonely man, divorced, broke, childless, in a London hospital in 1991, on your birthday. I was there. I'd heard he was dying, and paid him a visit. I wanted to confront him at last. He claimed he'd never intended for Hank to hurt Nora. She'd surprised him, he said. He'd told Hank to find homes for you two. As far from England as possible, but he had no idea where you were. Apparently Hank had contacted a couple of adoption agencies, met your parents at the Dublin airport and handed you off. It was a relief to know you hadn't been harmed."

"How did you know he was telling the truth?" Billy asked.

"I had cut off his morphine. I wrote Martha right away to tell her Titford was dead. There was no longer any need for her to keep my secret. But I didn't give her any way to reach me. I was too ashamed and I didn't want her to get caught up in my problems."

"She missed you," Yolanda said.

"I'm sure she did, and I missed her."

• • •

"You shall rise from these ashes, Miss Scarlett." Jack O'Malley raised his martini glass to his sister, Kathleen Hamilton. They were sitting in a quiet little bar not far from his apartment in the Hell's Kitchen neighborhood of Manhattan. It was a cool, breezy afternoon. Powerful storms had thundered throughout the night, drenching the dregs of raging Republican protestors.

Kathleen's kids and her mother, Mary O'Malley, were back at the Waldorf. The night before, Kathleen had had a long discussion with them about Bob's announcement, most particularly the part about his relationship with Jonathan Jones.

"Well, I guess this takes the pressure off me," Robert V had said.

"What does this mean? Is he still a Christian fascist?" Martha had asked.

"I'm so humiliated," her daughter, Mary, had said. "How can I face Boo after this?"

Kathleen's mother, Mary, had been the most upset. She had so hoped to visit her daughter in the White House. "In my day, we kept these things private. Why did he have to tell the whole world? If he's gone this long the way he is, why does he have to blow up your marriage and ruin his chance to be president?"

Bob had left a short message on her phone. "Kathleen, I'm so sorry for doing this so publicly and for deceiving you all these years. I truly love you. I won't be coming back to the hotel tonight. I figure you could use some time alone before we talk."

Kathleen raised her glass. "Thank you, Jack. But I'm fine. I didn't want to be First Lady, and we would have divorced if he had won the election, so, in one way, I was prepared for this. It was a huge relief when I heard him speak. I realized I didn't love him anymore. Although I'm proud of what he did last night. That took guts."

Jack sniffed. "It takes guts for anyone to come out. I wouldn't give him any medals. I always wondered about Bob. Something was off. He was too perfect to be a straight man. A classic closet queen."

"I do feel sorry for him," Kathleen said. "This was his whole life. He is still the father of my children. What does he do after this?"

Jack drained his martini and signaled the bartender for another. "He'll be fine. He's rich and handsome. He can have any gay man he wants. I wonder if his brother is single. I've always thought your husband was hot. I mean, with a makeover and everything."

Kathleen laughed. "Thank you for coming out with me. I needed this."

Jack gave her a kiss on the cheek and a hug. "What you need is a refill. Barkeep, another mint julep for Miss O'Hara, please."

• • •

Yolanda answered her cell phone. She smiled. "Martha's ready for company again."

As they rose from the table and headed inside, Billy pulled Lizzie aside. "I figured out everything except why Martha married Robert. What was she thinking?"

Lizzie shook her head. "That's a story for another night. Let's just say Robert thought he had finally caught the woman he'd been chasing since her debut into Atlanta society at the Piedmont Driving Club. And Martha, as Mrs. Robert Hamilton III, do-gooder for the Red Cross, got the career she wanted, working undercover, catching Commie spies, while she traipsed around Europe."

Josh held back as the others left to go upstairs. He smiled at

Lizzie. "So what do you think? Am I your Henry or Nora's Brendan?" Lizzie's eyes twinkled. "Well, there's only one way to find out. Come with me to the powder room."

Once the door was closed, she asked him, "Now, would you please turn around, drop your trousers and bend over?" Josh figured since she was his mother, it would be all right to bare his ass. When he bent over, Lizzie yelped, "Oh, Henry! There it is! There's your birthmark. The little red heart!"

"I always thought it looked more like a strawberry," Josh said, smiling, as he pulled up his pants.

• • •

Bob Hamilton arrived in time for dinner, and, later that night, Bob and Martha had their first moments alone. "I'm sorry," Martha had struggled to say.

Bob was holding her hand. "Don't apologize. You did nothing wrong." He hadn't slept for two days. He was exhausted, but strangely at peace.

Martha handed him an envelope that Yolanda had retrieved from the safe. Inside he found a letter she'd written to him the preceding New Year's Day. It said:

> *If you're reading this, I'm either dead or dying and I've failed to tell you the truth about who you are and where you came from.*

After explaining in great detail the story of his past, she wrote:

> *Because your father and I feared for your life, we kept Lizzie's secret and raised you as our own. After Titford's death, I had no good excuse to keep the secret. I could blame your father, but, in the end, it was my own lack of will. You deserved better.*

> *You may already know that I have tried to sabotage your career, not only because of what you stand for, but also because I was trying to keep your past a secret. I wanted to save you the pain and embarrassment of learning from others that your father and I had lied to you.*

255

*I hope that you can forgive me and understand that I acted
out of love for you.*

Love,

Mom

Bob began to cry halfway through the letter. When he finished,
he looked into Martha's eyes and said, "I love you too, Mom. Now,
more than ever."

July 20, 2012

"Well, that went better than anything we could have planned,"
Phinneas Graves said as he muted the news coverage of Emily
McIntyre being led out of a New York courtroom in an orange
jumpsuit.

"In some ways." Angela Patterson said. She closed her file and
set it on Phinneas' desk. They were sitting in his office at CIA
headquarters.

"Thank you, Angela for all your hard work. I know how
distasteful it was for you."

Angela shrugged. "I feel badly about Webber. I wish I'd known
McCormack was working for McIntyre. He might still be here."

Phinneas nodded. "Sad creature. Webber."

Angela glanced over at the television. She smiled. "Phinneas,
turn it up."

Phinneas chuckled as he picked up the remote. On the screen,
Roger Webber was belting out *Delta Dawn* as an immensely rotund
Bette Midler. The tagline across the bottom of the screen read, "Roger
Webber, Manhole Bar, Toronto, 1995." In an eerie, soulful voice, he
sang, "Did I hear you say he was meeting you here today? He's gonna
take you to his mansion in the sky."

• • •

"The Leopard Christ?" Eulalia Gibson asked, thinking she had a
bad connection.

"Yes," Rosie said. "That should make you happy. My publisher
loves the title."

Rosie was lying naked on her back in bed. Natalie Jordan was curled up next to her, smiling as she listened. They were in Natalie's old bedroom in her parents' home. The parsonage of the Mount Horeb African Methodist Episcopal Church in Philadelphia. The girls had just finished making up.

"Christ was a man, not a wild animal," Eulalia protested.

"Jesus was a man. But spirit has no gender or form, Momma. You've always said God is everywhere. Why can't she be a pretty spotted cat sometimes?"

Eulalia smiled and shook her head, as she sat down slowly at her kitchen table. "Oh, child. You never do things easy, do you?"

Rosie was stroking Natalie's cheek. "What's easier than the truth revealed?"

Eulalia closed her eyes and rubbed her forehead. "Now, you're a prophet?"

"What? You think God only speaks to angry old white guys?"

Eulalia laughed. "No, Rosie. I'd pick you over them any time."

Just then, the big cat appeared out of nowhere and leapt onto the bed. She nestled against Rosie and closed her eyes.

John Myers lives in Chicago's
Andersonville neighborhood,
where he enjoys his passions for
politics, meditation, good food,
and good friends.

Photo by Doug Birkenheuer,
www.BirkenheuerPhotography.com